THE
DEFIANT
Heart

BEPPIE HARRISON

CAMDEN HILL PRESS

This is a work of fiction. Names, characters, places, and incidents are products of the author's imagination or are used fictitiously and are not to be construed as real. Any resemblance to actual locales, organizations, events, or persons, living or dead, is entirely coincidental. England and Ireland do exist, of course, but it is only in the 21st century that the ancient enmity has at last settled into a wary but welcome peace.

The Defiant Heart
Copyright © 2015 by Beppie Harrison

Published by Camden Hill Press
ISBN 978-0-9862408-0-5

Cover design by Dar Albert, at wickedsmartdesigns.com
Formatting by Author E.M.S.

Published in the United States of America

For all the dream-dazzled hard-working fellow authors
I've met since I turned to fiction
with thanks for all you've added to my life
(partial list only!)
Michelle Celmer, Shirley Jakway, Deborah Trickey, Maje Brennan,
Beth Szabo, Sandy Marshall, Dory Jensen, Stacey Joy Netzel,
Kathy Crouch, Janette Harjo, and Nancy Mayer
and love for what we all share.

TABLE OF CONTENTS

Other Books by Beppie Harrison

The Heart Trilogy

The Divided Heart

The Broken Heart

The Rebellious Heart

The Grandest Christmas

Acknowledgments

There may be writers who retreat into a closed room to produce their books; I am not such a writer. I wrote this book sitting on the living room couch with family life surging around me, and so my first and largest thank you has to go to my remarkably patient family, who were willing to live over and around me, tolerating my blank stare and mumbled "What?" when they tried to talk to me, and willing to repeat whatever they had said a minimum of three or four times before I returned from Ireland where my mind was planted and accepted the reality of Michigan and whatever their problems happened to be.

This time I have a special thank you for Helen Nazzaro. I was looking for an editor for this book and I had heard wonderful reports of her skill and patience. I wrote to her, and to my complete amazement after some backing and forthing, she told me that she and her partner James Price were setting up as publishers, and asked me to be their first published author. I cannot begin to explain how wonderful they has been. One of the unavoidable parts of being a writer is the loneliness of being alone with the words that you've put on the page. Helen has helped me, again and again, by being a wholly supportive presence who believed in me more than anyone has done before. Working out all the issues has not always been easy, but with unshakable good will on both sides, we have learned to know and trust each other. I look forward to the years ahead working with her and James, and Ken Trickey, who has been a creative support on the promotion side.

The irreplaceable, as he has been now for more than forty years, is my husband. When we said "for better, for worse," neither one of us could have foreseen how difficult it could be at times—we've both had our spells of serious medical problems—but then again, we had no idea how wonderful "for better" could be. Let me remind him, then, that he is the center of my world, along with the four children we've been privileged to raise.

This book talks about love. What I know about love I have learned from the remarkable people who have surrounded me from the very beginning. Let me thank all of them, those still with me and those who have gone before.

County Donegal, Ireland. 1812.

THEY WERE ABOUT AS SORRY a bunch as he'd seen.

Diarmaid MacGuinness ran a hardened hand through his hair, hair that was still as bright a red as it had been when he'd been a lad. He'd not spoken a word to the men yet; perhaps he was being a mite unfair. Unpromising they might be, but his job here was to turn them into a secret cell of men dedicated to the job of evicting the English from Irish land. Not now. Not until there were cells like this all over the country, when they could gather the power to convince the English that the end of their rule had come.

He glanced back at them. There were—what? Eight of them? No, ten. A couple must have crept in when his mind was elsewhere. 'Twasn't one of them sitting straight up as if ready for business. They might have been so many heaps o' dirty laundry, the lot of them, slumped on their stools, peering at him sort of sideways like, more like sulky schoolboys than the warriors he needed.

Donegal was as far north and west as you could go and still be in Ireland. Worse, it was too close to Ulster and all those damned Protestant Scots the even more damned English had planted among them. That's even what they called it: plantation. Tossed out the Irish who'd owned the land for generations, and given it to stubborn Scots and more English, as if there were not too many in Ireland already. There were some of the plantations even in County Donegal itself, taking up the best of the land, of course, and the good Lord and 'is saints knew Donegal had hardly any good land to begin with. Peat bogs, yes, they had those, crowded between mountains and rocky spurs leading down to the sea. Made it logical to suppose that the Donegal folk would be as eager as the rest of the Irish to overthrow the English and take back their own land.

Instead they sat there, great lumps that they were—though some of the bulk had to be the layers of badly fitting clothes that kept some cold from their bodies, because when you looked in their faces too many of them were gaunt and thin.

And more than half of them had filthy bare feet.

Diarmaid lifted his eyes to study the inside of the roof. Pity had no place in his heart. Pity would keep these feeble excuses for Irishmen where they were. He needed men, and he would make these useless clods into men if he died in the process.

He allowed his eyes to sweep over them again until his gaze stopped abruptly on one of the smallish ones. Sweet Mother of God, that was no man at all. It was a woman—no, a girl. What the hell was a girl doing here in this falling-down shed, hidden, he hoped, from the eyes of the constabulary behind two or three sod houses also on the point of collapse?

He reached out swiftly and, grabbing the cloth around her shoulders, lifted her to her feet.

"Who in God's name are you?"

She barely came as high as his shoulder, but her eyes blazed back at him as fiercely as if she was six feet tall.

"Nobody said you had to be a man to come," she hissed at him.

"I thought ye had some common sense." His voice snapped and the others straightened up, just a bit. Diarmaid glanced at them with the first stirring of hope, then let his eyes settle back on the girl.

"I have no use for you," he said. The words were final as he meant them to be.

"Then you're the fool."

He had turned his head, dismissing her, but his attention jerked back. She had shaken the scarf from her head, and he was a bit taken aback to see her hair was as red as his. Her face was dirty, but out of it flashed eyes of the sharpest blue.

"You know nothing about me." Might've been a cat, the way she spit that out.

"You're female."

"So's half the human race. Your half's made a bloody mess of things, it looks like. Maybe you could use some of that common sense you talk about. Respect it when you see it, maybe."

'Twas not often Diarmaid MacGuinness found himself without words, but it happened now.

The girl knew it, too. She cocked her head and stared at him. Daring him, like.

Diarmaid met her eyes for a moment and then turned away to look at the man—this one at least was a man—sitting at the far left.

"Name?"

The voice was a mutter.

"Speak up! You're a man here."

"Patrick McGurk."

Diarmaid's eyes switched to the one sitting next.

"Seán Doherty."

With a nod, he encouraged the rest. "Jack Loughlin." "Charlie Mullan." "Liam Doherty." "Seamus Bonner." "Cathal Sweeney." "Brian O'Donnell." "Donncha Ward."

That was the last of them. The girl stood where she was but did not speak.

The silence bristled between them. Diarmaid did not allow himself a glance to see if she was still watching him.

It was war he meant to prepare them for. It would take a war to sweep the bloody British back across the Irish Sea to England where they belonged, and there was no place in war for a woman.

Even without looking he realized she'd tossed her head, quick like. He stood where he was, reconsidering. He might have no need of a woman for fighting, but he might need quickness. Assuming he could badger this unpromising bunch into shape to fight, he would need someone to take messages from one place to another. 'Twould be possible the English would be less wary of a female.

He spun around to face her, and she blinked. *Not so sure of yourself, me darling?*

"You have a name?" The words snapped out.

Her chin lifted again. "Muirne. Muirne Coyle." She was still standing.

"Sit down then. You're here now. Can you keep your mouth shut or are you like all other females, flapping the news about?"

Her eyes flashed. "I been to the pub and to the washhouse. I know where the gossip is, and it's not those doing laundry."

He feared for a moment that his mouth quirked up a bit, and turned away just in case. The men were shuffling about a little, and he had to hold their attention. As he looked over the men he realized she was still standing and wheeled back to face her again.

"I said sit. If you can't follow orders, get out."

She sat.

From then on it was more routine. Really a business of figuring out which men would follow and which would wander back to their fields or their looms, more frightened of what they might lose than angry enough to risk winning.

Diarmaid had been all over western and northern Ireland facing groups like this, feeling out what sort of strength existed should a miracle occur and the opportunity for an uprising come unexpected like. The networks had been mown down like grass after the disaster of 1798 when the few Protestants with a brain or two worked with the desperate Catholics to reach for freedom from the bloody English. Even the French had come aboard. Well, as far as agreeing to help, that was. Hadn't shown up when blood was on the line and the well-armed English, already in place, swept unforgivingly over the land, wiping out every suspicion of rebellion. Good men who knew nothing of it had been killed, nastily, mainly because the damned English couldn't be bothered to find out what really happened. Wipe the half-human Irish out, that's all it was to them.

So now of course there were two problems. The one of securing arms again was the lesser one. Diarmaid knew of one store no one else could access, and if he had one, there were others. The real problem was the men. Men who weren't dazed by hunger, by the constant cold, and despairing that their lives could ever be different. Was that what ailed these silent men in Donegal? The only one showing life among them was a girl, for God's sake.

He cast a scornful eye over the huddled lumps, and then reminded himself they'd at least had the gumption to come. How many men lived roundabout here, in this odd collection of dwellings they called a clachan? Certainly as many as thirty or so. And of the thirty ten had shown up. Well, nine. The tenth had been the girl.

Nine was still better than one or two. Or none.

"Why'd you come tonight?"

It wasn't the way he'd ever started before. Usually he started by talking about a free Ireland. But these men were a different lot, and he was curious. What had drawn them away from their sorry hovels?

The men shifted on their stools and looked at each other.

One o' them—Cathal Sweeney, was it?—muttered something.

"Speak up. No point talking as if you don't care if you're heard."

When the man spoke louder, it was in Irish.

Diarmaid glanced around at the others. "Everyone here speak Irish?"
All but a couple of heads nodded.

"English?"

Hesitation. Then they all nodded, unwillingly, most of them.

"When we get rid of them, we can speak what we please. Now, it's better to know what they say to each other. There's a place for Irish, and we'll use it, but not now." He turned back to Cathal Sweeney. "Tell me again, in English."

"I hate 'em. They took my da's land, what belonged to him and my gran'da. Set the stupid Scots on it." His worn dirty face brightened briefly. "When do we get to killin' them?"

"Not tomorrow. Not the next day either, most likely. We wait and watch and plan. When we get the chance we strike. But only when we know what's to happen next. 'Tis easy enough to thrash around, but they're trained and ready. Thrashing's no threat to them. The ten of us's no threat to them."

"Eleven," Muirne Coyle called out, cool as you please.

Diarmaid's eyes switched to hers and she gave hard stare for hard stare.

He continued as if she'd not spoken. "There may be times for hit and run, but what we need to do now is plan and build some strength so we're of some use." Now he was back giving the speech he'd given often enough before. 'Twas his uncle in Galway'd told the others Diarmaid had the power of drawing ordinary men into the struggle. That was what had set him on his travels, starting groups here and groups there, handfuls of men who were like seed corn planted among the powerless men about them. Stupidity was his biggest obstacle. He'd known his share of daft great fools before he'd come west who thought flailing about at the English worked, as long as you could disappear afterwards. What men like that never considered was that the English didn't care if they wreaked their vengeance on the ones who had attacked or on some poor Irishman who happened to be handy. Wiping out other Irishman did no good at all.

Rebellion only worked if it was smart. That was what Diarmaid had come all the way up to cold and rocky Donegal to teach. Could he do it? He'd done it before. The men he'd left behind in Galway had other jobs to do.

Time for him to do his.

By the end of the meeting, maybe an hour, maybe less, he had some feeling about these nine men with enough gumption to show up. Heroes they were not on the face of it, but he didn't need heroes yet. What he needed were men who were willing to be patient and develop cunning and trust in each other—the kind of trust that made a man care as much about the life of his comrade as about his own. The process had started. Whether it would blow up in a fit of temper or drunkenness or problems that had not yet surfaced no one could know.

But it had started.

Of course the red-headed Muirne Coyle was standing just inside the door when Diarmaid was ready to leave.

"So?" she asked.

She was smaller than she'd seemed when she was standing at a distance, the blue of her eyes even more striking close-up. But dear God, was she dirty!

"Where do you live?"

"Here."

He glanced around the bare interior of the shed. He'd picked it because there had been no sign any poor fool lived here. Of course, hard to tell in these parts. People lived places the dear Lord himself wouldn't see fit for an animal.

"What, in here?"

She shook her head, impatient like. "No. Over there." She pointed over at one of the sod heap-like dwellings he'd hoped would hide the light from the lantern in the shed.

The sod heap was sad enough itself.

"Where's your mam?"

"Dead." There was not a whisper of sorrow in her voice. She might have been talking about a stone that had fallen in the wrong place.

Diarmaid felt his eyebrows rise.

"She wasn't good for much. Me dad's not much use, either." No trace of regret or complaint in her matter-of-fact words.

For a fleeting moment he thought of his own father, dead in the Revolt of 1798, and his own mam, running all the grand aristocrats in that massive stone big house in County Meath. Ran his life as well, or tried to, but he needed the shelter she provided. They'd hired her as a cook, but she knew more about what was happening roundabout the house and the neighborhood than the prissy housekeeper—or, as far as that went, the earl and his lady for all their gold.

Muirne Coyle still stood there, expressionless.

"Ever wash your face?" Even Diarmaid was surprised by his question.

She shrugged. "What's the point?"

"Don't you work?" Surely whoever hired her had to notice.

"Course."

"Doing what?"

"Cuttin' peat."

He was surprised again. Twice now. Cutting peat was hard work, a man's job.

"You're not a man."

Her mouth quirked. "That's twice you've noticed."

"Who hired a girl like you?"

"Knew I could do the work. Didn't care what's between me legs."

Diarmaid's head jolted upwards. Not a flicker of expression crossed Muirne's face.

"If you come back here, wash your face. You're an Irishwoman. Take some pride in it."

She stared hard at him, taking his measure, and then nodded her head. One sharp nod, and then turned and disappeared into the shadows round the sod heap she'd pointed out.

Great. He had nine volunteers of doubtful value and one gem. And the gem happened to be female.

God help them all.

'TWAS NOT YET FULL DAY when Diarmaid crawled out of the half-collapsed empty sod house he'd taken over as his quarters, but with the cold wind blowing across him—reasonably warm though his clothes were—lying in was hardly a temptation.

At least he wasn't taking up space in somebody else's house.

He straightened up, absent-mindedly cursing the stiffness in his back until he managed to flex and stretch the cramp out of it. 'Twasn't a bad day, for all that. Couldn't see it from here, but you could smell the sea, which wasn't far distant. Have to get closer before you heard the crash of the waves, a sound he'd learned to like. Unfamiliar to him at first, coming as he did from the east side of Ireland where the sea just lapped at the shore most of the year. Only in winter storms did it show its strength. In any case, he'd lived mainly inland.

He took a deep breath of the salty fresh air. If County Donegal was as far west and north as you could go and still be in Ireland, the Inishowen peninsula, where he stood now, was the farthest west and north you could go in County Donegal. Had he been over-optimistic to think that the bitterness against the English would be sharpest here? Sure and almost all the land worth anything for growing had been seized out of Irish hands and given to the plantation folk—Protestant, all of them, hard-eyed and suspicious, most of them. The night before he'd seen flashes of anger from the men of the clachans, but had these folk endured too much to use that anger and rise against their oppressors?

Hard to tell. It would take time, sure enough, and it was his job to be patient enough to spend the time. Pity that patience was not one of his strong points, although sure indeed he had more than he'd had before.

His stomach growled, reminding him of breakfast.

Memory was a wild beast, hard to ignore. Without even properly thinking of it he could taste the bacon and eggs his mam dished out in the earl's kitchen when the wind howled without. Safe inside the stone walls of the big house all was sheltered and warm. Bacon and eggs and thick slices of wheat bread, not the monotonous oaten stuff they ate here. Oaten porridge in the morning or sometimes oaten bread (but that— what they called scones—was not too bad with butter), potatoes with salt and buttermilk for dinner, with luck a bit of fish. The fish they called "kitchen," which was anything beyond the monotony of potatoes, porridge, and oaten bread. Most often there was no kitchen. Then the same bread and porridge again for supper.

God knew he wished for wheat, but for the present he'd better be satisfied with oats. The question as always was where to get it. In this dismal place there was no shop. He'd heard tell there was a shop in the parish, but the man who'd told him couldn't explain where it was, or at least not so as Diarmaid could make sense of it. So far he'd made do, given invitations to eat at somebody's fire—even in Donegal, the folk were as generous as they dared be—but no one had spoken up about today, and he ought not count on anything as chancy as that.

His stomach growled again. Might be it was time to think about a fire of his own. There would certainly be enough ventilation in his sod heap—or piece of sod heap—and could be a fire would keep him a bit warmer through the night, which would not come amiss. All he'd need was a circle of stones, and the saints in heaven knew there were enough of them. Since about half the roof had fallen in, he'd have no need of a chimney, at least.

He was sitting on a pile of stones, now that he looked down at them. The ground would do as well for sitting, and the stones could be converted into his new fireplace. He picked one of the bigger ones up— sweet Mary, it was heavy!—and grunting just a little, made his way back into what he was calling his place.

He had about half the fire circle made when one of the men from last night wandered past. Donncha Ward, was it? Nah. Liam Doherty.

"Whatcha doing?" He bent a bit to follow Diarmaid's progress into the sod hovel.

"Figured 'twas time to build a fire," Diarmaid said after he had dumped the stone and come back out for another.

"Have any peat?"

Diarmaid shrugged. "Nah. Thought I'd go over to the turf fields and buy some."

"Won't be dried out yet. Me wife's been careful like and we have some to spare, if you like."

Diarmaid folded his arms and contemplated young Liam. Well, younger than he was, if that meant anything. "Kind of you. I'd be grateful, but only if you let me pay you."

Liam's eyebrows went up and down. "I don't take pay for kindness. Mayhap I can throw in a bit of oats and butter to get you started."

Diarmaid started to speak and then shrugged. God bless the Irish. "I'll take it then with thanks."

"Come with me."

They stalked along together, making their way down something that probably passed for a road, but could equally well be called a footpath.

"Not much traffic along here?" Diarmaid asked.

Liam shrugged. "Horses, now and then. Carts only come from Derry. Thick wheels they have, but after a rain they may stay a while in the mud, like it or not."

Derry was a piece away. Not so far it couldn't be walked, and since it was the closest town of any size there must be a fair bit of back and forthing. For a moment he considered moving his operation on in that direction—no. 'Twouldn't do. No point hoping he'd find more success if he pushed farther east. The English had too tight a grip farther that way, with their prissy-faced Scots growin' crops on Irish land and set to stay forever.

"Round here," Liam said. He turned off the road and ducked into a small stone dwelling. Stone? Diarmaid was impressed. Inside was small enough. There was a fire burning there, but the chimney was only a rod creel bunged into a hole in the roof. The smoke made its way through the opening at the bottom of the reed basket. It crawled up from the fire along the gable wall to reach it, which accounted for the tendrils of smoke hanging about the rafters. Hard to miss the strong smell of oats in the smoke.

Liam looked about with some pride, and nodded his head toward the bedroom off to the right. "Me brother Seán stays with us," he said.

Diarmaid took a quick look. Small enough, the room was, just barely the length of the bed, and whoever slept there had to push the door open and use the space in the doorway to put his feet when he got up. Nobody there now.

Still, it was a stone house, and on either side of the fire were kitchen beds—outshot, Diarmaid'd heard them called. Had boards all around the side, a sliding door facing the fire and on the top a roof that made space for storing things out of the way. He looked at Liam with respect.

"'Tis nice here," he said.

Liam beamed at him with pride. "'Tis. Me wife's a good 'un. She makes fine butter, and spins 'til deep in the night by the fire. It was a good day's work, marryin' her." He knelt down and scrabbled around by the side of the fire, then produced a basket with a handle, and a few lumps of peat piled within it. "That should hold you for a bit. 'Tis sure the rest of the lads can add some to it when it gets low."

"I thank you." Dear God, the goodness of the Irish, for all they could be stupid as stumps. Sometimes it seemed to Diarmaid he had more of that kind to deal with than was fair, but it was Liam and his like that made all the arguing and fussing and even real fighting worth the time and bother it took. Their sort deserved far more than to be considered a short step up from animals, to be spoke to with contempt by the useless English who ruled their lives.

He looked away and tried to take a deep breath quiet enough so Liam would not hear it. Settle down, he told himself silently. When there's nothing can be done now, no point in bristling. Wait. The time, it will come. Then this bloody cauldron of bitterness and anger will be of some use.

He was just turning back to Liam when the corner of his eye caught some motion, and he looked around to see a woman, a young one, coming into the house.

"Lizzie!" Diarmaid could hear the lift in Liam's voice. "This be Diarmaid MacGuinness, come up from the south to lend a hand."

His wife. She was plain but sturdy, and her smile looking at her husband made her face warmer, like. "Welcome, Diarmaid," she said. "Did you get food to eat this morning yet?"

"I ate some already," Liam told her.

"Then what's left will go for him." With a quick deft motion, she pulled out one of three bowls, dipped a spoon in the pot, and dished out porridge near to the top of the bowl.

"Hey, there," Diarmaid objected. How far did that potful have to be stretched? Dammit, he needed to find a source of oats, if that's all there was, something that was not the makings of somebody else's meal.

Lizzie turned around, the bowl in her hands, and gave it to him with a spoon in it. "Eat and stay strong," she said.

The bowl was warm in his hands. He dipped his head in thanks, and began to eat. Food fit for gods it was not—how long did it take to get used to the eternal oats?—but it slaked the growing hunger in his belly. Which was the point, was it not?

"Where in the south were you?" Lizzie's voice was polite, but plainly curious.

"Been far as Dublin, but mainly Meath and more recent, Galway. Connemara as well," he added as an afterthought.

"Mmm." For a moment he saw what might be a hint of something wistful on Lizzie's face. "But travel's hard, innit it?"

"The way I do it, on foot mainly? That it is." But it was the only way to learn what life was most truly like for the people he'd come to find. All you learned from riding in a coach was if the springs were any good.

"How far do you get in a day?" Liam moved toward his wife—to hush her?—but Diarmaid shook his head and Liam stopped where he was.

"Depends. On weather, how hot or cold 'tis, who I meet."

"Must be grand to be free." Lizzie's voice sounded wistful, and Diarmaid saw Liam's eyes switch to her. But that was a woman's life, was it not? For no good reason the dirty face of Muirne Coyle flashed into his mind. Would she wind up doing women's work in a house like this someday? Somehow it seemed less than likely.

Well. He'd have to spend some time giving thought to Muirne Coyle one of these days, but today did not have to be one of them. Where would she be today, anyway? Most likely out in the peat fields, cutting along with the men.

He handed his bowl back to Lizzie and heard his own self saying to Liam, "What about that Muirne Coyle, then?"

Liam's mouth quirked into a crooked grin. "She's one of a kind, no fear."

"She never had a fair turn at anything." When Lizzie spoke up, both men turned to her in some surprise. Liam's eyes moved from her to Diarmaid, and he reached for his cap.

"We'll go out," he said.

Diarmaid nodded at Lizzie, who looked straight at him.

"Ta for the porridge." Her face softened into a smile and she nodded and reached over into one of the baskets on the kitchen bed roof behind her. She took out three scones and wrapped them in a loose bit of cloth and handed them to Diarmaid.

"See if you can get a bit of butter and heat those on your fire."

Diarmaid wrapped the scones a bit tighter and put them in the basket with the peat. He looked first at Lizzie, then at Liam. "Thank ye both."

Liam shook his head and half smiled, looking at Lizzie. "No one's going to starve if she has food."

She looked back at him straight. "You have the right of it," she said, turning then to Diarmaid. "Don't be put off by what they say about Muirne Coyle. She works harder than three men. Her da dodges the revenue police so as he can make poteen and drink most of what he makes. If t'were not for Muirne he'd have wasted away from hunger long since."

"Enough, Lizzie." Liam opened the door and checked over his shoulder that Diarmaid was coming along behind him.

Diarmaid turned in the direction toward his half-collapsed sod heap. "Thanks for all," he said.

Liam nodded. "I'm off to see to me cows. Two of them we have. If Lizzie makes butter she'll bring a bit of it to you. She makes grand butter."

Diarmaid shrugged his shoulders. "Thanks is a poor word compared to all you're doing for me. I do have some money—"

Liam's half smile vanished. "Keep it for the cause. When do we meet again?"

Diarmaid shrugged again. "Not sure. A day or two? I'll pass the word."

Liam gave a quick nod and turned away.

The two men walked off in different directions, Diarmaid toward the sod heap, remembering the days when he'd been the one bringing food from the big house where his mam worked, wrapping it in cloths around his body so that the hungry men who prowled the roads then would not know it was there to be stolen. Times changed. Back then he'd been the giver; now, it appeared he was to receive.

It was more comfortable to give.

He bent to set down the basket with the peat and the wrapped scones, looking about for a place to put the scones. One advantage his makeshift dwelling did not possess was any place to keep anything safe. Even in its prime, the sod house had not run to cupboards. As he did not take to the notion of having a stray dog eat up Lizzie's scones, he stood there fuddled like, trying to figure what to do.

How many dogs were around, he wondered. Not many, was his best guess. From what he'd seen, there was little enough food to make it unlikely there were many who would keep an animal around for pleasure. Could be Lizzie's scones would do fine tucked under the straw he was using for a bed. He thought about it for another minute or so, and then shrugged and knelt down again to push the scones in their wrapping under the straw.

He settled back on his heels for a moment and allowed himself a bitter chuckle. In that big house back in Meath where his mam was, even the lowest servant had a bed of some sort. The English earl and his lady and their two daughters slept on finest linen, of course, smooth and soft to the touch. Rich they were, and the fields of their estate were fine and fertile, growing lush crops to add to their wealth.

It was only here, on the rocky soil where they had been pushed when all the good land was taken by the Protestants that the Irish were allowed to scrabble for a living. And then accused of lack of skill in farming, blamed for their inability to feed themselves.

The sour taste of outrage welled up in his mouth.

"Diarmaid MacGuinness, sir…"

It was a soft voice, a woman's voice he heard, and when he turned, saw Lizzie Doherty looking round the fallen part of the roof to see him.

"Miz Doherty," he said, scrambling to his feet.

She held a pan in her hand. "I should of thought before. The peat you have'll be of no use without something to light it." She extended the pan toward him, a glowing lump at the bottom.

He grabbed the pan by the handle she offered him, and dropped the burning embers onto the peat he had fortunately already placed in his stone circle fireplace.

Lizzie leaned over to watch, and then straightened up, smiling. "That'll catch now," she said with satisfaction.

"'Twas good of you," Diarmaid said.

"Should of thought before," she murmured again. "That should burn slow and steady now."

"I'm more grateful than I can say." He handed the pan back to her.

She was still watching the smoldering peat, and then looked up at his face, with a shadow of the same smile he'd seen her give Liam.

"You've come all this way to help us," she said. "Let us help you when we can."

She dipped her head in a kind of a bow, and then retreated rapidly back out of sight, her pan in her hand.

Left alone, Diarmaid rubbed his face with his hands. Could be he had not slept all that well the night before. Might be that explained the rush of warmth and weariness he felt now.

But by God, he was willing to give the rest of his life—or even to lose it—if that would help give back to these people their own green and lovely land.

MUIRNE COYLE LEANED ON HER spade for a moment. How was it possible to be cold and hot at the same time? Her feet felt frozen from standing on the chill turf. The soles of her shoes were near wore out, while the rest of her sweated from the hard labor of cutting blocks of what would be peat. Well, was peat, but it would need the drying before anyone could burn it.

She rubbed her face with one hand and then groaned a little. Dirt on her face again. Damn it all to hell, she'd washed her face this morning—how had that arrogant know-all from the south dared suggest she lacked pride as an Irishwoman? She'd been so burned by his stupidity that she'd even complained to Seán Doherty about it, and she wasn't one to complain about much. She glanced up to see Seán, his shoulders and back working in a steady rhythm, one line over. Might've been a bloody machine.

But she could cut as much, or more than he could, so she jerked up the spade and plunged it back into the thick turf on which she was standing. 'Twas still early enough so that the thrust of her arms and back felt good, the good burn of exercise. By the end of the day she'd be aching like an old woman, but, saints be praised, she wasn't there yet.

And it was a good day, another blessing. The sky arched like a great blue bowl overhead, a few scraps of cloud drifting across. The kind of day it would be a pity to be stuck indoors. Thank God she was not one of those women hitched to some man; sentenced to spend her days inside with some bawling babe, each day just like the day before, just like the day that would come next.

She still owned her own self.

She thrust in her spade the next time, forward, then straight, then forward again. Once you fell into the rhythm it went on and on, easy like, until the muscles rebelled and the pain began. She was still young enough, not yet twenty, so that she could get in a good few hours first. She glanced back to see the crooked row of peat blocks behind her, each one where it had been tumbled off her spade just before she dug into the next.

When her eyes moved forward there were two shoes standing just beyond where her spade was working. She followed the legs coming up out of the shoes to the shape of a man looming above.

Oh, bloody hell. It was the southerner.

She peered up at him, closing one eye against the sun that shone into her face when she looked that direction.

"What d'ye want?" She spit out the words.

"You washed your face. There's just that one bit o' mud, and it's fresh." He grinned at her.

She plunged her spade back into the earth, folded her arms, and stared up at him, squinting only a little in the sun. "So? What d'ye want?"

"Came to talk to you a little."

"Not now. I'm working." She unfolded her arms, grabbed the spade again and sunk it into the turf the barest distance from where his feet were standing.

"Hey! Watch my feet!" He danced backward.

"Get 'em out of my work, then."

He shook his head, back and forth, a half grin on his face. For a minute he said nothing, then, his face dropping any trace of amusement, he snapped out, "You serious about working with us?"

"Think I had nothing else to do yesterday but go hear you talk?"

He looked at her for a moment, intent like. "Dunno. Might have come by for the entertainment."

"Better shows elsewhere."

He lifted his head and straightened up. In the sun his shadow stretched a lot farther than hers did. Damn. Why did women have to be small?

"Need to know. More, I need to know now. Are you with us?"

"You said you had no need for me."

He looked fussed. Fair enough. She *felt* fussed. He looked away and then back at her. "I may not, may do. 'Tis why I want to talk with you."

"Not now. This is me work."

The southerner—of course now his name was fled from her brain—nodded. "When then?"

She sunk her spade into the turf. "Tonight?"

"Where?"

She cast him an irritated look. Did she have to figure it all out herself? "Where you were last night."

He nodded, and without a word of farewell, ambled away down toward the edge of the field. Muirne looked after him, halfway between tossing a wad of peat after him—her arm was strong, and most likely she'd hit him—and giving thanks to whatever saints were paying attention that there was someone willing to give his life to the cause, to make Ireland as it should be.

Nah. She'd not waste her time doing either. She pulled out her spade and sunk it back into the black thick peat.

Since it was turning spring, the days were longer than they had been and shorter than they would be when summer came in. Long enough so that by sunset Muirne's arms and back sang with the pain of hours of digging and lifting. Carrying her spade, she trudged back toward the sod house her da called home.

Home. Funny word, that. The Dohertys—Seán and his brother Liam and Liam's wife, Lizzie—had something you might call home. Stone built, it was. Floor was dirt, just as it was in the sod house, but Lizzie kept things straight. At least any time Muirne had happened to be there, the fire was warm and the beds were neat. Liam had even put hooks in the wall so that Lizzie had a place to put the pot and the pan when she wasn't cooking. Kept the rest of her things—the bowls and plates—in the outshot bed they wouldn't be using before they had a bairn. No need for bedding yet in there.

Her da's house? No bedroom like Seán had at the Dohertys' place. Most nights her da had had too much poteen to care where he fell asleep. Most often 'twas on his coat he'd tossed on the floor by the fire. Muirne had made a bed for herself with a pile of straw flattened out. One thin quilt she tossed over it, and another she pulled over herself for the nights that sometimes were cold even with the remains of the fire glowing nearby. Such clothes as the two of them had they kept in piles, Muirne's neater than her da's. All work clothes they were. There was only a Protestant church down the road a piece; none of the Irish needed church clothes as there was no chapel nor place to say Mass in. The wandering friars would use the Mass rocks scattered round the hills. Word would be passed beforehand about where to go, and people would gather, casual like.

So the sod house might not be much like a home, but it was a place to rest. Well, it had a roof. Last year the rain had come in so bad her da got fed up and paid a couple of lazy good-for-nothings with poteen so they'd climb up with him and make it sound. So that was good. That morning Muirne'd taken a couple of cooked potatoes with her for her dinner during the break at work. Most o' the others went home to get something to eat, but there would be no one at the sod house unless her da happened to be there, and if he was he'd not be alone. Muirne was not about to hand out food to half the wastrels living roundabout. 'Twas better to eat her potatoes cold in the field. Might be there was some porridge left over from the morning. She'd have that for supper, and there might be buttermilk still there, she thought.

It was as she turned the corner, the makeshift door ahead of her, that she remembered the damned southerner.

Bloody hell. She'd told him she'd be there in the shed to talk. Talk? What about?

For a moment she hesitated, and her shoulders hung limply. She was so tired; it had been a long day. But so would tomorrow be, and the day after that. 'Twould be better to settle things with the southerner tonight and get it over with. She'd have a bite to eat first. That usually gave her a push forward.

She straightened up again and pushed the door open.

Muirne still hadn't remembered the southerner's name after her meal when she went round back of the sod house and headed for the shed there. She could see no light and for a moment thought with real venom that if he couldn't be bothered to be there when she'd told him to be, there was no point in having anything more to do with him.

But when she walked into the shed, there he was, rising to his feet in the dimness. She blinked, waiting for her eyes to adjust to the partial darkness. Gradually the room, such as it was, came into greater clarity.

There was the pile of stools they'd sat on the night before. She wondered as she waited how he'd come across so many.

He had just two set out now, and gestured toward one of them for her.

"Muirne Coyle, is it?" he asked.

"'Twas that last night and I'm not about to be changing me name."

Although her tone had not been friendly and had not been meant to be, a flicker of something like amusement passed over his face.

"Sit down then, please, Muirne Coyle."

"An' what's your name again? It dinna stick in my mind." She spoke sharply, although she knew it was a kind of laziness that she'd not remembered, rather than it being his fault.

"Diarmaid McGuinness."

Not a bad name. She'd make a point of remembering it this time. Nodding a little, she sat on the stool. 'Twas a pity there were not many chairs in her life. She could have used something to rest her tired back against.

He sat as well, his hands loosely linked together, leaning on his thighs.

"We've not had the best of starts," he said, his eyes looking into her face. "Would you like to begin again, or shall we just agree we'll not get along and you can go home and rest your weary bones?"

Muirne met his eyes straight on and considered. 'Twas true enough her straw pallet seemed to be calling to her, but God knew she loved Ireland. Although she couldna see sensibly how anything would ever change, the idea that it might was a bright dream on long days.

"I'll stay." She said it swiftly and folded her lips so she'd not change it.

"That's good." He nodded sharply, as if the subject was closed. "Then I need your help." He pulled a piece of paper out of his pocket and unfolded it. From what Muirne could see, it was the list of names from the night before.

"Do you read?" he asked.

Her head moved slowly up and down, her eyes studying him.

"I do some, not a lot," he confessed. "I'm working on it. Can you read the names on this list? I'm not sure they're spelt as they should be."

Still wordless, she reached out for the paper, and he put it in her hand.

She peered at it, but the light was too dim to read.

"No one can read in the dark," she said. "Have you a candle or some sort of light? We're a bit low on them." Which was an understatement. Between them Muirne and her da generally had only a single candle, most often a stub, and not always that. Practically speaking, the fire was the only light in the house once it went dark outside.

Diarmaid looked about as if he half expected one would materialize somewhere in the dark shadows. He looked toward the door. "Can we take it outside? It's not full night out there yet."

'Twas certainly the only way she was going to be able to read anything. Holding the slip of paper firmly between her fingers, she led the way out the door. As soon as they were back in the twilight outside, she looked at the words on the paper again. This time they were clear.

"It's the names of those what were there last night." She looked over at him, waiting for further instructions.

"I know. What I'd like you to do is go over them, read them out, and tell me what you know about them. Who's reliable, who's likely to be a bit rash—that sort of thing."

She glanced up at his face and nodded, then looked back at the list.

"Patrick McGurk," she read, looking again at his face. "Big man. Not the smartest, but oncet he gets set into something, doesn't stop till it's done."

Diarmaid's face was intent, absorbing the information. "Next?" he asked.

"Jack Louglin. One to watch. He'll never come out the short end of a bargain."

"Honest?"

Muirne considered. "Mostly."

"Next?"

"Seán Doherty. Solid gold. Lives with 'is brother and 'is wife. Works on next row to me most days."

"I got a chance to talk to Liam," Diarmaid said.

"Solid gold there, too. He'll go as far as needed to help you."

"Yes." Diarmaid's grin flashed and for a moment he was near to a handsome man.

Muirne continued. "Has to be watched careful like to make sure he doesn't give away what he needs to someone who needs it worse."

"That's him."

An answering smile flirted around her mouth. "Married Lizzie O'Malley who's as bad as him or worse."

Diarmaid shrugged. "Next?"

They went through the whole list. As the sky darkened and the words melted into the page, Muirne had to rely more on her own recollection of who sat where and who sat next. She liked watching Diarmaid's face as he absorbed each lot of information and tucked it away somewhere behind his eyes. She was quite sure that if she asked him the next day or maybe two months from now all the facts would come spitting right out, not a one forgotten or changed by the remembering. She'd never seen a man like that before, except maybe one priest who'd come by long years before. For a moment she let herself remember what the priest had been like, and wondered what had befallen him in the years since.

"Thank ye." His voice came out of the darkness now. "'Tis the knowledge that takes me a long time to gain. This lets me start."

He was only a dark shape now in the blackness of night all around them.

"Start what?" Muirne heard her own voice, sounding softer now that all the light was fled.

At first he did not speak, but she heard no sound of him moving away.

Then, his voice softer, too, he said, "That's what I don't know meself yet. I know what I'd like it to be."

She waited, but when he didn't speak again, she asked, "What?"

His voice was still gentle. "I'd like to leave a knot of trustworthy, devoted men who'd be prepared to come forward when we manage to build a force that could strike a heavy blow against the English. Trained men who know not to lose their heads should a gun be pointed at 'em or their brother. Men who know enough to keep their mouths shut and do as they're told. What we need is a disciplined force to face the English and not a bunch of fools running about doing whatever they think is needed but who have no idea of what all may be going on in the places they cannot see." The gentleness in his voice had sharpened as his words went on, until at the end he was speaking with more force than he'd had at any time she'd heard him before.

"Will some die?"

This time he did not pause. "Most likely."

"The good ones?"

"Sometimes 'tis the brave ones shot down and the stupid ones live on."

"Then what's the point?"

"That's why we have to work to find the brave ones, the dedicated ones, so that they can overpower the English. The English have the power now. They are not going to go away until they are shown there is wave after wave of Irish that will keep coming until it can be proved to them their time is over. It will happen, but it will not be easy." His voice had changed, somehow. His words were cold, hard, coming out of the darkness. Muirne felt the chill of them, redoubled by the chill of the night itself.

All at once she wanted the quiet of her straw pallet not far from the fire in the pitiful shelter of the sod house.

"'Tis time for me to get back," she said. "Morning comes early."

"That it does." Abruptly Diarmaid's voice was gentler, easy, as it had been before. "Get back home. Thanks for your help. I am grateful to you."

Should she say "That's all right"? or "Glad to help"? Or mayhap just leave quietly and go back between the houses to her own front door. She stood there, uncertain.

"Be on your way." There were the words, and then the crunching sound of his feet moving over the ground to wherever he was going next. The clouds above made it so dark that she could not see where that might be.

She stood where she was until the crunching sound had grown quieter and finally was swallowed up in the low murmur of noises all around. The sounds of people speaking some distance away, a few steps of someone else going somewhere, in the distance the bark of a dog.

She was alone now, as she usually was. She turned, and there was the sound of her own feet walking in the darkness. She thrust out a hand as she turned the corner to go between the houses, and when she felt the cold damp of the sod knew she was heading the right direction.

She could count steps from here. She counted and then turned, the blackness of night still absolute. Then she put out her hand for the door and the familiar wooden boards were under her fingers.

When she pushed the door open, she was home. Her da was not there, but that was nothing odd. Perhaps he would come later, perhaps not.

In the light of the fire she could see all as it always was. The piles of their clothes, the stones surrounding the fire. The pot for porridge the next morning pushed back from the fire against the wall. Her pallet, waiting for her.

It was all as always, and yet in some indefinable way she felt change creeping toward her.

DIARMAID HAD TO KEEP REMINDING himself it was never easy. When he looked back at the other spots where he'd started a knot of good men, he should remember he was looking back at how it finished, not how it began.

Here in Inishowen he was only at the start. Two more meetings had gone well; the third never got underway. To start with, only five had showed up for those two meetings unless you counted Muirne. Diarmaid briefly debated, but then counted her even though she never pulled her stool up with the rest of them, but stayed in the background. She listened intently and if he said something she thought was unwise or daft, she'd tell him about it, but afterward, casual like. The next time nobody came round. Had he been unclear in telling them when it was to be?

By the time of the meeting that wasn't, at least Diarmaid was getting himself a bit settled. He'd resolved the food problem when he realized the place to get what he wanted was Derry. It was the better part of thirty miles away, but men and women walked it in the ordinary course o' things. He'd walked distances like that many a time himself. The way should be obvious, and he could always ask. More, he'd get a look at what the east side of Donegal was like. Everyone he'd talked to said that was where the good land for planting was, and it was thick with Protestants. Certainly the Scots and English that had been planted there were still there. The ones given land along the western coast had almost all given it up as a bad deal.

Most of what he saw was what he thought he'd see, from what folks had told him. The land in east Donegal was gentler, more forgiving. There were plenty of fertile fields, well prepared for spring planting.

There were proper houses, even some big houses like ones he'd known in County Meath. 'Twas flat, even, not like the part of Donegal where he'd settled, just back from the coast, where there were hills and crags and bogland good for nothing but peat, and where even ground running up the sides of the hills around the stones had to be used for growing potatoes and oats so there'd be something to eat.

Would it have been better for him to start recruiting there? In Galway they'd spent hours in one pub or another arguing it over. Would they be more successful working where the common folk were most downtrodden and had more reason to throw themselves against the injustices of English rule, or would it be better to start where life was easier and even the poorer Irish had more strength to call on, not having to use every shred of endurance just to get from one day to the next? Once he was committed to doing the recruiting himself, Diarmaid had not wanted to argue for the easier course lest some idiot say he wanted the more comfortable place to live himself. He'd been on the side arguing for the west of Donegal himself then.

But now—well, now he knew how being hungry all the time wore down a man's strength. How slaving like a navvy every day but Sunday carved away the ability to get angry enough to be willing to take on anything else. You might have the right of it, and blame the bloody English and the Scots and their land grab for the sad thing you call your life, but given the merciless run of your days be too exhausted to do much about it.

Thinking was one way to pass the time as he walked. Wasn't much in the way of towns or clachans—the pattern of thatched cottages or sod houses in a cluster surrounded by the fields shared out among the people living there—the further east he went.

The pattern broke up into what he was already familiar with. There were villages in the distance—well, they looked more like villages, straggling along short distances, not like the close spacing of the clachans. And the fields: the fields were more like what he'd seen elsewhere in Ireland. Fields stretching out from what was clearly a farmhouse. And the pattern of big houses was there, too, complete with lawns and drives and gates.

Not that he was alone on his walk to Derry. There were groups—well, two or three walking together—and solitary figures ahead of him. Some of them he caught up to and passed, sharing smiles and greetings as he walked by. Others kept up a steady pace ahead of him, remaining just at the edge of the distance he could see.

"You're the southerner," a voice said behind him.

Diarmaid turned to see who it was. Just that momentary hesitation, and for a bit he lost the rhythm of his stride.

"I am," he said, trying to pick it up again. His legs wanted to continue on the pace he'd established, and there was still far enough ahead so that he didn't like the idea of slowing down.

"Going to Derry, then?"

"I am," he said again. Well, where did the fool think he was going, walking along this road?

"How's it going, then?"

Diarmaid cast a quick glance at him. The other man'd caught up now, and they were moving at the same pace. Who was he? He looked just the same as dozens of others. Bearded, not in first youth because his hair was going white at the temples. His clothes not as shabby as many Diarmaid'd seen, but more so than he was used to in Galway and farther south.

What was this stranger asking about? The walk to Derry? His health? Surely not how his work was going. He'd not knowingly seen this man before and he was not about to develop a loose tongue at this late date.

"Not that far to go," he said.

The stranger's eyebrows went up and back down again. "You plan to stay there?"

"No." His plan was to pick up what he needed in the way of staples, load them into the bag he would carry on his shoulders, and walk back to his clachan. If he turned out to be too weary to get back all the way, he would find a spot to sleep. But how that concerned anyone else, he could not see.

The stranger nodded. "It's a fair distance. I'd not thought a southerner would want to do it twice in a day. There are places to stay."

Diarmaid cast a quick look at him. "Thank you. I've walked this far and more in the south."

The stranger nodded, as if that was what he had expected him to say. "You have reasons to get back?"

"I plan to return to where I'm staying." Diarmaid did not look at him again. He was not over-fond of questions, but at this point there was naught he was doing that was needful to hide. Still, he had no need or desire to answer questions.

He lengthened his stride just a wee bit.

The stranger kept with him for another few minutes, and then gradually fell behind. Diarmaid said nothing more, nor did the other man, and Diarmaid did not look behind to see how far behind him the stranger was now. He must have settled back to whatever his initial pace had been.

Odd, that was what it was. Next time he wrote to his uncle in Galway, he just might mention it. Certainly there'd been times when he'd needed to melt away rather than attract official notice, but that was not the case now. Was this some curious stranger who might have seen him at the clachan and wondered about him? Possibly. Had someone heard his casual invitation to the first meeting and wondered what was going on? Or was someone just looking for some company on a long walk?

He'd assume that for now, at least, although he didn't want company himself and was relieved the man'd fallen back. But he'd remember his looks, and keep an eye out for him. His mother's son was no fool.

It was as easy as he'd thought it would be to pick up the food he wanted from a proper shop where he could pay without creating obligations he'd feel if it was offered to him. Once he had it packed away neatly in the pack on his back he stopped in a pub—good that there was one right on the corner—and had a beer and a meat pie. Hot it was, and tasted good. Seemed a long time since he'd had anything so ordinary. It was going to take a long time for him to ask for a bowl of porridge once he got out of Inishowen.

Coming out of the pub, he realized dusk was not far off. It must have taken him longer than he expected to make the walk. Either that or he'd not taken into consideration that he was so much farther north now, and night came on earlier here.

Standing on the corner he looked around. God in his mercy had planted an inn not that far down the street. A grand place it was not—just as well, as he had only the money he'd been given when he left Galway, and he'd used much of that buying his food for the next week or two—but there were coins in his pocket. He could begin walking; of course he could, and there would be fields all along the way where he could sleep, but after thirty miles of walking today, more or less, his legs were reminding him that they'd like to stretch out on something meant to be slept on, however hard and thin it might be.

Without quite deciding to do so he found himself walking toward the inn.

When he reached it the old crone at the desk showed no interest in anything but the coins he produced when she told him the price, and directed him up a staircase that had seen better days to the second door on the right.

It was about what he expected. Plain, with a bed and a chair and a rickety table with a wash basin and an ewer. A chamber pot under the bed. He took a quick look around and then locked the door behind him. Fine. The decision to stay had been made and he discovered he was grateful to know he'd have a night in a proper bed.

The only surprise, and it was a welcome one, was that the ewer did indeed have water in it. Not hot—miracles not likely to happen—but not icy cold either. Diarmaid pulled the shabby curtain to one side and looked out at the street. It was nearly night now, but in the windows of the buildings and houses there was a light here and there. He remembered the total blackness of night in the clachan and thought that at least there the stars were bright in the sky.

When there were no clouds, of course.

He set down the bag—that would be heavy on his shoulders for the walk home—and pulled off his outer clothing. Must have taken him all of ten seconds. Another five to fall into the bed, which creaked ominously, but that was all he remembered.

When he opened his eyes, it was morning.

Muirne had escaped the sod house early and made her way down to the shore. It was Sunday, and her da was flat asleep on the dirt floor of the sod house, with a couple of his drinking mates collapsed around him, all of them snoring and choking a bit in their sleep. They had not been there when she'd fallen onto her straw pallet the night before. In fact, she'd not laid eyes on her da for two days or so, but now a fool could tell what he and t'others had been up to. The place reeked of poteen, probably both from the making of it and the drinking afterward.

For a minute or two when she first roused she'd felt cold anger that this was her life. There were men about worth something, but all she had for a father was this drunken sot. She wisht she could keep that anger long enough to drag him out of the door and leave him to freeze outside, but the pity of it was t'would be a waste of her time. If she really thought he'd die, it might be worth it, but spring was coming on, and the day dawning now would be too warm. And oh, dear mother of God, the fuss it would make. Not that she believed anyone would blame her. She could argue that he'd collapsed out there all on his own. No one in the clachan would be inclined to question it.

Still, by the time she'd opened her eyes the spurt of anger had waned. What was the point? Her life was what it was. Nothing was going to change.

She'd crawled from under the flimsy quilt and pulled on the outside clothes she'd taken off the night before. The fire was smoldering still: she searched quietly but thoroughly for what might be about, and when she found a scone her fingers closed around it and she stuffed it into a pocket. For a moment she thought of emptying the sludge at the bottom of the porridge pot onto the fire, then shook her head and walked away. He was welcome to what was left of yesterday's porridge if he wanted to eat that—tasteless and gluey it would be—and the pleasure of putting out the fire wouldn't be worth letting the house get even colder than it was already.

She went out of the door, closing it behind her, and looked around at the new day. As far as she knew no traveling friars were about. If there was to be a mass said up on the hills in one of the spots hidden by rocks, word flew around days in advance.

It would be a bit of a walk to the beach, but what would she do if she hung about here? She hadn't laid eyes on Diarmaid for two, three days now. He'd disappeared before her da had. Had he given up on them here as a hopeless task? She couldn't blame him if he had. Too many of the lazy bastards hadn't seen fit to show up. Why should he care about them if they couldn't bother to come work with him?

'Twasn't as if she cared, either. True, he'd given her a glimmer of hope, just the wisp of a dream that someday things might change. But hope was a fool's game, and dreams lived about as long as soap bubbles. She'd known that even as she listened to him.

She met no one during the hour or so—probably a bit less—that it took her to walk to the shore, nor was anyone else there when she picked her way across the rocks to the stretch of sand. 'Twas mostly habit that had her scanning the breadth of the beach to see if by some chance a fish or two had been washed ashore during the night. It happened sometimes, and a fish with their potatoes for dinner would not go amiss.

No fish today, however, and she could not claim to be surprised. Today had given no indication pleasant treats might be lurking. Still, the fresh ocean air blowing her hair was a welcome change from the sour smell she'd wakened to in the house. The sun was making a good try at warming the air, and she was free of the peat bog for the day. She could lean back against the rocks and feel the sun and the wind against her skin.

The rocks were sharp and unwelcoming, but she managed to wriggle into a place where nothing seemed to be poking her. She must even have dozed off, because when she lazily opened her eyes Diarmaid was standing there.

For a minute she just stared at him. "Where did you come from?"

"I been to Derry."

"Oh." She was vaguely aware that part of the rock was pressing into her hip, and shifted just enough to ease the discomfort. "Wondered where you'd gone."

"Did you?" Was he asking, or had he just said, "Did you." The pleasure of the sun that was now warming the rocks as well made her disinclined to fuss at him, or anybody else, come to that. She closed her eyes again.

"How'd you get there?" she asked without opening them.

"Walked."

"And back?" She did open her eyes then to look at him. "That's a fair piece."

"That it is."

"When did ye get back?"

"Yesterday." He grinned at her. "Went to bed early last night, I promise you."

She tried to settle back again into the pleasure of just lying there, the warm rocks around her, the waves tumbling gently onto the beach, but her conscience niggled at her.

"Have you had anything to eat?"

He laughed, and abruptly, seeing him there with the wind ruffling his red hair—red as hers was—he was wonderfully pleasant to look at.

"Cooked myself an egg for breakfast."

Her eyes opened wider, and she struggled to a position that was a bit more erect. An egg? Those lucky enough to have chickens saved the eggs to sell. Cash money was too valuable to pass up for the pleasure of eating an egg yourself.

"Why?" The word burst out without her meaning to say it.

"It tasted good." He cocked his head. "I have another one. Have you eaten anything yet?"

She remembered the scone, and wriggled far enough free of the rocks to retrieve it. She pulled it out to show him.

"That's hard as a rock," he said.

She shrugged.

"I have some bread as well. Wheat bread."

"Where did that come from?"

"Derry. Come have the egg and some bread and let me talk to you about some plans I was thinking of."

She stared at him with disbelief. He wanted to talk to her? It was even stranger than the offer of egg and bread, which made her mouth water just to think of it.

He reached out and grabbed her hand, pulling her to her feet. "Just one condition."

Instantly wary, she looked at him.

"There's a mess o' water right here. Wash your face."

For a moment she trembled on the edge of fury. Then, for no good reason she could have given him if he'd asked, she started to laugh.

Diarmaid tossed his head back and laughed with her.

Muirne crouched at Diarmaid's side as he boiled her egg. He offered her a good thick slice of bread, but she said she chose to wait until she could have it all together. He slipped another chunk of peat into the fire before he put the pot on, but peat-like, of course, it would take a bit before it gave up its heat.

Her gaze was fixed on the water in the pot, waiting for it to bubble up around the egg. Diarmaid found himself concentrating on her face, instead. When 'twasn't so dirty, he could see how fine her bone structure was, how well-shaped her eyes. He'd seen the intense blue at once, but had not noticed the smooth curve of her eyebrows above them. So many girls like her, forced to work as hard as she did (and he'd done enough turf cutting to know himself it was weary work), gradually thickened, like, their girlish look vanishing bit by bit until they were as stolid and silent as their mothers.

Not Muirne, although her life was harder than most. She'd had nothing good to say of either of her parents, but when it came to other people more than not she'd say whatever was good or useful about them. In Diarmaid's experience most people were not like that.

He wisht he had something more to offer her than working with him to try to shape some unlikely downtrodden men whose lives had taught them to keep their heads down and out of trouble into proper Irishmen with a sense of what they were worth. The sad knowledge he'd gained here in this forlorn clachan was that it was just as well that he wasn't trying to raise a corps of men who would be capable of bravery and making decisions any day in the future he could see directly ahead.

"It's boiling," Muirne whispered by his shoulder.

"Right." He watched the pot, hoping more than he usually did that the sense of time passing his mam had taught him would work this time. This egg was to be right for Muirne. He watched it in the pot, a solitary egg tumbled around in the boiling water, remembering the racks full of eggs in the kitchen in the big house where his mam was cook.

No. Couldn't let himself be distracted. Keeping track of time in his head worked only if he gave it his full attention. Only then.

At exactly the right moment he whipped the pot off the fire and set it on the hard packed earth by the side of the stones circling his fire pit.

Muirne still watched him.

For a moment he hesitated, glancing around to see where he'd put the hot water when he'd cooked his own egg earlier. Hot water was not something you just poured out on the ground. Where had he put it before?

His eye fell on the jar he'd found somewhere around here—couldn't remember where now. Not that it mattered. The rim was chipped and it hadn't been worth much when it was whole and new. But the sides of the jar were thick.

He poured the still barely boiling water into the jar, hearing the slosh of the water he'd put in there before. He kept just enough back in the pan so that the egg didn't plop into the jar with the water.

Setting the pot back on the ground, he handed Muirne the jar.

"Wrap your hands around that. It'll warm them up for you."

She had been watching what he had been doing intently, now she glanced up at his face and grinned at him as she took the jar and did as he said.

"That's nice." For just a moment she lifted the jar to warm one cheek, but set it back on the ground almost at once, her hands still around it soaking up the warmth. "Nice for hands, too hot for me face."

Diarmaid had but the one bowl and one spoon, and now was glad he'd taken the time to wash both after he'd eaten before. He pulled out his knife and neatly split off the top of the shell. The yolk was unbroken, and he almost grinned himself with satisfaction.

"There ye be," he said, handing her the bowl with the two parts of the egg and the spoon inside.

She set down the jar to one side and took it. Deftly she spooned the cooked white out of the top of the shell, then the rest of the egg out of the bottom. The yolk trembled for a moment and then split, wonderfully soft yellow over the bottom of the bowl.

Muirne glanced around, searching, and Diarmaid handed her the bread he'd cut before.

She took it and tore it into pieces, dipping the pieces into the yolk before she popped them into her mouth.

After the first two or three bites she looked over at Diarmaid—her attention had been entirely on the bowl, the bread, and the egg—and sighed and smiled at the same time.

"That's grand."

For a reckless minute he wished he'd bought half a dozen eggs instead of the two when he'd been in Derry. But he'd been afraid they'd break on the long walk back. Two was worth the risk; six would've been foolhardy.

There they sat, the two of them on the dirt floor of his half-collapsed sod house, while he watched her savor the rest of the bread and egg. As there got to be less and less at the bottom of the bowl she ate more slowly and ran the tip of her tongue around her lips to make sure she was not missing a speck. She'd planned it out careful like, he could see, because at the end she still had one piece of the bread to run around the inside of the bowl to pick up every last bit of yolk, wiping up what the spoon couldn't capture.

Then she set down the bowl with the spoon, licked clean, set inside it.

"I thank you," she said with careful courtesy.

He grinned. Mainly at her, but partly at the delicious thought of her in his mam's kitchen, with all that was to be eaten there. Wonderful food she'd never tasted, and lots of it. Not like a single egg. He was willing to take odds she'd never imagined such quantities of food existed. All for— how many of them had there been in the big house? Four? Five. Yes, five it was. The earl and his lady and the two girls. Lady Anne and her sister. Oh, yes, and the old lady as well. Five.

And the servants of course. But even so he'd been able to take as much of what was left over as he could carry for the settlement just across the boundary of the estate, where they were just this side of starving. The earl's tenants did all right, as it happened. Yes. 'Twas important to be truthful about it. That earl made sure his tenants had food and reasonable shelter.

'Twas true many of the English didn't seem to care. But that earl made sure the tenants paid their rent—well, of course he did—but he made sure they had enough to live like human beings.

Diarmaid shook off the memories and looked up and laughed.

Muirne was now leaning back against the wall next the fire, and she sat with her hands folded over her belly, looking like the cat that'd been in the cream. Her glance slid over to him. "You laughin' at me?"

But her voice was lazy.

"Not really." He got up to his feet, walked across, and sat down, as she was sitting, back to the wall. "So what's going wrong?" He could hear that his own voice was easy, but somehow purposeful at the same time.

She had closed her eyes, but she opened them. "What's going wrong?"

"The group." Well, really, what was supposed to be the start of a group by now, but wasn't.

She nodded, her eyes still closed. For a bit neither of them spoke. Then she said, "They want something to do."

"It's too early for that. We have to know we can trust them, and we don't know that. They don't know they can trust each other."

Muirne opened her eyes and tilted her head to one side. "Some of them we can. Liam we can, Seán, too. Patrick, Seamus, I think. Donncha."

"Charlie?"

"Charlie's a wee bit light in the brain. Trusts everyone. Can do whatever he's told to do, but doesn't know nor care why. Kinda like a gun. Has to be pointed so it'll go off—but it would go off just as certain if he got pointed wrong."

"Cathal?"

"Maybe someday. Not now. He and Nellie just got married, and he doesn't see much more than the tip o' her ear."

Diarmaid nodded. "Brian?"

Muirne shrugged. "Dunno. Sort of like Charlie, but not as good-tempered."

"Jack?"

She looked up at him straight. "No. Told you about him. Out for Jack, first and last."

Diarmaid's mouth quirked. "No redeeming qualities?"

"Not a one." Her voice was hard. "He came just to see what was going on. He wouldn't stick."

Diarmaid sighed. "You see what I mean? We're not ready. Have to be a unit first before we set off to be anything else."

She shrugged again. "Biggest problem is that none of them b'lieve anything can ever be different. Even me. Talk's cheap, but talk's dangerous, too. We hear some talk, yes, but nothing changes, except that them that talk usually don't last long. Mebbe they get impatient; mebbe the English get tired of listening to 'em. For sure and the rest of us wisht they'd be still. Hopin's hard work. Better just keep your head down and get through the day, one after another. Eat something, sleep somewhere, and do it again. Get children, get old, and know it'll be just the same for your children when you're too tired and die."

The sound of her voice, low and forcing his attention, came to an end and stopped, although Diarmaid could have sworn it still hung in the air.

They sat, the two of them side by side against the wall, in the silence for a bit.

"I have to try," Diarmaid said at last.

Muirne did not turn her head to look at him. "I know."

He sighed. "So Liam, Seán, Patrick, Seamus, Donncha."

Her head nodded.

Diarmaid continued. "And Charlie and Cathal should they come."

"Charlie might. Cathal won't."

He could feel his mouth bending into the start of a smile. "Nellie won't let him?"

Her elbow dug at his ribs. "It's kind of nice. Leave 'em be."

"If he's not there, not much I can do."

"No." But her voice sounded dissatisfied, like.

He leaned forward a little, glancing at her. "What did you think I would do?'

Her shoulders jerked up and down. "Dunno. Make him come somehow."

He settled back. "Making a fuss is the last thing I should do. D'you think I want people paying attention to me?"

"You think people don't already?"

There was that chill feeling down his back. People taking notice—the last thing he wanted.

"No."

She actually laughed, just a little. More like a giggle. "Maybe in a town you can come in and out w'no one paying you a bit of attention. This is a clachan, and we all know each other and our mothers and fathers and their mothers and fathers. Not usually past that, but there are those long-lived ones who do. Old Eithne—I've never asked, but I'd wager she'd know something about me great-grandmother if ever I did ask."

Could be that starting out in a Donegal clachan was not the best idea they'd ever had, when they were back in Galway discussing it. A bit late to change now. What was it they said? The dice was thrown already.

"So what do they say, then?"

She was still grinning. "Don't quite know what to make of you. Say you keep to yourself. Say you have red hair."

"There's a bit of news."

She laughed again. "There's those that wonder if we're related, except they can't figure out how that could have happened as they've known my family ever since ever since. An' there's a lot o' other Irish with red hair as well. Maybe not as red as ours, but red even so."

"Me da had dark red hair when he was young."

She made an odd dismissive noise. "Mine doesn't. Just as well. I've no ambition to be like him."

He opened his mouth to ask her something—maybe when her mam had died, maybe if her da had ever done anything but make poteen and drink it, ask her what it had been like when she was a child. Sure they could not have left her so much to herself as her da did now. Then he shut it. What if the asking upset her somehow? Surely it did not matter enough to be worth tilting the trembling balance he suspected she managed to keep.

Safer to tell her something about his people.

"I played at being my da until I decided 'twould be better for me to carry on his work than play it as a game."

"Where was that?" Her voice held genuine interest.

"South and east o' here. Not far from Drogheda."

Muirne shook her head. "I've heard of it, but have no idea where it be."

"The River Boyne runs through it. Getting silted up now, the opening to the sea, but it's still a port."

"Like Derry?"

He nodded. "A bit."

"Is that where your family is?"

"Just me mam now."

"Where's your da?"

"Dead by the hands of the English."

She nodded. "How does your mam get on, then?"

He grinned. She had not expected it, and for a moment her mouth fell a bit open. "Me mam is the cook for an English earl in one of them big houses. Runs a great kitchen like her own kingdom and knows more about what's going on than the earl or his lady."

She laughed back at him. "Like you, then."

He hadn't thought of it quite that way, and was surprised by his own pleasure.

"Naah. She runs circles round me."

"Doubt that." She fell quiet for a moment and then scrambled to her feet to look out the door Diarmaid had pulled over from the bit of the house that had fallen down, and now used as a sort of obstacle to close off the part where he was living. It would not close all the way.

"'Tis dusk," she said, surprise strong in her voice.

He scrambled to his feet to look out. "'Tis," he said with equal surprise. How many hours had they been sitting here?

"I better get back," Muirne said, and with only a hint of hesitation, pulled the door open enough to get past it and disappeared from sight.

Diarmaid walked over to the door and watched her back vanish into the gathering darkness. She'd not have far to go; she lived close to the shed where they'd had the meetings and his house was not far from there, but in the other direction. All the buildings of the clachan were close together.

What an odd day it'd been. He could hardly count the things that had changed.

WHEN MUIRNE CAME INTO THE sod house, only her da was there, sitting leaned up against the wall as she and Diarmaid had been. Unshaven or on the way to a beard—hard to tell which. Looked lumpy and awkward under his variety of clothes, his pants pulled on over shabbier pants, shirts over other shirts that were torn and worn, jacket over the top. To defeat the cold, she assumed.

She glanced at the fire, but it was glowing. Looked for the basket with the peat, then walked over to toss another lump on the fire.

"Seen fit to come back then." 'Twasn't asked as a question, more a grumble. Poteen, not so strong as it had been, was still what she smelled first, but his tone was not that of a happy man. Had it all been drunk already, then?

"I'm here."

"Where you been?"

She opened her mouth, without thinking, like, to answer and then shut it. Why did she owe him an answer? Where had he been the two, three days he'd been missing? Of course she could guess he'd been up in the hills working on the poteen—the Revenue Police were making a proper nuisance of themselves, and distilling in the same place for long was a fool's game. Better to keep moving and finding spots close to inaccessible.

But how did her knowing that give him the right to ask her what she was doing? She earned her own way out in the turf fields. Any time he wanted to know where she was all he had to do was walk that far.

Of course today had been Sunday, but that didn't change much.

"Where you been?"

So now he was angry. He sort of heaved about a bit, as if he was trying to get up to his feet. More sober he might be, but not enough to take command of his legs yet. He fell back against the wall. "I'm your da!" he shouted at her.

"So I've been told."

She breathed out her rising anger to keep it down. What use would it be to answer with fury? He was still far from being able to grasp at common sense. She could roar back at him, he'd get incoherent with rage, manage to get up to his feet and lay about him with a stick. Suppose he even managed to catch her with a blow or two. She'd fall to the dirt floor, he'd get scared he'd done her a real injury and stagger off to brood about it, and in the end she'd get back to her feet, doctor herself whatever needed mending—so far, thank the Lord, he'd never broken a bone of hers or anything—and life would gradually go on. In two, three days he'd come back, having blurred out his memory of all of it, and life would resume in the ordinary pattern.

It all had happened too many times, like a game they were tied into playing. What if she would not play it? She stared at him, knowing contempt was in her eyes.

He made another attempt at getting up, fell back again.

"You was with the bloody southerner!"

Her look changed to honest surprise. How the hell did he know about him? Far as she'd been aware, her da had been up in the hills or drunk as a lord all the time since Diarmaid had come to town. Sure and nobody could know about them spending today together yet—and if any did know, why would they think to say anything? 'Twasn't as if her da had a fine reputation for trustworthiness or ordinary friendship. He was a ranting, useless old sot—all he was good at was making poteen. Most people, most sensible people, stayed well out of his way unless they needed to buy some of his goods 'cause no one else who was more reasonable had any.

"So what?" She kept her voice more curious than challenging.

"I'll not have a bloody whore for a daughter!"

He might as well started in speaking Welsh or Turkish. She stared at him in amazement. His accusation was so ridiculous she had not the words to challenge him.

"Get out of here! I'll have nothing to do with you!"

This time he managed to get to his feet, but without his stick was staggering around, nearly falling in the fire.

Well, let him. Burn to a crisp, if he wanted.

He bent over, nearly collapsed again, fought for his balance, and grabbed up her straw bed with the quilts.

"Get out of this house!"

She was still watching him with wonder.

He staggered toward the door. "Couldn't be bothered t' come home and feed your poor da anything for dinner, then?" He looked over his shoulder at her, imperiling his balance so that he near to fell over again, but kept going.

So was he serious, then? Muirne moved quickly to scoop up the porridge pot and a couple of potatoes with one hand and her pile of clothes with t'other.

Still bawling with rage, he pulled open the door and, leaning on it, tossed what had been her bed to the bare dirt outside.

"Get out and don't come back! Not tomorrow, not never."

He was still hanging on the door as she passed him, but let loose using the free hand to grab her arm and give it a vicious jerk.

She swallowed her gasp of pain as she heard the door slam behind her.

In the darkness, she sank down on the pile of straw and gritted her teeth to get past the first agonizing throbs. Pray God he hadn't managed at last to break it. It was her right shoulder—how the hell was she to sink the spade into the peat tomorrow?

More to the point, what was she going to do now? Pity she hadn't thought to grab a candle—there had been one there, she was sure. The pain pulsed through her shoulder as she tried to think what should come next.

For one thing, even given the agony of her shoulder, she couldna stay where she was. True, he might collapse into sleep or into a drunken fog, but the whole excitement of throwing her out of the house might have spurred him into wakefulness, and if he came out in search of more poteen or support from the drunken fools he passed his time with, he would not be pleased to find her still there.

The Dohertys? Sure, and she could go there, but what then? They had not the space nor food for someone else, particularly if that someone else had a bad shoulder and could not work for a day or two—worse, for a week. They'd take her in for tonight, maybe, but since she'd have to think of something else tomorrow, she might as well worry out a plan now.

She listened for what she might hear going on inside the sod house. Silence.

Hoped he'd collapsed again. As far as that went, she hoped he'd died, but that was too much to count on.

Muirne stared into the blackness, trying to think, trying to ignore the steady throb. Why couldn't blessed Mary pay attention when she was needed? She tried to summon up the words she'd murmured with her rosary, back in the days when she'd had it. Where had it gone? She'd never known.

"Holy Mary, mother of God, pray for us sinners now."

The shed. Of course, the shed. No one used it at night, and it wasn't far to get there. Slowly, trying to not to use her shoulder any more than she had to, she gathered up her clothes, the quilts and the straw—well, as much of it as she could grasp in her left arm, and tried to reach for the porridge pot with the potatoes with her right. No, that wasn't going to work. Not now, anyway. Maybe tomorrow, when the pain was not so sharp.

Two trips, then.

She managed to get to her feet, and stumbled toward the gap between the sod houses toward the back. Pity there wasn't the full moon tonight. She could have used it. But there was some—'twasn't a real fingernail moon yet, and when she got to the back she could see the dark shape of the shed. She made her way there, slow but steady.

Inside was pitch black, of course. No windows. Who would waste a window on a shed? Someone had put the stools out of the way—Diarmaid, for sure. Who else would it be? She shuffled her feet through the blackness to find a bare spot where she could drop her armload.

Had to get back as fast as possible. If her da did stagger out of the house and see the porridge pot and potatoes there, he'd take them back in a second.

Holding her right elbow in her left hand helped. She walked as quickly as she dared through the darkness—which was, to be fair, not as dark as in the shed—down the gap between their sod house and the next one.

Well, his sod house now, she supposed.

Turned the corner, and praise be to God, the pot and the potatoes were still there. Grabbed them up with her left hand and turned to hurry back between the houses. The pain in her shoulder was sharper when she let the arm dangle loose, but it was not far to the shed. Maybe she could fashion some sort of cloth to hang around her neck that would support the elbow for the time being.

She was there. She didn't slow her steps until she was safe inside, the door pushed as close to closed as it would go. She dropped the pot, and the potatoes rattled against it. For a moment she froze, listening for an answering sound, but there was none.

She longed just to stop now, to sit and let the pain wash over her, but there was more to do. Shuffling along with her feet, she found where the straw had landed, and the quilts. The clothes as well, but those she just pushed out of the way. She'd deal with them when there was some light. She patted out the straw, as much of it as she could find, hunting with just her left hand, and tried to arrange it into some kind of a bed, but there wasn't as much as there had been, so in the end her bed was only long enough for her body down to her hips.

Couldn't be helped.

Spread out the bottom quilt, unwillingly grateful her da'd grabbed the two of them, and then tried to work out how to get the other one over her. In the end—she was too impatient to to spend much time on it—she lay down on the straw bed, as far as it went, and pulled the top quilt over herself as best she could.

She closed her eyes, wondering how long it would take her to fall asleep, given the steady throb of her aching shoulder, but she must have been wearier than she'd thought.

When she opened her eyes, there was morning light. Diarmaid was standing there, looking at her.

"What the hell?" Diarmaid said. How could it be she was here, in the shed?

Muirne blinked at him for a moment, as if she wasn't sure herself why she was there. She'd made sort of a bed for herself, but there was more straw and clothing scattered all over the dirt floor. She started to push herself up, but instead of a smooth movement she fell back, gasping. Her face went fish belly white.

Diarmaid dropped to his knees beside her. "What happened?"

She closed her eyes and he waited for her answer. With a sick thud, he realized she must be in severe pain. How could she have injured herself, and if she had, how did she come to be in the shed of all places? Could someone have attacked her? Who—and why? He'd watched her walk away just the evening before, and she hadn't far to go. But something had happened.

She took a deep breath, and looked at him, her eyes brilliantly blue in the ghastly whiteness of her face. Her words were a whisper. "Me fool da. Angry he was that I did not cook him his dinner—because it was Sunday, I guess—and he threw me out. Gave my shoulder a twist as I went past." Carefully, using her left arm, she tried to push herself up to sitting.

Diarmaid leaned over and tried to help her, but when he touched her right arm, she gasped again.

"Not there." She tried a faint smile at him.

He grasped her firmly, one hand on either side of her chest—she was thin and light as a bird—and lifted until she was sitting. "Better?"

She nodded.

He started to ask her what happened again, and stopped short. Her fool da had attacked her. What was he, drunk then? Not that that mattered now. Chances were the feeble excuse for a man would remember nothing of it. Most likely the stupid clot had no idea this morning that Muirne might be in pain.

He fought back the impulse to go drag him from his house to show him what he'd done. The important thing now was coping with Muirne and what she was to do next.

"He'll have forgotten about it, most likely," Diarmaid muttered. "Will be wondering where you are."

Muirne looked up at him and he was taken aback by the hardness in her face.

"I haven't forgot. I'm never going back."

His words burst out before he had a chance to check them. "What'll you do then? You can't stay here." He caught himself, when she turned her face away. "I mean, of course you can, but it's a godawful place to try to live. Not even a fire."

"Mebbe I'll make one."

"Not here." Felt like his mind was running in a dozen different directions, trying to think out what choices she had. "Best you come to my place with me. It's fallin' down, but it's got most of a roof, and a fire."

She shook her head. "Can't do that."

"Why not?"

"Not your problem."

Diarmaid sighed a sigh of purest exasperation. "Ye can't take care of yourself, as things are. Who else is going to do it? The King of England, mebbe? Could be he's just waiting for you to drop by and ask."

She was glaring at him now, even as she was supporting her right arm with her left hand. "It's no concern of yours."

His anger flared as rapidly as hers. "Of course not. I just happened to come by to see if all was set for a meeting, and here you are with your stuff all over. Guess I'd better toss you out and tidy up."

She struggled to her feet and bent over, using her left hand clumsily to start to gather the straw and her quilt. "Don't bother. I'll leave myself."

He was angry enough to grab her by her shoulders and shake her, but good sense blossomed in time.

"Muirne. Don't be daft. Just sit down a bit and we can work out what we'll do."

She'd had some color come back into her face, but when she stood up her face had whitened again. Her left hand was back supporting her right elbow; it was clear that it pained her to have her arm hang loose from the shoulder.

She stood there looking at him, swaying just a bit.

He surveyed her for a moment, trying to think what might help. He had seen more than one who had an arm in a sort of sling. She was much smaller than he was. Perhaps he could rip the sleeve out of one of his shirts and it might be long enough to support her arm and wrap round her neck. He turned around to sort through his belongings to find a shirt—preferably an old one that would tear easily.

"What you're doing?" Her anger seemed to have faded a bit, as well. Not herself yet, but at least he need not worry that she would fling herself out of the shed and run away from him.

"Let me see if this fits." He took a likely shirt—'twas not as if he had a great number to choose from—and stepped over to measure a sleeve against her arm. She started to step away when he approached, and then, when it was clear he did not mean to touch the arm, she stopped where she was.

"What are you doing?" Same question again, but this time less challenging.

"See if this will work as a sling." The sleeve was not quite long enough to extend from her shoulder to her elbow and double back around her neck. Perhaps the length of cloth from the back of the shirt would do it.

He ripped the sleeve away from the shirt, and took the back of it to measure again.

"You spoilt your shirt!" She sounded almost as appalled as if he'd torn one of hers.

"I have another. This one's old." 'Twas, and it ripped easily when he tore it. He got a nice broad strip of cloth and gently settled her elbow into it before he wrapped it around her neck. There was enough to knot it, although he would have preferred a pin. But he had no pin, and the knot would not prick her.

It comforted him somehow to see some of the pain in her face ease as the sling took the weight of her arm.

"Thank you." Her voice was a quiet murmur.

"'Tis there a doctor anywhere about?"

Muirne shook her head. "Not within ten miles or so."

He nodded. He had no way to carry her except on his back for a walk that long, and being bumped along on his back would most likely be agony for her. 'Twould be better to let her rest and see if her shoulder mended up by itself. He could not say he had great trust in doctors in any case. He'd been bashed about a bit from time to time, and he had always healed up. Chances were she would do the same.

But of course she could not rest here. She needed to be where there was some warmth, and a better bed, where he could look after her. There was no one else to do it.

"Then needs be you come to my house where there's a fire and I can make you a better bed." He spoke as gently as he could, fearful of her Irish pride flaring up again.

But it seemed the pain of moving about had tamed her some. She touched the sling with her left hand, and offered a crooked smile.

"I wisht I had a better idea," she said.

"'Tisn't one," Diarmaid told her and began gathering her possessions together, wrapping the smaller things in what remained of his shirt.

She watched what he was doing, but did not reach out to help. It was plain her energy was fast slipping away.

"I did take the porridge pot and two potatoes," she pointed out after a moment.

He grinned at her. "That's fine. I have only one small pot, so we can use yours as well." He pressed her clothes on top of the potatoes in the porridge pot, and gathered what straw he could into the quilts.

"There," he said, and gave her a quick, searching look. "Can you walk?"

She nodded.

"Then we'll be going."

And as simply as that, she followed him to what would be, for the time at least, her new home.

BY THE TIME THEY WERE in the part of the house still standing, having pulled the door across the opening where the roof was collapsed, Muirne was breathing hard, as if she had walked a mile or two at speed. All her strength seemed to have disappeared into nothing, like the light in the evening. She leaned against the wall, trying to hide the quick in-and-out of her chest. She held back drawing in a new breath, trying to slow it down, but the panicky feeling made her long to gulp fresh air. Sure, and Diarmaid would notice if she did that.

Luck was with her. He was too busy trying to remake her bed to look in her direction. The trouble was that between her da tossing the straw and quilts out of the sod house and the problems her shoulder had given her carrying them from the sod house to the shed, and then Diarmaid moving them yet again, there was not enough straw left.

He must have decided the same thing, because he rocked back on his heels, and looked at her, as he had not since they had arrived there. Had been a waste then, all that time she'd been trying to keep her breathing closer to what it was usually like?

"We need more straw," he said, his voice telling his surprise.

Muirne nodded. "I know. Me da threw it out the door, so that lost some, and then I think I lost some going to the shed." After a moment, she added by way of apology, "It was dark."

She leaned against the wall and watched him try to smooth it out so there were no bare spots. He got it even but none of it was thick enough to offer much comfort. He got back up to his feet, frowning.

"Let's put you on my bed while I go fetch more straw," he said. He stooped to pick up the quilts, and lay the first one over whatever it was he had spread out on what he was using as a bed himself. When he had the bottom quilt arranged, he reached out for her left hand and tugged lightly on it to bring her closer so that if she just gave up the struggle to stay erect she could stretch out on the makeshift bed. She sank down on it, hesitated for a moment, and then lay her head down, her left hand protecting her shoulder as the sling fell away.

He spread the other quilt over her. She tried to find words to thank him, but managed only a drowsy smile. It was so much easier to lie still and let the pain settle into a faint ache.

He was still fussing about with something, but it was too hard to keep her eyes open. It was so much easier to let the world drift and even the ache fade away.

Had he crept out past the door leaning at that odd angle? She was too close to sleep to care.

When she roused, Diarmaid was whittling something with a pocket knife, sitting leaning against the wall. He had built up the fire, so that instead of just the smoldering peat that had been burning when they had come in there were now flames leaping over peat piled higher.

Muirne gazed at the fire, mildly interested, as she tried to remember where she was. Oh, yes. She was here in Diarmaid's house. She moved her shoulder tentatively and established that the pain had not drifted away. But was it a bit less insistent? It might be.

"You back?" Diarmaid's voice asked her.

"I am." She started to try to sit up and the pain rippled through her body. She allowed herself to sag back.

"Better just stay there," Diarmaid advised, not moving from where he was. "All we can do for your shoulder is rest it. Let's try that for a day or two, and see if it does any good."

Her impulse was to jump to her feet and protest. This was what? Monday? And she had not gone to the turf fields. Not that she could have—she was not stupid, and it was obvious that her shoulder would never let her pick up her spade, let alone plunge it back into the earth. So. One day's wages gone. But how, short of a miracle, was she to work tomorrow? 'Twas all very well for Diarmaid to talk of a day or two.

How was he able to keep himself? She stared into the fire, the flames dancing over the black heaps. 'Twas a grander fire than any she'd built.

"Are you rich?" She heard her own voice asking it.

Well, at least it made him laugh. A full, rollicking laugh.

She could still hear the traces of it when he finally spoke. "That's an interesting thought," he said. "What made you ask that?"

She tried to put her left arm under her head to lift it some so she could see him better, but it was sharply clear she needed her left hand to support her shoulder. Only that muted the pain.

Diarmaid frowned. "You need a pillow," he muttered, looking about. "P'haps I can figure something when I get you over to your bed."

"Me bed?" Muirne looked around, and belatedly realized Diarmaid had fetched enough straw from somewhere so that there was a great fat bed-shaped pile of it on the other side of the fire.

"Sure, and all the time you slept I sat here twiddling me thumbs."

She considered what he'd said. "Then I was asleep a while?"

He clambered up to his feet and stood over her. "Your body's working on healing. The best thing for you is sleep." He grinned down at her. "We missed out on porridge this morning—I do have oats for tomorrow—and the taters you brought are cooking for dinner. I got the straw and then begged some buttermilk from Lizzie Doherty. You need food for healing now. She told me where to go to fetch more milk."

Muirne's head sagged back down on the bed. Diarmaid towered over her, his face frowning with concentration.

"If you'd let me lift you as I did before—" he started out, tentative like.

She frowned as well, trying to remember. When had he lifted her? In an odd half-memory, the feel of his hands on her sides, lifting her, flashed into her mind, melting out again.

"Did you?"

He nodded. "You just hold your elbow and I'll carry you over."

She'd never liked anyone's hands on her, not even back when she was a wee thing, as best she could remember. But this was Diarmaid's bed and it was clear she could not remain here. If she had to get up, anything would be better than her trying to lift herself.

She gave him a sharp nod to show her willingness.

He bent over and as soon as his hands wrapped around her sides she remembered the sense of safety. More than safety, perhaps, but there was no point drifting off in that direction. He had her standing on her feet before she'd had time to brace herself. She tried to swallow her gasp of pain as he propped her up against the wall, but once she leaned back and held still, it was better. The roof came down low, and Diarmaid would never have fit under there, but she was much smaller.

"You just stay there whilst I get this bed made up," he told her, stripping the quilts off the place where she'd been. Then he went to the straw, taking some off one end and laying it on the floor, separate. He set the quilts down as they'd been before, the one covering the rest of the straw and the other on top of the first.

She started to take a step forward, holding her elbow, but Diarmaid shook his head.

"Stay where you are," he ordered.

Still intent and busy, he scrabbled with something by the fire. When he stood up, he had something like a flour bag in his hands.

"I'll be back in a minute," he said, and walked out. Obediently, she settled back against the wall, puzzled. She could hear odd sounds outside, sort of a light thumping that went on for a bit.

When he came back, his eyes were laughing. He gave the bag another shake, and a small cloud of flour flew up, and settled back on the bed, the floor, and the bag itself.

"Sorry," he said, chuckling. "There's no getting rid of all of it. If your hair sudden-like goes white, it's not old age. It's flour."

She only understood what he meant when he filled the flour bag with the straw he'd taken off the bed and shaped it into a sort of pillow.

"There," he said. "There's a bed for me lady."

He laid the pillow at the top of the bed, and came over to her, lifting her again, his hands strong but gentle, and carried her over to the bed, where he set her down, lying on the quilt over the straw.

"Oh," she sighed, and for the first time looked straight up into his eyes. The intensity was like a shock through both of them. Frightened, Muirne shut her eyes. To her relief, his hands slid away from her—but did she imagine it, or did some of the warmth linger? She was afraid to think so.

But when she opened her eyes a moment or two later, he was once again just plain Diarmaid as she had come to know him.

That was better. She dared not trust flashes of excitement, but the comfort he'd provided wrapped around her as the pain eased. The thick straw yielded just enough to suspend her in softness, more than she'd known any time before. The quilt smoothed over most of the straw prickles, and the flour bag pillow supported her head so that she could look around the whole room.

Diarmaid unfolded the other quilt over her.

"This is grand," she whispered.

He took a sweeping look over the entire arrangement. "It'll do for the time being." He gave it all a quick nod of approval and went back to the side of the fire where he'd found the flour bag, searching again.

Now, her head propped up by the pillow, Muirne could see what he was doing as he moved around the part of the room they now shared. He seemed to have some sort of box there, and he was sorting through whatever was in it.

He pulled out what looked like a pad of paper, dipped back in the box, and his hand came out with a short pencil. He sat back down, his back against the wall, and propped the paper against his knees. For a minute he looked into space, his eyes concentrated, and then he started to write on the paper.

The question "What are you doing?" rose to her lips, but she folded them closed. He had taken her in because neither of them could think of any other place for her to go, but she had not the right to ask him about what he might happen to be doing. If she needed to know, he would tell her. She had to trust that.

The room was so quiet she could hear the gentle hiss of the fire and the scratching on his pencil as it moved over the paper. Outside there were few noises. Why so few? Somewhere in the distance a baby cried. That seemed more ordinary, and it was, after all, an ordinary day to everyone else.

As would tomorrow be. And would she still be lying on this bed? That was impossible. You earn no wages unless you work. She would not suddenly assume that Diarmaid, in making sure she had a place to stay, also took on the responsibility of feeding her. Yesterday, and the wonderful egg and bread, was something extra. Special. Today she had brought the potatoes and, of course, the porridge pot. If she'd thought of it, she should have brought some oats with her as well. Not that she'd had time.

But tomorrow, what could she offer? She still had a few pennies, if she could find where they were among the mishmash of her few possessions she'd grabbed as her da was throwing her out. Then Diarmaid had squashed everything into the pot when he moved her out of the shed. 'Twould be some sort of miracle if they had not fallen somewhere along the way.

Her hand went searching to see if by some chance the coins were still in a pocket of the clothes she was wearing. She tried to shift her weight to allow an easier hunt, and her blasted shoulder let her know that moving jarred it. Plainly it was not healed yet.

Muirne shut her eyes tight and waited for the surge of pain to subside.

It did, but as always now, it seemed, left a nasty aftertaste of the soreness. It would gradually loosen, but she still did not know if she had anything to pay for food for her to eat. Nor was she about to search again.

How did Diarmaid keep himself? She had asked him if he was rich. She remembered asking, but she didn't remember what he'd said, if indeed he'd said anything. The way he lived made no sense, but she knew little about rich people. She did know there were some round about—landlords and all—but they lived well away from common folk such as she was. And Diarmaid? At times he acted as if he was common as well, but he was different. She could not explain just what the difference was, but it existed. She knew that.

How did he happen to be here?

That was the other puzzle. She'd never seen him before, nor had anyone else—at least anyone else she'd had the chance to ask. One day he wasn't there, and the next day he was, easy and pleasant, chatting to people about the clachan and how it was managed and what changes might make it better. Well, everybody had ideas on that and sometimes they had tried out one o' them, and sometimes something got a little better. More often it didn't so they went back to whatever it was they'd done before.

It was out o' that the meetings began. Diarmaid had not said trouble might find those who came to them, but it didn't take a wise man to suss out that might be the case. At first curiosity brought them out, but she was not surprised there'd been fewer and fewer. Cowardice was much easier than standing up to be a man.

And now instead of getting on with that, Diarmaid had to be distracted with the shameful fact that her own stupid da would rather slash and twist than figure out what the hell was going on and in his drunken uselessness had left Muirne unfit to care for herself for—for how long?

She stirred restlessly on the straw bed until the pain reminded her to stay still.

Dear God. She didn't have the time to lie about like this. Even if she found her pennies they'd do her no longer than another day. By tomorrow she had to be able to work in the turf fields, and she was completely, helplessly terrified that would be impossible.

What was she to do?

With her shoulder as it was, she was not even sure she could manage a walk as far as the beach again. If she was able, she could just keep walking into the water until it overtook her and tumbled her under to certain death. A man had done that some years ago. Just got up one day and walked into the water, and that was the last they'd ever seen o' him, although word was that later they found his body on the rocks down the shoreline a ways.

He'd had a wife and children, as well. Muirne didn't know what had happened to them, except that they no longer lived here in the clachan. She hoped they'd had somewhere to go.

If she walked into the water, there would be nobody left behind.

For no good reason, she started to laugh. At least she wasn't that desperate yet.

Diarmaid looked up.

"What?" he asked. He held his papers in place against his knees.

She started to shrug, and then stiffened before she moved too much. Her shoulder twinged, but that was all. Maybe 'twas going to heal.

"Nothing," she said.

"You taken to laughing at nothing?" But he had a smile lurking as well.

She nodded, carefully. "Can't tell what might happen next."

He stood up, stretched. "Might be an idea to have it be dinner." He walked over to the fire, added another lump of peat absent-mindedly, and picked up the porridge pot. "I can use this. It's bigger."

Muirne watched him, thought about the way he was tossing peat on the fire. "I asked you before. Are you rich?"

Before he had laughed. Now he sort of turned about to return her look. "Why?"

"I don't know what to think. You don't work. You put peat on the fire like it grows free on some bush. You went to Derry, brought eggs back, soft bread. I don't know anyone else who does things like that."

One of his eyebrows lifted. "I don't work?"

"Not as far as I can see."

He walked over to her, squatted down beside her. "Can you keep what I tell you to yourself?"

She frowned at him. "Who would I tell?"

He shrugged. No pain there, Muirne thought enviously. "If I knew, wouldn't have to ask."

"I don't talk." So what if there was pride in her voice. What she said was true.

He gave her a hard look, then nodded. "There's some of us down round Galway who don't like British boots on Irish soil."

She went on watching.

"Some has time and some has money. The folks what has the money give it to them that has time, and we go about laying foundations."

"Foundations for what?"

He shrugged again. "Don't know exactly yet. Picking up where the poor souls of 1798 gave it up."

"They didn't give up!" Muirne flared. She'd heard about them. "They were murdered by the bloody English."

He nodded. "Yes. So next time we do it different. We're learning how."

Her words nearly tumbled over his. "I want to help."

"Then your first job is to heal."

She moved her head restlessly. "How do I do that faster?"

He grinned. "Do what I tell you."

"Damn you," she said, sort of absently. Her gaze returned to his face. "You must know. I have no money and no time."

"What do you spend your time on?"

"Cutting turf!" She came near to shouting at him.

He shook his head. "We don't have place in the movement for those who shout. 'Tis too important others not hear."

"I only shout at you," she muttered sulkily. "I need to eat. Only way I can get money is cutting peat."

"You can't do that for a while. Better think of something else."

Did he have any idea of the panic his words swept up? What else had she been worrying about ever since it happened? Nothing else. Just that.

"I don't know how to do anything else." How she despised admitting that, and to him.

"You can work with me."

"And earn a wage how?"

"I have the money they gave me. If you work with me, it's for you as well."

She settled into the pillow, staring up at the roof, bewildered. Just like that. One of God's miracles, done just for her. Up 'till now God had never taken any particular notice of her existence, as far as she'd been aware. She'd never had a miracle before. Not one.

Diarmaid rose to his feet and went to prepare their dinner.

IT DID NOT SURPRISE DIARMAID that immediately after their meal Muirne fell asleep. He was sure she'd not expected to work so hard to eat. Her right arm and hand were almost useless, and since it seemed she was strongly right-handed, eating left-handed was not only slow, but left her with food dripped here and there down her front, which she obviously found embarrassing and frustrating.

All things considered, he was relieved when sleep overtook her almost as soon as he took her bowl and spoon away. Once he'd taken care of what had to be cleaned up, he could sit back against the wall and consider how he was going to use her, as he'd so recklessly said he would.

Well, perhaps she could write. If so, he could have her produce the record of what he was doing. That would be useful. His own writing was a bunch of letters and small sketches—really a way of awakening his memory more than writing as such.

Someday he would learn. He had promised himself that for how many years now? The more capable he came to be at recording things that would remind him of what needed to be reported, the less important his learning to read and write seemed to anyone else. There were always ten things more important for him to do than the wholly self-indulgent business of learning to read, to write so that anyone could understand, not him alone.

Nor was it entirely anyone else's fault that he was still technically illiterate. He'd heard that word, asked for the letters, and written it down at the beginning of his notebook as a challenge to himself. But then there had always been something else more urgent, and the notebook with "illiterate" written was succeeded by another—in which he wrote "illiterate" again, just as carefully. How many notebooks were there now? Twenty? Twenty one? All with that word on the first page, and it still as descriptive of what he was as it had been in the first one. Every page thereafter filled with his approximation of letters and sketches, each reporting something only he could understand. And the pity was, some of them in the first books even he could no longer decipher. Bits, perhaps, and sometimes the bits held together well enough for him to remember what the whole had been.

If she could write...

But she had common sense, and a clear understanding of what had to be done to move forward. She could untangle a senseless dispute and point out to everybody where they'd gone astray and haul them back to the central purpose. He'd seen her do that more than once—probably even as many as three or four times in the early meetings.

The meetings. By damn, the meetings were becoming more and more pointless. Liam and Seán and Patrick were willing to follow where he led. They did not need persuading. The others? A bunch of will-o-the-wisps, they were. With you one day, not to be found the next. He had not had that problem in the past, at least not to this extent. Was it because the situation in Donegal was so much more desperate? Yes, he'd seen poverty before. But it had been surrounded by those who were managing to scrape past. Here the desperation was universal.

Not the landlords, of course. Never them. But their tenants were almost worse off, because what little they had could be ripped away—and was—with bare notice. The whole system was different here. They called it rundale.

Elsewhere, a tenant held a patch of land, and as long as the tenant paid his rent, how he managed the patch was up to him. Here it was more communal and equal, one tenant with another. 'Twas a two-field plan: in the center was the clachan, or what might be considered a village. The sod huts and more permanent houses round about him now were the clachan, and beyond them was first a ring of land farmed each summer. Oats, barley, and potatoes were the usual crops, far as he could tell. Beyond those fields was a second ring, for grazing animals, kept a safe distance from the unfenced fields. The inner ring was divided into strips, some better farmland than others. From time to time, the strips got shifted around, so that those who had poorer land generally had more of it, and then the next year—or whenever they were reorganized—they would have more fertile land, but less of it. Then in the winter, the livestock was brought into the inner ring, where their manure would re-fertilize the land to prepare for the crops the next year.

Seemed a sensible system to Diarmaid, although he heard murmurings that some of the landlords considered it old-fashioned, and longed to bring in more up-to-date ways of leasing the land, although from what he heard the goal was more to increase rents than to provide better for the tenants.

But there was a basic fairness to rundale. Was that why the farmers were reluctant to change it, although what it seemed to mean in practice was that everyone grew just enough to sustain life, never enough to improve it? Did these men he was trying to deal with think it was safer than trying something that might upset the system entirely?

He glanced over at Muirne, still sleeping, curled up now like a kitten under her quilt, but her hand still wrapped protectively about her shoulder. This was now the second day since her stupid bastard father had whacked it, and when Diarmaid thought about it, he felt his blood might have boiled with his fury.

If he had any trust that her father might take care of her, he'd go fetch him and force him to look after her until she could cope on her own. But that seemed unlikely at best, and it was perhaps asking too much of Muirne to allow her father near her, whether Diarmaid stayed to enforce the caretaking or not.

In any case, Diarmaid had his own decisions to make. First, if Muirne could help in any way, was there any point to struggling on here, or would he do better to return to Galway and consult with t'others about where it made the most sense to concentrate efforts? He was not quite willing to admit defeat yet, but the thought was not far distant.

It was the rustle of straw that alerted him.

Muirne had managed to use her left arm to push herself to a sitting position, but now was supporting her right arm with her left hand, as she had been doing.

"D'ye know what happened to me sling?" she asked. "Mayhap if I had that I could get up and be a bit o' use."

"There's no need for that."

Her eyes narrowed a bit. "Mebbe not for you, but there is for me. I've had enough of bein' a potted plant. There's nothing wrong with me legs except they feel queer from not being used."

He could not help the quirk of amusement on his mouth. Well, she had a point there. Would he have expressed it so politely had it been him laid up for close to two days, completely helpless?

"For a bit, then."

He gathered up his papers, tucked them back into the box, and stood, looking around the small space they shared. "It's still light," he remarked, looking past the crooked door into the roofless space beyond.

"Spring's coming. Wisht it would come faster."

"All impatience, that's what you are." He leaned down to lift her by her sides as he had done before, and although he was prepared for it this time, the urgent wish to wrap his hands around her lean, frail body was hard to resist. He deliberately kept his eyes focused on the bed, where her feet were scrabbling around to find somewhere solid to land. The last time he had looked into her brilliantly blue eyes, and he could still feel the pulse of—of what? Lechery, most likely. He was in no position to desire her. Not when she depended absolutely on him as she did now.

Fatherly. That's what he should be. Priestly, even better. Never stick your hand in a fire. You get burned every time, and deservedly so.

"I'm standing up!" She squealed with delight.

"That you are. Mind if your knees feel weak, and sit down. A useless shoulder's bad enough. No need to go breaking anything else."

Her eyes flicked to meet his instantly. "You think it's broken, then?"

Damn. Why could he not govern his words a bit better?

"Don't know. We'll have to see. Shoulders are funny things. Sometimes they slip out and then slip back—hurt like hell while they're out, but settle to a dull ache and get better once back where they belong." He'd seen that happen once before. Only once, and by accident.

"D'ye think if I moved it about that might happen?"

"For God's sake, woman, don't be stupid!" What possessed him to let his mouth flap like that? Who knew what the crazy girl might do if she took it into her mind? That she had the courage to face whatever pain was necessary he did not doubt for a moment. But what if it was broke? If she made it worse, would her arm be dangling or some other unnatural thing, and how could he get her to someone who would know what to do about that?

He made sure he had her attention and glared at her. "Don't you dare do any crazy thing that might need more fixing than it does right now."

"I'm not stupid, and it's my arm. I know how it pains."

Still looking straight into her eyes, he would have felt happier if she didn't have her chin cocked up and her mouth unyielding. Right now he felt almost sorry for any British soldier who might someday be faced with her in this mood.

"Use the good brain God gave you."

"I am." She stepped away from her bed, then turned back to move the top quilt back. "Oh, there it is." She picked up the sling he'd made from his shirt that had been covered by the quilt, and slipped her arm through it, ducking her head so that it could settle around her neck.

To his surprise, she walked, a little unsteadily at first, toward the crooked door.

"Where you going?" he demanded.

"I need to see Lizzie Doherty." When he opened his mouth, she countered swiftly. "Woman stuff."

Blocked, he subsided. He could hardly ask what woman stuff. Didn't want to know, was the truth of it. He nodded, shortly, and reached out to get the door open so that she didn't have to pull on it.

As she slipped past, he opened his mouth to say, "Don't stay out too long," but providentially closed it. He feared it would do no good with Muirne with her mouth set the way it was. Dear God, it was like dealing with an unexploded firework. Who knew but that it'd go off when you least expected it?

As Muirne had expected, Lizzie was alone in the house.

"Muirne!" she said, her voice equally split between anxiety and welcome. "Diarmaid said you'd hurt yourself."

"Well, he said it wrong. It was me miserable da. He told me to get out o' the house, and gave a nasty twist to my shoulder as I was leaving."

"Ach," Lizzie groaned. "P'rhaps that explains it."

"Explains what?"

"He's gone. Not seen for a couple o' days. Not distilling—the McLaughlin's been looking for him."

Muirne shrugged with her left shoulder only. "Better him than me. As far as I care, next time I see him I'll be on me way to heaven and he'll be going straight to hell."

For a moment they just looked at each other silently.

Muirne lifted her chin and tried to smile as if nothing unpleasant had been said. "Wanted to thank you for the buttermilk."

"He wouldn't take it but he paid me some for it, you know," Lizzie said. "He's a good man."

"He is that." Out of plain respect for the truth, Muirne had to say that much for him, irritated though she still was.

"How's the shoulder doing?"

"I'd like if it'd heal faster. I still need this sling Diarmaid made me, and there's no way I can cut turf until it settles down on me some."

"Seán said he told them up there you were poorly but would come back when you could."

Muirne absently chewed on her lip. "That was good o' him. What'd they say?"

"He says you're a good worker, and they didna say much. He thinks if you just go back when you can all'll be well."

If she intended to keep her job, that'd better be sooner than later, Muirne thought. Good of Seán to do what he could, though.

"Tell him thanks from me if you see him sooner than I do," she said, moving toward the door. A proper door, one that was set in a frame.

"Take care." Lizzie's voice accompanied her out of the house.

Outside, Muirne hesitated for a moment, trying to consider what she should do next. What she needed was to be far away enough from people so that she could do what she intended to do without people being close enough to hear. If she yelled, she didn't want anyone to come running to see what was happening. She walked far enough away so that she was out of sight, and tried running her left hand over her shoulder.

Yes. There would be pain. But she could feel a knob on her shoulder that had never been there before. If she gave it a good shove, would it slip back where it belonged? Surely it was worth a try. 'Twas good of Diarmaid to say she could help him, but the truth was that it would be better for her to be self-supporting, as she had always been since she was big enough to know she was on her own.

She walked purposefully away from the houses of the clachan, up one of the hills that hemmed it in. The fields of the rundale wrapped around the hill as well—there wasn't enough flat land to share out. She soon had climbed above the farmed land, and made her way among the stones to find a place that was private like. Probably at some time or other her useless da had had his poteen still up here—it was hidden away just as he liked it.

She sat down, gritted her teeth, and before she had a chance to think about it, pressed hard with the heel of her left hand, right on the knob.

The pain near to killed her. She didn't know if her body flew apart or her head exploded—either or both seemed equally likely. After the worst of it blew past, her face was wet with tears and she was shaking all over, but the knob was gone, and even through the agony she could feel whatever had been wrong was now right. She sank down to her knees in the dirt and let the pain that remained wash over her. She leaned her head against a rock and let go: quit fighting for control, quit trying to define the pain, just quit. Sooner or later—unless she starved to death first—she would take back command of her own body. In the meantime she would exist the way the rock did. Just stick where she was and endure.

Time passed. It must have, because in and out of the clouds, the sun was sliding down the western sky. Muirne lay with her head against the rock, watching where it had been.

"What in the name of all that is holy are you doing up here?"

It was Diarmaid, and from the sound of his voice he was furious.

Well, three cheers for him.

DIARMAID HAD BEEN SEARCHING FOR the better part of an hour. He'd gone straight to Lizzie, who told him Muirne had been there, but was gone. He checked her da's sod house—no sign that anyone had been there; the fire was burned out. He finally figured out which were her footprints in the dust, and followed them, most of the time. They would disappear, and then he'd have to check in every likely direction until he picked them up again. The track led up and up the hill, up winding around the stones. There must be other people came up this way, because there were other footprints besides hers, but he saw no sign of anyone until he was searching behind one o' the rocks the way he'd been searching all the way up and around, and there she was.

At first he thought it was just a pile of her clothes, until he looked more closely and realized she was there, too. Her head was tipped forward, resting against a smaller stone than the great one hiding her.

She didn't move when he yelled at her. He darted over to her. People didn't die of a broken shoulder, he was sure of it.

He fell to his knees. "Muirne," he murmured touching her shoulder—the left one; the right one had her whole body curled around it.

Her face turned slowly toward him. Her face was that fishbelly white again, her face was dirty, only this time it was windblown dirt that had stuck to her wet face. Her eyes slowly opened, and the brilliance of the blue was again startling against the dust and her pallor.

"It's healed," she whispered.

Healed? Had she said something was healed? He could barely sort out any words. "What's healed?"

The faintest wisp of a smile drifted across her face. "Me shoulder. I mended it."

"You what?"

A frown, just as faint as the smile, followed it. "Don't shout at me."

He opened his mouth to say he hadn't, when he realized he had. "I'm sorry. What did you do?"

She straightened, just a bit. "There was a knob. I pushed it."

He stared at her, not comprehending.

"Where?"

"Me shoulder." Pridefully, smiling at him, she moved the shoulder. "See? Still twinges a bit, but I can move it. Couldn't, before."

Diarmaid rocked back on his heels. Mind what you say, he told himself. What he wanted to do was explode with fury that she'd taken such a chance. Hadn't he told her not to? What use was she if she never followed orders?

She was watching him out of the whiteness of her face, although color was returning. Watching him warily.

He kept still, reminding himself that whatever he was about to say was important. What would he have done in her position? The very same damn thing, and he knew it.

"Was it bad?" His eyes stayed on her face, and he saw her eyes flicker. She hadn't expected that.

She kept their eyes locked together and nodded, once, sharply.

"How is it now?"

She took a deep breath. "Sore. But it's healed now. It's different, and I can move it."

He nodded slowly. God in heaven, she was brave, all right. Without thinking, he laid his hand on the back of her neck, and was surprised by the bumpy knot of the sling. It was still hanging there, useless now.

"Ye don't need this now," he said, and untied it. It fell in her lap.

"Sorry 'bout your shirt." Muirne picked the sling up with her left hand, looked at it for a moment, and then handed it back to him.

Diarmaid noted she was not yet using her right hand routinely, but he supposed that was to be expected. Her shoulder must still be painful, just from the time the knob—whatever bone that was—had been sitting there out of place. Probably swollen all around, although he doubted Muirne would let him touch it to check.

Well, he didn't need to. She had not been able to use that arm at all, and now she could. That was all he needed to know.

"Come back now. We'll cook a bit of supper. I've even some kitchen for you." It felt queer to use the word that way, but Muirne knew what it meant. Her eyes brightened.

"What, then?"

"Another egg."

"Where'd you get another egg?" No mistaking the excitement on her face.

"Miz Dooley heard about your shoulder. Fair vexed she was with your da. She has chickens, and she said she had a good lay today, so she brought one over."

"She's a kind woman," Muirne murmured. She stood up, rocked for a moment, and he steadied her with the hand still on the back of her neck. She shook it loose. "I'm all right. 'Twas just a bit wobbly on my feet."

She did seem to have her balance now, and that ghostly pallor had turned into normal color. Dear God, the pain of pressing the bone into place must have been terrible.

"Let me just keep a hand on your elbow—the left one," he added hastily. "Makes me feel better about comin' down the path with you."

He expected she would flare back at him, but she nodded instead, and they set off on the way down the hill. Across they could see the sun had slid behind the mountains behind, and it was dusk. Still plenty of light to get back safely.

But holy mother of God, what a day.

'Twasn't until later they had the chance to talk. Muirne was hungry, which made sense, since eating with her left hand had been more frustration than nourishment. Then, too, there was the plain pleasure Diarmaid got from watching Muirne eat her egg. Not a scrap of it was overlooked, and every speck was relished.

She noticed his close attention, and did not care for it. "You're watching me like a hawk watching a mouse," she objected.

"I'm not about to eat you," he said as mildly as he could manage.

One of her eyebrows lifted in disbelief. She licked the spoon with care to make sure every dot of yolk had been consumed, and laid it down.

"That egg was even better than the Derry egg," she said.

"Fresher."

"Oh, aye." She stretched a bit and it must have pained her because her face tightened for a moment and then relaxed.

"How's the shoulder?"

"Not good yet but better than 'twas."

He nodded. 'Twas a great relief to him that she would tell him honestly how she felt, but he daren't say that to her. The last thing either of them needed after today was a giant row, and they were both almost certainly tired enough to find themselves in the middle of one.

It had gone full night now, but past the crooked door Diarmaid could see some pale light shining. The moon? It had been a day for the sun and only trailing bits of clouds, and so it might indeed be the moon looking down on them.

"Is that the moon?" he asked, half tempted to go out to see.

Muirne had gone over to her straw bed and was fussing about with it.

She shrugged her one-shoulder shrug. "Go see and then tell me about it. I'm weary enough to settle into me bed now." She was in fact halfway there already, still favoring her right side, but moving freely enough compared to what it had been. She wriggled her way under the top quilt and pulled the pillow over, punching it a bit.

"This pillow was a kind thought," she said as she settled her head into it.

Diarmaid watched her as she nestled her way in, but the temptation to go out and see what was making that light was too strong to ignore. "I'll be back in a moment," he promised, and made his way past the leaning door.

It was the moon, a full one hanging in the sky like a giant golden globe. He'd not seen such a fine one for many weeks—even months, most likely. For a moment he was sore tempted to get Muirne to come out to see it. Something so grand seemed as though it should be shared. But sure and she was exhausted by now. Pain wore a person down worse than a wakeful night, and he'd had enough of both to know that for a fact. No. He'd let her sleep. But he took some time himself to just stand there, watching the wonder of it. Hard to believe that in this miserable clachan, where there was so little of the good things of life, there would be the luxury of the great golden moon.

When he came back in, as quiet as he could manage expecting she was asleep, she was sitting up in her bed like she was waiting for him.

"You still awake?" he asked.

She was frowning, thoughtful like. "What happened to the meeting then?"

He frowned back at her, dredging his memory. Meeting?

"Tonight," she insisted. "Wasn't there to be a meeting?"

The remembrance burst out in his head, like a rocket going off. Yes. He had planned for a meeting tonight. Muirne and her shoulder had wiped all memory of it out of his head. But if he'd not been there, why had no one come to find him to ask? Or had they all heard of Muirne and her da and figured he was too busy dealing with that? For sure and everyone must know by now she'd taken refuge with him. 'Twas not the sort of thing to pass unnoticed.

"Oh, my God," he said. And was it not worst of all that she was the one to remember, and not him himself?

She just sat there on her straw bed watching him, the thin quilt gathered in her lap.

So what to do now?

"I'll go see if anyone came." Although how he could tell that now when anyone who had come would long since have gone if they had any sense, he didn't know. Ah yes, the great Diarmaid MacGuinness, the masterful leader of men, turns out to have less grasp of what his job is all about than the dimmest of the men he was supposed to enlighten.

The moon hung on in the sky and he gave it not a glance as he scrambled to the shed. There it sat in the moonlight, with not a soul about. He came to an abrupt halt at the door. Of course, empty inside. What else did he expect?

There he stood, scrabbling through his mind to figure out what to do next. This Donegal business had been ill-starred from the start. Had taken him longer to get here than they'd expected, any of them, although part of that was because things went better in Connemara than planned. So that time had stretched out. O' course, at the time the delay had seemed more fortunate than anything else, and he could not say even now that he regretted getting to Donegal only as winter was giving way to spring. Early spring was cold enough, God knew. Couldn't say even now, when he was getting used to the place, that he wished he'd been here through a bitter winter.

How many men would have come here tonight? There'd been nine o' them at the first meeting, but the number had steadily dwindled. He'd kind of figured that he'd see how this meeting went before he made any plans for later. What if for this cursed day they'd all been there, and went away discouraged because the great man, the southerner, couldn't be bothered to show up?

"Hey."

A voice came out of the darkness. Diarmaid turned round, and there was Seán Doherty, him of the strong shoulders and great grin.

"Was there to be a meeting tonight?"

So what was Diarmaid to say? Yes, but I didn't come? Instead he just nodded his head.

"Damn it, then," Seán said, but his voice was still pleasant. "'Twasn't sure. Knew Muirne Coyle was poorly."

"She was, but she mended it. Shoulder bone slipped loose and she pushed it back."

Seán gave him a steady look. "Must have smarted some, that."

"Not half. She's asleep now, I hope. Plain wore out."

"Does she want me to say something at the turf field tomorrow?"

Diarmaid shrugged. "I don't know. Can't think she'd try to work tomorrow, but mebbe if it seems to be healing up fast she'll be game to try the next day. She's hard to figure out."

Seán nodded, grinning. "So anyway, I came by here just to see, but nobody was about. Figured everyone else knew, and went home meself."

At least it was not Diarmaid's worst nightmare. There had not been a roomful of men sitting there waiting. But the idea that nobody had bothered to show up left him in a worse position for sure. Was this remote Donegal hamlet or clachan or whatever you chose to call it going to be his first, his only failure? If it was, would it not be better to make his way back to Galway to consult with his uncles and the others there now, rather than later? Sure, if there was no reasonable prospect of success it made no sense to spend more money than he had already done.

Seán's good-hearted, hopeful eyes were still on him. What about him, and Liam, and those other few who had supported him?

What about Muirne?

"Go on home and get some rest." He heard his own voice, sounding firm and kindly and sure of itself. "We'll talk more tomorrow."

Seán nodded. "G'night, then. Give me best to Muirne, if she's awake."

"I hope not."

They turned away from each other, each walking by the light of the moon back to his place.

So if he did leave to go to Galway, what about Muirne? She could stay, of course, in the house—such as it was, not that an abandoned collapsing hovel was a great refuge—and he'd leave her some of the money he still had. Part of it he'd need for his own trip south, but there should be enough to keep her for a while here, surely long enough to let her shoulder heal. If one o' them had to skimp, far better he be the one.

After all, it was not as if he had any obligation to see to her. He wished now he'd not said anything about her working with him. Could be she'd be looking forward to doing that, rather than brute labor out in the peat fields. Well, the situation had changed, hadn't it? She'd be able to take up her old life now, once her shoulder mended. Could even be that she could move back into the sod house she and her da had shared. He'd not been seen for a couple of days—mebbe he was shamed by his burst of temper, as he should be. Mebbe when he came back from wherever he'd gone, almost certainly to distill a new batch of poteen, he'd have gotten over whatever the trouble had been.

He felt his own footsteps slowing as he got closer to the half-fallen house where he and Muirne were sheltering.

He stopped before laying a hand on the door, laid loose across the opening created by the fallen half of the roof. Must not make a sound. Wouldn't do to disturb her if she was getting some o' the sleep she must need. Tomorrow would be soon enough to talk.

DIARMAID CAME IN AS QUIET as if he'd been creeping into some grand cathedral, late for Mass.

Muirne was already sitting up in her bed. She'd had some serious thinking to do. At first she'd thought she'd just drift off to sleep, but when Diarmaid had remembered the meeting, he'd looked so misery-stricken that she couldn't get the picture of his face out of her head. 'Twasn't that she hadn't tried to sleep, but somehow her aching shoulder and his miserable face got mixed up together and wouldn't leave her alone.

Sure and her shoulder was no longer a major problem. True, she could not remember anything that had been near as painful, but it was going to be all right now. The knob—surely the bone that had been jerked out of place—was back where it belonged, and now she was certain all she had to do was be careful for a bit and let everything settle down.

That part was easy.

Diarmaid was the hard part. Somehow she'd come to be another load on his back, and she wouldn't have it. When he'd said she could work with him, it had been like a whole new door opening. But back then, of course, she'd needed the new door. If she'd done something terrible to her shoulder—or, more accurately, if her damn fool da had done something terrible to her shoulder, she would've had to think in new ways. But as soon as Diarmaid had told her about shoulder bones slipping out of place, she'd known that was what had happened. And she'd known how to mend it.

So the new door wasn't needed, now. It would be grand to work for the hope of a free Ireland someday, even if matters went so that she would never live long enough to see it. But it was one thing for her to work for Ireland maybe someday down the road from now when she had some strength of her own to bring to the battle. 'Twas an entirely different business to huddle under Diarmaid's wing. She had no skills, no experience. If she were still a cripple with a useless arm, and if he coulda proved she could do something he needed doing, she might have had to take his offer for a time, if she could not support herself any other way. But the circumstances had changed.

Could well be—well, 'twas—that hacking up peat was not the pleasantest way to earn your keep, but she'd done it with no one's help, and as soon as this bloody shoulder settled down she'd be able to do it again. Way back as far as she could remember, she'd known to rely on anyone else was a mistake. Problem was she'd come to like Diarmaid, which made relying on him even more stupid. He didn't need her leaning on him, and she sure as hell didn't need to learn to lean.

She'd never counted on anyone else, and she wasn't about to start now.

"You're still awake." Diarmaid's surprise was there in his voice.

"I am."

"Is your shoulder paining you?"

"Nothing compared to what it was. I'm fine."

"So why aren't you—well, I thought you were tired."

She shrugged. Her shoulder still didn't like her doing that, but there was a big difference between a passing stab of pain and the agony it had been. "Did any of the men wait around for you?"

"Only saw Seán, and he said he'd come by and no one else was there."

"Oh." Dear God, that must've been disappointing to him. She wanted to ask if anyone could've been there earlier, but that would be like pressing on a bruise. He was a proud person, and the way this group was going smelled a lot like failure.

She wriggled around a bit so that she was facing him square.

"So what are you going to do now?"

He ran his fingers through his red, red hair (same color as hers, it was), and she suddenly remembered him doing just that before the very first meeting they'd had. The one when he'd said he had no use for her. Had he been uncertain then, starting off on a new project? Could be. Could be he was uncertain now, not sure whether to push forward or call it a bad deal and go elsewhere. Had to be lots of places in Ireland with people eager to work with a man like him.

He jerked one shoulder and came to sit down on his bed. Not like usual, erect and interested. He seemed tired, like. Sagging some. Even his voice had less energy.

"Haven't decided. If they were all like Jack, or Charlie, or Cathal, it'd be easy. Walk away and work somewhere else."

"Cathal's all right," she said quickly. "Eyes clouded with love for a bit, that's all."

He grinned, and for a minute the uncertainty she'd felt in him since he walked in seemed to have eased a bit. "Trouble is it's now that I'm here."

"True enough." She'd known—of course she'd known—that he was not about to stay here forever. But it gave her an odd sick feeling to think he might be going now. Her fingers played with the folds of the quilt in her lap.

He took a deep breath. "Doesn't need to be decided tonight," he said. "Don't know why I should be tired clear through. You're the one should be exhausted."

"Not scared tonight. Now it's just a matter of lettin' it get better." She hitched herself down the bed, and pulled the straw pillow into position.

"Getting scared doesn't help anything." She couldn't see him from where she lay, but his voice came out of the darkness.

"What a stupid thing to say," she retorted. "Hadn't been that scared, never would dared do it." She paused for a moment, remembering. "Hurt like hell."

He chuckled, but it was sympathy, not jeering at her. "Don't know anyone else who would've done it. 'Tis something to admire, your courage."

Muirne let the warmth of his words wash over her. Could be he'd be gone tomorrow. But she could remember he'd said that for the days to come.

When Diarmaid roused in the morning, Muirne was asleep. The fire was still barely alive, so he threw a bit more peat onto it. That was close to the end of their peat, but they'd done well with it. The supply Liam had given him had lasted the first day and into the second, and then when it became clear that Muirne's da had not returned to the house, she had gone over and collected as much peat as she could carry with her left arm.

Diarmaid had frowned at her, she'd looked at him blandly, and suggested he go get the rest of it.

Thus the problem of heat—and some light—had been neatly solved. But it was clear on this new day that some decisions could not be delayed. Either he needed to find a new supply, or he needed to get started returning to Galway. The same could be said of food. They had enough for today, barely. If he left, he could take most of the oats with him, although to tell God's truth, the notion of existing on oats alone was a grim prospect. And Muirne? Well, if she remained behind, he could go buy her an egg or two as a farewell present. She'd have some money to keep herself until she was earning again.

"If she remained behind"? The words suddenly clamored in his ears. Was he saying there was a question there? Had he gone daft? He knew the wisdom others had told him, and as time went on, he'd told yet others. He travels fastest who travels alone. Not so much now, but in the past and certainly in the future he'd need to be up and moving away without having to counsel with someone about the decision.

Wives and children and all the rest of it wasn't for a man like himself, who had to answer to the needs of the movement all over this blessed land of Ireland. Wives and children were for staying in one place, and oncet a man had acquired a set of his own, it was his responsibility to keep them fed and sheltered. His own responsibilities were different. Any fool could see that.

Still—Muirne wasn't a whole batch of a family. She was one woman. One girl, really. Life hadn't been easy for her, and she did not seem to look for it to become so now. But she'd given him two happier days than he could remember having before. She was good company. Even when her face had been bleached out with pain, he'd been glad she was there.

Glad he was there.

'Twasn't that she was so beautiful she knocked you sideways. He'd always thought beauty was a lush and buxom woman, with flowing clean hair and a fresh scent about her. Muirne was plain dirty, although he had t'admit he'd been touched by her effort to keep her face clean. Her hair was as red as his was, and he'd never thought that would tempt him. He'd once been dazzled by eyes as green as Ireland, with just a faint ring of gold. Muirne's eyes were blue as the dark ocean smashing up against the western rocks, and yet he liked looking into them even more. The rest of her? She was probably shaped more like a boy than like a female, but when he'd had his hands on her, helping her lie down or get up again, he'd felt a rush in his blood.

71

Although, if he did take her with him, did that mean she'd be more than a companion?

It occurred to him mebbe he'd do better not to take that for granted. They'd shared the same house these two days and at no time had she given him a flirtatious glance. Could be that was the way they'd go on. And if that should be the way it stayed, well, he'd still be glad he'd taken her out of the miserable poverty of the clachan. She'd do well in Galway, and he'd be proud to tell his uncles and the rest about her abilities and her bravery. She could read, for God's sake, which was more than he could do. For toughness he'd match her against any man he knew.

And she made him laugh. On the long road back to Galway, that would make hard days easier. Life these last years had been lonely, if he was strictly honest.

But oh dear God, was he losing his mind?

"Porridge's ready."

He jerked about, ripped out of his reverie. There she stood, in the same strange collection of clothes she'd worn when she went to bed the night before. Her hair was wild and straggly—for the first time he wondered what it might be like if she brushed it. Her eyes were as blue as ever, but she looked irritated.

"You intend to come in and eat it, or shall I bring it to you so you can go on staring at the hills there?"

"I'll come." For no good reason he was grinning at her.

"Well, do. We've only the one bowl and I can't eat till you do."

"No reason why you couldn't have yours first," he pointed out as he followed her through the crooked door set against the collapsed bit of roof.

"Next time mebbe I will." She went to the fire, a nice healthy one now with the extra peat, and scooped out porridge into their single bowl. "There. Eat and grow strong."

He took a mouthful or two. "That's what Lizzie Doherty said."

"Some words get used twice." She sat down on her bed, watching him eat.

He ate two more bites, and then plunged the spoon into the porridge, sitting down on his bed. "I've had an idea."

"Why don't you eat your porridge and have your ideas later?"

"Are you hungry?"

"What d'ye think? It's been a long time since that egg."

He clambered to his feet, scooped up a great mouthful with his spoon, and stuck it into her astonished mouth.

"There. Will that hold you for a minute or two?"

Still surveying him with suspicion, she swallowed. "For a bit."

"I think I'm heading off to Galway today," he said. "D'ye want to come with me?"

Her face went blank, and she simply stared at him. There was still some porridge by the side of her mouth.

Diarmaid ate two or three more spoonfuls, glancing over at her from time to time.

It was as if she'd gone frozen.

"It'd be best if ye could find an answer before noon." He kept his tone easy.

She opened and closed her mouth a couple of times before she said anything. When she did, it was one word. "Why?"

He took a deep breath. "Don't know as I've got the whole answer to that."

"I'll take part." Her eyes didn't move away from him.

He tried to decide what part would be best to give first. Mebbe he should just give them as he thought of them, although that might be dangerous. He'd only seen flashes, but he'd be willing to make a substantial wager that Muirne Coyle had a temper. For some reason, that made him want to grin, which would probably not be wise just then.

"It'd be company on the road. I'd like the men in Galway to meet you. You're smart and brave. You can read. I don't like to leave you here when God alone knows where your da has gone. You've never seen any part of Ireland but Donegal, and it's a bare and cold patch indeed. I like you. I like to hear you talk." He spit the words out as fast as he could say them, barely pausing between one thought and the next.

Muirne looked as astonished as if he had suddenly transformed himself into a bear. Or a fine Dublin gentleman.

"Dear God in heaven," she said.

Well, that could have been worse. Diarmaid returned his attention to the bowl in his hands, eventually scooping up the last bits with care.

"D'ye want me to wash it out before I give it to you?"

Muirne blinked as if she'd just wakened, stared at him for a moment, and then shook her head. "It's all porridge. Don't bother."

He spooned out what remained in the pot, and handed the bowl and spoon to her.

"Ta," she said absently.

He let her eat about half of it before he spoke again. "Well? D'ye have anything to say?"

She looked up at him, the spoon midway. "No," she said, her voice uncertain. "Mebbe are you crazy?"

"Wondered some meself. No, I don't think so."

"What would it be like?"

What a very Muirne question. He sat thinking for a minute, maybe longer. "Don't know, exactly. It'd be a lot of walking. We'd sleep where we could, eat what we could find or buy. Some o' the countryside's plain beautiful, some's just miles to get past. Once we get down Connemara way I've got some friends will take us in for a day or two."

She nodded. "What'll you tell the folks here?"

He sighed. "That's the hard part. I was thinking I'd try to get Liam and Seán and mebbe a couple of the others together and tell them to keep what we talked about to themselves, and that I need to go down to Galway to talk to the leaders there. That the time will come when they're needed, but it's not yet. That they should keep an eye out for others from other clachans who might want to join us—not now, but in time."

She listened intently, her head cocked, and then nodded again when he was done. "Yes, that should do."

He frowned. "Not sure if I can get them all together today. Might be we're here until tomorrow."

Muirne cast a glance at him. "Haven't said yet if I'm going."

Exasperated, Diarmaid snapped, "Well, are you?"

A satisfied smile started small and gradually spread all over her face. "Course I am. Setting off on an adventure beats cuttin' turf any day of the week."

He was astonished at the swelling of the glow of relief in his chest. So they'd set off together, and what came of it would come, he supposed. Sure and his uncles in Galway would be a bit surprised when he showed up with a little thing of a Donegal girl with wild red hair and an unconquerable spirit.

But they'd like her. He was sure of that.

GETTING HOLD OF LIAM DOHERTY, at least, turned out to be easier than either of them had thought. When Muirne took the bowl and spoon out to wash them, she nearly bumped into him stepping tentatively into the part of the house where the roof was down.

"Sorry," he said, moving back out of her way. "Diarmaid?"

"You need Diarmaid?" She had not yet pulled the door back into place.

"Need to talk to him." His voice sounded uneasy, and it caught her attention

"He's right there." She started to point with her right hand and the shoulder twinged. "In there," she said instead.

Liam nodded, and they edged past each other, he going in and she out. The jug of water was out there, and as she washed the bowl she tried to hear what they were saying. They must have been speaking quietly, because she could barely hear a low hum of voices

She finished as quickly as she could, and went back to the door, still open into the part of the house they used.

Liam had his back to her, but Diarmaid was facing her. Tall and narrow he was, but his face was no longer easy and calm, as it had been. He watched Liam intently.

"I didn't hear more," Liam was saying. Muirne stopped where she was, in the doorway.

"Likely there was no more to hear." The intensity of his gaze was in his voice as well. "Can't say I like what you did hear."

"Nor me." Liam shifted his weight uneasily.

Should she speak up or pretend she'd gone stone deaf? Muirne hesitated there by the door, but she must have moved somehow, because Diarmaid's eyes found her.

"Odd bit of news," he told her.

Her presence officially noticed, she walked into the room. "What, then?"

"Liam here heard some curious talk."

She switched her gaze to Liam, who glanced back at Diarmaid before he spoke. "There was some fellow wandering about asking questions. Wanted to know if anyone knew of a red-headed southerner round about. Well, he happened to talk to Michael Connaghan, and Mike, he shrugged and said p'rhaps he might be up in the hills making poteen wi' Muirne here's da. Didn't give 'im your name, just your da's," Liam told her, and went on. "So last seen, the fellow was climbing up the hill paths." He shrugged, and added, "Thought it was right clever of Mike, since he knew well Diarmaid was down here, and the curious bloke can wander up and down a lot of hills before he finds Diarmaid up there."

"Be even better if he's Revenue Police and finds me da," Muirne muttered.

Liam grinned. "Wasn't in uniform, or Mike would not've given him a word."

"What did he look like?" Diarmaid's question was casual.

"Much the same as anyone else, Mike said." Liam stared hard at the fire, clearly trying to pull up whatever Mike Connaghan said. "Dressed ordinary, not shabby like. Bearded. Not a real young man, since his hair was going whitish round here." He touched his own temples.

Diarmaid gave a bark of laughter with no cheer. "Sounds like the man who tried to talk to me on t' way to Derry."

Muirne kept silent, this being his business, but found herself wondering what man. Diarmaid had never said much about his walk to Derry, certainly nothing about anyone he'd met. Liam's eyebrows lifted briefly up almost to his hairline, but he didn't speak either.

"Well, seems like a good thing you and me are leaving for Galway today, Muirne," Diarmaid said. "Thanks for the news, Liam. 'Twould be just as well if he was kept wandering around the hills for a bit t' let us get safe out of Donegal."

"I'll pass the word." Liam nodded briskly, showing no sign of interest that the two of them were leaving together. Would be different when he got home with Lizzie, Muirne was willing to bet. She wondered if she'd have a chance to talk to Lizzie herself before they left, to explain it to her, like. Or mebbe 'twould be better to leave it alone. Least said, soonest mended. Hadn't she heard that somewhere?

"Just don't have anyone who went to any of the meetings talk to him," Diarmaid was instructing Liam, the two of them wandering to the door together. "Any of you can write?"

Liam scratched the side of his nose. "Jack, I think."

Muirne shook her head. "Not Jack."

Liam glanced at her. "Think Donncha can, a bit."

"Muirne can," Diarmaid went on. "She'll write when we get there and have a chance to talk to them in Galway. We'll send it to you, and you give it to Donncha if he can read and write. If he can't, send it back to me and I'll find another way to reach you. By the way, 'twould be good if during the winter any of you find a chance to learn to read and write. The talking's good but when we're out of shouting range this would be better."

Liam nodded.

"I'll leave you in charge," Diarmaid said, and Muirne watched him, trying to work out when his voice had changed from casual and friendly-like to giving orders. There must have been a moment, but she'd missed it. She stood silent, not wanting to interrupt them.

"Well, you and Seán," Diarmaid added. "I'll say the two of you in case anything happens to one or t'other. Best rule is to say nothing unless you know you're alone—helps that you live in t'same house. No more meetings. Don't know what this fellow with the white temples is up to, but the less he finds out, the more likely he'll wander off somewhere else. We'll just go t'earth for the time being."

Liam glanced around the house again. "Best you be off," he suggested.

Diarmaid nodded, looking around himself. "Tell Lizzie to make use of anything we leave behind. We can't take it all, and t'would be better if it didn't look as if someone had been living here."

"You can put whatever you don't need or have no room for in my da's house," Muirne said. "He's got no idea of what was there and will never notice."

Diarmaid looked at her with a small smile and nodded in approval.

"I'll let you get started then," Liam said. He went to the crooked door, and looked over his shoulder. "Safe travel."

"Thanks to ye," Muirne said, as he ducked down and out.

Diarmaid looked at her. "Ye don't have to come, y'know," he said. "This makes things a bit different. For a couple of days we'll have to be more careful than I'd expected." He took a deep breath. "They don't know about you. Hope they don't know much about me, either, but you've got a blank slate."

Muirne felt her lips twitch with a smile. "You asked me to come, and you're not going to weasel out of it now."

He was fighting a smile as well. "God save me from women," he said, and then turned to look at their possessions, spread on the floor. "Let's see. Most important to take is food. Put on whatever you have that's best, not what's on the point of fallin' apart. What shoes do you have?"

She kicked up her foot, and he frowned.

"Don't know if those'll make it," he said. "If we have to buy others we can do it in Donegal town or Connemara way."

"I can walk barefoot."

"We'll hope ye won't have to. Them's that do it all the time can walk just as far with no shoes, but that's not you." He picked up the pack he'd been wearing on his back from time to time, and the first thing he put in it was his box that stayed by the side of his bed.

Watching him, she got an idea, and shuffled through her clothes to find the bag she'd had. There was a handle on each side, and she tried slipping the handles over her shoulders. Without meaning to, she made a soft whimper of pain as the handle pressed against her right side.

"That's no good." Diarmaid was looking at her. Had he been doing so all along? "Mebbe in a few days it'll work, but for now carry it with your left arm. Don't put too much in it."

Muirne nodded, and keeping her own eyes fixed on what she was doing, filled the bag with such clothes as she had. She was not short of shifts, so she discarded the worn ones and kept two in relatively good condition. Her stockings ranged from tattered to whole, so she kept the best ones without reference to color—they'd hardly be seen beneath her skirts anyhow. She had only one good shawl, but two neckerchiefs, and of course her everyday gown. Today she happened to be wearing what people called a bedgown, although here women wore them during the day. It was of coarse linen, so it was warm. She'd worn it a lot recently.

Since it seemed to her she was pruning her wardrobe severely, it was discouraging to see how quickly the bag was not only filled but bulging. 'Twas not heavy to carry, however, so it had been worth discarding the things she had. She'd wear her cap on her head, but at the last moment she tucked her second-best cap into the bag, along with a couple of potatoes lying by the fire.

Diarmaid had been busy at the same time, and when she was stuffing in the potatoes and glanced up at him, he had his coat on, and the backpack on his shoulders.

"Anything particular you want to keep?" he asked, looking around.

Why would she want to keep anything? None of what she had had been new, as far as she remembered. 'Twas all old, and worn, and reminded her of misery. Much better to leave it behind and take as little of it as she could.

Diarmaid took a quick look over what she was leaving, and dipped down to pick up the tattered blue shawl. "You might need this for warmth," he said.

She looked at it with no enthusiasm. "There's no room in the bag. Besides, it's falling apart."

He grinned at her. "I'll fit it in mine," he said, and did.

She looked around. The bowl was missing, and the spoon, so he had probably taken them. She looked at the porridge pot, and then at Diarmaid.

"Should I take that?"

He looked at the pot and at her bag, obviously calculating. "Could you fit some of your clothes inside it? If we could make a fire, we could cook in it."

She swallowed a sigh, and dropped to her knees. She'd folded everything carefully, but it did not take that long to reorganize it all, with the shifts and stockings in the pot, her cap and the potatoes on the top. When she lifted the bag now, it was heavier, but carrying it would still be nowhere as much work as she did daily cutting peat.

She gave a momentary thought to her spade, but decided she'd just leave it for whoever happened to need one.

"Ready?" Diarmaid asked.

She nodded, and followed him through the crooked door, not taking the time to close it.

It didn't matter now.

Walking through the narrow passageways of the clachan, Diarmaid tried to keep Muirne in front of him, but her legs were shorter than his, and he kept slowing down lest he outpace her. What always struck him as odd was the seeming emptiness of the place, although it was now full light of day. Made a certain amount of sense, of course. The farmers were out on their strips, planting or preparing to plant. Would be only the women at home with the children, each family within its own place. Many of them would be spinning or weaving as well. For doing laundry, there would be the communal wash house, but he didn't know where that was.

Muirne would know, but there didn't seem to be much point in asking her now. Her jaw was set, and she seemed determined to keep her legs moving as fast as she needed to, keeping up with him. For her sake, he should slow down, but he had no desire to be seen in the clachan by the mysterious man with the white temples. He had never—to his knowledge, that is—been identified before. If the bearded man knew his name, likely he would've used it. Even so, mebbe t'would be better to lie low for a while once he was back in Galway City. Perhaps he might even take the chance to go back to Meath and the big house there, see his mam.

He glanced down at his side, at the girl scuttling alongside of him. It wasn't safe to slow the pace yet, so she'd just have to keep up. To keep himself from worryin', he went back to plotting the future. If he did take Muirne to Meath, what would his mam make of her? Well, t'would be sensible to get her to brush her hair before they got to the big house.

She'd not like that. He almost missed a step, rethinking. Muirne glanced up quickly at him, as if she wondered if he'd had some problem. He grinned at her and they both kept walking.

He'd leave it to her. Most likely when Muirne saw everybody else in Connemara, or Galway, come to that, she'd start brushing her hair herself. Probably had no brush or she'd do it now. If he saw her making an attempt to smooth her hair down, he'd make sure she got one—once they got down to Donegal Town they'd be passing through towns with shops. He'd a thousand times rather have her figure it out than explain it to her. It was as she was in the clachan that he'd found her remarkable. He was not about to change her.

It seemed certain to him when she saw everyone else scrubbed and smoothed over she'd do the same.

They were on the dirt pathway now. People called it a road, but he'd never seen anything on it but people walking as they were, or, now and then, men on horseback. Not many of them, either. Whatever it was called, the pathway crossed both the inner circle of planted land, and the outer circle for the livestock before it entered the broader road, the one he'd followed himself to Derry. Assuming the bearded man was still scurrying up and down hills looking behind stones, the road should be safe enough.

Even so, he'd only feel truly safe once they'd turned off the road going to Derry. They needed to be heading south, past Lough Swilly and away from the Inishowen peninsula. Then they'd be only two of the many on the road, with wagons and coaches and farm vehicles of all sorts to make their way around.

"Can we stop a minute?"

He turned to see Muirne had already stopped and was sitting on the ground behind him, taking off one of her shoes.

"Feet hurting you?" he asked.

She shook her head. "Stone in me shoe." She shook it out. Getting a look at the sole of the shoe as she did so, he could see that it was no wonder a stone made its way in. There were a couple of holes in the sole itself and the sole had pulled away from the top of the shoe in at least one place. Would she get to Donegal Town before the whole thing fell apart?

"There." She sounded satisfied as she fastened the shoe around her foot again and scrambled to her feet. "Ye don't need to stop, you know," she said as she caught up with him. "I'll catch ye up if it happens again."

"May happen to me," he told her as they went on together.

"Then ye'll have to catch up with me." He got a glimpse of her guileless smile before he turned to face the road ahead. He wasn't used to this business of traveling with a girl, just the two of them. Well, wasn't used to traveling with a girl at all, come to that. He was usually alone, or perhaps with another man—once or twice it had been two. Having his companion be a female made all the difference.

Didn't bear a lot of thinking about. He lifted his chin and kept walking.

Muirne wished she'd had a look at the map. She knew he had one; when his box had been lying open in the sod hut she'd seen it there. Course then she'd had no idea she'd be walking away from the clachan forever, and certain she didn't need a map as long as she stayed there. But she'd left now, and every step was taking her places she'd never seen before, for all that so far it looked much like where she'd been. 'Twas a long way to Derry, that she knew. Was it that they must get there before turning south?

Time would go faster if they talked, but walking took breath out of you. If you tried to walk and talk at the same time you'd slow down. But she'd like to know about the places where he'd been, and the places where they were going. Galway City—he'd said that. So Galway was a city, not just a town. She'd never seen a city before. Never seen a proper town, either. She'd liked to listen to the tales of them that'd been to Derry, with streets full of houses and a river running through it. Was Derry a city or a town? Shops, streets of them, she'd been told. What would such a street look like? And churches with spires tall enough to see from a distance. Odd, that. They'd be Protestant. But there were chapels there, too. Strange it would be to go to Mass in a chapel. But since they'd broken all the chapels and the monasteries up when Cromwell came, many long years before, 'twas now only the traveling friars who said Mass up behind the stones on the hills. O' course in Derry might be different

Still, she'd been told Mass was Mass wherever, and like enough that was right.

A rabbit scurried across the path ahead of them and she followed it with her eyes. Now where could such a creature come from, and how far must it go before it found cover? Brave little thing, daring men and beasts everywhere, all of them seeing it as a tasty dinner. It disappeared under a line of low bushes, and she wished it well as she walked beyond, now looking around for other creatures. Way ahead down the road two men had a dog, and she watched it lope along with them, taking brief runs off to the side now and then. Dogs liked to run, she knew that much.

It would be nice to have a dog, except for having to feed it. Hard enough to feed the people. You'd have to save some out for a dog. But 'twould have been good to have one for company back there. Life would be different now, when there wasn't the rhythm of days out in the peat bog and coming home to deal with her good-for-nothing da. The change had already begun. She was walking away from all of that now, step after step.

"Getting tired?" Diarmaid's voice broke into her musing.

She glanced over, thinking out what to tell him. Of course she was getting tired—made out of flesh and blood, wasn't she? She'd been a whole lot tireder in the peat bog day after day. O' course in the peat bog she knew how long she had to stick at it, knew when she had to slow her pace a bit so she could finish the day. Didn't know anything about this adventure. How far were they going today? How far had they gone?

She asked him that.

Diarmaid pursed his lips, clearly calculating. "Mebbe ten, fifteen miles."

"So today—how far did you think we'd go?"

"I wanted to get to Buncrana at least, and we passed it just a bit ago, so that's good. I'd like to make it past the bend in Lough Swilly, and find a spot to sleep there. Then we'll go on south to Letterkenny. That's the way I came."

Good. She hadn't slowed him down. How long would that fellow Liam had told them about wander round the hills looking for Diarmaid? What mattered more now, where would he look next?

"That man Liam said was lookin' for you—will he come this way?"

Diarmaid shrugged. "That's why I'm looking to get past the bend of Lough Swilly. The road to Derry goes straight east toward the River Foyle. Could be he'll go back there. Mayhap that's where he come from—it was on that road I saw him. Think he's likelier to go east than south." He grinned at her, his usual cocky grin. "Hope so."

The grin went a way toward settling her. So 'twould be some farther, but she still was strong enough so she wasn't like to have to stop. She took a deep breath, looking round. She'd always been told the east part of Donegal had better land for farming than the rocky hills and marshy bits she was accustomed to, and seemed 'twas true. As they walked, t'were now fields wherever you looked. Good fields, seemed like. Still some stones about, but few compared to what she was used to.

"Startin' to look a bit different," she said. Talking did make the time go faster, helped her notice less her legs were getting a bit tired.

"Lots of changes." Diarmaid glanced over at her. "We'll be walking by the shore for a piece, coming down past Sligo, that way."

"Walking right on the beach?" She heard her own voice rise in eagerness.

"Not right on the beach." He was looking at her again. "We could, but the main thing is to get to Galway City as soon as we can. 'Tis faster to stay a bit inland."

"Oh." There'd been beaches to walk in Inishowen, and when she could, she'd escaped to them. Even just to sit on the sand and watch the waves come rolling in, one after another. Made her think strange thoughts about eternity. The waves always had rolled in to those beaches, always would.

But who knew what wonderful places might exist once you went south of Inishowen? The strange fact was that she, plain old Muirne Coyle, was traveling now, like all these folks before and behind them on the road. She put her head down. She'd feel a fool if Diarmaid happened to look over and caught her marching alongside him with a great silly grin on her face.

So her legs were getting tired. She was on her very first adventure, and as never before, tomorrow held a promise of being different from today.

12

BEST TO START OUT AS you mean to go on. The words kept rumbling through Diarmaid's head as they set about arrangements for the first night. He'd be the one to decide where they'd eat, where they'd sleep. Thanks to all the saints, they'd reached the bend of Lough Swilly that went round Inch Island. Not only were they beyond the turning for Derry, but Lough Swilly was turning into River Swilly, far enough from the sea so it was all fresh water. Made life simpler. Good thing in general, that.

They'd found a reasonable stopping place with some grass that would do for sleeping, and a barer patch where he'd set a fire with twigs fallen from the bushes round about. Then they set Muirne's pot on three stones over the fire and cooked the potatoes for supper. Muirne told him to save the water and they'd boil up some oats in it in the morning, so not only did they have something in their stomachs for tonight, but the promise of breakfast tomorrow.

Not having traveled with a woman before, Diarmaid wasn't sure whether all women would be so sensible, or if he was just fortunate Muirne had looked after herself most of her life. He couldn't see a way of asking her that, so he just sat by the dying fire, feeling fair satisfied with the way the day had gone, all things considered.

"Clear night tonight," Muirne said, looking up at the stars above, getting brighter and brighter as the sky darkened.

"'Tis," he agreed. She was sitting with her left arm propping her up so she could lean back to have a fine view of the sky. "How's the shoulder doing?"

"'Tis all swings and roundabouts, isn't it? My left arm got so tired of holding me bag that I thought it might fall off, but it didn't, and my shoulder's getting better." She gave him a quick smile. "Thank ye for asking."

"Ye did well today."

She glanced at him, and looked away. "'Twas good of you to let me come." When she looked back, her eyes had a mischievous glint. "Wonder what me poor old dad is doing without his porridge pot."

"Blessing your name?"

She laughed out loud. "Unlikely, I'd say." She looked up at the sky again. "What do you do when 'tisn't a clear night, but turns rainy?"

"Wish I had a tent?" They both grinned at each other. "No, really, I have a bit of oiled cloth that helps some—put it over my head, and try to pull the rest of me under bushes or find some farm outbuilding so I can get out o' the rain. All depends on what's around when the rain starts. Sometimes I've had to walk some to find shelter."

"How big's your oiled cloth?" Her eyes still had that glint of causing trouble for the sake of it.

"Not that big," he teased back. Pity they hadn't had time for much in the way of readying themselves. Not that he could have oiled another much larger cloth without having days to get it ready. He'd just have to make a mental note to start looking for somewhere to shelter earlier in the day when it was grey or rainin' already. Walking in the rain wasn't wonderful, but sleeping out in the rain was impossible unless you were so weary you could near go to sleep on your feet. Although he'd done that on occasion, as it happened. He just didn't like the idea of asking a woman to do it, even when the woman was nothing more than a feisty girl who looked as if a strong wind might blow her away.

No, no doubt about it. Traveling with a female was different from being on his own, or with other men. Couldn't say he'd then paid a lot of attention to whether they had rain on their faces or not.

"The fire's near out, isn't it?" Muirne gathered herself up to her feet. He couldn't help but see that she used only her left arm to push herself up. "Over here is where we sleep, right?" She went straight to the grassy piece he'd had in mind.

"That's the spot." He clambered up to his feet as well, and went over to the pack he'd carried on his back. "Here you go." He pulled out the shabby shawl she'd said she'd leave behind.

"What's that for?"

"Put down under your head. That way if you roll over you'll not find your face in the grass."

She looked at it, clearly considering what he'd said. "Suppose so," she muttered, sounding more dubious than grateful.

"Ye'll be glad of it."

She lifted a skeptical eyebrow. "So you say." She put out her hand and took it, anyway, and with it went over to the grassy patch. "You going to sit there by the fire all night?"

"Most likely not." His plan had been to let her settle herself, and then when she was placed and hopefully on the way to sleep—for they had indeed walked a fair distance today—he would pick a spot close enough to her so that if she needed him during the night, he'd be there, but far enough away so everything stayed matter-of-fact. That had been the plan, but he hadn't expected her to call him on it. "I'll be there in a bit."

"Suit yourself."

She was far away enough so that he could only see the general shape of her as she pulled the other shawl out of her bag and laid it down on the grass, making herself a bit of a bed. She took the shawl he'd brought for her and wrapped it around some piece of clothing she brought out of her bag as well, and then set it as a pillow at the end. Despite his resolve to treat her as he had his male companions in the past, he could not pull his gaze away from admiring how slim and graceful she was, taking off her shabby coat so she could use it as a blanket.

He forced himself to take some notice of the fire he was supposed to be tending, and when he'd stirred it with a stick, he glanced back, and she was only a dim shape on the grass.

Traveling with Muirne was going to have its temptations, no doubt about that. There was no way that he could protect himself entirely with good intentions. He'd have to be careful. Like tonight, he'd make sure that his sleeping place was far enough distant so that if he reached out a hand he wouldn't touch her.

He was not quite sure he'd keep his hands to himself in his sleep.

Muirne was the first to wake in the morning, wondering how long he'd sat up there by the fire. He was sleeping face down in the grass, spread-eagled as if the cold had not bothered him, with nothing over him except the clothes he'd worn the day before. Even had his shoes on.

She reached for her own shoes, looking them over for a minute before she put them on her feet. Many a mile they'd walked before she'd set off on this journey. How far could she go before they gave up altogether? The idea worried her, perhaps more because she mustn't share the worry with Diarmaid. He had money with him, yes, but that was to build up the cause, not to provide shoes for anyone happening to be around him.

Well. That would have to be a worry for another day. Each shoe was still in one piece this morning, praise the Lord.

She walked quiet as possible over to where the fire had been. Pity they'd had no peat with them—it'd be easy to rake up and find a bit of fire still living. But this poor fire was dead as dead. She could, and would, gather more dry sticks, but unless Diarmaid had left his flint there—well, miracle of miracles! There it was, with the steel. So she could make breakfast. Have to tell him not to leave it about like that.

She glanced back over her shoulder at him. So defenseless and unguarded he looked. Nothing like the person he was in the day. Were all men like that?

She wondered for about two seconds. Her useless da was not. When he was asleep he usually looked even worse than he did when awake—lying on his back, mouth open, sprawled like a shabby doll some child had thrown on the floor. Snoring. Usually smelled of drink as well. Had he ever been young and energetic and mebbe even good-looking? Ever had some interest in more than gathering barley to make poteen or finding some poteen ready made to drink?

Not that she could remember. What had her mam seen in him? Right down discouraging it was to think she came of those two. Her thanks went to Mother Mary that she could see nothing of herself in his face. Couldn't remember her mam's face well enough to know if she took after her.

T' only reason they let them stay in the clachan was it was her mam's family that had started it, a couple o' generations ago or whenever it'd been. And, to tell the truth, because o' his poteen. Everyone said he made fine poteen. He said 'twas mostly because o' the copper still he used—that was his special treasure—but allowed as how the gift ran in the family.

How splendid. Some families had a gift for weaving, or could carve wood into smooth shapes. Her family had a gift for poteen.

Gathering enough sticks for the breakfast fire was a quick job. Lucky Diarmaid'd left his backpack lying near, so she could pull out the bag of oats. Once the potato water from the night before was set over the new fire on the stones still in their places, it was just a matter of waiting. Waiting for the water to boil, waiting for the oats to cook.

She pulled her knees up and wrapped her arms around them, watching where Diarmaid slept. This was a strange new way to start a day. Yesterday—no, yesterday her life had already taken a surprising turn. She'd need to go back more days than one. As many as twenty, could be.

So then twenty days ago she had thought her life was as 'twould always be. Cooking breakfast for her ungrateful da, picking up the spade and walking to the turf fields. Cut peat all day, and come back as the sun was sinking. Cook supper whether her da was there or not, and when she tired of staring into the fire, lie down and sleep.

Never enough to eat, never enough sleep. Oh, mebbe every now and again a ceilidh with dancing and singing. That would be nice, but that would make the night shorter, and the next day in the turf fields seem longer. Hard, it was. Living was hard.

Then came this southerner. Diarmaid, she knew now, but first he'd been a red-headed southerner who talked about the chance that some day this hard life might be different. Ireland could be run by the Irish, not by the English, who now had all the money and land and made all the rules. Those meetings—they'd opened a different world to her. Why so many of the men had drifted away she puzzled over. Mebbe they just were tired at night and couldn't be bothered to come. From what she'd seen, 'twas men who crumbled first, and women who stuck at it, getting old and tired and shapeless but still doing what had to be done.

Mebbe nothing would change. Mebbe change was impossible. But it glittered, just out of reach.

"A smile's a great thing to wake up to."

Diarmaid's voice broke into her brooding so sudden that she jumped a bit.

He laughed. He'd rolled over so he was no longer face down in the grass, but she saw grass marks on his cheek.

"Good morning," she said, polite-like, like that would cover up her surprise.

He came up to his feet in a single smooth motion, one hand rubbing his cheek. "Guess I have to make up me mind whether I fight to shave every day or if I just get scrubbier and scrubbier looking."

She looked up at him. He looked—well, he looked unshaven now, but that 'twasn't the end of the world. "Leave it as 'tis. The bearded man won't be lookin' for someone else with a beard."

He raised one eyebrow. "That's true enough. The only thing is that growin' a beard's an itchy process."

Oh. She'd never thought of that. "Do as you please, then. You will anyway."

"You a grouch in the morning?"

She hoped he was teasing. She'd put the oats in the boiling water a time since, and so instead of answering she stirred the pot to see how the thickening was going. Still some to go.

"I made breakfast," she pointed out.

"And I thank you." He came over to inspect the porridge. "Looks about right."

"Still thin." She tilted her head to look up into his face. "If it's me cooking, I say when it's done."

He grinned. "Fair enough." He dropped into a squat across the fire.

She inspected him more closely. "You're scruffy, but not bad. Why not leave it until it's driving ye mad, and shave then if you have to?"

"Ye willing to risk madness?" The grin still lurked.

"Oh, go away and leave me to me porridge." She stirred it with extra energy. "Get me the bowl. I think 'tis ready now."

They still had only the one bowl. She filled it, and handed it back to him.

"Doesn't seem right that you cook it and I get to eat it first," he grumbled.

"'Tis the way the world works, far as I've seen."

"With luck we get to Letterkenny today. We can get another bowl there. Maybe a bit of kitchen to add to supper."

She pressed down the small burst of enthusiasm at the thought of kitchen. Might happen, might not. She sat there, watching him eat.

Letterkenny. She needed to remember the names of new places she was going. Had anyone in the clachan ever gone as far as Letterkenny? Most likely not. Not her da, for sure. What would he say if he knew she was here? Not that he had anything to say, after whacking that bone out of place. 'Twould be interesting to know if anyone told him she'd been in pain.

Diarmaid had been good to her, though. What would her da have to say when he found out—if he cared about finding out—that she'd gone off with the southerner? Bit unlikely to think he'd come off after them, grabbing Diarmaid and tellin' him he had to marry her. Just the idea of her puny, full-bellied da reaching for Diarmaid gave her a smile.

"What's funny?" Diarmaid scraped the last of the porridge out of the bowl, and came to his feet to bring it over to her. "There. You, now."

"Doesn't matter," she said. She took the bowl and scooped what was left of the porridge into it. To her surprise, Diarmaid grabbed the pot off the stones and carried it over to where there was a streamlet feeding into the lough, to wash it out. His hands must be tough as leather, although they hadn't felt all that rough when he'd touched her.

Would he touch her again? She kept her eyes on his back as she spooned the porridge into her mouth, a quick mouthful at a time. 'Twasn't so delicious she'd pause to savor it. Porridge was what kept you alive, that's what 'twas.

She'd never had a day start like this. It was unlike anything she'd known, so she had no way of telling what might happen next. Would Diarmaid touch her? She thought she'd seen hints that he'd like to. Would she like it? She'd liked the way he'd looked at her, and that was a first. Up to now, the only ones who'd reached for her she'd shoved and kicked away. 'Twas going to be her choice before she was anyone else's.

She'd emptied the bowl. She up and walked over to where Diarmaid had been washing the pot—he was on his way back, now.

"Done?" he asked. He reached for the bowl and handed her the pot. "Put it back in your bag now. We need to be off."

"I can wash it meself."

"Sure and you can, but it takes longer to get the pot in your bag than it takes me to tuck away the bowl."

"And the spoon."

"And the spoon." For a moment he hesitated, looking into her face. "You in a bad mood this morning?"

She glanced over at him, in surprise. "I'm not in a bad mood."

"Just as well. You look better with a smile on your face."

She looked down at her feet, embarrassed. "Don't see what how I look has to do with anything."

Her right hand was loose, and he caught it, running his thumb over the back. "Has a lot to do with everything, wouldn't you say?"

She grabbed it back. "Don't know what you're talking about."

He laughed, and they moved past each other. Now what was all that about? 'Twould give her something to puzzle over as they walked.

Only then did she notice that when he'd taken her hand, her shoulder had not protested.

DAY 'TWASN'T AS NICE AS it'd been the day before, but grey rather than rain. Diarmaid squinted up at it speculatively. Could always be the weather would improve as the day went on, but the clouds sort of lay up there in the sky as if that's where they intended to remain. Living in a sort of shelter for the past few weeks had made him soft, it seemed. He'd walked many long miles in rain and never given it a thought. So why was he wondering about rain that wasn't there now?

Could be it was yet another way of worrying about Muirne. Not that he saw any reason he should worry about her. He'd known she was tough and strong. Hadn't known that, he wouldn't have given her the choice to come or not. He didn't have time on a long walk like this to mess around with someone who needed to be looked after.

But then she'd never asked him to do so. So why was he fussing about it in his head anyway? Mebbe it was just another way of thinking about her.

He glanced over at her now, wondering where her mind was taking her. They'd fallen into the pattern of walking more swiftly in the morning, generally both of them silent, off in their own thoughts. It was as the day wore on that the tiredness crept in, and they fell into conversation, the talking making the last few miles easier.

Letterkenny had been both useful and an irritation. Had taken them three miles out of their way—they could have gone straight on toward Ballybofey, but they needed to stop where there were some shops. Oilcloth ready-made they needed, for one thing. And of course a second bowl and spoon so they both could eat at the same time. He'd some concern about her shoes: seemed to him there wasn't a lot of wear left in them, but Muirne insisted they were fine. Since they were past Ballybofey now, he just hoped they'd last as long as Donegal Town, which was where they were presently headed.

Donegal Town, and then Ballyshannon and by the coast road to Sligo.

The names of places were coming to be more familiar to him. Now he had to think out whether it made sense to head off to Connemara, or 'twould it be better to head straight south to Galway City. The road to Galway through Claremorris and Tuam was more level. Connemara was all up and down, over hills and mountains. True, Connemara was close to his heart and 'twould be good to see if the organizations he had put in place were still whole and waiting, but 'twould be faster and easier taking the flatter route to Galway, and he wanted to warn them there. If his presence had caused a flutter of interest, made more sense to let Donegal be for the time being. The few who'd been willing to work with him had enough sense to keep their mouths shut, and that would be what those in Galway City would want them to do.

He sighed, and her head turned toward him.

"Troubled?" she asked.

Diarmaid shook his head. "Not really troubled, quite. More deciding that 'twould be better for us to head straight to Galway City from Sligo, and leave Connemara for another time." He shrugged. "Good people there you'd like to meet, but I'm thinking it's all up and down walking to get there. Makes it beautiful, but it's tiring for a body. We'd probably do better to go straight to Galway City and take our rest there."

Felt like her eyes were searching his face.

"I could do the up and down walking, you know. Good Lord knows I got used to it in Inishowen."

He grinned at her. "'S not toughness I worry about. 'Tis how long it takes. That bearded man with the questions could've been anybody, but if'n they're wandering among the clachans looking for trouble, 'twould be just as well if there's none to find, and I need to let them know in Galway."

She was watching him closely, but she nodded and her face turned back to the road ahead of them. "So where we going for tonight?"

"Donegal Town, I hope."

She glanced at him over her shoulder. "Does County Donegal go on past the town, then?"

"Some, just a bit. Why?"

"Donegal goes up north past where we were. Toward Malin, I've heard? And we've been walking—what? Three, four days, and there's still more of Donegal to come?"

He laughed a little. "Long, stretched out county Donegal is, sure enough. True, most of the t'other counties are smaller. But we're close to putting Donegal behind us."

Her mouth quirked. "An' a queer feeling that gives me. Donegal born and never set foot out of the place. D'ye think the people down south will be able to tell?"

"An' what difference would it make?" Their pace had slowed, and he almost stopped, wondering what she would say.

"Can't say 'cause I don't know." 'Twas about as straight an answer as he could have asked for. She went on. "I'd just as soon they not think me a fool for not knowing much about anywhere else."

"I'd have a word or two for anybody who said you were a fool."

She gave him a long look, and shook out her bright red hair. "Then I'd better keep it to meself if anyone says so."

How had he not seen that she was a beauty from the very beginning? With those direct blue eyes and a face—now it was generally clean—that was fine-featured and lively, she made him catch his breath every now and again.

Like now.

They'd been walking for an hour or so, mebbe some less, when the rain began. It was a hard persistent rain, the sort that settled in to stay. At first it wasn't too bad. Diarmaid looked over at Muirne when it began, and they both shrugged and laughed. Sure, and today was going to be dismal—might as well prepare to enjoy it.

P'rhaps they picked up speed without deciding to, but they moved right along through the rain. There were others on the road as well, and few of them had found much of a way to stay dry. Horses and their riders were wet; the carts carrying heavy goods like iron for blacksmiths had water dripping, and the roads, dirt and ill-kept, got muddier by the hour. Diarmaid saw one coach pass them, on the way to Derry, perhaps, and those inside were dry enough, but the people sitting on the roof and the driver were sodden.

Usually, somewhere around dinner time, they had stopped to eat something, although they saved the hot meal for supper, when they had settled in for the night. In the rain, there seemed to be little point to stopping. They'd bought some buns in Letterkenny, and Diarmaid had them in his backpack, so he managed to pull out two and handed one over to Muirne and took the other himself.

Wet the buns were, of course, by the time they got to their mouths, but they'd be wet anyway, Muirne pointed out, once they were to swallowing them.

"I see a shed," she said, pointing. "'Twouldn't it be better to lean against that to eat the buns? At least we'd have a bit of roof to shelter us."

Diarmaid followed the line of her finger and nodded. It did just cover them from the rain, and 'twas a relief not to have the rain hammering on their faces. Muirne put her bag behind her, where it had as much protection as she could manage, and Diarmaid slipped his backpack off his shoulders to give them a bit o' rest.

He leaned back against the wall o' the shed and closed his eyes. "There's naught so splendid as travel, is there?"

Muirne giggled. "Brings you close to nature."

He opened his eyes and looked at her. "Close to drowning's more like it."

She shrugged, and Diarmaid was impressed in passing that there was no shadow of pain crossing her face. "Ye trying to believe it never rains in Inishowen?"

"I don't remember a drop." He couldn't help the lift at the corner of his mouth.

Muirne just looked at him over the top of the bun half in her mouth. "Sure and you're right." She leaned her head back against the wall as he had done, chewing for a moment, her eyes distant. "If I had three wishes, two of them would be for the rain to stop."

"And the third?"

"That'd be telling, wouldn't it?"

"Ha," he said, his head still back against the shed. "A girl w' secrets."

"So says the man with none."

He chuckled. Pity 'twasn't possible to stay here and talk nonsense. He'd not known a girl like this one before. Well, perhaps except for the Lady Anne, but that had been impossible from the start and he'd known it. Girls were timid or simpered or tried to flirt. Not this one.

'Twould be pleasant to stay here and rest a bit, except for the rain.

Muirne's red hair had escaped from the shawl and was straggling down her forehead, most likely dripping into her eyes. He wisht he had a dry kerchief to wipe the rain away, but of course he did not, at least not where he could get at it without soaking everything else in his backpack.

Well. There were sunny days and then there were days like this. He pushed himself off from the shed, and picked up his backpack, sliding it up his arms to his shoulders. Muirne, without saying a word, picked up her bag and stepped out into the rain.

As they set off again, he wisht he'd thought to dig out the map, just to look at it. It 'twas at the top of the backpack, just so as he could pull it out easily. He'd like to know how far it was to Donegal Town, assuming he could figure out where they were now. O' course it didn't really matter. Whether he knew exactly how many miles remained, they had to walk however many it was to get there. Somehow the little break had made it seem wetter and their legs more tired. Would they have done better not to stop?

'Twas common sense that 'twas better not to fall forward on your face in the mud from fatigue. He rolled his shoulders, shaking his head. If he were on better terms with the dear Lord, he'd beg him to give them a dry day tomorrow.

Could be her shoes were falling apart altogether, but as long as they clung to her feet somehow she'd keep walking in them. Seemed to be as much water squishing through them as she was stepping in, and every step was wet.

She'd certainly worked the turf fields when it rained, but usually when it settled into an all-day rain, the way it was now, even the men in charge got fed up with the wet clear through, and sent them home early so as they could go as well. And even when working in the rain there had always been the spade and cutting through just right so that what you left lying on the ground behind you were blocks o' the same size. You had something to think about besides the rain sliding down your face.

She brushed her hand across her forehead, impatiently.

Traveling, o' course, was different. Couldn't say as how she'd given a lot of thought to what Diarmaid had had to go through, walking all the way from the south to Inishowen Never having walked any comparable distance herself, she'd had no thought of how difficult it could be.

P'rhaps she should have. But even if she had considered it, she still would have come with him once he asked her. Mebbe it was miserable right now, but she still felt just a faint flutter of excitement that she, Muirne Coyle, was doing something. Something other than getting married to some poor man with horizons as narrow as her own, cooking and washing for him and having his babies and knowing there was nothing for any of them but more of what her life had always been. Never quite enough to eat, never enough warmth to sit down and sink into it, never enough sleep because each mornin' was a twin to the mornin' before, greeting the first light with the knowledge you had to pull your body out of whatever was serving as your bed. Truth be told, the only thing that made up for the cold of winter was long winter nights. Couldn't cut peat until the sky was light enough to be able to see it.

Couldn't really blame it on the man she might marry, neither. If life with him would be long and hard, life on your own wasn't much to brag about. There were some of them, skinny spinsters who clung to their brothers and their brothers' wives, always coming at the bottom of the list. Endlessly helping with the children as they came, one after another. Fetching water. Like as not spinning away night after night, until you'd be so tired you'd find yourself dozing off by the faint light of the fire. Doing the dirty jobs, just so as you could stay.

So what would her life be like, now? Couldn't say for sure, 'cept that it would be different. So she was marching along with the rain tippin' down, wet through to the skin—she must be that, by now—and where they would sleep tonight she could not imagine. Hadn't Diarmaid said something about sticking his head under the bushes to keep it drier?

If he could do it, so would she.

An' even this being Ireland, it couldn't rain forever. Sooner or later there'd be a dry day and she'd be dry and warm all over. An' they were heading south, were they not? South meant closer to the sun, whenever it chose to show itself.

"Hey, Muirne," Diarmaid said.

She was more than half surprised to hear his voice. Buried in her own thoughts, she'd been, stumping along as if she was the only creature on God's wet earth. She turned her face toward him.

"I've been thinking."

"Odd that. So have I." The words snapped out without her giving much thought to them.

"Ha ha." His voice was not amused. "Doesn't seem likely to me the rain's going to stop tonight."

She started to tilt her head upward to look at the sky until she realized that would simply mean more rain in her face. "So? What did we get the oilcloth for, then?"

"Not for nights when rain's pouring down like out o' a spout."

Muirne kept walking. Neither of them had slackened their pace at all.

"I'm thinkin' this would be a good night for an inn."

Now she did slow down, and turned to face him. "An inn?" Could she have heard him right?

"I'm thinking it might be worth sleeping dry and warm for one night. And have a supper that's not potato and oats over a fire."

She brushed her wet hair to one side of her forehead. "So where's an inn?"

"Must be one in Donegal Town. Even think I remember seeing one."

She came to a stop, forcing him to do the same, looking back at her. "Would you do an inn if you was alone?"

He tilted his head back to look at the rain, pulled off his cap and squeezed it, water running down his arm. "Raining like this? I'd sure given it serious thought."

"I can sleep out, you know."

"Then mayhap we'll have you sleep out and I'll stay in the inn." His lips were twitching.

"Most men have no sense about money."

He looked first surprised and then indignant. "What do you mean?"

"'Tis it the womenfolk who hand out shillings for poteen? I don't think so."

He groaned and turned around to continue walking. "'Tis not the same thing, and you know it."

She followed him. "Well, tell me this then. If you spend for an inn and supper tonight, is there still enough to get us to Galway?"

He groaned again but kept walking. "Have a little faith, woman. D'ye seriously think I'd spend my last pennies here in Donegal when I know we've got days of travel ahead of us?"

Muirne didn't answer, but kept walking. What did she think? From what she'd seen o' men—and her own dear da was the prime example—it seemed to her not at all unlikely that any man would think in the short term rather than worryin' about tomorrow.

But was Diarmaid different? She'd never known anyone like him, that was for certain.

"All right," she told his back. She hadn't yet caught up. "I trust you."

Diarmaid spun around, his arms out like a crazy man's. "Dear God," he shouted, "a miracle right here in the rain! She trusts me!"

Muirne tried not to laugh, but it was hopeless, and the more she laughed, the more he laughed with her. They wandered down the road together, laughing like two lunatics, and the rain continued to fall.

IT TOOK A COUPLE OF hours more to reach Donegal Town. By that time, he was certain sure that his clothes were sodden all the way in to his body, and his feet squelched in his shoes with each step he took.

It was an embarrassment when they arrived at the inn.

Inside, of course, it was dry. There were two sets o' doors at the entrance, and he hesitated inside the first one. He pushed the second open and took a look at the floor. Wood, it was, and nice wood at that, with a runner of carpet just in front of the desk.

He spoke over his shoulder to Muirne. "You stay here. 'Twould be better if I could find a way upstairs without dripping all over the place." He opened the door, and then hesitated. Looking back at her, he said, "I'm thinking 'twould be better if I call you my wife."

Women had often been incomprehensible to him. So was Muirne now.

"I haven't a ring."

Ring? There they were, dripping water like two drowned rats, and she thought the innkeepers would be looking for a ring? Half the married women in the clachan wore no ring—never had, most likely.

"So stuff your hand in your pocket," he ordered and shut the door between them, standing careful, like, so he was dripping on as little of their floor as possible.

The man at the desk—the innkeeper, he hoped—looked up when he heard the door shut, and his eyes widened some.

"Me wife and me got caught in the rain," Diarmaid said unnecessarily. The man nodded. "We need a room for the night. Is there some way we can get upstairs without wetting the whole place?"

Must've been the innkeeper. His face relaxed considerable when he realized these guests at least had some common sense. He nodded. "Come follow me. There are service stairs that you can use."

"Thank ye, sir." Diarmaid bobbed his head for courtesy, and turned back to open the door.

"Come w' me," he told Muirne. Silly girl, she did have her left hand in her pocket, and was carrying her bag with her right hand. But no sign of discomfort; Diarmaid relaxed a little more.

She slipped through the door after him, and followed him as he followed the innkeeper, who led them up the service stairs, plain scoured wood and windowless. When he opened the door to the next floor, he pulled keys out of his pocket and unlocked the first door. It looked a pleasant room with a window overlooking the street. There was only the one bed, as Diarmaid had expected, but there was a soft chair and carpet on the floor. One way or another they'd make it do.

"Very nice," he said.

Muirne stood just behind him, silent as a rabbit, her glance flicking around the room.

"Would ye prefer I pay ye now? We'll be having supper here, if that's possible."

The innkeeper looked relieved that he'd have the money in his pocket at once, and nodded with extra courtesy. "That would be excellent, sir. Just the one night?" He named the sum.

Diarmaid heard Muirne catch her breath behind him. He dug in his pocket and produced coins, which he counted out and handed over.

"Sorry they're a bit damp," he said.

The innkeeper, all beaming hospitality, made a sweeping gesture with his other hand. "Unavoidable, sir. It's been a right terrible day."

"That it has," Diarmaid agreed. He and the innkeeper nodded their heads to one another, and the innkeeper loosened the key from his ring and handed it to Diarmaid.

"Supper is ready when you wish to come down." He nodded again, and stepped around Muirne to open the door and disappear into the hall.

Neither of them spoke for a moment. When Diarmaid glanced at her, Muirne was standing where she'd been, nervously licking her lips.

"Well, I'm not about to stand around soaking wet." His voice was firm with no nonsense, as he meant it to be. "We've seen enough of each other already." Although in fact they had not. He was still wearing the clothes he'd worn leaving the clachan, and from all he could remember, so was she. Yes, they'd slept in the same place but both of them had always been clothed.

He turned his back and with determination began to strip.

Once naked, he dug in his backpack to find the other clothes he'd brought. They were faintly damp, but that was still a great improvement over what he'd shed. He started to pull them on, damp or not.

He had not heard any noise in the room. None at all. When he was once again decently clad, he took a swift look over where she had been standing.

She was there yet, back now turned as well, but she'd only stripped off her outer layer. Or layers? He had no idea what or how much she'd been wearing, but even in his quick glance he could see how much thinner she was than he'd thought she'd be. Dear Mother Mary, there could hardly be much but skin over her bones.

Even so, he found his body was beginning to stir. Time to give his mind to other things.

Pity that when he'd turned about he hadn't given a thought to what there was to look at. Given how slowly and uncertainly she was moving, if he'd thought to be looking out the window he could have memorized the whole of Donegal that was visible through it. Instead there was naught but a blank wall to capture his attention. That and the knowledge that Muirne was there, near to him, and now that he was listening, there was the sound of wet garments plopping on the floor.

How many layers had the girl been wearing? He cast a quick glance over his shoulder and immediately returned his gaze to the blank wall. Lord have mercy, she was indeed thin, but not as skeleton-like as he'd feared. Her naked back was pale and narrow, but there was the slightest flare of her hips, and even with the single glance, he could see the grace of her body as it moved.

How could it be taking her so long? Was she trying to kill him?

"Been staring at this wall for quite a time now. Are you ready?"

She squeaked. "Not yet."

"Hurry it up, would you then? I'm hungry as well."

"Me clothes are damp."

"So are mine, but they'll dry quicker on my body and if there's a fire downstairs we can sit by it and get warm clear through. That'll help." He took another quick look. At least she was no longer naked, but he had the uneasy sense that the picture of her slender body was well and truly set in his mind now anyway.

"'Tis hard to pull on damp clothes," Muirne complained.

He chose not to answer, still staring at the wall.

"There's a fireplace here," she said.

"Are you dressed yet?" He was afraid he had not stripped all the impatience from his words.

"Yes," she said in a small voice.

He turned around. She was indeed dressed, but clearly what she had been wearing were her finest clothes and what she had on now would be second-best. Or third, more likely. The pulling off and pulling on of her garments had left her hair wild and disarranged—surely not entirely standing on end, he hoped.

He had made sure to bring his brush with him, and as he inspected her, it seemed her hair was the only thing he was in a position to improve.

"Let me help with your hair." He hoped his tone sounded as bland as he meant it to.

She ran her hand through the back of it. "It's still wet and it's a mess."

"Not as bad as all that," he soothed, although of course it was.

What was needed was a towel. The one he had was not dry enough to improve her hair significantly. There was a small wardrobe in the room, so he went to look into it. The day of miracles had clearly not passed, because there was a towel. Ragged, but dry.

"Here's a dry towel." He could hear his own triumph. "Here, Muirne, you sit here on the bed."

She followed his directions. He took the towel and set to drying her hair, even darker red, now that it was wet, like his own. Walking through pouring rain was obviously not the best way to wash a body's hair, but judging by the grubbiness that came off on the towel, the downpour had done a fairish job. There was even some shine to it now. He went over it with the towel two, three times, and took the brush to it.

She sat quietly, only a murmur now and then when the brush hit a knot in her hair.

At last he stepped back to see what improvement he'd managed.

She lifted her chin, looking up at him anxiously.

"You're beautiful, d'you know that?" His voice was rough—even he could hear that.

She touched her hair on one side with careful fingers. It fell onto her shoulders now, and there was a bit of a curl in it. Either the wash by the rain or the brushing had brightened the golden lights in the red as it tumbled down the back of her head.

He had already seen that her face was pretty—her features small and dainty, and of course those blue eyes blazing out at him. Only now they weren't blazing as he'd always seen them. Muirne looked soft and shy.

He took a deep breath. To do anything else courted danger. He looked around the room instead, but there was nothing like a mirror.

"Pity." His voice was back to normal. "Can't see a looking glass anywhere. Seems a shame for you to look so nice and not be able to see it yourself."

Her hand went up to her hair. "Feels nice."

That it did. From now on he'd do well to let her brush it herself.

"Ready for supper, then?" he asked.

"I'm ready." Except that she wasn't heading for the door. Instead she was peering into the fireplace in the room. "Would they build a fire in here for us?"

"Suppose so. Why?"

"I'm thinking our wet clothes won't dry without one. And how can we pack them in our bags as they are?"

He nodded, thinking it over. Good thing she was there. He supposed he'd have thought of it sooner or later, but 'twould be a better idea to get the clothes started drying while they were eating their supper.

"You ready?" he asked again, but this time she appeared to be.

They went out together and stopped off at the desk again. Diarmaid noticed with amusement that she'd put her hand back into her pocket.

"Me wife told me our clothes will never dry out without a fire in the room," he said to the innkeeper.

The innkeeper nodded. "I can take care of that."

Muirne leaned toward him and asked, softly, "Would you happen t'have a rack we could borrow?"

The innkeeper turned toward her with an expression on his face that caught Diarmaid's attention. He 'twasn't at all sure he approved of it, since it made it perfectly plain the man had noticed Muirne was nice-looking. She was Muirne, after all, but not someone for just any man like the innkeeper to take notice of. Course he hadn't seen her much when they came in first. She'd stayed in the lobby between the sets of doors while Diarmaid had done the talking.

But then 'twas also true that Muirne as she'd looked when they came in had little in common with the girl standing by him now.

"Me wife might have one you could borrow," he told her while Diarmaid watched him more like a hawk than he'd want to admit. "It's just for the night, is it not?"

"That would be very kind of you," Muirne said in that soft voice. All too much like a purr for Diarmaid's taste.

The innkeeper beamed at her. "I'll just run up and get the fire going while you're having your supper," he said with more enthusiasm than was strictly necessary.

Diarmaid took her elbow in his hand and guided her off toward the room opening off the main room there, following the sounds of voices and the low clatter of dishes.

"Isn't that kind of 'im?" Muirne asked as they walked across the central room.

Diarmaid muttered something. "That's the kind ye have to look out for," he added.

"How so?"

Diarmaid avoided answering by making a business of settling her into a chair at an empty table. They had maybe four or five tables there, with other people at two of them. Whatever they were serving smelled fine, not a bit like oats.

Muirne was near to embarrassed by her appetite. She didn't know if she'd ever had anything so nice as the stew—great lumps of tender beef mixed with onions and carrots. It warmed her all the way down. She finished one bowl and when asked if she wanted another, made what she feared was a spectacle of herself by eating that one, too. Good bread came with it, too, which worked well to mop up the last bits of gravy in the second bowl.

Diarmaid watched her with more of a grin than she thought was necessary. He had a second bowl himself as well.

"Better than oats in potato water, 'tisn't it?" he asked between mouthfuls.

She had already pushed her empty bowl away. Had she eaten that greedily? "Still good that we have potatoes and oats to eat when we leave here. It's bad for me to taste this that's so much better," she added.

"Wait till you taste what me mam can cook." Diarmaid had a kind of secret smile he only used sometimes. He used it now. "They have all the finest foods there at the big house—plenty o' meat, nice salmon, chicken that cooks up well."

"An' you get to eat it?"

He shrugged. "All of them's that's in the house gets fed out of me mam's kitchen." He grinned at her. "O' course, they didn't always know I was there."

She watched him finish his bowl, wondering what 'twould be like to slip in and out of a big house, having your mam there. What would the grand English people think of having the son of the cook there come in and out? Or he said they wouldn't always know. How would he get in— or out—without them knowing of it? Or would there be lots of other servants who would let him in? She couldn't picture how people in the midst of grandeur might live their lives.

Just imagine. Never hungry, never cold, never worried about what the next day might bring. Soft beds, nice clothes, someone to do your bidding. How strange 'twould be.

She looked back at Diarmaid. Sudden-like a rush of pure tiredness came over her. Like a puppy, she thought. Give 'em a good dinner and they'd roll over into sleep. Her belly was full and warm, and all she could think of was a place to sleep.

She daren't close her eyes or she'd go to sleep here at the table.

She must've looked drowsy, because Diarmaid laughed.

"There's pudding yet," he said.

"Pudding?" And where was a girl to put it? Had she known that she mightn't have taken the second helping.

"I'll tell them to bring it straightaway," he said, and got up to go off and talk to somebody. Muirne was hardly awake enough to know where he went.

But he was right. He came back with some sort of custard over apples. She was not able to eat it as fast as she'd eaten the stew, but little by little it vanished.

"Ooh," she said, laying down her spoon at last. "You think mebbe I'll pop?"

He was looking at her in an unfamiliar way, his eyes warm. "Hope not," he said. "We've got a mile or two yet ahead of us."

"Not until I've had some sleep," she protested. She looked around at the windows, but it had gone dark outside. "Is it still raining?"

"Don't know, but as long as it stops by tomorrow morning, it can rain all night for all I care."

She closed her eyes in weariness, and then suddenly they were wide open.

"What are we to do?" she whispered urgently. "There's just the one bed."

"We've been sleeping close to each other for how many nights now?"

"But not in one bed."

"True enough. But we'll sleep the night through—we're both tired enough, I'd say."

"What—what about the innkeeper?" She was still whispering the words.

Diarmaid laughed out loud. "D'ye think he's going to come up to the room to check? He thinks we're married." But he was keeping his voice low as well.

Muirne sighed. This was not the way it should be working out, but she was too tired to argue about it. She'd just wear all her clothes to bed. She'd been doing that all along, after all, even when her bed'd been naught but a shawl.

After all, she should be safe enough. Sheer exhaustion had given her limbs of lead. Once she got to bed, she wouldn't be able to stir.

15

DIARMAID HAD BRACED HIMSELF FOR a battle against temptation, but it turned out to be less than a skirmish. When he unlocked and opened the door, Muirne walked past him like a sleep-walker, straight to the far side of the bed. She kicked off her shoes, pulled back the covers, and climbed in.

Diarmaid was still by the door.

He had barely reached the near side of the bed when Muirne sat bolt upright.

"Hell and damnation," she said, quite clearly. She climbed out of bed and picked up the wet clothes dropped across the floor and arranged them with remarkable speed all over the wooden rack the innkeeper had indeed provided in front of the fire.

She then marched back to the bed—Diarmaid was not certain sure her eyes were open—pulled back the covers again, rolled into a ball under them, and if she had not been asleep before, was certainly asleep within seconds.

Diarmaid sat on the edge of the bed, grinning, and followed her example. Could not have been as much as five minutes since they walked into the room that he was in bed as well, his resolutions to get an early start the next day dissolving in his mind as sleep overtook him.

He was certainly not prepared to be awakened some time later by the sound of Muirne's passionate weeping.

She was still curled into the tight ball, and he leaned over her to try to see her face, to ask what had disturbed her so. She struggled away from him, thrashing with her arms and legs as well, once she unrolled from the ball.

"No!" she shouted at him.

Thinking of the people who might be in the next room, he covered her mouth with his hand. To his indignant surprise, she bit it, hard.

"What's with ye?" he demanded, keeping his voice as low as he could, confused as he was. He peered at her more closely, looking past the tracks of tears down her face, and realized her eyes were still closed. She was still asleep.

"Here, Muirne," he murmured, gentling his words. When she started to thrash again, he wrapped his arms around her. "Wake up, a ghrá, 'tis all well. I have you and I'll hold you safe." He rocked back and forth, until he felt her suddenly go boneless in his arms. He pressed his mouth against her temple. "All is well, little one. There's naught to fear."

She moved in his arms, but it wasn't the mindless struggle of before. When he looked into her face he could see that her eyes were open now and she seemed to know where she was. He had moved a bit away to see her better, but she suddenly wrapped her arms around him and clung like a frightened child.

"What 'tis it, Muirne?" he asked, running a hand up and down her small narrow back. "Was it a bad dream? Or what?"

She leaned back for a moment to look into his face, and then curled back up against him. "Nightmare," she said into his chest.

"You're awake now." He ran his hand over her hair, now nearly silky. "It's all right, pet. You're safe. You're with me, and nothing can harm you."

Her head moved against him, as if she would burrow into him. Then all of a sudden she lifted her head, and pressed her mouth against his. He'd been trying to govern himself, and it was all of a sudden as if a fire broke loose, exploding through both of them.

There was nothing he wanted so much as her. He could not kiss her often enough, nor tire of the way it felt when his hands moved up and down her body. The wonder of it was that she seemed to wrap herself around him as if she could not press herself close enough to him. They were both fully dressed, and they might have been both in a dream as they gradually stripped the clothes first from one and then the other. In one way it felt as if it took forever before they were both naked, and in another way he would not have wished to lose one moment of the slow delicious process.

"Now," she whispered against his chest, and nothing in the world seemed as logical and inevitable as to do what she wished.

Even in the aftermath neither of them seemed ready to let go of the other. He lay on his back with her face pressed into his chest, and waited.

"Who was it, Muirne?" he asked. He'd not been the first, but she'd not seemed to have experience with what they'd been doing. 'Twas like something had been done to her, not with her.

She shook her head and seemed to try to bury herself even deeper within his arms. "Don't matter," she muttered. "'Twas not by choice."

"Then it matters even more." His hand ran over her hair. "Was it that your nightmare was about?"

She would not look at him, but her head moved up and down. Her words were muffled. "...not often," was all he heard.

He straightened up a bit and leaned over her. "What?" His voice was at once tender and determined.

"Not often, nightmares." The words were so mushed together he had to think for a moment to understand.

"The nightmares—you are not troubled often?"

She nodded.

He pulled her close again, his chin resting on her head. "Is it that you want me not to ask about any of it?" He had never felt so helpless.

To his surprise she pulled away to shake her head. "'Tis better to tell you. I've never said a word. Not to anyone. I cried out, truly I did, an' he would not stop. Was too strong, and he smelled..."

He closed his eyes to block the pictures in his head. Dear God, if it were possible to run back to Inishowen he would start now and keep running north across land and loughs 'til he had his hands around the bastard's throat.

The words were on his lips but he struggled to gentle his voice. "Who was it, then?"

She took a deep breath and then whispered. "Seamus Brady. One of those drinking with me da. Drunk then, of course." She shuddered.

"Was your father there?" He could feel the anger climbing within him, higher and higher until he feared it would choke him.

She shook her head, then shrugged. "He was there, of course, but stupid drunk as well. I don't remember. In the nightmare..." she hesitated "in the nightmare he's sleeping."

Diarmaid looked over her head to the wall beyond. Seamus Brady. What was her father's name? He'd never known, nor seen him. Well, might have seen 'im not knowing who he was. What was his name, then?

Had to be something Coyle. He wisht he had his hands around the bastard's neck. But the truth was, both Brady and Coyle were far behind them now. If only he had known this before they left the clachan, they would have paid for what they'd done. Now? Too far to go back and God alone knew what he would find if he did.

Muirne was under his protection in any case now. Much as he wished for the satisfaction of grinding their faces in the rocky soil until their heads disappeared, sure it had to be more important to stay with her now to keep her safe. Would he ever run into either of them again? Most likely not, but pray God in heaven if there was justice, they would, in time, rot in hell.

He smoothed Muirne's hair away from her face. "You're mine now, Muirne Coyle. Whatever happened before, this changes everything."

She looked at him straight, her lips trembling just a bit now. She nodded.

In some distant part of his mind Diarmaid rejoiced that he did not have to argue with her about it. If she was willing to let him shield her, he would put all the ugliness behind them. Let the good part of this night be their new beginning.

That he would remember forever. Given enough love, her horror from the past must gradually disappear, and although he had not known it before, he had enough to wrap her around.

But this, this place, this night, he would remember forever. The plain room with the fire, the familiar fragrance of the peat fire drawing him into the beginning of something he could not yet name, but knew would be the core of the rest of his life from then on. The shape of their clothes on the rack by the fire, the glitter of the flames brightening the walls and the windows: he would never forget any of it, nor his own awestruck wonder knowing all the pieces of his life were falling into place.

What would his mam have to say?

How long before he would be able to take her to Kendall House in Meath where his mam ruled the kitchen? Not as soon as he'd like. There was what he had to do in Galway City. He had to have some time with his uncles, time to report and to set out to them how the situation there was somewhat the same as what they'd thought, and how it was different. How desperate the poverty was. How beaten down too many of the people.

That he had left because of the presence of the man asking questions.

To let them meet Muirne, and to make it clear that his life would change. Oh dear Lord, how it was changing already.

Yet it could not change utterly. He would not give Muirne up: that was the new reality. But neither would he walk away from the goal he had dedicated himself to from the time he'd been old enough to understand. The fight for Ireland, for his land's freedom had always been the flame in his heart. Always would be.

Somehow he had to fit the two together. He needed time to put the pieces of his life together, the new and the old.

His arms tightened around the girl he was holding and, still half absent-mindedly, he dropped a kiss on her head.

"Ummm," she murmured.

"A ghrá," he said in response. His love. He'd never used those words before. Somehow he'd known the time would come when he needed them. Now they could be part of his life, day after day.

She nestled a bit closer. "Diarmaid?"

"What, love?"

"When you said this changes everything, did you mean *everything*?"

He looked down at her head, warm against his chest. "What are you asking, then?"

"It'll not mean you give up the fight for our land to be free?"

Was she afraid that he would, or that he would not? But there was only one honest answer he could give.

"That I cannot change. I will never rest easy while the English hold our land."

"Oh." He could not mistake her sigh of relief.

"Did you think I could walk away from that?" He pulled away a bit so that he could see directly into her face.

She sat up, brushing the hair off her forehead. "It was for that I came to you. I'd heard loose talk before, but there had never been one to say it was possible. 'Tis mainly because of that I made up me mind to come away with you. D'ye think those in Galway will be like you at first, saying you had no use for a woman?"

Of course she would remember that. He remembered as well. He had indeed spoken those words.

"I did work out ye're not the typical woman," he said, but he didn't like to recall that first meeting. Not all of it, at least.

"Could be the typical woman's more capable than you give her credit for."

He chuckled weakly. "Could be." And would she be telling him that to his dying day? Seemed well more than likely.

"Well, this woman is either to be part of the fight or she walks back to Inishowen."

Would she? He discovered he did not doubt it for a moment.

"So tell them so in Galway," he said, visualizing for a moment what his good uncles and the others would say when faced with Muirne Coyle the Fierce.

"Have you not told them yet?"

Diarmaid swallowed the impulse to groan. "Muirne, my love, you will be the end of me. When have I had the chance to tell them that you exist? If it has slipped your mind, I'll call to your memory that we left the clachan in a sort of rush. You do recall that?"

Her grin flashed. "Perhaps a wee bit of it."

"You can choose. When we get to Galway and meet them, shall I say, 'This is Muirne Coyle, the fierce woman from Donegal who will tell you how it all is to be done,' or shall I begin with 'This is Muirne Coyle, my dear love, who is to be my wife'?"

She cocked her head, considering in all seriousness which she would prefer. Diarmaid, who'd meant it as a tender joke, waited with more anxiety than he'd expected for whatever she would say. Would she always catch him one-footed like this?

"How about 'This is Muirne Coyle from far Inishowen in Donegal who has come to join our fight'?" she suggested. "Then you can say 'She will fight with me,'" she added at the end, as an afterthought.

He took a deep breath. "Or might I say, 'She will be my wife and fight with me'?"

Her face crinkled into a smile. "That will do. As long as you say the other first. If we go into battle, a ghrá, I will not be sheltered behind you. I will walk at your side."

The endearment warmed his blood almost as much as her determination chilled it. In a sense it was fair. For certain sure, he expected she would accept him as he was. It had just never crossed his mind that Muirne would demand the same. Women and men had always occupied different spaces in his view of the world. Now this woman, the only one in the world for him, expected him to change that. How could he fight forward if she fell behind beside him? It did not bear thinking about.

"But what if you have a babe at your breast?" His voice was a challenge. He meant it to be.

They were sitting separate now, facing each other. He almost could touch the intensity crackling between them.

"Is that what you want of me? A mother for your children?"

Her strength was what had caught his attention first. He had to remember that. He did not want a woman, a wife, to hold him back by her need to lean on him. But he'd never considered the price he must pay to stand back and let her be who she was.

Let him deal with her challenge first.

"No, I do not want you as a wife solely to give me a child. But it does happen."

"Then let us take steps to make sure it does not."

That he could agree to. Not to have a son—or a daughter!—now would suit both of them. But never? 'Twas good fortune they need not decide that now.

"All right. Agreed."

Her intensity dissolved into another smile, and, almost shyly, she reached out for him.

"Not again, my temptress. We have a long walk ahead and dawn will be creeping through the curtains all too soon." He wrapped his arms around her, and coaxed her to lie down with him, pulling the covers over them both.

He did not allow himself to sleep until he heard her breathing become regular and slow. Even then, feeling his love for her like yet another blanket wrapped around them both, he still lay awake, staring into the distance, torn between joy and trepidation.

16

AS IF TO MAKE UP for the relentless rain before, the northwest of Ireland for the next few days put on a splendid display of sun and fat playful clouds that drifted across the blue sky, changing shape as they sailed past. Now a ship at sea, now a bear reaching for its cub, now a fat old man dissolving into a bowl of apples. Muirne amused herself by watching the shapes shift and alter overhead as she walked.

Diarmaid walked by her side thinking his own thoughts, she guessed.

She'd never gone on a long walking trip before. As far as that went, she'd never strayed far from the boundaries of the clachan where she'd been born. Nor, as far as she knew, had anybody else who lived and farmed there,'cept for an odd few who'd gone to America.

So odd it was to discover that while she and t'others stayed in the clachan year after year, other people were making their way along the roads every day. Like the old man in a horse-drawn cart who was slowly passing them now. 'Twere two young children bobbing around among the great bags in the cart, laughing and chattering with each other, calling to their grand-da. He nodded and they waved at her as the cart lumbered past. She smiled and nodded back.

Walking was easy now, at least until afternoon. Her legs got into a rhythm, a pattern, one foot swinging forward and then the other. Thank the good Lord, she could wear the bag as a backpack now, her arms threaded through the straps. Backs were more fitted for carryin' a weight than arms. Every day as the shadows from the afternoon sun stretched out more, her shoulder would twinge a bit, and every day she'd debate whether 'twould be better to make her shoulder grow accustomed or whether she should carry it using her arms, changing from one to t'other as they tired.

Thought o' asking Diarmaid his opinion, but he fancied himself the great master of all enough already. After all, choosin' whether to tire her shoulder or her arms was her decision, and she meant to keep it that way. She glanced over at t' side of his face, his look concentrated. On what?

Pity it was that falling in love with a man made a woman tolerate dwellin' under his thumb too much o' the time.

But it did make the nights nicer. She ducked her head to hide her grin, should Diarmaid pick that moment to turn round. O' course, life being what 'tis, he did.

"So what's striking you funny?" he asked.

Caught. She turned the grin on him. "Nice day, good walking weather, sun's shinin' warm, not hot."

"Lucky we are."

She nodded, looking around. "Nice country here." She'd never seen such gentle land. Pretty it was in the sunshine, fields neatly divided with lines of bushes. Looked like good land, too; no rocks and boulders to be worked around.

"Most o' Ireland's more like that." Diarmaid slowed his pace to look around, and discovering she was passing him, Muirne did a curious half step that set them both to grinning.

"About to fall over?" It was the voice he used when he teased.

"Not me." She did a bit of a jig to show him she was still balanced.

"In Galway we'll find a ceilidhe and dance a step or two," he promised.

Galway. It glittered in the distance like the Promised Land. A proper city. What would a city be like? She'd seen towns now—Letterkenny was one and Donegal Town another. Of course Donegal Town would always shine in her memory, but getting to mysterious Galway was still exciting. Not only as journey's end, even though it would be at once the end of the long walk and the slightly fearsome start of whatever her life might be in the time to come.

She wished she could take Diarmaid's hand, just for a minute to remind herself she was certain of him, but they had given that up. The day after the glow of Donegal Town they had tried walking hand in hand, but it hadn't taken more 'n an hour to find they each had their own rhythm of walking and staying separate like was easier. There were the nights to lie wrapped in each other's arms and to whisper their words until the fatigue of the long day walking tricked both o' them into sleep.

How far had they gone so far? 'Twas a kind of game she played with herself. She never asked him how much farther they had to go. Instead she made her own guesses, timing herself by where the sun had got in the sky. A game for fine days, of course. When the sky was blanketed with clouds neither she nor anyone else could tell behind which one the sun hid.

They were surely due another day of rain. Since the day when it had bucketed rain on them all day they'd had only random showers. One night a quick rain had come upon them and Muirne woke up fighting with it. God alone knew what she'd been dreaming. Diarmaid, laughing, had asked her, but with the best will in the world she could not remember it. The dream had fled with her waking. All she had was her wet face and a sheepish memory of trying to beat off the rain with her fists.

"Got me a fierce one, I have," he'd said, and wiped her face with a cloth from his pack.

She was not yet used to tenderness. She felt her bones might melt with it.

The towns were more frequent now. They were indeed walking close to the shoreline, but only caught a quick sight of it every now and then. When Diarmaid had told her that they would be taking the shortest road to Galway and would miss Connemara, she'd felt a bit like a treat was being snatched away. Instead he'd promised they'd stop at a beach, but now the shore was within reach she remembered that even with the rack before the fire their clothes hadn't dried all through from the long rainy day, and they would not have any rack—or any fire that would last a night—and so, mebbe, it was better not to think of splashing in water, however much she'd liked that back in Donegal.

Donegal seemed very far away now. Sometimes as she walked she wondered when she might see it again. If she might see it again. Wondered, too, if her da had realized that she was gone, now. Would he care, or had the drink scoured all feeling out o' him?

There was a lot of time to think as she walked.

Their days had fallen into a pattern. Waking early, one or t'other of them. Whichever 'twas would rebuild the fire and set the porridge to cooking. The shops in the towns they passed through now had bread for sale, and sometimes Diarmaid would buy bread instead, toasting it over the fire on a stick. He liked that a lot, but Muirne still liked the feel of the porridge in her belly in the mornings. Felt as if it gave her more power in her legs for walking.

Midday they might stop for a bit and eat some of Diarmaid's bread.

As the sun started to sink behind the hills—if there were hills—they'd begin looking for a place to stop for the night. What they needed most was to have water somewhere near, a brook or riverbank where they could scoop out some water with the porridge pot. Sometimes as they waited by the fire for the water to boil, Diarmaid would tell her about how he'd make her a cup of tea when they reached Galway. Tea, he said, was dear, and 'twas better for them to save their money while they were still walking.

Muirne had never tasted tea, not proper tea. All she'd had was what they called tea in the clachan which was whatever herbs some of the old women had been able to gather, chopped and boiling water poured over, to give some taste as the water cooled. Diarmaid said his mam always had a pot of tea, real tea from India, at her elbow in the grand house where she was the cook in the kitchen.

He'd not talk of it every night as they waited for the potatoes to cook—sometimes now Diarmaid would buy a couple of carrots as well and cook them in the pot as well—but Muirne loved the nights when she sat leaning alongside him and he would tell her wonderful tales of that kitchen. How there were great pieces of meat, and fresh fish, and always a sweet after dinner, only their dinner was in the late afternoon, not midday. Bowls of eggs they had in that kitchen, and cream, and sweet biscuits to nibble on with tea. 'Twas like a dream she might have had when she was young and hungry, but he promised her it was true, and she would see it someday soon. When his business in Galway was done.

There was one night she knew she would never forget.

Had been cloudy, but not raining, not even sprinkling, and when they found a flat grassy spot right by a shed—but no one round about—they'd set about the usual business of choosing a place for the fire. Couldn't always plan on finding the stones that were all around in Donegal, but Diarmaid had found a chunk of green wood that would do to hold up the pot.

While he was messing about with that, Muirne had wandered off around the shed to see what it could be used for, mainly to be sure that no one would be coming out to see who'd set the fire and to chase them off into the night that was coming to be dark.

Inside the shed were some chickens.

Muirne peered around the half-open door at them. How in the name of all the saints had somebody left chickens to fare for themselves? After looking around again, she dared to step into the shed. There was barely enough light to see anything, but there were nests on the floor and on a shelf, and wonder of wonders, in one of the nests were two eggs!

Breathless with the miracle of it, she stood marveling until she came to herself and decided that the chicken, having laid them, had no further use for them, whereas she and Diarmaid most certainly did.

She reached out for them.

One of the chickens flew at her. Clearly it did not agree with her, but Muirne was not about to let a chicken win. She cupped her other hand over the eggs, and scampered out of the shed, toward the fire.

"Diarmaid!" Even she could hear the excitement in her voice.

He came to his feet, and started in her direction. By then 'twas dark enough that she didn't see the anxiety in his face until he had nearly reached her.

"Look! Eggs, Diarmaid! Eggs."

He laughed like a lunatic and wrapped his arms around her.

"Watch out for the eggs!" She wriggled out of his hold, protesting. Thank the Lord, they were both still whole.

That was a lovely supper. Diarmaid popped the eggs into the boiling water with the potatoes, and took them out in time so that they each had a delicious soft egg in their bowl, and when the potatoes were ready they soaked up the last of the yolks still there.

It never happened again, but even just once was a little miracle Muirne liked to remember.

She kept up marvelously well. Diarmaid liked looking over and seeing her there beside him, her eyes secretive and absorbed with her thoughts. Sometimes he was tempted to suggest that they slow down just a bit so that she could tell him what she was thinking. He was always surprised and interested in what she had to say when he asked her. Small she was, and had not much of a life behind her, but her mind was quick and he would never have thought of half of the things she was puzzling over as they walked.

But she was right. They walked faster when they walked silently side by side. Had it been so when he'd walked with one of his companions in the cause? He couldn't remember. Sometimes when the road had been up and down over hills, their pace slowed out of weariness for the last hour or so, and they talked then. Those were the times he would catch himself marveling at what she'd been noticing, what she'd been thinking.

He was dazzled by her, that's all there was to it.

But what he sometimes was considering, as he walked, was how the two of them were to craft a life together. That they would he had no doubt. But he had never had to give a thought to anyone else as he went about filling his responsibilities. If he needed to pick up and travel two days to be useful somewhere else, he did so. Maybe a word to the landlord, if he was renting a room, but nothing more. More often, could be what started out as a pint with friends would turn into an all-night meeting, working out the strategy for some minor poke at the authorities. They had not the organization nor the resources for anything more, but they could perhaps delay or dispose of some letter or document that would have the British, puffed up and pompous as they were, scrambling around to figure out what they had done with it. Such a game would not greatly inconvenience the British, more's the pity, but it gave heart to those who waited restlessly to act, to do something, anything decisive that would bring their goal a little closer. They needed that. Saints be praised, *he* needed that.

But what would Muirne be doing while he was off giving a sharp tug to the British lion's tail?

"What do you do during the days?" he asked idly, as they walked.

"Work." She looked at him strangely, as if the question was a lunatic one, which—when he thought about it—it probably was.

"No, I mean..." His voice trailed off. No, this was not the way to get to the heart of the problem. "There be no peat bogs in Galway town or most o' the other places I might be. I was wondering what you'd be doing when I was busy."

"Working as well." She snapped out the words.

"Doing what?"

"Whatever needed doing." She was still watching him, and her feet moved in the direction of her eyes until she veered off sharply to keep from walking into him. "You of the opinion only you have skills folk are willing to pay for?"

Too late he saw himself sinking into a pit that might be hard to get out of.

"That's not what I was saying."

"Then p'rhaps you might tell me what you meant to say instead."

Dear Lord, the woman was quick to bristle. Not her words nor her face were all that friendly, it seemed to him.

"I meant that Galway is a city and it's different from what you're used to."

"And I'm fitten only to cut peat?" She did not give him the chance to answer. "I can read a bit, which is more than some of us can do. I can count money, as well. There's shops in Galway, right? A city would have enough shops, seems to me, that there would be one o' them could use someone who could read and keep the till and was honest and hardworking." She speared him with her glance again. "Even if it was a woman."

"A grá, that was not me meaning."

"A grá right back at you. Don't you think I'll be sittin' idle waiting for you to cast a glance in my direction. If I get fed up with it all, I know the way back to Inishowen, and I can make me own way there, too."

"Muirne!" His exasperation was such that the only word he could think of was her name.

"That's me name, and you must be Diarmaid." She picked up her walking speed and for a moment he had to scramble to keep up with her.

Were all women this difficult, or had he the bad luck to love the only one that was? Dear Lord, he couldn't even remember what misstatement he'd made to get himself into this fix. But there she was, the holder of his heart, her temper flaring as bright as her hair. Holy Mary, Mother of God, he wished he could shake her until her brain rattled.

"Suit yourself," he spit out, and they stalked on, side by side.

That night their supper was silent except for necessary words, and when they lay down, they were not curled close together. As she usually did, Muirne fell promptly into sleep.

Diarmaid lay awake, staring up at the clouded dark sky.

He hoped to God it wouldn't rain.

SHE WAS NO MORE TALKATIVE at breakfast. The porridge was made with the minimum of words between them. They ate it in silence, packed up wordlessly, and set off walking.

Irritated, Diarmaid wondered why this seemed to happen so often. 'Twasn't just women, though he'd be glad to think so. But there'd been times with the lads when what had seemed to be a perfectly cordial conversation suddenly took a wrong turn midstream. First thing you'd know people'd be silent with each other or try to settle whatever they thought was the problem by taking punches at each other. It'd go on until something else happened. Mebbe it took a bit of an emergency or just enough time passing so nobody remembered whatever had started it. At that point, and with no explanation, matters came normal again.

Was that what it was like with women, or more precisely, with Muirne? P'rhaps if he'd spent more time with girls, like, and less with angry young lads he'd know what to expect and would be better prepared to deal with her.

As it was, he wasn't of a mind to deal with it now. But there'd been good days, the two of them walking along together, and he'd a far side rather have it like that than like now, with her locked in her thoughts and him locked in his.

"Ah, damn it all to hell." Muirne's voice was loud and irritated. But now not at him, it seemed.

He looked over, startled, to realize that she had stopped behind him. She was sitting on the ground pulling her left shoe off her foot, without unfastening anything. The shoe had finally simply fallen apart. The shredded bottom and torn top o' the shoe were now two distinct pieces.

Walking back toward her, he looked around. Nice enough countryside, he supposed, but not much in the way of villages or shops. Pity the shoe had not collapsed when they were passing through Sligo. There was enough of a town there so that there might even have been a place to buy second-hand shoes. Damnation—his worn purse of money was growing light, and it would still be three or four days to Galway. How would they manage for food if they had to buy shoes for her, new ones?

She had taken off the other shoe when he reached her. "Better walk with two bare feet than try to do it limpin' on one side." She glanced up at him. "It's sorry I am."

He squatted down next to her. "Nothing to be sorry about. You and I both know those shoes had not many miles left in them when we left Inishowen. The miracle is they brought you this far."

She looked down at the sorry remains of her shoes and a fleeting smile crossed her face. "Well, that's true enough. A quick prayer of gratitude, then?"

"Don't think we have to go that far." He shrugged and straightened up. "Tobercurry can't be too much ahead. We can see what we can find there."

"Let's be on our way, then." She rose gracefully to her feet, and looked down at them, wiggling her toes. "At least I need not worry about these wearing out."

Diarmaid stood looking at her. He did not like the idea of her walking the distance they had ahead of them barefoot, and yet he had to admit that many of the women he'd seen when in Inishowen had not worn shoes. In fact, now that he thought about it, hadn't he seen a couple of women barefoot on the road to Derry with their shoes hung around their necks? Shoes they'd probably put on once they came close to the city.

But Muirne was no ordinary clachan woman, hands and body thickened by years of unrelenting heavy labor, day in, day out. She was still young and supple, with her body—even her feet—shaped as the good Lord meant a woman's body to be. He'd give her his shoes to wear, except that his feet were so much bigger that her feet would slide around within, and she'd most likely end with blisters. 'Twould be better to just get on with it, and hope they'd find some shoes for her as soon as they came to a settlement of any size.

'Twas pretty enough countryside here. Just a pity there were so few folk about.

They started off again, but now he was looking down most of the time, checking out the surfaces they walked on. Watching for stones, uneven spots, anything sharp that might cut her.

Probably walking slower, as well. He wished he did not feel so irritated about it all. She was not to be blamed for it. When those shoes had been purchased however long ago it had been it was certain sure no one had thought she would be walking some 300 miles in them. Clearly 'twas not his fault, either, unless he were to come to the conclusion he should have foreseen something like this happening, and insisted early on—Derry? Letterkenny?—they buy some sounder shoes at any of the second-hand stores both towns would certainly have had.

With determination he lifted his eyes to look at the horizon. In this gently hilly landscape there was no sign of anything different ahead from what he could see looking from side to side. No little gathering of houses that might indicate the outskirts of a village or town. Just farmland stretching out to the right and to the left.

"How're you doing?" He couldn't help that his voice sounded anxious. He was anxious.

"I'm fine." She glanced over at him, cheerful as ever. Well, as ever if you left out last night and the gulf between their points of view. What had the problem been? His brooding over her bare feet had scrubbed his mind clear of everything else. Whatever the disagreement had been about, he'd better stay away from it. He was learning just from his anxiety about Muirne walking without shoes to figure that arguing with her was something he should avoid whenever possible. How did he manage to get himself into such a sorry situation so unknowingly and with such speed?

"You sure your feet not bothering you?"

She smiled at him. "Look, Diarmaid, don't worry so. You must've seen there were a lot o' women with no shoes in the clachan. Not one o' them appeared to me to have died on account of it."

He grunted, and said nothing for a bit. Just went on walking.

Kept eating away at him, it did.

"Sure, and they'd been walking with nothing on their feet for years. Soles probably as strong as—as—" now he'd started talking about it, he groped for a suitable comparison "—as leather." He wished he coulda thought of something better.

"That may be." Her voice was still comfortable and she still had a half-smile on her face. "But the soles of those shoes weren't much good for a while now. 'Twas mainly the sides of my feet what got protection, and I'm not walking on that part now."

He couldn't figure out if it'd be better if she wasn't being so cheerful about it. If he was having to do this walk in his bare feet, he'd have a word or two to say about it, and that was for sure. As far as that went, how come it was the women in the clachan with bare feet, but every single man was shod and expected to be kept in shoes?

Spend too much time thinking about that sort of thing and he'd wind up like Muirne, complaining about matters that were as they were and had been, most likely, for centuries now. How was a plain man to work out which of the customs were sensible and which were not? Men and women were different. Didn't take a wise man to figure that out; babes of two or so who could barely talk could see the differences between 'em. So only made sense that they should be treated different as well.

Still, the thing that niggled at him was thinking how women were softer and needed more protection than a man. So why was it women who always seemed to get the short end of the stick?

He threw the problem away from him and looked back at the horizon. They were coming to the crest of the gentle hill he'd been looking at before, and to his delighted surprise there did indeed seem to be a few houses at the bottom of the shallow valley before the road lifted a bit to roll over the next hill.

"Are you looking down there?" He nudged Muirne with his elbow.

"S'only three or four houses," she answered sensibly.

"Houses have people in 'em, most times, and people wear shoes."

She giggled. "A ghrá, if they wear shoes, they're on their feet, not to hand out to total strangers passin' through."

The sound of the endearment on her lips was surprisingly comforting. Last time she'd said those words, affection had been the farthest thing from her mind. Would be good to find out that she was like him. About most things, anger was a passing storm, like in the summer when rain would belt down out of the heavens and five minutes later, be past and gone.

"We'll see what happens," he said, hoping. At worst whoever lived there could tell them the closest place where shoes could likely be found, especially if it was off the main road. So they followed the road down, Diarmaid finding to his irritation he was still keeping watch over the road surface, so much that he almost walked into her two or three times.

When they came close to the houses, he had the nightmare feeling that all the people were hiding in their houses or had simply disappeared. There seemed to be nobody moving in sight.

It was with great relief he saw a woman hanging laundry on a line outside her cottage. Striding out ahead of Muirne, he went straight to her.

"Excuse me for bothering you, but we need a bit of help here," he said as politely as he could. "Me wife's shoe fell apart just back up the road a piece, and we're on to Galway City. It's a long way to walk barefoot. Is there somewhere near about where we might find some shoes for her?"

He glanced over his shoulder and saw Muirne was glaring at him again and had stuffed her hand back inside her coat. 'Twas for sure unfortunate she took such exception to him claiming her as his wife. If she looked at it logically, to say such was simply sensible. And, as he was to wed her soon as they reached Galway, 'twas not all that far from truth.

The woman finished hanging the towel in her hands, and turned to look first at Diarmaid and then at Muirne. "So what happened to her shoes?"

"They wore out." Muirne spoke plainly. "We've come from Donegal."

The woman's eyes widened. "That's a far piece."

Muirne's answer was brief and to the point. "'Tis."

The woman bent over to pick up another towel out of the basket to hang it, and then dropped it back and straightened up. "Your feet look smaller than mine. Don't know as I have a shoe that would fit you, even an old one."

Muirne nodded politely at her. "Thank ye in any case."

Diarmaid stepped forward. "Would there by chance be anyone living round here who might have a pair o' shoes we could buy? Someone with feet about her size?"

The woman rested her chin on her hand, considering.

"There's one," she said after what had seemed a long time of pondering.

Diarmaid looked at her with interest, and waited.

"Don't know as how she'd be willing," the woman said slowly. "Kitty Kelleher's boy passed mebbe five months ago. They'd just bought him new shoes, as I remember. 'Course he was buried in the new ones, but she was telling me t'other day she hadn't the heart to clear out his things. If she still has 'em, they might well fit. He'd been poorly for a while, and was not a great big lad. They'd bought the new ones 'cause she thought his feet were growing. Took it as a hopeful sign, poor woman." She sighed heavily. "So 'twas not that the old ones were wore out. But they'd be boys' shoes," she added, looking at Muirne anxiously.

"Doesn't matter," Muirne said quickly. "But I'd not like to bother her. Poor woman. Mayhap she wants to keep what she has of him close."

"'Twould be foolishness," the woman said. "Life is as 'tis, and he's gone. You're still here and if you could fit 'em, seems most sensible to me. It's a long walk to Galway still, an' you must have walked far already."

Diarmaid and Muirne looked at each other quick, like. Diarmaid wisht he knew whether he should ask which house was Kitty whatever's house, and whether 'twould be better for him to go or for it to be Muirne. Muirne didn't seem to be much worried about them being a boy's shoes, but would she be comfortable wearin' a dead boy's shoes? There was no way to ask.

"I'll just run over to Kitty Kelleher's and tell 'er the problem and see what she says. _If_ she still has 'em," the woman added cautiously.

"That would be kind o' you," Diarmaid said, meaning it.

"I'll be back." The woman nodded to them both briefly and skittered off, moving her considerable bulk with surprising speed.

Diarmaid and Muirne stood there, uneasily, unwilling to talk in case the woman might suddenly reappear and take offense at something that was not meant to be hurtful. Diarmaid shifted his weight from one foot to the other, and Muirne, not seeming to pay attention, rubbed her bare feet back and forth on a patch of grass.

The waiting time seemed to move slowly, as waiting time always did. One of them caught the other's eye a time or two, and they would both smile a wary smile, and then go back to trying to pretend it wasn't important if the shoes were to be given after all, or, indeed, if they would fit. Diarmaid wished he remembered how far it would be to the next village or town. He'd been down this road before, but not more than once or twice, and had been on so many other roads since. Sometimes it seemed that all the roads blended into each other, and trying to remember any particular one was like trying to pick out just one thread in some woman's embroid'ry piece.

He hated seeing Muirne's bare feet walking along the road—kept imagining that they'd be cut and bleeding, and she'd keep walking because that was what Muirne'd do. Nightmares were bad enough at night; seemed unfair to have them bothering him during the day when he was wide awake.

It was the voices that let them know the woman was coming back, and someone with her.

"This is Kitty Kelleher," she said as soon as she was close enough to be heard. "An' Kitty, these be the two I told you about."

"I be Diarmaid MacGuinness and this is Muirne, my wife." Somehow he knew that if he gave her the name of Muirne MacGuinness she would object strongly, and this wasn't the place he wanted to deal with that. Seemed calling her his wife was bad enough.

They exchanged a quick glance of relief. Kitty Kelleher had a pair of shoes in her hand.

"These are my son Thomas's shoes," she said. "I didn't know what to do about them. Mebbe I was being prompted to save 'em for you." She smiled tentatively at Muirne. "If they fit, o' course." She handed the shoes to Muirne.

"Thank you," Muirne murmured, and sat down on the grass patch.

"Oh, wait just a moment," Kitty Kelleher said, and fished a pair of stockings out of her pocket. "They're mended—he was hard on socks, somehow—but they should do for th' time being."

"It's so good o' you." Muirne looked up at her with real appreciation in her eyes.

"Try 'em on, then."

Muirne pulled on the socks first, and then, somewhat warily, put on first one shoe and then the other. She scrambled to her feet.

"Do they fit, then?" The woman they'd spoken to first was clearly eager to know.

Muirne was wiggling around her feet, checking the fit. "They fit fine," she said.

Dairmaid could see the relief on Kitty Kelleher's face.

"Thomas will for certain be surprised when he looks down from heaven and sees his old shoes on the feet of a pretty woman," she said. "It's better so. I didn't know what to do about his things."

Diarmaid pulled his coin purse out of his backpack. "Let me pay you," he said.

Kitty Kelleher shook her head firmly. "I'll not take it. This is Thomas's gift to your wife."

Muirne looked at him, her eyes begging him somehow.

He scoured his mind. Then he opened the purse and took out two pennies.

"Then light a candle for Thomas from us next time you're at church," he said, and handed her the pennies.

"That'll be two candles," Kitty Kelleher whispered.

"One from each of us then," Muirne said.

"I'm Síle Doherty, and 'twas a good wind brought you here," said the other woman. "Walk on in peace and may you reach Galway well and in good spirits. The saints be with you."

Kitty Kelleher surprised both of them by abruptly giving first Muirne and then Diarmaid a close hug.

"Be on your way now, unless you choose to spend the night here. You'd be welcome."

They exchanged a quick glance and then both of them at the same time thanked her and told her they needed be on their way.

Even so, it took a bit longer for them to break away and walk far enough so that they felt free to speak to each other.

"Did you hear her?" Diarmaid asked.

"Who?"

"Kitty Kelleher. She called after us. Said, 'Thomas's shoes, keep them safe.'"

Muirne chuckled and looked down at her feet as she walked. "They're not beautiful, but I'm grateful for them all t'same." She looked over at him, smiling. "An' you're right. 'Tis easier to walk in shoes than barefoot."

She reached over to grab his hand and for a while they walked like that, soaking up the late afternoon sun.

18

IT FELT AS IF EACH step brought them closer to Galway. Of course that had been true from the time they set out from the clachan, but it was only now that Muirne began to think of it as real. The day after the drama of Thomas's shoes (that was what she would call those shoes forever, she admitted with a lopsided grin) had been a smooth, ordinary day, mile after mile falling away under their feet.

It made it that much more irritating that she woke on the next day as worn out as if she had just finished a long day's walk, instead of being at the beginning of one. Usually she had no problem jumping up to her feet to get started with the fire or the porridge, whichever needed doing at the moment. This morning she lay looking up at the low clouds covering the sky and tried to think why sitting up would take such an enormous effort. She counted to five once, then to ten twice before she managed it.

Finally on her feet, she went over to where Diarmaid crouched by the fire, stirring the porridge. He glanced up at her.

"You doing well?" he asked.

"Just tired this morning." She forced herself to smile back at him.

His look at her sharpened. "We've not started yet. You're tired already?"

She shrugged. "I'll be fine."

He went back to paying attention to the pot, casting a glance over at her more frequently than he usually did. She started out squatting next to him, and then because that made her legs ache, flopped down to sit on the grass, early morning dew and all. There she waited passively for the day to somehow turn back into a day like the others. She had shoes; it was not as cold as it had been. Mebbe real spring was coming, when they could count on good day following good day.

Except by then they would have reached Galway, and the long walking days would be over. What would she do with those hours? She'd almost forgotten what she did with her time. For a bit she frowned, trying to remember.

"Oh yes," she said out loud. Diarmaid looked at her, clearly puzzled.

"I was thinking what I used to do at the clachan," she explained, afraid he'd see she was embarrassed. "The turf field. For a bit couldn't think of it."

His face broke into a smile. "Just as well. Not much to remember, was it?"

She shook her head slowly. But some of it she did want to remember. The freshness of the air when they first came out to the fields when the morning was new. The satisfaction of the shovel cutting into the turf early in the day, when her body welcomed the power of her own strength. The patience of the donkeys while the peat lumps were loaded into the baskets, one on either side, fastened together across the donkey's back. The sky when it arched blue over them on a cloudless day. Joking with Seán Doherty, working the next row over. Hard work, yes, and she'd be glad to lose the memory of bone-deep tiredness at the end of the day or, worse, when the afternoon was not half spent and her back already ached and her arms were beginning to shake with weariness. Didn't look as if she'd do that ever again, which made her wonder if it would be something better or worse awaiting her in the future.

"You plan to eat any porridge this morning?" Diarmaid's voice, calling to her.

"Oh yes," she said, pushing herself up from the ground. Thomas's shoes had been fine the day before that. Why did she feel as if they'd somehow gained lead soles overnight?

She scooped all the porridge out of the bowl and swallowed it, even if she had a moment or two of wondering if one or two of the mouthfuls were going to make the return trip from her stomach without stopping to stay. Not her stomach, too? There was no time for her to be sick, any more than there'd been time back when she'd been cutting peat. Even less time now, because Diarmaid was impatient to get moving, and they had to stay together.

She climbed back to her feet to take the bowl and spoon over to the nearby brook to wash them out.

"I'll do that," Diarmaid said. He watched her with extra keenness. It made her uneasy.

"I can do it."

"Didn't say you couldn't. Just said I'd do it for you."

She shrugged again, and handed over the bowl, the spoon lying in it. She wouldn't sit down now, no matter how much she wanted to. Should she, Diarmaid would never leave off fussing at her.

They set off very much the way they did every morning—maybe it took a wee bit longer, but not much—and as usual they didn't talk much. This morning she was grateful because it seemed to take all her energy just to walk. There was none of the early morning lift she was used to, the sense of satisfaction they were putting miles away before she began to feel as if the walk would last forever.

She plodded along. She didn't look in Diarmaid's direction mostly because it was easier keep her eyes looking straight ahead and keep her legs moving. That she knew how to do. She was used to it seeming harder and harder to keep tossing off each chunk of peat, and move straight to the next as the sun slid down the sky. Maybe she and Seán had been joking and laughing earlier in the day. As the afternoon wore on, they were both silent, plunging the spades in, lifting the peat out, over and over and over again.

Just to lift one foot and then the other was not much work, not when she thought back to that. She reminded herself about that over and over as she swung one tired foot down after the other, and then the first one up and down again. And this was just morning! Today's walk had hardly begun.

She tried not to look at Diarmaid. Didn't like seeing the worry in his eyes. Wasn't much used to that. In fact, before now, she couldn't think of anyone else, except maybe someone like Lizzie Doherty, who would worry about her. Good people, who included her in their world. But now there was Diarmaid and he was worrying about her. She could see that, even considering as how she was doing her best not to look at him.

He shouldn't look so worried.

She was going to keep going. She wasn't about to quit, if that was what was worrying at him. She'd just keep it to herself that her legs were more tired than they had reason to be. She'd been tired before and worked through it. She'd do it again.

She lifted her chin.

"Are you slowing down now?" she called to him.

Muirne had kept up with him all day, had to give her that, and it was only another two or three days to Galway. Was bustling around now with the pot on the fire he'd set. She'd pushed him away and told him she'd do their supper. Potatoes, of course, but they'd had some chicken the day before and there was some left over. Diarmaid'd carried it in his backpack wrapped in two sheets of newspaper the fishmonger had given him. The fishmonger said the chicken was fresh that morning and the weather still cool enough that a body needn't worry it wouldn't be good later that day or the next.

Smelled fine today, cooking with the potatoes.

Just then Diarmaid happened to glance in Muirne's direction and caught her unawares. She'd shut her eyes for a moment, it seemed, and he was jarred by how drawn and weary her face was. Then her eyes opened and she saw him lookin' at her, and she smiled the same warm smile she'd had all day.

For the first time it crossed his mind to wonder which one was a mask, like. The weariness she'd seemed to have early that morning, if he remembered right, or the smile she'd had the rest of the day? And if it was the smile she was hiding behind, how could it happen that from one day to the next she changed so suddenly? Was she sickening for something?

"How you be?" he called over to her.

"Fine!"

What else had he thought she might say? He continued to watch her, studying the way she moved. Took her a minute or two to see what he was doing, and then she turned, just a bit, so her back was in his direction.

Mebbe what he'd better do was make sure she was covered tonight—he could use his coat; sky didn't look like rain—and once she was asleep, check to make sure she wasn't warm with fever. What he would do if she was he would have to think about. They had most likely about 60, 70 miles to go, and the only town on the way—and that a small one—would be Claremorris. There should be a doctor there, but that'd be close to 20 miles away.

But p'rhaps she was not sick at all. Could be he'd just dreamed it all up in his head because she was dear to him now, and he was fussed when it seemed that anything could be wrong. Could be she was just tired. It was the end of a long journey, after all, and although he had walked all over the north and west of Ireland—and a reasonable amount of the east, as well—he'd done it at first in more gradual stages. For her, poor thing, it was the whole 300 miles or so for her first long journey. Now that he gave it some thought, he wondered if she'd had any idea how far Galway was, when he'd asked her if she wanted to come with him. Most likely not. He could as well have asked her to come with him to the far side of the moon.

Mebbe it was just all the days of walking that were addin' up for her now. Well, no more than two or three days and they'd be in Galway. He'd make sure she got a good rest then.

"You have any interest in supper?" Muirne's voice—irritated, like—broke into his thoughts.

He scrambled to his feet and went over to where she was holding a bowl of potatoes and chicken in her hand, stretched out toward him.

"'Course I am. Smells fine," he said.

"That's good. I'd already asked two times before." Her voice sounded bad-tempered.

"'Tis sorry I am," he answered promptly. "My thoughts had gone wandering a piece, I guess, and my ears with them. I did not hear a word."

"You should clean your ears, most likely." But she was smiling at him and came over to sit with him, her bowl and spoon in her hands.

The mush of potatoes and chicken was better than anything he'd had since—well, since the dinner in Donegal town.

"This is wonderful," he said, pausing just a moment in spooning the mixture into his mouth.

"A bit of kitchen makes all the difference." Muirne's speech was slightly muffled by the food in her own mouth.

Kitchen. Well, now, should he say something to her about how nobody would know what she meant if she said that here in the county of Galway, even less in the city? Well, not today, most likely, if she was sickening. Even if she was just more tired than she'd been before. But he'd have to figure out some way of explaining it to her before they were with his uncles and the rest, who were used to meals with more variety than what they had in the clachan, or for all he knew, the whole of the Inishowen peninsula. What they called "kitchen" in the clachan was just an ordinary part of a meal down here.

But then there was this: did he want her to change, when he gave it some thought? He looked over at her, neatly eating her dinner, staring into the distance. What could it be she was looking at? P'rhaps they would keep "kitchen" as a word to use between them. Only the two of them would know what they meant by it. Their children would sigh and roll their eyes…

His mind came to a sudden jerking halt. Children? What was he doing, giving a thought to future children? Had not the two of them decided, right away, there would be no children? Had he not been taking steps to make sure there would be no children of this journey, even travelling all this way with only the two of them?

He ran his hand through his hair, troubled by the waywardness of his thoughts.

"What's wrong?" It was Muirne's soft voice, the one that in his mind went with evenings and a fire and the warmth of being close to her.

He looked at her, startled. "Naught, really. Just sitting here, letting me thoughts run loose, and then surprised by the corner they turned."

"You don't choose to tell?"

Had the soft voice sharpened? He stretched with deliberate laziness.

"Can't let me thoughts think they're so important." He smiled, a lazy smile to match.

She stretched, too, but on her it wasn't lazy. Maybe he was just watching her too careful, like, but seemed to him the tightness about her today, the odd way she'd swung back and forth between being bright and eager and being worn near to the nub, all of it was trying to hide something. Wished he knew what 'twas.

She stretched again, and then suddenly seemed to go limp, somehow, and sunk down onto the grass. "I'm so tired," she whispered.

Took no more than a second or two and he was beside her, pulling her into the support of his arms. "I know." His voice was quiet. "Been tired all day, haven't you then?"

She got some way toward stiffening indignantly, but then melted back into his arms.

"I have," she admitted.

"Better now?"

"For now, I guess." Her head was heavy against his shoulder. She sighed a deep sigh, and curled a bit closer to him. "The chicken 'n 'tatoes was good."

"That it was." His head rested against the top of hers. "Just before you settled here, I was thinking I should clean out the pot. No reason to keep it as 'tis, is there?"

She made a comfortable humming sound. He liked it, even not havin' an idea what she meant by it. They sat as they were for a bit, and then she lifted her head. "Do y'think porridge would be good with what's left of the chicken 'n 'tatoes?"

"You mean cook the porridge in the pot as 'tis?"

She nodded sleepily.

Well, why not? All mixed together in the stomach, didn't it? Had to admit that at this point he'd be glad to have the taste of oats masked by almost anything. Why not chicken and potatoes?

"We'll do it," he whispered to her—seemed to him she was half asleep already. Holding onto her with his arm around her, he tried to reach with the other arm for where her shawl had fallen. Not very neatly he laid it out on the grass, and then rolled her out of his arm and onto the shawl, staying as close to her as he could so she'd not be awakened by the sudden cold.

In a perfect world, he'd get up and put some water in the pot, but as luck had it, he'd put the lid on it. 'Twas not on the fire, which was dying down and away in any case. S'posed there was no really good reason why he could not drift off to sleep beside her, keeping her warm in his arms. He'd deal with the pot in the morning.

That was his last clear thought.

The next morning could have been the day before's morning run through a second time, the only real change being that the chicken and potatoes from the night before had formed a fine crust on the bottom of the pot, and even with bringing the water he'd added that morning to the pot, with the oats, it was taking some scraping to get it off the bottom and mixed in.

Then, too, in the morning he was less convinced oats mixed with potatoes and chicken was the making of a fine breakfast.

Muirne was still fast asleep, curled up into a ball like a kitten, with her nose pressed into the shawl under her. As she'd been the day before. He cast the odd glance at her as he stirred the porridge over the fire. She'd never roused when he'd wakened or when he'd been picking up branches from the ground around them, breaking the big ones, and built the fire.

He kept an eye on her, seeing when she first opened her eyes and, disbelieving, closed them again. He watched as she rolled over onto her back, looking up at the sky, bright with morning light. After a bit—longer than she usually allowed herself in the morning—she rolled over and up to her feet, looking around with what looked like dissatisfaction. Stood there for a moment, and then sat down again to put Thomas's shoes on her feet.

When she came to see what he was doing, she looked at the pot with no great favor.

"Want your porridge?" Diarmaid asked her.

She wrinkled her nose, but took the bowl and spoon he offered her. Somewhat to his surprise she stood to take the first mouthful or two, then sat rather abruptly, frowning.

He'd dished out his own bowl, and tasted his first spoonful. All things considered he decided chicken and potatoes, however delicious on their own, did not really add much to oats. Made the taste even a bit nastier, was his private opinion. But food was food, and a body needed it. He continued to eat with determination.

When he'd finished, he looked over to see what she was doing. She was sitting with the bowl in her hands, but not much eaten from what he could tell.

"Not hungry?" he asked.

She shook her head, keeping her lips pressed together.

"Take a bite or two, love. It's not good to start a long walk when you're empty inside."

She gave him a quick look, but what she'd meant by it he could not tell. Her lips were still tight together. After a minute or two of watching her, and her not meeting his eyes, he turned back to the pot.

"This is going to take a bit of scrubbing," he said, and took the pot and his bowl over to the brook they'd stopped beside. It did indeed take some vigorous work with the spoon to loosen what stuck firmly to the bottom. He had just about finished when Muirne appeared silently at his side. She had her bowl and spoon in her hands, and he took them from her. Although the bowl was sure in fact empty, he would have waged money that not one more bite of porridge had gone down her throat.

For one moment he considered going over to hunt for where she'd dumped it to show her he knew, but then he thought what would be the good of it? She was not going to eat it. He knew that, and so did she.

Something was wrong. He had no idea what it would be, but Muirne was not herself. Well. They'd be passing through Claremorris, and it was a town. With luck, and with him saying a prayer along the way, there would be a doctor there. Whether Muirne chose to see the doctor or not, she was going to be taken there. He—he, Diarmaid himself, was going to get some answers from someone. Someone who knew enough to tell him if this was just exhaustion at the end of a long, long walk. Or something worse.

He was not a stupid man himself. She would put up one hell of a fight. If he had to present her bound and tethered, he would do so.

He grinned a little to himself. Should he perhaps make sure he had some rope first?

19

THEY WERE CLOSER TO CLAREMORRIS than Diarmaid had calculated. It was only a town compared to some of the villages they'd passed through, but there was a greengrocer, and by some benevolent chance Muirne stopped to look at what there was there besides potatoes and carrots. There were two running the shop, a husband and wife by the looks of it, and Diarmaid managed to get the man back into the shop— which looked as if it was also the room in which the family lived—and ask him about a doctor. Diarmaid kept an eye on Muirne out in front, and the man, bless the saints, grasped that he wanted the information without her knowing. Even more fortunately the doctor's house was just down the main road. The man described it, and said old Dr. Kerrigan was a wonder at knowing which herbs were best for almost any ailment. He grew a fine bunch of them in his own garden.

When as if just wandering around, Diarmaid came out to the front, Muirne told him cautiously that they sold fresh eggs as well.

"She even has some hard-cooked already." Muirne's eyes were wide with the convenience of it.

"D'ye think you could eat that?" He almost added something about her having not wanted her breakfast, but re-thought it, and let his question go as 'twas.

She nodded, watching his face anxiously. "Have you enough money for it?" she whispered.

"No worry about that," he told her grandly, asked the price, and paid for two of them.

Muirne cracked and peeled one of the eggs right there, the greengrocer watching her with a hint of a smile, and ate it as they walked along.

"What you need when we're in one place is a chicken."

She looked quickly at him, and then smiled when she saw his grin. "Wouldn't that be grand? Eggs whenever you fancied one."

He raised one eyebrow. "For that we might need a flock o' them. Don't chickens just lay one egg a day?"

She shrugged. "I've never had one. Don't know."

They'd passed four houses. The greengrocer said it was the fifth. It was a well-kept cottage with a pleasant garden in front, so Diarmaid took a firm grip on Muirne's elbow, and turned her up the front path where he knocked on the door.

She looked at him, puzzled.

"Man named Kerrigan lives here," Diarmaid told her.

Fortunately a woman came to the door before there was time for any talk about who Kerrigan might be. She was motherly and well-dressed.

"Yes?" the woman asked.

"We'd like to see Dr. Kerrigan, if that's possible," Diarmaid said, managing to place Muirne just in front of him and more or less rush her through the door.

"Doctor?" Muirne asked.

"Just to make sure there's naught seriously wrong with you."

"I don't need a doctor," she hissed, but he played as if he'd not heard a word.

"Is the doctor here?" he asked the woman politely.

"He is." Like the greengrocer, she seemed to grasp that he thought there was reason for Muirne to be seen, and led them through a small parlor to knock on a door at the back of the room.

Diarmaid took a quick look at Muirne, hoping they would not have to wait long. Luck was with them, and while Muirne was still drawing an indignant breath, the door opened.

The man there, quite obviously Dr. Kerrigan, was white-haired and sturdy. He looked at the two of them with a question in his eyes.

"This is Muirne Coyle, my—she's to be my wife. She's not been well for a day or two. She has reason to be tired as we've walked from Donegal, but it came on her so sudden-like." He hoped not all of his anxiety was in his face. "She's not eating much, either."

The doctor looked over at Muirne, inspecting her.

"I just ate an egg." She sounded defiant.

"But naught else," Diarmaid put in.

"The porridge was horrible."

Even anxious as he was, Diarmaid found his mouth quirking. "Not the best, p'rhaps. Mebbe it's too much to put chicken and potatoes into it."

"Sounds terrible," the doctor said, opening his door wider. "Come in with me, Muirne Coyle, and we'll see what we can do." He looked over at Diarmaid with what might have been an invitation to join them, but Diarmaid shook his head.

He had managed to get her there. Now it was up to the doctor to see what the trouble might be. The woman—the doctor's wife, he thought likely—turned her attention to him.

"Would you like to take a seat?" she asked, directing him to what looked like a most comfortable chair.

"Yes, thank you," he said, and sat down.

Now all he had to do was wait.

Muirne eyed the doctor suspiciously. What had gotten into Diarmaid to take her here? So she'd been tired. So she'd not eaten breakfast, but the porridge had been a better idea than it tasted.

"Tired, are you then?" The doctor pointed at a chair and, warily, she sat down on it. He pulled up another chair to sit opposite her.

She considered saying nothing, but there was something commanding about him. He just waited.

"Yes," she admitted.

"For how long has this been happening?"

She shrugged, and when the doctor's eyebrows went up, said unwillingly, "Just a day or two. Came on me sudden like."

He nodded. "Anything else?"

She hesitated. "Well, felt a bit sick to me stomach this morning. The porridge wasn't good, but Diarmaid ate his. I was afraid it'd come right back up if I swallowed it."

"How long since you left Donegal?"

She put her head back, thinking about it. "I'm not sure. We've just been walking. Mebbe a week, two weeks? Seems like forever."

"And sleeping out?"

"Mostly. We had one night in an inn. Donegal town, that was."

Dr. Kerrigan nodded thoughtfully. "And when were your last courses?"

"Courses?" She looked at him curiously. "What's that?"

He cocked his head to one side. "Monthly flow."

"Oh." She could feel her own hot flush, and right after it a cold chill because she suddenly realized what he was asking about. No. Couldn't be.

"When would that have been?" he asked gently again.

Muirne closed her eyes. Couldn't be. Not now. But when had her last time been? So much had happened in her life that even trying to remember was a blur. Before Diarmaid ever walked into the clachan? No. Must have been after that, but however it was, a long time ago. And when—when was the first time she and Diarmaid had…oh yes. And certainly she'd had no flow since then.

"Can't be," she said, but she could hear in her own voice that she knew it could be. That it probably was. Her hands moved almost automatically to her belly. It was flat, as it had always been.

Dr. Kerrigan smiled at her. "No, it's still too early to show."

"When does it?"

He looked at her appraisingly. "You are thin and strong. Probably not for several months. Say four or even five? But that's just a guess."

"Oh." So she had some time before anyone had to know. Did that include Diarmaid? How much would he know about women and their patterns? Would he notice if she had none? Might, might not. She couldn't guess.

"Is he—the young man, your betrothed?" For the first time the doctor sounded uncertain. "Is he the father?"

Muirne nodded. The doctor smiled with obvious relief.

"So," he said. "Is there anything else?"

She paused to think. "How long?"

His forehead furrowed. "How long what? Until the babe's birth? Seven, eight months I would think. That's a guess. Can you remember how long it's been or when conception might be most likely?"

She shook her head impatiently. "No. I mean how long am I tired like this? And have a mislike for food?"

"Oh." The doctor's face cleared. "Usually it's at an end after the third month."

She nodded again. Not that she'd kept tight track of a calendar when she'd been back in the clachan, but they'd been walking in a timeless space with no attention to the day or the week. How long had it been? She dinna remember. As long as a month? More likely, longer.

Dr. Kerrigan rose to his feet. "Anything else?"

She shook her head, words not coming easy to her. Now she had to plan what to say to Diarmaid.

The doctor ushered her out of his office, and Diarmaid swiftly stood up from where he must have been sitting.

"Congratulations!" Dr. Kerrigan said. "You're to be a father."

Diarmaid's face went blank.

Behind the doctor, Muirne's hands were rising to her face when she forced them to clasp each other at her waist. No, this was in no way how she'd thought to tell Diarmaid. She lifted her chin. What now?

Diarmaid stood, paralyzed like, for a minute or so until he shook himself loose.

"Thank you," he said. "And what do we owe you?"

The doctor seemed to draw into himself a bit. P'rhaps he'd expected they'd have some pleasant chat about it. But Muirne felt as Diarmaid seemed to. All she wanted was to leave this fine cottage with its cozy furnishings and get to where the two of them could puzzle out together what was to be done now.

She stared off into the distance while Diarmaid and the doctor concluded their business, and then, with a nod of farewell and a faint smile, she stepped out of the door and back to the road leading through the town to Galway.

They walked some way in silence.

"Well," Diarmaid said at last.

"That's a great help," she snapped.

He shrugged, with a smile as faint as hers had been. "It's a start."

She kept her eyes on the road.

He reached for her hand, and she let him take it, but it lay like a dead fish in his. "How are you?"

"Pregnant," she said. She tried to pull her hand back, but his fingers tightened around hers, and in what seemed to be unwilling response, her hand closed around his.

He shook his head. "That's not what I meant, as you well know. How are you—still sick to your stomach?"

She shook her head, not looking at him.

"Still tired?"

She nodded. "'E says I will be for another two months, like."

"Good thing Galway's close now."

For a few paces she said nothing, then she nodded again. "'Tis."

They walked along for quite a time in silence, a bit more slowly than usual because they remained hand-in-hand.

"Diarmaid?"

He looked over at her. It was unusual for her to call him by name.

"What?"

"How are we to go on now? I mean, how will it be? Will you be off on your own and me stuck here—or anywhere else—with the bairn?"

He stared down the road ahead of them, not knowing quite what to say. How would it be possible for them to have a free life, the two of them, if there was always a bairn there, needing them, reaching for their attention.

"I don't know, love. But there must be a way. We work together."

"What? A babe with you as we go around the countryside? We'd have to stay at inns. Can't put a babe to sleep on the grass."

He didn't want her to fuss about it. There had to be a way. He'd just not thought of it yet.

"No need to worry about it now."

She stopped dead. "There's every reason to worry about it now. Now's when we can do something, if we choose."

He'd stopped dead to stare at her. Surely she was not...she could not...

"There was a woman in Inishowen—mebbe even two. If there's someone in far Donegal there must be someone in Galway. Or round about."

"No!" The word came out in a shout.

Muirne backed up a step or two from him. Her lips began to tremble. "How am I to do without you? 'Tis our people, not just yours, struggling to find a way to live under the English heel. I thought we were to be in it together!"

"I'll not kill that little piece of you and me growing in your belly. We'll find a way that's not a sin. Are you crazy, woman?"

"I'd not thought you cared about sins!" she wailed.

"'Tis not that the priests say 'tis a sin, Muirne. It's because I know it's wrong down to the core o' me. So do you. There's you and me mixed together in that bit of a babe. We're what's started that new person. So we had a plan. Well, we need another plan now. Just not one that kills what we made." He leaned toward her, standing there in the road, almost in her face. "You'd not survive that, a ghrá. It's a fine idea, you may think now, but when it was gone from your body, when you knew you'd had it ripped out of you, it would eat into your soul. You know 'twould."

She looked at him warily.

"P'rhaps so," she said, the words coming unwillingly. "I just—I just wanted to put things back the way they were. Before." She turned toward him blindly.

He slung his arm around her shoulder and drew her close to him as they walked on together. "Not often that's possible, a stór, me treasure. Once you've jumped across the fire, there's no jumping back. But I'm on the far side of this fire with you, me love. Can't say I know yet how we'll sort it out, but we'll get it straight one way or another."

She nodded, her head rubbing up and down his chest.

His voice was a rumble in her ears. "Now next thing is to get us married. Now. Before Galway."

Muirne mumbled her agreement. Today, then? she wondered.

No. More likely tomorrow. Their feet went on walking, carrying them forward.

20

"Tuam, I think," Diarmaid said.

"Tuam? What's that?"

Muirne blinked at him across the porridge pot on the fire. Maybe it was because it kept happening every morning now, but although she was still tired and groggy, she didn't mind it so much.

Seemed strange to think of it like that, but now when she opened her eyes she was prepared for feeling as if all she wanted in the world was to roll back into sleep. She knew she would have to get up regardless, and that the porridge would not sit easy in her stomach, but if she ate slowly, it would stay there. If she didn't eat, she'd have to deal with Diarmaid fussing at her, talking on and on about the babe, and how did she expect to grow a healthy one if she wouldn't eat?

So she ate, slowly, dipping her spoon in her bowl, resting it on the edge until she was certain sure that the last mouthful was swallowed and safe in her stomach. Only then would she open her mouth for another. Slower than a man walkin' through tar, Diarmaid said it was, but given time, the contents of the bowl would disappear.

An' wasn't that what he wanted, she'd growl at him.

But then the cursed man would smile at her and like magic, most times, she'd cease her grumbling and just wallow like a pig in mud, glorying that there was someone, right across the fire from her, who cared about what she did. He didn't talk a whole lot about loving her, but at times like that she felt it like a warm coat over her back.

She'd never had that before. Not once that she could remember.

"You have the intention of finishing that?" Diarmaid was looking at her, across the fire. It was dwindling now—he'd stopped working to keep it alight some time ago, and was letting it die down so he could pour some water over to snuff the last of it out.

She tipped the bowl toward him so he could see.

"'S gone," she said.

"There's a good girl." He jumped up to his feet. "Give it me, and I'll wash it out with the pot."

"Yours washed already?" She got to her feet as well, without the jumping nonsense. Course she could've jumped, if she'd felt like it, but she didn't. Just as well, too. No telling what would happen to that porridge she'd coaxed down into her stomach if she started leapin' about like a frog. Prob'ly come right back up. Diarmaid being the kind he was would most likely look at her and sigh a little, and then stir the fire back into life and cook some more porridge to try again.

She walked over to where he was crouching, over a little patch of water, more like a puddle than a lough, but the water seemed fresh enough. A spring, mebbe?

"What's Tuam?" she asked. "You were saying something about Tuam."

He nodded. "Right. Think that's where we might get married today. 'S not far from here, so a short day's walking would get us there, and then we can see what it's like. It's the biggest town around, I've been told. Has a market square with a cross in it, so I figure there must be a priest around somewhere. Shouldn't take us too long to find him."

"Married," she murmured.

He looked up over his shoulder at her. "Married. 'Tis what I wanted in any case, but we have to make certain that babe you're carrying about has a name when 'tis born." He grinned. "There's reason to say that now, but we'd not have been in Galway long before I'd've taken you to the priest there in any case. I know where to find that one without askin'. There was no escapin' me, Muirne Coyle."

She stood square on her feet, laughing down at him. "An' you think I've been trying?"

He came to his feet and handed her the porridge pot. "Quit your teasing, woman, when ye know I can do naught about it. Go put that pot in your bag, so we'll be able to get started."

It was all part of the routine they'd been following ever since they left Inishowen. But the time was surely coming—not far distant, now—when mornings would start different, like. When there would not be this preparation for a long walk ahead.

"How far from Tuam to Galway?" It was not a question she had asked before.

He squinted, thinking. "I think just a day. Not a real long day, either."

She nodded. So p'rhaps one more morning like this? 'Twas hard to imagine this journey coming to an end.

Pouring the water on the fire, he looked over at her.

"Seems to me that standing holding the pot in me hands doesn't get it put away," he remarked, as if he were talking to the fire.

Muirne made a face. "Your mouth's flapping again," she said and went to fit the pot in her pack.

The weather was fair enough. Not quite overcast, but enough clouds about so that they couldn't see the sun all the time, even though as the days passed, spring came more and more into its own. All the trees seemed to be pushing out pale green leaves on their branches. And the chill in the air from the morning didn't bite as it had before, but melted into the day with the sun, even if there only were glimpses of it.

The road still rolled on endlessly before them. As it had been almost all the way, they were not entirely alone. Might be patches when there was nothing within sight ahead or behind, but most of the time there were a few people walking. Then, since this was farming country, there were the carts and men on horseback, and from time to time, men leading animals from one field to another.

The sheep generally looked right stupid, trying all to stand in the same place and bumping up against the others. Not that the cows looked a whole lot brighter, but they didn't usually come across a whole herd on the move. It would be a man or a woman, sometimes even a child, keeping track of one or two cows. Lots of the children'd be barefoot, which made Muirne remember the children of the clachan, not a shoe among the bunch of them.

Odd 'twas to think that clachan children'd grow up, and she'd never see them again, most likely.

She shuddered, as if someone had walked across her grave.

"What's that about?"

Diarmaid of course had to ask. He kept a much closer eye on her than she did on him, she was sure of that. What he thought about when they were walking she couldn't imagine.

'Course she could always ask.

"What do you think about when you're walking?"

He looked at her curiously. "Dunno. Why do you ask?"

"Doesn't anything go through your head?"

He chuckled. "Sometimes I s'pose not. Sometimes I think about the clachan in Inishowen and wonder how it might have been different if I'd done some things differently. Seems to me if something doesn't work as you hoped 'twould, you can at least get some good out of it if you learn something. So some of the time I'm trying to figure out what I didn't do that I should've, or what I did that would have been better not done."

She was surprised how cross she was that he should feel he'd failed there. "It wasn't up to you. Had you been able to stay I'm sure as I can be that you would have found the way to get the handful of them—you know, Seán, Liam, Seamus and Patrick. There was another: Donncha, was it? Even poor old Charlie. When you're planning for trouble, it's not a bad idea, I'd think, to keep someone around who's good at thumping. It's just needful to keep an eye on who he's thumping, that's all."

He smiled at her. "But I didn't get it done."

Her irritation flared. "You didn't get a chance, boyo! 'Twas wise enough to get out of the way when there's a stranger prowling around asking after you. Now, I think what you did makes great good sense. You didn't make a fuss to draw attention, you just drifted out of sight, quiet like. If he wasn't there to make trouble, he'd probably think he'd just missed you and try again another day—or, if he was the kind that's sensible, leave a message with someone as to where he is and who he is so ye could go find him if ye choose to. How's he to know anyone warned you? They'll ne'er tell him, I can promise you that. All he has any proof of is that he's unlucky to have missed you."

His lips were twitching. "Clear enough 'tis that I should've set you on him."

She glared at him. Foolish man. 'Twas too hard to keep up with him. First of all he's saying—if she had the right of it—that he was trying to figure out what mistake he'd made that there was not in the clachan the hidden group of men ready to stand up and be recognized when the need came. Then he's acting as if the mysterious man who'd asked pointless questions of him on the road to Derry might not really be a threat when he was driftin' around the clachan asking questions. Well, if he wasn't, then what was the harm in leavin'? An' if he was, then 'twasn't it better that Diarmaid left no organization behind him? The men, the good men, would still be there when Diarmaid had need of them. And in the meantime they were all safe. Wasn't that what was important? So why was he tryin' to find some mistake?

Men. They were a different breed, they were. She'd never understand them.

They walked on together caught up in their separate thoughts, both of them to be jolted back into the present when they saw Tuam ahead of them.

Diarmaid glanced over at Muirne, her head slightly bowed and heaven alone knowing what her thoughts might be.

"Here we be," he said.

"Not quite yet," she answered, a Muirne answer if he'd ever heard one. And she had the right of it, of course. There would still be a bit to walk before they came into the town. Proper town it was, too. Been there a long time. Over a thousand years old, he'd been told. At one time there'd been a castle there, but there were only shreds of it left. Would Muirne be interested enough to hunt about a bit to find them?

'Twould be a toss-up. Most likely would depend on how long it took them to find the small Catholic church he knew was there. There was a proper Cathedral that had been given to the Protestants when the English took over. When the English were routed, it would be fine to roust out the Protestants as they'd forced the good Catholics to leave. He'd like to see that day himself.

But for now must needs find the church he knew would exist. Easy enough to do: the fastest way was to stop some ordinary looking Irishman and ask him.

So he did so.

Muirne stood quiet at his side as he was given the directions, and when he reached for her hand, let it slip into his. Then they were on their way, on this errand he'd wanted to take since the moment he'd realized that whatever else happened in his life, she belonged there as well.

'Twas just as well he'd asked, because when they got there, without knowing which was which, he'd have had a hard time telling which was the church and which was the ordinary shop next door. The damned English decided to make it as hard for the Irish to find the place as they could, he s'posed. Wanted to make sure it was as plain and uninteresting as possible. They'd succeeded well enough, but from the worn threshold he stepped over, a lot of other feet had walked here and found what they were looking for. Gave him a certain sour satisfaction.

When the two of them walked in, the door eased closed behind them. It was a chapel, nothing more, but clearly loved and used well. The benches were polished to a shine, and there was a proper church smell inside. What the smell was, he'd never given much thought to, except to know that it was right. Smelled holy, that's what it was. Even when he was not always purely faithful about coming to Mass—and a lot of the time he wouldn't have known where to go—stepping inside the chapel, any chapel, comforted his heart somehow. This came down to him from generations of Irishmen who clung onto it no matter what the English tried to force them to believe. They'd burned them, they'd torn them to pieces, they'd hung them by their necks all as examples of what their Protestant power could do, but they'd never persuaded them. Catholic he was born and Catholic he would die, and now, in the quiet and scent of this chapel, his faith wrapped around him like a great cloak he might not always choose to wear, but always knew he possessed.

"Hullo, then." 'Twas a priest who came out of a door at the side. Must've heard the door open and close and come to see who was there.

"Father," Muirne murmured, in no more than a whisper. She crossed herself.

The priest smiled at her. "I am Father Maginn. What can I do for you, me children?" He was like so many priests that Diarmaid had known over his lifetime. Few there were that ever looked really young, at least that he remembered. Old, yes, he'd seen that. But most of them were like this priest here, men of an age that 'twould be hard to guess, somewhere between youth and old age. Eyes wise and mouth firm. He'd known hard priests, who could frighten a child, and gentle ones, who drew people to him with love. Father Maginn looked like one of the gentle ones.

"We need to be wed," Diarmaid said, his voice steady.

"Where are your families?"

Muirne lifted her chin in the way she had. "I have none," she said. "I come from Inishowen, in Donegal."

Diarmaid looked at her, keeping his face blank. Well, that was as close to truth as need be, he guessed. She'd never had much reason to cling to her father, and from everything she'd said after he struck her, she considered such connection as they'd had broken.

"Far from here," he answered the priest himself. "Me father's dead. Me mother works in County Meath, near to Drogheda."

Father Maginn nodded. "Does she know you are to wed?"

Diarmaid shook his head slowly. "We have friends to see and business in Galway. When that's done I plan to take me wife to Meath to introduce them."

The priest nodded again, as if he were striking items off on a list. "When was your last confession?"

Muirne spoke first. "Not since Inishowen. We've been traveling. Even when I was living there, I only spoke to one of the friars when I could. We've no chapel, just the Protestant churches there. When a traveling friar comes to say Mass we find the Mass stone in the hills to hide us. 'Twas there I made my last confession, but I don't know the date of it."

Father Maginn's eyes were warm with compassion. "'Tis not always easy to hold to the True Faith, my child, but I see you cling on best you can."

She murmured something Diarmaid could not hear, and the priest turned to him.

"And you?"

"I've been traveling," he said, and willed his eyes to tell the priest not to ask questions but to accept that he could not talk about what he'd been doing. "Could we take care of that here?"

"Of course." He led them over to the confessional, and disappeared behind it. Muirne looked up at Diarmaid questioningly, and he nodded.

"You go first," he said.

She slid the wooden panel open and then shut again. From outside he could hear only the soft sound of her voice, but none of her words. He moved away so he'd not be tempted to try to listen: this was no business of his.

'Twas not long before the panel slid open again with a squeak, and she stepped out, her lashes wet and dabbing a piece of cloth at her eyes. She did not look directly at him as she passed to move out of his way, but he could see her lips were pressed together.

He jerked his chin up and went through, closing the panel behind him. Perhaps it was as well to clear things with his God before he took the momentous step of marriage.

MUIRNE'D NEVER GIVEN MUCH TIME to imagining what it would be like to stand in a church to be married, mainly because it seemed so improbable that such a thing 'twould ever happen to such as her. Even if she had, she was fair sure she'd not have thought her mind'd be buzzing so from her confession that she wasn't really sure she'd heard it all. Oh, there were promises, but she'd known 'bout them before. When she sat and thought about it later, she wasn't altogether sure she'd been listening right then, when the two o' them stood in front of the priest.

Then there'd been the real surprise. Diarmaid had a ring.

Oh, if she'd thought about it, she would know wives wore one, even in the clachan. Plain gold circles, most of them. Whether they were real gold or just something that looked gold Muirne didn't know and had never cared enough to ask. But when the priest mentioned the ring, to Muirne's dazzled surprise, Diarmaid pulled out a golden ring that was not plain. He slipped it down her finger on her left hand, making sure the little point on it pointed down.

From that moment until Father Maginn told them they were man and wife, she fought with the temptation to look at the ring on her finger instead of paying even as much attention as she'd been giving to the priest before.

A ring? Where had he ever found such a thing? How did he happen to have it with him now, when it was needed? And 'twasn't a plain ring, but without looking at it closely, she couldn't see what the pattern was.

Only when the priest led them off into a little side room at the end could she see what she was wearing now on her hand. Diarmaid was giving information for the forms as Father Maginn filled them out on a desk. While the two of them were absorbed, she ran her thumb over her ring. 'Twasn't a new ring, that she could tell, because the pattern was almost smooth, worn down with time. It had two hands on it, reaching to clasp each other, and a heart in the middle, with a crown on top.

But then Father Maginn had finished the forms, and Diarmaid was pressing some coins in his hand, and it was time for them to thank him by the door of the chapel before they left.

"I wish you Godspeed," the priest said, as he opened the door for them.

"We thank you," Diarmaid answered, and they walked out. It was done. As easily as that it was done and they were married. A strange feeling, that was.

"Where did you get the ring from?" she asked as soon as the two of them had walked out onto the street.

He smiled. "'Tis me mam's."

"How did you come to have it?"

He took her arm, and they walked off together, him holding her close to him. This is my husband, she thought with sudden pleasure, and then she remembered it was just as well she was a married woman now. She already had a babe in her belly.

"The ring?" he asked.

She nodded. Better to think about the ring, she thought. Thinking about the babe still frightened her a bit.

"Me mam sewed it into me coat when I left for Galway. She said it was like a charm to watch over me when I would be far away from her."

"Did she wear it, before?"

"I think when I was young. I don't remember. But I do know me da gave it to her, and after he was murdered by the English she had to find work, so came into the kitchen at Kendall House as a cook. She couldn't wear a ring on her hand when cooking, so she made a little pocket on her aprons for keeping it. When I left, she sewed it into a pocket of my coat— told me 'twas the only way she had of keeping me safe. She even sewed it all round so I had to unpick the stitching to get it out." He picked up her hand with his and inspected the ring with her. "See the hands? That's for the friendship, you and me. Your hand in mine, that's the way it's going to stay. The heart is for love, and the crown loyalty—which to us, like it did for me da and mam, means we will stay faithful to Ireland as she once was and work for her freedom." He put his hand over the ring and looked into her face. "That's the promise I make to you."

Her feet had slowed until she was standing still, looking at her hand.

She looked up at him. "I feel twice married," she said. "Once there at the church, and once now."

He grinned at her. "Must needs I find more ways to get you even more married."

She shoved at his arm, and they looked hungrily at each other.

"Now you've another choice to make," he said.

Her eyebrows went up, just a bit.

"Tonight should be our last night on the road. Tomorrow we'll be in Galway, and then we'll have a proper bed—at the house of one of my uncles, most likely. Now would you like to have our last night at an inn—I have enough money left for that—or would you want to sleep out, as we've slept all t'other nights?"

She looked up at the sky. There were clouds, but they didn't look like the rain-bearing kind. She felt again the wash of remembering she'd had before, of knowing this travelling time with Diarmaid was coming to an end. They'd still be together—she had his ring on her finger to promise that—but it would be different.

"Let's have one more night like the others," she said so softly that he had to bend down to hear her.

He grinned. "Right, then," he said. "We'll find a shop to buy some special kitchen for dinner. What do you fancy?"

"Not chicken," she said. The chicken and potatoes had been fine for supper, but she could still remember the taste of the chicken-flavored porridge the next morning. No, 'twould be wiser not to have chicken again. P'rhaps some other time when her stomach was more settled. "Fish. A piece of fish."

His grin told her he remembered the porridge as well. "Fish it will be."

Close to the town square was the market, known as the Shambles, and it was there that they found two or three fishmongers. Muirne hung back, staying half hidden behind Diarmaid. She'd never bought any fish in her life. The only fish she'd ever had were what she'd found washed up on the beach, and although they'd not all been the same, she'd not known the names of any of them.

"Which should we have?" he asked, turning back to her.

She peered around him, looking to see if any of them looked familiar to her. One of them seemed more like than the others, so she pointed at it, very aware of the ring on her finger as she lifted her hand.

To the fishmonger, of course, she was no different from any of the other women in the market. He did not even glance at her as Diarmaid asked for the one she'd pointed at. He asked if they wanted it topped and tailed, and Diarmaid nodded, so he chopped those bits off and wrapped the part they wanted in some paper he kept at hand, and handed it to her. Diarmaid found the coins he wanted and gave them to him. He nodded, and his attention moved at once on to the woman standing next, who seemed to be right sure of what she wanted.

Muirne looked at her with a kind of envy as she tucked the wrapped fish in her bag. So many things she would have to learn! 'Twas easy to see that living in the south was a different business from what she'd known in Donegal. She sneaked a quick look at Diarmaid, who looked at his ease in this market, so wholly unlike anything she'd ever known. Would there have been a market like this in Derry? It would be the only place anywhere near the clachan where she might have gone one day.

But she had never done so. Would the day come when she and Diarmaid ever went north again to Donegal? If they did, she'd like to see Derry. She'd imagined what it might be like when she grew old enough to hear tales from others at the clachan. Derry had tall church spires, she'd been told. And a wall round it. Indeed, and there was a spire here at Tuam, although she'd only seen it in the distance.

"Have you ever been to Derry?" she asked as they walked away from the fishmonger.

She looked around, seeking the road they'd followed into the town and would now, she supposed, follow out of Tuam and on to Galway City.

"Just the once," Diarmaid told her. "I brought back an egg for you, didn't I?"

She smiled, remembering the taste of it and the soft wheat bread he'd had as well.

"Was that what turned your heart to me first?" he asked quietly.

She could feel the hot flush on her face, and turned away a bit to hide it. "I don't remember," she said in as soft a voice as he'd used. "It grew when my attention was not on it. One day you were a stranger, a southerner, and then you were more than that."

"I remember you from the first time I saw you." Here they were, walking through a whole mess of people, and he was sayin' things that warmed her face and her heart. In a market in some town she'd never heard of? One part of her wisht he'd stop, and another waited breathlessly for what he might say next. "Your hair was as red as mine and you had the dirtiest face I'd ever seen on a pretty girl."

"You!" She gave him a shove with her shoulder, hiding her face since she could feel it turning what was likely even brighter red. "It's cleaner now, inn't it? I wash't it this morning."

"It's fine." He laughed, and turned to a table they were passing, right at the edge of the market. "I'll have three of those," he said to the stall keeper, who nodded and took out three eggs from the great bowl of eggs, brown and white, in front of him.

Muirne could feel her eyes growing large. "Three?"

"There's three of us now," he said, counting out pennies into the stall keeper's palm. "One for me, one for you, and one for the babe. Lucky, 'tisn't it, that you get to taste two o' them?"

The stall keeper looked at her and grinned. "And the best o' good fortune to you," he said.

Just when her face had cooled down a bit, she could feel the blush climbing again. What 'twas he doing, telling strangers about the babe? As they walked away, she looked at him accusingly, hoping he'd know what she meant by it.

He did. "And why not?" he asked cheerfully. "You've got the ring on your finger now. We can tell anyone we like."

"An' we can keep it to ourselves as well," she said. "No need to make a fuss of it."

"If I could write, I'd make a sign. It'd say, this is me wife, and she's carryin' me child."

Was he going to be like this when they reached Galway and there were people he knew about? She'd never dreamed that Diarmaid, so silent sometimes, would be like a child with a new ball t'play with. Here they were in a public place and he was happy telling people he'd never see again.

Well, better that than have him ashamed of her. But she'd rather have it a bit more down the middle than off either side.

He'd been fitting the eggs into his backpack where they could stay safe and whole until breakfast the next day. Once that was done, he looked down at her.

"Can't help being happy, me love."

She glanced up, meeting his eyes, and then looked away. "Then just wait 'till we're out on the road again, and we can be as happy as you like. I just don't like knowin' folks are lookin' at me, even if they're smiling."

He took her hand, laughing. "Ever think they're looking at you because you're a pretty girl with red hair and blue eyes that stop men where they stand?"

"Oh, Diarmaid!"

He laughed even louder, swinging her hand with his. "We'll turn at this road here and soon enough we'll be back out on the road again. But this will be the next to last day. Tomorrow we'll have our eggs over a fire, and tomorrow night we'll sleep in a real bed. That'll be good, won't it?"

She nodded, and made the turn with him. Yes, sleeping in a real bed had its attractions—she remembered the night they'd had together in the inn in Donegal Town. But she must be silly clear through, because she'd still miss the smell of grass first thing in the morning, and the feeling she'd always had when she first woke to the sky and the fresh air knowing every day was not just a lot of walking but a new adventure.

'Course tomorrow might be the greatest adventure so far. When they reached Galway, and met his uncles, it'd be the start of her new life as the wife of Diarmaid MacGuinness. The Coyle name with all the unhappiness she'd known being a Coyle now belonged back in Donegal. In far Inishowen.

And there, as far as she was concerned, it could well stay.

THE QUESTION, OF COURSE, WAS how close they wanted to get to Galway city before they stopped. For this last night when they would be just two of them—their wedding night as well, as it happened—Diarmaid told himself he had to find the best spot. They needed to have water handy, of course, but the River Clare squiggled itself through the countryside. What they needed was a patch of grass, and enough small trees and bushes about so there would be sticks for their fire. A stone or two to hold up the pot wouldn't come amiss. Far enough away from the road so that they could be quiet, like, and on their own. Close enough so that they'd not have to walk a fair distance to get back to it in the morning. Bushes not only for sticks, but for privacy.

Given the distance between Tuam and Galway city, it shouldn't be hard to find such a place.

Found it hard, he did, not to keep his eyes fixed on his wife. That ceremony had been plain and short but a great difference it had made in his thoughts about who he was and what he was to do with his life. Ah, Ireland would always be his greatest love, and as his father had died in the attempt to wrest her freedom out of the grasp of the filthy English, so would that be the governing thrust of his own life. Always had been, and he'd been right careless—and knowingly so—about whether he might give up his own life in the struggle. Hadn't mattered much, had it? If flinging himself off some high rock would have made the King of England and all his putty-faced men repent for what they'd done to Ireland and step backwards, 'twould be richly worth while.

Only now things were different. Events might still turn so that he would offer up his life for Ireland, only now—dear God, now—he was so much more aware of the cost. There was his wife, pretty Muirne, with the red hair flying and the devil in her eyes, and even more important now, there was the child in her belly. How could he bear to give it all over to some stupid careless foray against odds he knew to begin with were going to sweep him away in the end?

What if that child in her belly was a son? How could he leave him until they'd had enough time together for him to teach his son what he had to know? He had to build in him that love for the very earth of Ireland, so as he could pick it up and with the feel of it in his hands and the smell of it in his nostrils know that it was his land, and he would love it and fight for it to the day he would die?

Could he leave Muirne to teach the boy all that, or must he stay with them to do the teaching himself, as his da had done until the merciless English swept down on him and killed him as if he'd been some roach climbing on their table?

More than ever he needed to talk with his uncles. Two of them there were, Patrick MacGuinness, who was his own da's brother, and Con Flanaghan, who'd been closest to his da's heart although he'd been a cousin, and the two of them the same age within a week. He s'posed that if you were to be strict about it Con was his cousin as well, but he'd called him uncle from the time he was a wee boy, and his uncle he would always be. The same passion that burned in his chest had always burned in theirs. Glad he was that he'd turned his back on the hapless fools in Meath and come to Galway, where there was not only Patrick and Con but cousins of his mam, who were there to aid and help him as well.

No, he'd not come here until he was a man, but Galway city would always be where he was most at home. This was now where he had to work out what he might have done different in Inishowen, what could perhaps be done by someone else, or even by him if he went back again. Had to figure out what lessons he should be learning.

But even more than the wisdom of dealing with men and causes, he needed to talk to them about his very own heart: how was he to fit Muirne and the wee one into the life mission he'd chosen? That was what he most hungered to talk about with his uncles, the older, wiser ones, who'd dealt with life a lot longer than he had.

"What's wrong with that spot there?"

Her brisk, matter-of-fact voice brought him back from the wanderings his mind had been doing.

He looked at it as if he had not seen it before, which was more or less the case given that his mind had been ranging from Inishowen to Galway and probably Meath and back.

When he looked at it, it struck him that if he'd had a checklist of what they needed, everything he'd checked seemed to be here.

There was a brook gurgling, and it seemed to be close enough to be useful and not so close that the ground would be marshy. There were some bushes and a young tree that looked as if it'd had some winter damage, with broken off sticks and twigs lying on the ground. There seemed to be enough stones lying around to make a fire circle, and the grass looked flat and smooth enough although there were taller grasses by the bushes.

"Well? Cat got your tongue?"

That was his girl, all right. Living with her promised to be an adventure.

He slid his backpack off his shoulders. "Looks just about perfect. Did you find it this way or run ahead of me when I was pondering issues of life and death and arrange it all for us to stumble across?"

Her smile spread across her face. "You're an idiot, then." It didn't go with her words, and he could hear the affection in her voice.

He crossed his eyes and flapped his hands by his ears. "And you married me today, you did."

Her giggle bubbled out of her. "I did that, and see what I bought into?" She shook her head at him, and, turning businesslike, picked up a stone.

"Shall I build the ring of stones while you find the branches or d'you want it t'other way around?"

"Stones are heavy." He took the one stone from her and walked over a step or two to pick up another.

"Sticks are scratchy." Her head was bobbing around between bushes and the ground under low branches of the tree. With her usual efficiency she was already collecting a respectable bundle.

Keeping an eye on her progress, he fussed around with the stones, having to collect more than he started with, as always. It seemed every time he made the fire circle he underestimated the number he would need. Of course in Inishowen where stones were everywhere, you could collect as many as you needed or more without havin' to move your feet.

Here in Galway it took a bit more effort.

But once the fire was underway, the end of the day took the same pattern it had taken day after day since the walk started. O' course it was lighter than they were used to. Not only were they a piece farther south, but the spring was more advanced as well. Thinking of that, Diarmaid found himself watching Muirne as she sat by the fire, feeding sticks into it from time to time.

"When will the babe be born?" he asked.

She glanced over at him. "Nine months, they say."

"An' how much already?"

A smile flitted across her face. "You should be able to guess as well as me. You was there too."

He grinned back. "I'd like it t'have been in the inn at Donegal town."

Her smile turned shy. "So what's it been since then? A month? Six weeks?"

If he'd been in one place—Galway, say—he'd've been keeping track. But in the clachan and then on the walk days just flowed into each other, and he didn't remember them separate, like, or what the weeks were they'd added up into. Still, now he wanted to know.

"So say six weeks," he said.

"A month."

He looked over at her and grinned. "Fine. A month. So eight more."

'Twas nearly April then. They counted it out on their fingers.

"December," Muirne said. "Pity, that. Cold and all the flowers and bright leaves gone."

The grass was dry enough so that Diarmaid stretched out on it, waiting for her to tell him the fire was ready for the pot to be set upon it. December, then. There'd be no lying out on sun-warmed grass in December. The thought occurred to him that he had no idea where they might be by the time December came around. Galway? Meath? Even Donegal again? It was not a thought he chose to share.

Donegal would be cold in December. Colder even than it had been in March? 'Twould be best if he never had to find that out. No, better to think of places like Meath, or even down farther south towards Dublin.

"Our babe would be kept inside for the winter months, would he not?" He watched her face as he asked the question, curious to find out how much thinking she'd done about this babe-to-be. Was it easier for a woman, like, to imagine the babe, to see herself caring for it?

"I suppose," she said. "Depends on where we are then. Fire's ready for the pot now. Are the potatoes ready?"

He sat up to look around for them. "They're not scrubbed, if that's what you mean."

She cast him a look of exasperation. "So what have ye been doing there?"

Not thinking much about potatoes, and that was God's truth. He picked up the potatoes and the cloth they used for scrubbing and went over to where the brook was. Would most likely be the last time he'd be scrubbing potatoes for a bit. Once they were in Galway with his uncles, things would fall into the normal ways, where the cooking was left to the women and the men had their own concerns to tend to.

As his hands worked on the potatoes, he looked over to where Muirne bent over the fire. For a moment he longed just to toss them to one side, to go grab her and swing her up in his arms, to glory in this time they had to just be themselves and be together, fitting into no man's—or woman's—pattern. Sure and it would all change, soon as they got back into stayin' in one place, fitting into the life of other people. And change again when the babe was born.

"Muirne!" he called over to her.

She turned, the setting sun making the wild curls on her head gleam redder than ever in its light.

"A mhilis—my sweet," he said. "Wisht I could stop the clock right now and be here with you forever."

She smiled at him. "Foolish." But her voice was gentle. "Hungry you'd be in no time, and askin' where your food had gone." But she stood up, and walked over toward him.

"Here." He handed her the potatoes, and watched her walk back and drop them into the bubbling water. So graceful she was, even with those boy's shoes on her feet. Thomas's shoes, she still called them. He came after her, swiftly, and wrapped her in his arms.

"I canna wait longer, me love," he whispered into her hair.

She pulled backward a bit, her eyes searching his face. "'Tis not even dark yet." She sounded puzzled by his words.

"And who to see us besides some sheep? An' they don't wait till dark, do they?"

She looked around, as if she expected to see some standing there with them, though they were in the next field over. Far enough so the bushes made them invisible, close enough to hear when they bleated.

He pulled her closer, so that he could feel the warmth of her body against his. "I want you. From tomorrow we must be ordinary an' civilized, like the rest of God's people. Tonight it's just the two of us, and if we choose to have each other while the potatoes are cooking, who is to say we must not?"

The soft breath of her giggle would have tickled his chest, had he not his shirts on, so he peeled them off, and pressed her against his naked skin.

And neither of them noticed the sun sliding down the sky to its setting.

Most nights they both were so tired that sleep followed almost as soon as Muirne lay down on the shawl she'd spread on the grass and Diarmaid laid out the old torn shawl he'd insisted on adding to his pack as they left the clachan. They'd both replaced the rest of their clothes, since the shawls only kept their heads and some down from their shoulders off the grass, and as often as not by morning Diarmaid had rolled entirely off the shawl and lay stretched out on the grass.

But this night they were both wakeful, and lay close together, the shawls lapped over each other. Muirne's head was cushioned by his shoulder as she stared up at the black sky above them, watching the tiny points of light they called stars scattered from horizon to horizon.

"Tomorrow we sleep inside, do we not?" Her voice sounded loud to her, in the silence of the night. Even the sheep seemed to have settled into sleep, although after she spoke, there was one last bleat that faded away.

"We do." Diarmaid's voice was drowsy. "Couldn't sleep outside in a town as large as Galway and expect to still have your possessions when you wake. The law abiding folk sleep at night but there's enough who are not that you'd be unwise to leave yourself undefended."

"Mmmm." She let the silence lie there about them for only a moment or two. "Tell me. When we get to the place where your uncles stay, are aunts there as well?"

She heard his sleepy chuckle. "An' a couple of extra ones."

In her eagerness to know, she lifted her head until his hand set it back where it had been.

"You're keepin' my shoulder warm," he muttered.

"So who are the aunts?"

He chuckled again. "Bound to know them all, are ye? Well, there's Kate—she's wife to me Uncle Patrick. And Auntie Rose, who's married to me Uncle Con. Not a real uncle, he's not—really a cousin by blood, but he was close friends to me da, and has been me uncle since my da was murdered. Then there's Auntie Lena and Auntie Rosanna, and exactly how they fit in the family I've never known, but they're there as well."

"Four of them. Kate and Rose and Lena and Rosanna," Muirne's voice murmured. "Is that all?"

"All?" This time he laughed out loud. "An' is four of 'em not enough for you? How many aunts do you have, then?"

"Me mam had a sister—Nora, I think she was—but I don't know what happened to her. She was there when I was a little bit of a thing. I don't know about me da. He's so mean I hope there's no more where he came from. One was too many to begin with."

The silence lay between them a bit longer this time.

"Do they all live in the same place?" Her voice was small, coming out of the dark.

"No, thank the Lord. 'Twould be enough to drive you mad. All the aunts have the gift of knowing what the good Lord would have them do every day of their lives, but none of them do the same things, so there's a bit of arguin' from time to time. Every day, in fact. But they'll not leave each other alone, either. Keeps the place lively enough."

Oh. If Galway was the place they were to live, she'd have to get used to that. How long would it take before they'd be able to have a house of their own? Or would they ever? P'rhaps when a man was devoted to the cause, as she had reason to know Diarmaid was, he'd be moving around all the days of his life and never have the chance to be anywhere long enough to set up a house and a home.

'Twas a good thing then if she could get her mind settled to that now, so she'd not be expecting more and wondering when it was to happen. She would never believe it had been a mistake to settle her heart on Diarmaid MacGuinness.

She stared up into the blackness above them and was about to frame another question when she heard the soft but unmistakable sound of a snore. Whatever she was going to be wakeful worrying about, her love Diarmaid had settled into sleep.

She shifted her head on his shoulder, finding the most comfortable spot, and lay there quietly, watching the stars in the black sky above, waiting for the next day to come and all the discoveries she'd be making then.

It was most likely very late by the time her eyes closed and she settled into sleep.

MUIRNE HAD PLAINLY NEVER SEEN anything as splendid as Galway.

Diarmaid watched her, hoping she wasn't aware of the smile he kept straightening out so she'd not think he was laughing at her.

"All the houses," she whispered, as they came down the narrow, winding streets leading to the Corrib River, running through the center of the city.

All the houses indeed. After a moment's deliberation, which he did not share with her, he'd decided to take her down to the river so she could see the city before he took her to his uncle Patrick's house. He kept a firm hold on her hand, discovering she kept stopping in the middle of the road to look about with amazement unless he was gently urging her forward.

"I never thought there'd be so many," she said.

"So many what?"

"All of it. So many houses, so many people—the streets just go on and on." She stopped again and looked all around until he tugged at her hand again.

"Look up that street there," he urged her. "That's where the St. Nicholas church is. Beautiful building 'twas 'til Cromwell came, killing and laying waste. Near 200 years it's been and that church's still ruined. T'English used it to stable their horses."

Muirne looked up the side street. "Horrible," she said. "Over and over again, it's horrible."

Diarmaid turned to look at the River Corrib, flowing steadily between its bush-covered banks down toward the Bay and the sea, as it had done in good times and bad. "He died in bed, himself," he said. "Sometimes naught is fair."

"Don't know what to think," she said. "To me all is still grand now. What must it have been like before?"

"I've only heard what me uncles tell. Not that they were around then, o' course. But it was a rich city back then, with a wall. Con says 'twill be again, but I don't know how long it may take, if I'll be alive to see it. But it'll happen. I promise you that."

Her face softened into a smile. "Then it will."

He took a deep breath and looked around. "You've seen the city—at least some of it. Shall we go find me uncles now?"

"And the aunts?" Her voice had an odd quaver to it.

Diarmaid pulled her closer to him. "A ghrá, don't worry. It will all be well."

She looked up at him, her face uncertain. "An' that you can promise, too?"

"Two days, and it'll be as if they'd known you forever."

She took a deep breath. "Let's go then. I'd rather have it happen than keep thinkin' it over."

He laughed, but he could tell from the tightness of her fingers around his that she was telling him her truth. They turned, and wound through narrow streets as familiar to him as the paths around the clachan had been to her.

The sight of his Uncle Patrick's house was like a kick to his belly. How long had it been since he'd been here? As they walked down the street toward it, he was remembering how last time he'd been just back from Connemara, where everything had gone so well. Was it still flourishing? In a way it was a pity they'd not gone that way, but all things considered 'twas prob'ly best they'd come here straight. Had been a long way as it was for Muirne, who'd for certain never done a walk like that before.

Was it the length of the walk that had her face a bit drawn now and her eyes anxious?

Diarmaid dropped her hand and lifted his to knock on the door.

There was the familiar babble from inside—most likely arguing about who was closest to the door—and then the door burst open.

"Diarmaid, me son!"

There was no missing the rollicking welcome in the voice. His uncle Patrick, as tall as he was but much better padded, threw his arms around Diarmaid and lifted him over the doorstep. He set him down in a hallway that was rapidly filling with everyone else who happened to be in the house at the time.

There was his aunt Kate, apron wrapped around her round belly, and the two spinster aunts, Lena and Rosanna, trying to make their way between the children bobbing and weaving between all the rest.

For a moment Diarmaid feasted his eyes on the look of them all, and then hastily looked round to see what had happened to Muirne. She was still standing out on the doorstep, her eyes as big as saucers and her lips pinched together. He reached for her hand and pulled her into the front hall with the rest of them. The front door creaked closed behind her.

"Have to have you meet somebody," he said loudly enough to stop the uproar for a moment or two. "This is me wife, Muirne."

In the place of the uproar there was sudden-like the quiet you'd expect in church.

Then his auntie Kate pushed her way through the children and all, and put her arms around Muirne.

"An' now you're wedded to one of Ireland's finest," she said. "Welcome to our house, Muirne. We're pleased by the sight o' you."

When he saw the shine in Muirne's eyes and her lips, on the edge of a quiver, he tugged on her hand, and Kate let go long enough for him to pull her into the shelter of his arm. "Lots o' people all at once," he said, loud enough for all to hear, quiet enough so that Muirne settled against him, and her lips bent into something very close to a smile.

Uncle Patrick approached official-like, and took her other hand. "Welcome, Muirne," he said in his deep voice that was so much like his da's that Diarmaid felt the lump in his throat again—all these years, and there was that damned lump.

"And where was your home, then?" Patrick asked gently.

"Inishowen, in Donegal," she said. "On our clachan. Don't know as how it had a real name: some people called it the clachan on the plain, but 'twasn't as flat as all that." When he heard her voice coming stronger and her words so plain and clear, Diarmaid found himself grinning at her.

It would be all right. He'd promised her, and it would be. Maybe hard at first, but you had to get past the beginning before everyone could settle.

Patrick was looking about to collect the children. Aidan, who was the oldest, had clearly had a growth spurt since Diarmaid had seen him last. Three boys there were, and then the two girls, Mary Catherine and Mary Margaret.

"This is me oldest son, Aiden," Patrick said, pushing him forward. Aiden hadn't grown into his body yet all the way, and looked as if his arms and legs were not connected quite right, but he bent his head and muttered some words of welcome.

"And here's Daniel and Lorcán." Patrick grasped both of them and pulled them in front where Muirne would be able to see them. "And the girls." He looked around, and located them behind two older women also in aprons, standing bright-eyed and beaming in the hall.

"Here they are," he said with relief, releasing the boys and grabbing the girls only slightly more gently to push them to the front of the crowd in the hall. "Mary Catherine is older and has the brown eyes and red hair, though not as bright as yours, Diarmaid—or yours, Muirne for all of that. When you have your first bairn, he'll probably be born with his head afire."

Muirne's eyes turned quickly to Diarmaid and then she smiled politely.

Mary Catherine dipped a bit of a curtsey, and elbowed her sister. "This is Mary Margaret," she said in a shy voice. Not quite as shy as Mary Margaret seemed to be, turning beet red and ducking her head.

"What a lot of people," Muirne said, her voice stronger than Diarmaid had thought it'd be. "Hope I remember all the names."

"You mean Diarmaid didn't have you practicing them, then? Shame on you, me boy." One of the women in an apron pushed toward the front, the other following her lead, and the children scuttled away before they were trampled over. "Only two to go. I'm your auntie Rosanna, and she's auntie Lena."

Muirne nodded at them. "I'm pleased to meet you all."

Diarmaid rested his hand on the back of her neck. No way to tell her now, of course, but he was so proud of her 'twas almost painful. He hadn't thought how hard this beginning would be, and she'd been polite and a proper lady, for all that her hair was still in wild curls round her head. But her back was straight and her chin up, and he wisht it was possible to wrap his arms round her to tell her how well she'd done.

"Makes no sense to stay here mushed together in the hall," Aunt Kate said in a determined way, and shooed the family, like a lot of chickens, into the front room where there were chairs to sit on and a table in the middle. This was where the family gathered in the evenings, as Diarmaid remembered with pleasure. After their supper, the table rapidly became covered with family amusements, left in a cheerful jumble. There were books, and a plate that looked as if it might have had biscuits on it before, and some colored pencils and a box with wooden puzzle pieces in it. Looking at her now 'twas hard to believe it, but aunt Kate was capable of a fearsome roar when 'twas time for all to be cleared away.

Diarmaid pulled two chairs close together and sat Muirne in one of them and himself in the other, keeping his arm around her shoulders. For the time he was richly content. He had a wife—almost more of a wonder to him now he was in the midst of his family than it had been before— and the long walk was done. Maybe tomorrow, or p'rhaps later today, he and Patrick and Con would have to deal with the way he'd bolted from the clachan in Inishowen with the work unfinished and not as he'd liked to have left it. But that'd draw in other men, and wasn't needed until later. For now he was home.

Diarmaid's arm was warm around her as she sat listening to the chatter of the voices. Hadn't been as bad as she'd feared, but of course the hard parts were to come. She was made cautious by the size of the house, for one thing. How many rooms could be within it? All these people—did they all live here? And food! They must be rich indeed to feed them all. How many were there?

She counted. There were Patrick and Kate, and they had five children and all of them looked well-fed and healthy. So that would be seven, and the two aunties, and then herself and Diarmaid. Eleven in all. Eleven!

There might be as many as that in some families in the clachan, but if there were, 'twas likely most of the children would be sent off t'work for the farmers in the east of Donegal. They'd work from May until November, when rents had to be paid and they'd bring home their wages. At the May hiring fairs, little children—young as seven, some of 'em—got hired to work as herders for sheep or cows. If they were like thirteen or fourteen, they could get more pay, being hired for most jobs an adult would do: milking, or plowing, taking goods to market, becoming laborers to do whatever was required.

But these children were still at home, and it didn't appear to Muirne they'd be off to a hiring fair in a month or so. It was all very strange. Were all city folk so rich then?

The buzz of voices went on, all the children (and the aunties) wanting to tell Diarmaid what they'd been doing while he was gone. She tried to listen, but kept finding her attention straying to looking around what she could see of the house. There was this front room, where they were, and then through a wide doorway into another room right behind it. Didn't look as if it had anything that'd serve for a bed, either. Where did all these people sleep? And what would anybody need two front rooms for?

Course when they'd come in the door was in the middle of the house, so perhaps there were bedrooms on t'other side. But where was a kitchen? Maybe behind these rooms? That'd make the house a deep one. From the outside 'twas plain it was tall enough for a storey above— mayhap that was where people slept. What if there was one bedroom for the girls, and maybe the aunties as well. Is that where she'd be put to sleep, and Diarmaid with the boys?

She hoped not.

Diarmaid's arm was warm around her as she sat listening to the chatter of the voices. Hadn't been as bad as she'd feared, but of course the hard parts were to come. She was made cautious by the size of the house, for one thing. How many rooms could be within it? All these people—did they all live here? And food! They must be rich indeed to feed them all. How many were there?

She counted. There were Patrick and Kate, and they had five children and all of them looked well-fed and healthy. So that would be seven, and the two aunties, and then herself and Diarmaid. Eleven in all. Eleven!

There might be as many as that in some families in the clachan, but if there were, 'twas likely most of the children would be sent off t'work for the farmers in the eastern parts of Donegal. They'd work from May until November, when rents had to be paid and they'd bring home their wages. At the May hiring fairs, little children—young as seven, some of 'em—got hired to work as herders for sheep or cows. If they were like thirteen or fourteen, they could get more pay, being hired for most jobs an adult would do: milking, or plowing, taking goods to market, becoming laborers to do whatever was required.

But these children were still at home, and it didn't appear to Muirne they'd be off to a hiring fair in a month or so. It was all very strange. Were all city folk so rich then?

The buzz of voices went on, all the children (and the aunties) wanting to tell Diarmaid what they'd been doing while he was gone. She tried to listen, but kept finding her attention straying to looking around what she could see of the house. There was this front room, where they were, and then through a wide doorway into another room right behind it. Didn't look as if it had anything that'd serve for a bed, either. Where did all these people sleep? And what would anybody need two front rooms for?

Course when they'd come in the door was in the middle of the house, so perhaps there were bedrooms on t'other side. But where was a kitchen? Maybe behind these rooms? That'd make the house a deep one. From the outside 'twas plain it was tall enough for a storey above—mayhap that was where people slept. What if there was one bedroom for the girls, and maybe the aunties as well. Is that where she'd be put to sleep, and Diarmaid with the boys?

She hoped not.

His fingers tightened around her shoulder and she looked over at him quickly. Had she missed something? She'd wandered a long way off in her thoughts—should've been payin' attention to what was going on in this room. She glanced around, hoping she could figure out what they'd been talking about.

"It was a right long walk," Diarmaid was saying. "I'm still proud that Muirne did it all—she'd never done a walk like that before." He looked at her and his face crinkled into a smile. "She walked right through a pair of shoes, she did. They fell apart on her feet, and we were then in a bit of—would it have been County Galway then?" He half turned to ask her.

She looked at him blankly. She'd no more known where they were than how to fly to the moon. She shrugged. "'Twas a little place, w' no shops. But I don't know where it would have been. Three, maybe four days ago."

Diarmaid swung his arm around to pick up her closest leg to show them all her shoes. Muirne could feel her blush starting from her chest and mounting up to her cheeks. Her shoes weren't even a girl's shoes. They were Thomas's shoes, and had done her right well, but what would all these people who seemed to have so much think of her walkin' through the city with a boy's shoes on her feet?

"These be Thomas's shoes," he said. Well, at least he'd remembered the right name.

"He'd been a sickly boy, but his mam'd bought him some new shoes just before he died, so he was wearing those, and when we came along with Muirne here walking in her bare feet, his mam gave her the other pair so she'd not have to walk all the way here w' nothing to protect her feet. Good shoes, these have been."

"Not beautiful." Muirne wanted to make sure they all knew she knew that.

"How exciting!" Mary Catherine said, eyes shining.

Mary Margaret peered around her sister. "But the boy was dead!"

The two aunties and Kate all spoke at once, all saying more or less the same thing in different words—that it was wonderful some use could be made of the shoes.

"I'm sure 'twas a great comfort to his mother," Kate said. "I would think the hardest would be feeling that nobody remembered him, that it was as if he'd never been. Now I'm sure Muirne here gives him a thought whenever she puts 'is shoes on, and now all of us will think of him when we see her wearing 'em."

Muirne met her eyes when Kate looked over at her, like she was checking Muirne agreed with her.

"It's true," Her voice was quieter than Kate's had been, but Kate smiled at her, nodding in agreement.

More time must have passed than Muirne realized because it was shortly after that that Kate gathered up the aunties and headed for the kitchen, saying that she had dinner partway done, but everyone would be hungry and she'd have little for them if she didn't go to work on it now.

There was general agreement that a bit of dinner would not come amiss, especially from her three sons. She collared Lorcán, the youngest of them, and dragged him along, saying that what he clearly needed was peeling a potato or two.

The kitchen must be at the back of the house, Muirne decided, hearing the voices retreating in that direction, and then a low hubbub of talk continuing from there. She looked at Diarmaid and whispered to ask if she should join them, but he shook his head.

"Another day, p'rhaps," he said. "Today you'll be a guest."

He didn't lower his voice at all, and Uncle Patrick—if it was like that for Muirne to address him—shook his head.

"There's plenty of them out there," he said. "We should make sure you have a good rest for a few days. 'Tis a fact that I'd need it if I'd walked half as far as you have. And is it true as I expect that this great lad here was bounding off ahead of you most of the time?"

Everyone laughed even as Muirne protested that hadn't been the case at all, and then it was a great succession of stories about Diarmaid as they'd known him in the years since he'd come to Galway, and from there to stories about his mam, Maeve, when she was a girl…

Muirne was right startled when Kate appeared in the doorway to say that dinner was ready to be put out and they'd all better have a quick wash of their hands and come to the table.

Those who'd been sitting and talking jumped to their feet, and all trooped back to the kitchen, Muirne the only female among them. All the rest were scurrying around the kitchen and carrying dishes to the table in the room behind the front room where they'd been sitting. There was a great table there, and chairs had been lined up along the walls and were now pushed into place, so there was room for all of them. The water to wash their hands with was poured from a bucket into a pottery bowl, and there was a towel by the side to wipe the water away afterwards.

It felt good to have clean hands. Muirne took a quick look at her gold ring, shining on her finger as she walked back to the table.

Diarmaid took a chair—the table was round, so Muirne wasn't quite sure where she was to sit, but Diarmaid pulled her into the seat next to him. Mary Margaret, quiet with shyness but her eyes bright with excitement, slipped into the seat on her other side. Took only a minute or two for everyone to find a seat. The bowls of food were all out on the table with big spoons already resting in them.

Muirne looked over the table and felt her eyes grow large.

She bent over toward Diarmaid. In a whisper, she said with wonder, "There's nothing here but kitchen!"

"Auntie Kate's coming with the potatoes," he said, as if that was what she had been worried about.

"But look!" Her whisper was urgent—she could hear that herself. "Look at that—there's bacon 'n onion—and is that sausage? With the potatoes. An' over there—what's that? Carrots? All at once?"

"Well, there's a lot of us," Diarmaid said, not in a whisper.

Kate came in with yet another steaming dish. "Here's some nice colcannon." She set it down on the table, close to where Muirne and Diarmaid sat.

"That's got cabbage and onion in it, with the potatoes," Diarmaid told her.

"There's so much," Muirne marveled.

Kate looked at her, and shook her head. "There's a lot of us here," she said. "Believe me, it'll all go."

Patrick's eyes swept round the table. "Give thanks," he ordered, and all of them mumbled a short prayer—Muirne couldn't quite catch the words—crossed themselves, and then fell on the food, the boys starting to help themselves first.

"Now wait, ye savages," their father ordered. "We've a guest here."

Aiden's shoulders drooped a bit, but he stuck the spoon back into the great bowl of sausages and bacon with the potatoes and pushed it over in Muirne's direction.

"That's Dublin coddle," Diarmaid told her.

They must be rich, she thought, as she helped herself to a spoonful.

"Now, you'll need more than that," Kate told her.

Muirne looked up at her, and then obediently put more onto her plate before she pushed the bowl—far too heavy to carry, it seemed—over in Diarmaid's direction.

Turned out there was some soda bread that was delicious with butter as well.

"Do people eat like this all the time?" Muirne asked Diarmaid as the meal went on and she was urged to take second helpings. She was sure she'd be sick if she did, so she thanked them and moved the bowls on.

By this time she could tell that they were looking at her with badly-hidden curiosity.

"At home, our food is much plainer," she said, glancing at Diarmaid to make sure it was all right for her to talk about it.

"There's not much round Inishowen for people to eat," Diarmaid explained. "Mostly there we ate oaten porridge for breakfast and dinner, and potatoes plain for dinner, with buttermilk if we had it."

"And a bit of kitchen for dinner, if we had some," she put in quickly.

Everyone looked puzzled.

"You know, something extra," she added. "Mebbe a bit of fish, or meat if you had some. Or carrots," she added, as she passed on the bowl full of them.

"Kitchen?" one of the boys said and giggled.

Kate fixed him with a look. "Enough of that. People have different names for things in different places," she said sternly. Then, looking at Muirne, she said, "Life sounds hard there."

Muirne shrugged. "Things are as they are." Her voice sounded small even to her own ears. She could not help but be aware of the eyes staring at her.

"Well, you can eat up here," Patrick said, and firmly guided the conversation in another direction.

AFTER DINNER, THE FAMILY WENT in different directions. One of the boys—Daniel, Muirne thought, though it might've been Lorcán—was sent over to Con's house to tell him that Diarmaid had come. The aunties took over the kitchen once the girls had cleared the table, wiped it down carefully and then pushed it against the wall. To her surprise the top of the table tilted upward so that it fit near flat, and then the chairs were again arranged around the sides of the room so that it was clear in the middle. She could hear the splashing of dishwashing from the kitchen.

The whole business was overseen by Kate, with occasional corrections, and once everything was properly set where it belonged she turned to Muirne.

"Are you weary now?" she asked.

Oddly, she was tired. She had no good reason for it, she told herself. They'd hardly walked at all today. She hesitated, not sure what she should say.

Kate must have sensed her bewilderment. "I think bein' in a new place wears a body out. Nothing's where you're used to finding it and your mind's jumping around all the time to make sense of what's going on. Why don't we get a clean bed for you, and let you take a bit of a rest?"

"I'd like that." She turned to tell Diarmaid where she was going, but he was sitting with Patrick, his face intent as he listened and talked, and rather than push in where she wasn't needed, she turned back and followed Kate down the hall.

There was a staircase just before the kitchen, and she climbed the stairs after Kate, looking around as she went. The stairs were well-worn, probably by many feet from the looks of them. When they came out on the floor above there was a central hall with what looked like many doors, all closed.

Kate stood for a moment, obviously running over possibilities in her mind.

"We have a spare room here," she said. "Patrick has people coming from time to time—mainly others who work with him." She gave Muirne a quick wary glance as if she was not entirely sure of what she might know.

Muirne straightened herself and lifted her chin. "I came south so that I could work with Diarmaid." She spoke with pride as she meant to. "We only decided to wed after—after we'd come part of the way." Kate had looked attentive when Muirne hesitated, but Muirne couldn't help that. It had happened as she'd said. Had they talked about marriage before the day the rain poured on their walk to Donegal Town? She couldn't remember.

"However it happened, you couldn't have chosen better," Kate said. She threw one of the doors open and the two of them came into a room with enough space for a wide bed and a wardrobe. There was a table with a basin and a ewer for water; under the bed was the chamber pot. There were fresh curtains at the window and the room was wonderfully clean with a small rug at each side of the bed, and the smell of furniture polish and soap all round.

Muirne looked at it all, turning around as if she wanted to see every corner, but mainly so as she could fight back her tears before Kate saw them. Suddenly her own eyes saw not the tidy room she stood in but the grubby sod house where she'd lived since she could remember. Almost like they were before her now, she could see the stone circled fire on the dirt floor, and the straw bed she'd made for herself. The worn pot they'd used for porridge, the same one she carried in her bag now.

Kate, who mercifully hadn't noticed she'd lost Muirne's attention, was showing her the shelves in the wardrobe, asking if she needed more space. Muirne could think only of her bag, with the few tattered pieces of clothing she had carried from the clachan pushed down inside the pot. What was she to do here in this city? Kate was not grandly dressed, but her clothes were neat and Muirne could see no patches. What Muirne had would not begin to fill even one shelf in that elegant wardrobe.

But dressed as she was, how could she walk around in this city of Galway? Her clothes were torn and patched, nothing out of the ordinary for the clachan, but what would she look like if everyone here dressed as nice as Kate? Muirne even wore a boy's shoes—a dead boy's shoes, in truth, but she turned that thought away. They were Thomas's shoes, and she was still grateful for them. Always would be.

Still, before she worried about what to wear she had to thank Kate for the use of this lovely room.

So she did, making sure to mention how fresh and clean it was. There was even an extra quilt—a pretty one, too—at the end of the bed.

Kate ran her hands down her apron, looking pleased, and blushed a little.

"It'll be wonderful to have this for the time being," Muirne said. After all, she didn't want to give Kate the idea that she and Diarmaid had come to stay there permanently. Although what they would do permanently she had no idea herself.

"It's simply good to have you here." Kate's voice was warm with genuine welcome.

"But what will you do if one of those who usually stays here comes?" Muirne hadn't given a thought to that until this instant.

Kate thought about that for a moment or two, and then to Muirne's great relief, giggled.

"I don't know, to tell the truth," she said. "but 'tis not all that important. Usually they're not much more than lads. I suppose we could put Lorcán in with the girls for the day or two and put a couple of mattresses out somewhere for the other two boys, and then let whoever it is have the boys' room. Or if it is someone older or fussy, send them over to Con and Rosie and let them sort something out."

Her grin was so infectious Muirne found herself giggling with her. She'd never had a sister. Was this something like what it would be with one?

Kate picked up the top of the bed coverings to peer under ("just to make sure it's all clean," she said) and then moved toward the door. "You'll not take a rest while I'm here," she said. "I think you should just have a lie-down and if you go to sleep so much the better. I'll send Diarmaid or someone up if you're not down by suppertime."

Muirne nodded and obediently sat down on the edge of the bed to take off Thomas's shoes. The door closed with a quiet snick, and she pulled her stockinged feet onto the bed and lay down. It was wonderfully comfortable—a great improvement to her straw bed, even after Diarmaid had made it up with about twice the straw she'd been able to use in the first place. What went into these beds to make them so luxurious, like? Pity she was too tired to try to investigate. Seemed very long ago now but it was still true that when she wakened this morning she'd been sleeping on the ground. As she had the night before, and how many nights before that? She didn't remember.

Now she was in a world where everybody slept on beds of one sort or another.

She had so many things to think about. Not just the clothes, although she would have to talk to Diarmaid or Kate about what could be done with what she had. There was no way she wanted to shame either one of them, which she probably would do unless she just stayed here in the house. She supposed she could do that. Would Diarmaid object if she did? Did a husband have the right to say anything about things like that?

O' course, she'd never been married before, but it was worse than that. She couldn't pretend she wasn't learning that the way they'd lived in Inishowen—more exactly, in the clachan—was nothing like the way people lived in the rest of Ireland. So did she have to learn how to live all over again like a backward child? And if so, how would she learn? Who would teach her? She couldn't follow Kate around like a puppy, lonesome though she might be.

The hardest part was to learn to be on her own again. These weeks with Diarmaid had been something she'd never known before. She'd had a love, yes, but almost more, she'd had a friend. O' course she'd had friends in the clachan, but they were friends like Seán and Liam and Annie. Her life bumped into theirs, but mostly she was on her own. The weeks with Diarmaid they'd been together all the time.

'Twasn't going to be like that now. He was with the men. If she wasn't being pampered on her first day, she'd be with the women.

She was so tired. Mebbe that was why she felt like putting her face in the pillow just to have a quiet cry now she was alone. She didn't know quite why. She just felt silly weepy. She'd walked for so long to be here and now she was, all she wanted to do was to hide and cry.

She wished her busy brain would stop so she could sleep. She was so very tired.

There was the sound of footsteps in the hall. Mebbe. That's what it sounded like to her. She turned her head into the pillow and closed her eyes.

She was not in the first bedroom Diarmaid tried, idiot that he was. So sure he was that he remembered this house he'd thrown open the door that led into Patrick and Kate's room. 'Twas a mercy they were both downstairs where he'd left them and so he'd saved himself a red face from bursting in on something no one else was to share.

He found her in the next room over, which if he'd had the wit of a worm would have been the door he tried first. He himself had stayed in that room before. 'Twas well known among all of them working for the cause that there was a place to stay—more likely, to disappear into—at Patrick's house. The window looked only out at the back garden. As long as reasonable caution was taken, a hunted man could find a night or two of good sleep and good food, thanks to Kate, a rest on his way to create a bit of chaos, and then disappear into other refuges across the land.

'Twas not a hunted man in the bed now. Just a smallish sort of woman—could hardly call her a girl now she was breeding—her face half hidden in a pillow, but on the bit of a cheek you could see there were tear streaks. He walked quietly around the bed to where he could get a better look at her.

She was tired, Kate had told him. Tired from the journey which he knew well himself had been a long one, even considering he had made a business of walking all over Ireland himself. Walking all day and sleeping rough was nothing new to him. 'Twas to her, though, which he should have remembered. Would have been hard even if he had not carelessly planted a babe in her belly, but there it was. He had done just that, and instead of tempering the pace, they'd kept on the same as before, or close to it. No wonder now they'd reached their goal she'd crumbled. But he should have been the one to see her wilting, to have held her hand on the way upstairs, 'stead of leaving it all to Kate.

He took care when he sat down that he not bounce the bed, and looked again at her face. Why had she been crying? He'd had little to do with women—most he'd met had been the wives of men he worked with one way or another. Oh, there'd been one long years ago, but there'd been no way anything could have come of it. Be that as it may, he'd not seen tears on any of them, and that it should be his own wife's cheek streaked with tears made him ache.

What was he to do for her? How they would manage waiting for the birth of their babe he did not yet know, so there was little point in talking about it to her or she'd worry. Patrick had been concerned about the state of those new groups in Connemara, the ones that he himself had brought together. The trouble was, as it had probably been in Inishowen, was that there was not enough to do to keep restless young men willing to wait as they had to until enough strength to act had been built up. They were angry, as they'd every right to be. To be asked to continue to suffer the scorn and indignities the English dished out until enough men had been gathered in was hard enough for the ones who'd seen rebellion crushed over and over. Seemed like it was impossible for the young and unruly. All they wanted was justice with a good helping of revenge.

But what good would it do to have spurts of rebellion here and there when the English had strength to stamp out one after another? There had to be enough at once, so that even the English with all their power would be forced to see Ireland would never rest under the English heel. See the men they dismissed as incapable of learning, of discipline could show both. Thought the Irish were a surly uneducated mob more given to drink than planning and sense, the English did.

But how was he to reconcile his need to work with the Irish with what he knew his wife deserved from him?

He leaned over the bed just to brush a lock of her bright red hair that had tumbled over her face, and was taken aback when her deep blue eyes opened.

Her sleepy smile let loose a bubble of such relief in his chest he might as well've floated straight up to the ceiling.

"Here ye are." Not the brightest thing to say, but at least a start.

"Kate thought I was tired."

No reason not to run his finger down her face, so he did. "You've been crying?"

She shrugged as well as she could, lying down as she was. "I guess Kate was right."

He nodded, and gave way to the impulse to kiss her soft lips, just lightly. "You've every reason to be. Patrick told me I should be shamed for having walked from Donegal so fast, when I had you with me."

Her eyes widened with alarm. "Did you tell him I was carryin'?"

He shook his head. She relaxed back against the pillow. "I s'pose they have to know sooner or later, but I'd rather it be later, meself." Her voice sounded quite firm.

"Why?"

"Dunno. Just seems more proper to have some space between tellin' folks you just married and then there's a babe on the way." She struggled up to a sitting position. "If you see my meaning," she added.

What he wanted was to gather her into his arms, but he thought this might not be the time. There was still supper to get through, but he was ready to be with her in a proper bed. He just wasn't quite certain where she was in her head now. Tired, yes. Glad to be here? He'd been so relieved to be back with Patrick and all it hadn't crossed his mind that this was another strange place for her. Stranger, probably, because all she'd known before was the clachan, and this plain but comfortable house was a long stretch from the mainly one-room houses back in Inishowan.

One of his jobs, now he'd gotten her here, was to remember that.

"Something on your mind?" he asked. She wasn't exactly frowning, but her face was heading in that direction.

Her mouth jerked a couple of times, as if she was on the point of sayin' something, and then went still.

"Tell me."

She shrugged again. "It's me clothes."

He looked at her without speaking. What was she talkin' about? They were the same clothes she'd worn all the way here.

She must have read his thought in his face.

"Never mind," she murmured.

No. Wait. This must be something important to her. If it was important to Muirne, the girl he loved, it had to be important to him, no matter how puzzled he might be by it.

"What about your clothes?"

He was right. It was important. She looked at him with pleading in her eyes.

"Can't you see? I'm all patches and darned places. No one else is. If I go out, that's all anyone will see. And my hair is all over the place." She shook her head and her eyes were bright again with unshed tears. "Don't want to shame you. Don't want to shame me, but look at me. Take a walk and look at people walkin' in the streets. It's different, that's all. Mebbe I should have stayed in the clachan. There everyone was dressed like me."

Diarmaid sat and thought about what she'd said. Trouble was, of course, he was a man, and clothes were what covered his body and kept him warm. Hadn't thought much further than that. But what she thought had to matter.

"Should I talk to Kate?"

Muirne said nothing, just looked at him.

"What would you have me do?"

She shrugged. "Anything you do will cost money."

Money? Was that the problem?

"I have money," he said.

She looked at him blank-faced.

"Did you think the only money I had was that in my purse?"

She stared at him for a moment and then nodded, dumbly.

"Well, 'tisn't. I have more here." He was suddenly immensely glad that that was true. 'Twas money hard earned last time he'd been in Galway. He'd unloaded hookers, the sailing boats with broad black hulls and thick masts that flew white or rust-colored sails. Peat, cattle, beer— he'd unloaded all of them. He dug ditches where ditches were needed. He carried timber for houses, slates for roofs. Whatever was needed, he'd given his back and his strength to. And saved the coins he was given in a great pot, here at Patrick's house. All he had to do was dip his hand in, and Muirne could have the dresses she longed for. Didn't matter to him whether they were patched or not, but it did to her. That was the important part. She was his now.

"Shall we go shopping tomorrow then?" he asked.

She pressed her lips together. "D'you s'pose I may borrow something from Kate?"

Well, she was smaller, but he thought most likely with dresses they could probably be drawn in or let out.

"I'm sure she'd be willing. How hard would it be to get it to fit?"

"Doesn't matter." She gave him a shy smile. "Don't mind it being a bit on the big side. I just don't want to have patches and holes in what I'm wearin'. People don't look like that in the streets here."

The light was back in her eyes. Was that what all the problem had been about? 'Twas true that men and women were different sorts.

"What about shoes?"

She looked at him in surprise. "Thomas's shoes are fine."

"What about some lady shoes while we're in Galway? When we get to walking, Thomas's shoes will be fine. But here in the city, I'd like you to have lady shoes."

The smile she gave him might have come all the way up from her toes—Thomas's shoes were by the side of the bed.

Something had come right. Somehow he'd known what to say, and it'd met her need. It was a good omen. They'd found a way to meet each other.

"How about some supper then?" he asked.

THE STRANGENESS DID GET BETTER. The weeks added up, and between Kate and Con's wife Rosie (who turned out to be as warm and friendly as Kate), Muirne had clothes she was not ashamed to be seen in. It seemed Rosie had gained some weight and insisted she had clothes she hadn't been able to wear for months.

Muirne had smiled gratefully and said nothing about her baby. It wasn't a problem for now. She was still slender as a sapling, and although mornings and her stomach didn't seem to mix well, otherwise she felt fine. She was getting more restful sleep at night in their bed, which probably helped with the tiredness, although sometimes she wondered if it was more a matter of her getting used to it. Muirne glanced over casually at Diarmaid when Rosie suggested she borrow the dresses that didn't fit now, and he had shown no expression. When would Diarmaid be ready to tell them all that Muirne was expecting a birth as well? These were his family, the ones to whom he was closest, and so it was his decision. At least that was what Muirne told herself.

Diarmaid took her to the shops for the purchase of lady shoes. Kate insisted on coming with them to make sure he was not taken advantage of. She said Diarmaid's knowledge of shoes and their prices was only a little better than that of a trout, and shoemakers in Galway were no fools. Diarmaid did not look entirely pleased that Kate thought he could so easily be taken advantage of, but Muirne suspected that what Kate said was most likely true. She was certainly not an experienced shopper in a place like Galway herself. In the end Kate did take charge, and the shoes fit and to Muirne's eyes were unbelievably fashionable. Muirne, the peat cutter, wearing such wonderful shoes! When she lived in the clachan, the possibility of such a thing would never have crossed her mind.

But Kate bustling along with them did mean that Muirne's chance to spend time with Diarmaid on their own was lost. She missed him so when days passed and she only saw him at meals in the middle of everyone, or when they climbed into their bed, and he so tired that he would nuzzle into her neck like a cat might, and fall asleep.

Truly, she'd not expected to have days and weeks of exploring Galway with him, or even just of following him about as he did his business. 'Twas important that as few as could be knew of what he and Patrick and Con were doing. 'Twas obvious, that. There were so many English about. She saw them striding down the streets, suspicious masters of the city and its people.

Ironic, in a way, Kate told her, because back in history when Galway was still a walled city, the walls were built really to keep Irish peasants separate from the safety and comfort of the city. The city's loyalty and that of the 14 tribes, or merchant families, who controlled it, belonged to the Crown. But in 1652 that loyalty cost them dear when Cromwell and his men, having no truck with the Crown or Charles I, the king whose head they'd chopped off in 1641, wreaked havoc on the city for its support of the Royalists. Diarmaid said it just went to show that the English considered the Irish no more than trash to be swept away. After the Battle of the Boyne of 1690, which guaranteed Protestant dominance over the whole of Ireland, Galway as a fine great city withered to a shell of what it had been. Or so Diarmaid told Muirne.

She listened with awe. If 'twas a shell now, what must it have been like then? Even after weeks of following Kate or Rosie around the narrow curving streets or down to the quays along the rivers leading out to the sea, she was still impressed with what was left. She'd be scrambling along behind the two of them, a basket on her arm just like the ones they carried. It still struck her how unlikely it was that she, plain old Muirne Coyle, would be walking through streets hundreds of miles from Inishowen and the clachan. That if she took the wrong corner she was learning how to get back to where she'd been. Some of the shopkeepers were even coming to know who she was, even though she hardly dared say a word beyond a shy whisper naming what it was she wanted to buy.

'Twas almost as if she was more of a daughter to those two busy women, sure of themselves as they bustled around their houses. Which was fine, because of course she was younger than either of them, but what would they say when they found that she was increasing? She hoped Diarmaid would say something soon, for she felt as if in a way she was telling a lie even as she lived under Kate and Patrick's roof day after day.

'Twas not until a rainy day in May that she was able to set matters straight.

Patrick and Diarmaid and presumably Con were off wherever it was they did their mysterious business, and Muirne was sitting in the front room, trying to practice her writing so it would look less like chickens walking across the paper and more like letters anyone would recognize. She had come to think perhaps she could be greatest help to Diarmaid by helping him learn to write so that anyone could read it. But she needed to improve her own ability before being rash enough to suggest helping him.

Kate came in to join her, her sewing basket full of socks needing mending. With her came the smell of bread baking—or was that from the kitchen?

"I think the boys have toes that wiggle more than any other I've ever seen," she said, sitting down and pulling her needle out of a piece of cloth where she had several of different sizes lined up ready for use. "Can't explain how they get all these holes in them any other way." She looked over at Muirne curiously. "An' what might you be up to?"

Muirne's first impulse was to hide the sheet of paper she was working on, but then she gave a moment to sensible thought. If she was goin' to spend some time on improving her writing, Kate was bound to see it one place or another, and it made no sense to tuck it away like a secret.

"Tryin' to make me writing a little easier to read," she said.

"Oh, and you write then?" Kate asked with some surprise.

"Not as well as I should. But there was a schoolteacher, a long time ago now, close to the clachan where I lived and I went to school for a piece of time." That classroom seemed very far away now. Far away and years since she'd been there.

Kate picked out a stocking and pulled it over her left fist so that she could mend the hole with her right hand. "I never had the chance," she said. "I doubt I would've been much good at it in any case. I was never much at sitting in one place for very long."

But she looked as if she belonged where she was now. She had brown hair that had to be very long indeed, because she plaited it and then circled the plaits around her head. 'Twas much like a crown, Muirne thought. And she had brown eyes and a pretty mouth, and the easy sense that she was content.

Muirne wondered if Kate ever felt restless, or if her days gave her enough of what pleased her so that she never needed to look around to see what else there might be.

Would she herself ever reach that state of mind or would she always be wanting just to walk far enough to see what lay around the corner? Or to look out the window to wonder at what was there? Seemed almost as if Kate only looked out to see if the children were coming home from school yet.

Sometimes Muirne wondered if when the babe in her belly was a school child, would they still be here, her child walking home with the others? If not, where they might be, and what Diarmaid might be doing then. The same as he was doing now, trying to work out plans for rebellion? Then God protect him and keep him safe. Seemed unlikely to think the English would not take an interest in what he was doing if anyone made a misstep and word of what the Irish were doing reached their ears. As they might have happened already, back in Inishowen.

Could it have been Jack Loughlin who laid an information with the police, by chance?

She considered the possibility, frowning, but the more she thought of it, the less likely it appeared. She could not see where the advantage would be to Jack, and she'd never known him to do anything that was not to his personal benefit.

"Something wrong?" Kate asked.

Muirne's head snapped up. She'd been so deep in her own thoughts she'd near forgot that Kate was in the room with her.

"Not really. Just sitting here givin' a thought to one of those we knew back in Inishowen."

"Not a pleasant thought, looks like." Kate's needle flashed in and out of the stocking.

"He wasn't a pleasant man. One of those who keeps a sharp eye out for what's his own." She straightened her piece of paper on the book she was using to write on. "Came to the first meeting Diarmaid held, but my guess is that he couldn't see enough advantage in it to him, or not enough soon enough, and he didn't come again. Can't say that I felt sad about it. I didn't think folk like that was what Diarmaid needed, to be honest."

She glanced over and saw that Kate was looking at her sharply.

"Mmm," she said, looking back down at her sock on her fist. "Well, you're far enough away now that 'tis unlikely he could do real harm."

Muirne felt a prickle of dread. She'd not thought that a possibility.

"I don't know," Kate said. "I've always thought that's one of the few things I could do to help the cause—mebbe listen and watch to see if there's risk Patrick might not consider. It's their business, true, but mine as well, once I have children to keep safe. It'll be the same for you, now."

It took a minute for Muirne to think out what Kate had said. Puzzled, she laid down the pencil and puzzled, looked over at Kate. Had Diarmaid told her of the coming babe? "Did Diarmaid say anything— tell you?" she asked.

Kate glanced up and met Muirne's eyes for a moment. "It's not hard to tell, once you've had a few of your own," she said, turning her attention back to the sock. "But you're such a thin little thing I thought p'rhaps I was imagining it." There was a smile lurking around her lips now. "But I guess I'm not."

Muirne shook her head. "No."

"Any idea when the birth will be?"

She went on shaking her head. "Not for certain. Haven't had any but Diarmaid who knew, and he knows less than I do about it. Maybe December?"

Kate gave her a quick look from top to bottom before her eyes returned to the sock on her fist. "About two, three months along, then."

Muirne nodded. "'Bout that, I think."

"Have ye talked about where you'll have it?" Kate knotted her thread and pulled the sock off her hand to inspect it, drop it to one side of her on the couch, and pick up a new one.

"No, not yet." She tried to smile easily at Kate. "It's a bit hard to find time when there aren't a lot of people about."

Kate chuckled but not light-heartedly. "'Tis true enough that. Gone all day, they are, and when they get back there's supper with everyone there, and them so tired so early that they fall into bed with nary a word shared."

This time the smile was easy. So 'twas the same with Kate and Patrick? That was a comfort to know. Not her business, of course, but still—'twas good to know that it was not her alone who'd done something wrong.

Kate checked how much thread she had in her needle, and then looked up at Muirne. "You know you're welcome to have the babe here. Might be good to have me and Rosie to help."

How good it was to be able to talk freely!

"I know that Diarmaid wanted to take me to meet his mam in County Meath, but I don't know if that was to be just a visit or if he'd want to stay there for a while." She shrugged. "I know she's the cook in one of the big houses there, but I don't know if she has a place where we could stay, let alone give birth to a baby."

"Nor do I." Kate's voice was rich with concern. "If I had the deciding, I'd have you stay here."

Muirne opened her mouth to say "So would I," but shut it. She didn't know what Diarmaid wanted, and that would be more important than Kate's opinion. She was a wife now, and had to remember he was where her first loyalty should lie.

Wasn't that expected of a wife?

Kate shrugged, her shoulders loose. "Well, the luck is that you don't have to have the arrangements all made for many months. We'll just wait and see what Diarmaid has planned, if he's done any planning. Or maybe he and Patrick have been talking and have it all worked out."

Muirne took a quick look at Kate. Perhaps Patrick was that sort of man, but she knew she would be rocked back on her heels if Diarmaid had done any practical thinking about the birth of the baby. Patrick had had five children born, and could be expected to know what was required. Diarmaid—not quite the same. But 'twas always possible that Patrick, being his uncle, knew that and had sat him down and talked to him…

"No," Kate said, as if she knew what was in Muirne's mind. "Me Patrick is a love of a man and I'd not trade him for another, but for him, as for most men, I think, birth is something that surprises him every time it happens. You'd think with five growing up and flappin' their wings around us he'd be a bit sharper on what's going on, but he's not. And get to childbirth and he doesn't even try to be. Just looks around for someone to tell him what he's supposed to do."

Muirne tried to swallow the smile bursting to get out on her face, but it didn't work well, and Kate took one look and started giggling. Then they both laughed so hard that tears were springing from their eyes. P'rhaps this business of havin' a baby wouldn't be so bad if someone was round to laugh about it with you.

"Always nice to see the ladies enjoying themselves." 'Twas Patrick's voice.

They both sat straight up, hands unsuccessfully trying to muffle laughter, eyes wide with surprise as Patrick, Con, and Diarmaid walked into the room. Patrick and Diarmaid looked much like each other, being the same height, with the same red hair, but Patrick a good bit heavier. Clear it was to see they were related. Con, who'd been Diarmaid's father's friend, was different. He was shorter, and had brown hair matching the freckles across his broad face. The hair now was touched with grey but the twinkle in his brown eyes never seemed to die out entirely.

"And what were you enjoying so much?" he asked.

Kate shook her head, waving her hand in front of her face. "By the time we explained it, t'would no longer be worth so much as a smile," she said. "You came in a minute or two late."

Muirne looked at her with admiration. What a clever way to avoid telling what could not be shared!

"Why're you back so early?" Kate asked.

"We got tired of spending all our time with each other." Patrick spoke as blandly as if it'd been the truth. "Thought we'd come back to the two of you who're much better looking."

Diarmaid was looking at Muirne with something in his eyes that made her uneasy. There was something that concerned him, and she had no way to guess what it might be.

"So you've seen us. What's there to tell?" Muirne tried to sound light-hearted, but even to her own ears it didn't come out quite like that.

It was Con who spoke. "Diarmaid had a bit of news that changed what we were thinkin' might be our plan." He looked directly at Muirne. "Seems there's someone around increasin'."

"No!" Kate sounded as shocked as if such a thing had never occurred to her. "Muirne, you should have told me!"

What she'd do to Kate when she had her alone! Knowing all three men were looking at her, Muirne tried to find somewhere to put her face without collapsing into helpless laughter again. She looked away from Kate to Diarmaid.

"So how does that change plans?" she asked. Better keep her mind on what might happen next. Giggling about it was all very well and good, but she felt like a feather being blown around by one gust of wind and then another. What had their plan been before? What was it now?

"Diarmaid wants to take Muirne to Meath to meet Maeve, and quite right, too," Con said. "She needs to know all that's going on, and this's not the sort of thing for a letter unless there's no other way. But there is."

Patrick nodded. "And given that there's a babe on the way, they can't just set off on foot as they did before."

Muirne's eyes had followed whoever was speaking, but now she looked back at Diarmaid. What could he be thinking about all this?

His eyes met hers and stayed locked there. "So we're going on the coach leaving at two o'clock tomorrow."

Muirne glanced over to Kate, whose face was frozen by surprise, and then back to Diarmaid. Her husband. The one who now was to make the plans setting out what was to happen to both of them. Had she ever thought about how it would feel to be like a doll or a tin soldier to be picked up and moved from one spot to another?

Course not. He'd helped her escape her da and the clachan and then she'd fallen in love with him. And all this followed from that.

Kate stood up, peeling off the sock still on her left hand to replace it in the basket, and put the needle back with the others. "We'll need to put together some clothes for you," she said. "If you're increasing, the ones you have from Rosie'll not be much use for long."

"But will it matter what I wear where we're going?" She knew Diarmaid's mother worked in a great house, but she was one of the servants, wasn't she? So how grandly did the wife of the son of a servant have to dress? Surely no one would care, would they?

"It matters." Kate's voice was flat. "They're all rich people there, and even their servants have to be dressed according to their station."

"Oh." Muirne considered that. "An' what's me station?"

"Me wife." Diarmaid spoke up with firmness. "Who doesn't wear tattered clothes. I still have some money to spend. We'll go now and see what we can find—the stalls won't be closed yet a while, will they, Kate?"

"I'll go with you," Kate said. "Patrick, keep an eye out for the children. They should be home within the hour, and that's all of them. Be sure Aidan and Daniel remembered to bring Lorcán with them."

Patrick went over to Diarmaid and put some coins in his hand. "I'm your uncle, and you're to take this."

Con was right behind him. "This is what your da would do if he were here," and he passed what Muirne thought might be a bill into Diarmaid's hand.

"Thank ye both." Diarmaid's voice was husky.

Kate came over and put her arms around Muirne and held her close for a minute or two. "'Twould have been fun," she whispered in her ear. "But you'll be back. Trust me."

Muirne nodded, not daring to speak.

"Pick up your cape," Diarmaid said, but his tone was more a suggestion than a command. "Seemed to me 'twas a bit of a cold wind out."

Could not have been that many minutes before the three of them were walking toward the marketplace, to buy what would be needed for the trip to Meath. Muirne allowed herself one look over her shoulder at the place that so briefly had been home.

WHEN THE WIND WAS NOT blowing straight off the sea, and there was no rain, it was coming to be summer. Diarmaid held Muirne's hand tightly as the coach moved out of sight of the family waving them off, and hoped the weather would be better over on the east side of the country.

"Are there more family there?" Muirne's voice sounded smaller than usual. "Or is it just your mam?"

"Just me mam." He didn't even need to close his eyes to see her room. As cook, she had a room of her own close to the kitchen, small but homely. When he was growing up, he'd slept in one of the small rooms around the kitchen that would otherwise be used for storage. He assumed his bed was one of the spare beds brought down from the attic where most of the servants slept. As he'd grown taller, his feet had hung over the end. There'd usually been some spare stuff stacked just inside the door—chairs, or a chest or two: just something so that if anyone glanced in that's all they'd see. The bed was hidden at the back. A couple of kitchen maids who did know he was there had beds that folded out in the kitchen itself, but they kept his secrets like their own. The housekeeper and the butler had rooms in the basement where the kitchen was, but they were removed enough so that neither of them had known when Diarmaid was in the house.

He wondered if the bed was still there. Not that it would be possible for the two of them to sleep there. For one thing, the bed had been small for one growing boy, and for another, he'd always known how to make himself scarce. He'd known the kitchen and round about that part of the house well enough—even known the secret passages that no one in the earl's family knew existed, at least at the start. 'Twas skilled in disappearing one place or another when 'twas needful, he was. Not a skill Muirne had, nor one he wanted her to learn.

Surely 'twould not be beyond his mam's cleverness to find some place for them for a night or two, and then with her help they'd figure out something for after. For one thing, the steward John Bowyer, if he was still there, might help. He might be able to find them something for the next few months.

Not a proper tenancy, of course. That would commit them to stay, and he was not about to leave the cause and turn farmer.

But he had to find a place for Muirne.

If'n his uncles thought that Muirne ought not to be walking from one place to the next in her present state, then making sure a roof was over her head was going to be his lookout. Might not have thought about exactly that at the time, but when he'd said those vows and put that claddagh ring on her finger he'd taken on that charge as well.

Her hand was so soft in his. 'Twasn't as if she hadn't done her share of washing up and cleaning when they were at Patrick's, but then hadn't her hand been soft when she'd been at the clachan in Inishowen and digging peat day in day out?

"How do you keep your hands so smooth and nice?" Diarmaid tipped his head toward her. She'd seemed a bit quieter—mebbe tired?—during all the rush to be ready for the coach today and the day before.

A flash of a smile brightened her face. "I don't know. That's the way they are."

"Lucky for me. They feel good in my hands." There were two other people in the coach but they were on the opposite bench and more toward the other side, so that he felt sure if he kept his voice low they could speak to each other without being overheard. In a way it was good to have this chance to be here, just the two of them. They'd had precious little time alone together while they'd been at Patrick's house. There were children everywhere, and Con and Rosie had been over there whenever they could be as their children were grown and gone.

Ah. Muirne had had no chance to say goodbye to Rosie. The saints be praised, he'd forgotten that until right now. Well, for sure Rosie would understand that he was eager to get to Meath and introduce Muirne to his mother. Muirne seemed to.

He looked down at her, proud of the bonnet on her head and her nice clothes. Not grand—his mam wouldn't have expected that, but plain dresses—two of them—that had no patches or worn spots, and bright clean white aprons to wear over them. Long enough, too, so that unless you were looking close you wouldn't see Thomas's shoes poking out as she walked. He'd been quite ready to buy her another pair. Perhaps not proper lady shoes, but they'd be good plain shoes that were not clearly those a boy might wear. Muirne would have none of them. She said that Thomas's shoes were fine for her, and she thought he would be proud to know she wore them still.

He found himself smiling. He looked down at his wife—there was a miracle in itself—and murmured, "We've had a fine lot of adventures, haven't we?"

Her head tilted up to his, and his smile was reflected in her face. "We have. I was just thinking about Thomas's shoes, and how surprised he and his mam would be to know that they were in a coach goin' all the way to County Meath."

"Funny that." He felt the warmth in his chest. "I was just thinkin' about the shoes meself."

She stuck out both feet so they both could admire them. "That was a lucky chance, wasn't it? Which town was that?"

Took him a minute to recall it. "Tobercurry it was," he said.

She nodded. "Long way from here."

"Oh yes. Those shoes've walked more than a mile or two."

She rested her head against his shoulder for a moment, and then she must have remembered about the bonnet on her head, and promptly straightened up, using her hand to set it properly again on her head.

"It's good to be just the two of us for a bit." Her voice was little more than a whisper.

"'Tis," he agreed. Funny, that. 'Twasn't that they'd not been together. They'd slept in the same bed every night, and even on the nights when he was bone tired and only longed for sleep she'd been a warm presence in the bed with him, soft skin and even breathing that he could curl himself around as he drifted into comforting blackness. T'other nights they'd not spent much time talking.

But awake? No. They'd not had much time for that and when they were together they were with everyone else, too. He'd not noticed that particularly, although p'rhaps that might be one of the things helping to make up his vague dissatisfaction. Working in Connemara had been difficult and satisfying. Working in Inishowen had been difficult and—well, and difficult.

He'd even asked his uncles if they'd thought he'd been too quick to leave when there was someone there asking questions he'd no reason Diarmaid could think of to ask. They'd made it plain right then that what he'd done is what they would have had him do: come back to Galway as directly as possible, and consult with them there. The people in Inishowen were still there; nothing had been done that could be laid to their charge. 'Twas not that he'd left any damning evidence behind.

"There are times when it's convenient that you cannot write so that anyone but you knows what you mean," Con had told him, half-teasing, when they were talking about it.

Diarmaid's eyebrows had skittered up and then down again. "'Twould still be better had I paid better attention when I was in school."

Patrick shook his head, a half-smile on his lips. "Eh, lad, forgotten already? Remember what 'twas like in 1798? Went bad from the start, it did, and no one was faster or could hide in the blink of an eye like you did. It was you what told us where they was and where they was moving. D'ye remember how many messages you carried for us? I don't. Had you been sittin' in school proper like learnin' your lessons things might have gone even worse."

"They're all dead. How could things be worse than that?" Diarmaid spit out the words, fueled by the bitterness he'd felt all these years.

"Not all." Con got up and walked over to the window to look out. "I'm not dead. Patrick's not. And there was a handful of others. If you want to look for reasons, cast your mind back to the French. Had they come when they'd said they would…"

Patrick sighed. "Leave over, Con. We can spend our time and our strength re-fighting the battles of the past, or we can see what we need to do to win the battles next time." He turned to face Diarmaid more squarely. "And that's for you as well, me nephew. There's blame enough to be spread far wider than your shoulders."

"What's it like there?" Her voice was still very quiet. Because of the other people in the coach?

Diarmaid bent over so that he could speak to her the same. "Where do you mean?"

"Where your mam is."

"Oh." He straightened up and tried to summon up Kendall House in his mind's eye. "Very grand it is."

She nodded.

"Great big house built of stone, with green lawn all around it. 'Cept in the back there's flowers, in the spring and summer, like. There's two stories where the earl and his family live, and then one below with the kitchen and all the rooms that y'need to keep house. Then there's the attic on top with the rooms for those that work in the house."

"How many servants are there?"

He shrugged. "Dunno. 'Twasn't my place to be upstairs when people were about. I was to stay right round about the kitchen, help when I could. Mebbe lend a hand with rough gardenin' or work a bit in the back buildings." A grin lightened his face. "But there's secret passages there. Must've been the family what put them there in the first place, but there's been father and son owning the place for generations, and they've forgot. There's not a one of the earl's family now knows they exist, except for Lady Anne, and she doesn't know about all of them."

"How did she find out?"

"I made a daft fool of meself." He settled himself into a more comfortable position, his arm around Muirne so she'd be close to him, and his legs stretched out in front. "I was explorin' round—it was a rainy day, 'twas, and I was looking for something to do. In my wanderin' around, I'd found this long room that had pictures down all the walls. That day, I thought I'd take another look. Got to the end of the passage that went there, and was quiet and still so I stepped out."

"How did you get out?"

"'Twas a catch on the wall inside opened a door. Had a picture on the outside, so you'd not see the door was there. Problem was when you were in you couldn't see out 'til you stepped out. I waited for a bit listening, and heard nothing. So I hit the catch, came out and there was Lady Anne, right at the end of the carpet, taking a walk. She was turning around and there I was. I was fair flustered, I tell you.

"Did she see you?"

"Of course she did. I've got the devil's luck at times like that. She just looked at me with her mouth hung open a bit and I looked back and wondered what in the name of all that's holy I was to do next."

"What did you do?"

Diarmaid shrugged. "What's there to do? Hadn't had time to pray but the good Lord or somebody took pity on me and there was a clap of thunder loud enough to sizzle in your ears. So she looked over to the window, and I jumped back in behind the picture, snapped it shut, and leaned against the wall, hardly fit to breathe."

"What happened then?"

Muirne's face was as bright with interest as a child with a picture book. He smiled at her, and treated himself to running his hand down the side of her face, just once. Smooth as silk it was, and the way she looked at him—well, none of God's creatures had ever looked at him like that before.

She pretended to frown at him. "Finish the story. What happened then?"

He shrugged. "Well, that part I don't know, since I made my way back to the kitchen and made myself scarce for a bit. But one o' the kitchen maids told me 'twas an almighty carry-on, and they had the footmen and the rest o' them running around the house everywhere looking for a man w' red hair." There was a laugh lurking under his words. "I stayed where I knew none from upstairs would find me. Far as that goes, they had some of the footmen running around outside in the rain getting soaked to the skin. They'd have been none too pleased if they'd found 'twas me. So I stayed out of sight and waited a good few days before letting any but the kitchen folk see me. When I did go, I went out the back door and kept my distance from that long room."

"What did Lady Anne do?"

He chuckled. "Pity you're not likely to meet her. She's a wonder, she is. More curiosity than a cat. Once she figured out that the only way of explaining me disappearing was some way around inside the walls, she was set on exploring. I ran into her more'n once. Didn't know quite what to make of her, and she was as puzzled about me. Got to be a sort of friends, in a way. She didn't know anything about what life was like for the Irish, so I told her. Then o' course I had to get her t'hold her horses, because she would've shot out o' there and tried to set all to rights and that would've been a right mess. Her father was—is, I expect—a fair man, but there's lots o' English round about who are not, and they wouldn't of stood for it. All hell would've broken loose. I was takin' some of the leftover food in the kitchen out to the village beyond the estate, where good Irish men and women and their babes were starving, and she wanted to take that on and double, triple it, but if anyone had known of it, it woulda been stopped and the Irish would've starved even faster. Had a heart of gold, she did, but she didn't know what it was like, bein' Irish."

He sat for a minute, looking back into the past and the girl Lady Anne had been. "Brave little thing she was. Married now. Married the marquess over at Ballymuir, and she's got a bairn." He shook his head slowly. "Wonder what she'd be like now. Had this dark hair—lots of it, like, and eyes as green as the land of Ireland. Hair wouldn't stay where it was put. Half the times I saw her it was slidin' down one side of her head or t'other."

Muirne nodded, but she asked no more questions. They sat silently for a while, still about as close together as was decently possible in a public coach, when it occurred to Diarmaid that he hadn't really answered her question. She'd most likely wanted to know about his mother, Maeve, and where she worked, and what it was like there. Instead he'd told her a long story about Lady Anne who didn't even live there nowadays.

"Was it the house you wanted to know about?"

She nodded again.

"Well, it's a great grand house, that's about all to be said. Big rooms, half of them not used much. The front door might as well be in a church, given the size of it, and there's marble, like, on the floor. And a huge staircase. Bottom bit is broad enough for five or six people to go up at t'same time, then at the landing it splits, and half goes up on the left side and half on the right. All the big fancy rooms are up there—you know, for when they have balls and that sort of thing. The family's bedrooms as well, but I've not been up there enough to know much about that. Big long passageways and lots o' doors."

"Where's the kitchen?" Her interest seemed to have picked up again.

"Oh. For that you don't go up the big staircase. You go around to the back of it, and on t'wall behind there's a door through to one of the ways round the house just the servants use. A kind of plain passageway and the stairs to the kitchen come off of that."

"Do the stairs go up?"

"The stairs go down. The kitchen and all the places to keep stuff like dishes and linens for the table and the rooms for storage of food—" Suddenly it hit him that this was what he'd wished he could show her when they'd been back at the clachan and an egg had seemed wonderful beyond measure.

He moved a little free of her so he could twist round and see her face.

"A ghrá, you've never seen nothing like those rooms of food. There's wire baskets with twenty eggs or more. There's hams you'd not be able to lift. There's boxes with fresh bread made that day, five, ten loaves of them. There's jugs of beer and milk and whatever else anyone in the family might like to drink. There's chickens lined up in a row in the cold room. Chickens, and joints of beef, and—you can't imagine it, and how I wished I could somehow magick some o' it up when we were in Inishowen so you'd have all the food you ever wanted to eat." He paused for a moment. "Oh, and potatoes. Great sacks of potatoes. An' carrots and cabbage and peas still in t' pods and—and—and more than you can imagine. Just you wait, me girl. Me mam will take you around and you can have whatever you like. Whatever looks good to you."

"But that's for them that's upstairs, isn't it?"

He looked thoughtful. "Well, o' course it is, but they could no more eat all of it than a kitten could eat up a whole chicken, feathers an' feet. Besides, that's where we get our food as well. All that in me mam's kitchen is not just for them. It's for us as well." Diarmaid shrugged. "Oh, I s'pose there's fancy stuff just for the family and the other English that visit and dine there, but they don't eat the plain food you and me would eat anyway. It's the plain food that's what we like to eat that's free for the taking."

She nodded, but sure and all, she wouldn't be able to believe what he'd told her until she was standing there on the floors of his mam's kitchen herself, seeing how they always looked scrubbed clean on account of hours and hours spent scrubbin' them. And the table and the hot cups of tea they had there as if tea only cost a penny for a tin. Then Muirne could have a look around with her own eyes and see what he'd told her was true.

She looked up at him, but asked no more questions. Had he made her more scared of what she might find there than eager to see the riches? He pulled her close to him again and she sighed, a small very quiet sigh.

"Tired?" he asked.

She nodded.

"Then put your head down, a ghrá, and have a bit of a sleep. We've a way to go yet, and you might as well sleep while you can."

She nodded again, or perhaps 'twas that she settled her head against his side, and as the coach jounced along he felt her settle into sleep as her body slowly relaxed against him. Holding her close, he looked ahead down the road. They'd traveled many miles already, and there were miles more to go. Let her sleep through as many of them as she could.

Let him find a place for them to rest together. He'd never needed a place quite so badly. He had to find a place for Muirne to rest, to let their bairn grow till it was ready to be born, and finally somewhere she could give birth where she would know she was safe and unafraid.

He had to find that place. Now.

27

THE COACH BUMPED ALONG RUTTED roads becoming more familiar to Diarmaid, while Muirne slept bonelessly against his shoulder. These were roads he'd walked again and again in years past. He went over what he expected to find in his mind, hoping it'd work the way he'd planned. The coachman had agreed to stop at Slane, the closest spot to Kendall House along the route from Galway to Drogheda. Slane was no more than a village, but there he'd been known, and with luck there would be someone with a cart who could take them to the big house.

That would be fair easy to arrange. The cart could take them around to the back of Kendall House itself, where the door was that led into the kitchen. As long as that door was unlocked, it would be an easy business to slip in the back way. Then they'd go down the long painted wood hallway inside—he could still see it in his mind, if he shut his eyes—and come out into the great kitchen where his mam would be.

If the door was not unlocked, they'd have to walk all around the house to go up to the splendid great front door, as if they were important enough to be a part of the grand world themselves. Mr. Duncan, the butler and thus the most important of the servants, would let them in, Diarmaid knew. He'd have bet money that Mr. Duncan knew him, even though for all the years Duncan had been slippin' in and out the house he'd done his level best to escape Mr. Duncan's notice. But Mr. Duncan knew all that went on in the house. Diarmaid would not be greatly surprised to find that Mr. Duncan had worked out that it had been Diarmaid all those years ago when he'd had his unexpected encounter with Lady Anne.

In theory, there was naught to keep Diarmaid from walking right up to the door and asking polite like to go down to the kitchen to see his mother. Even so, it seemed somehow against nature. God knew the butler was not there to welcome members of servants' families into the house. Diarmaid couldn't quite escape the fear of the indignity if Mr. Duncan told him to go round the back to come in—he with Muirne there at his side.

No. 'Twould be much much better to let themselves in, quiet like, and not disturb the elegant decorum of the splendid entrance hall and the dignity of Mr. Duncan.

The saints of heaven must've had a hand or two on his shoulder, because all fell out just as he'd hoped. They did indeed leave the coach in Slane, and the coachman was friendly and helpful, getting their bags down from the top of the coach, and seemed pleased with the coins Diarmaid handed him. There was even a bench conveniently set there, so Diarmaid had Muirne sit with the bags around her while he went over to the blacksmith's shop to see where he might find a cart and driver.

He was just crossin' the road when he almost got run over by one. The driver pulled the horse to a sudden stop and shouted out, "Diarmaid MacGuinness, be that you back here at home again?"

Diarmaid stopped right where he was, and looked around with a grin. Steven McPherson it was, who'd kept him company on many a reckless stunt when they were both boys living roundabout. Steven vaulted down from his seat, his horse peering around to see where he was going, and threw his arms around Diarmaid.

"And where have you been these years?" he demanded.

"Here and there, here and there," Diarmaid said, his grin spreading from ear to ear across his face. "Galway, mainly, where my uncles are."

"So, Galway," Steven said. "A big city man, then, back to visit the peasants in the village?"

"None other." Diarmaid let his grin show how glad he was to have met an old friend first thing here, and pointed at the cart. "You spendin' time with the horse these days?"

Steven looked around behind himself as if the cart and horse were a new sight. "Well, and why not? He's not bad company. Don't drink and can't play cards and don't spend his time lookin' for the ladies. Better than a lot of the others round here."

When they got down to talking, turned out Steven had a wife and a small boy with another on the way. Diarmaid was just about to take him over to meet Muirne when somebody with a wagon and two horses, convinced he had important business, shouted to Steven to get his miserable gear out of the way of those with work to do. They shouted back and forth a bit, and then the wagoner realized it was Diarmaid MacGuinness standin' there so he climbed down from his wagon and the three of them chatted, remaining where they were in the middle of the road.

It was about then that Diarmaid remembered that he'd been going to take Steven to meet Muirne, and so he took them over to her, leaving both vehicles in the roadway. Their horses stuck there, patiently waiting.

Diarmaid grinned with pride now. Muirne greeted them with easy good manners, positively pretty as she was with her red hair peeping out under her straw bonnet. He hadn't really paid attention to how her belly was rounding now, but Steven saw it right away. He nodded politely when they were introduced. Once they stepped away back toward the road, he smiled like a man who knew what 'twas all about.

"Bun in the oven then?" he said, elbowing Diarmaid. "That's all right. Happens to us all."

His voice was loud enough that Muirne colored right up, and Diarmaid hoped he wasn't doing the same, although his ears were a bit warmer than usual.

"We need a ride to Kendall House," he said, making his voice as brisk as he could. "Could either of you—"

"'E's got business," Steve said, now giving the wagoner a shove. "But I'd be pleased to take you." He bent over to pick up the bags, and with Muirne coming behind, they all went back into the road to put the bags in the cart, and get both vehicles moving again. Just in time, too, because a carriage and four were coming down the road through the village.

Diarmaid glanced up at the carriage as it passed. It was a grand carriage, so it was not that surprising that out of all the people it could have been, it had to be Lady Anne. She wasn't looking out; she was absorbed with the child on her lap, so didn't see him. For a moment he stood where he was, watching the carriage bump off in the direction they would soon be taking themselves. Queer sensation 'twas, to see her just then. Queer and comforting, in a way. With all that had passed between them, she was safe in the world where she belonged and so was he, standing there with his bonnie wife and babe to come.

He watched the carriage going on until it took a bend in the road and was out of sight.

Still standing there, he was, still too close to the road for safety. He looked about, and placed his hands around Muirne's widening waist, lifting her up to the seat of the cart. She smiled at him, and he smiled back. Sure and the good Lord had known what he was doing all along.

He climbed up onto the seat himself, the bags safely behind them, and for a golden moment knew himself the most fortunate of men.

"Ready to go?" Steven bent around Muirne to ask.

"We're set," Diarmaid told him. The horse stepped out, and the cart jolted into movement behind, bouncing across the main street and taking the road directly across, following the direction the carriage had taken. 'Twas the last leg of the long trip from Inishowen they were starting now, and a short one it would be.

"We're almost there," he said to Muirne, leaning toward her to half whisper it.

She looked back at him, her eyes more intensely blue than ever, and then smiled shyly, as if to tell him she wasn't afraid.

Although of course he knew she was.

Had arriving at Galway been easier? It seemed now it had happened a long time ago. Muirne held on to the edge of the cart seat with two hands to make sure she wasn't bounced down into the road. She wasn't quite certain why she had been placed between the two of them. 'Twould have been easier for them to talk had she not been plunked in the middle.

But there she was, and although the cart was not bumping along at a high speed, she didn't like to think what might happen if she tried to change positions while they were moving. So she sat like a lump between the two of them and tried to concentrate on what the cart was passing as it jounced along.

It was about as different from Inishowen as she could imagine. Instead of the hilly, stony fields with mountains rearing up in the distance which she'd always thought was the way the world was, here the hills were gentle and rolling and the fields were full of growing things— she didn't recognize many of them. Everything was so green here. They were even lucky enough to have today be a fine day, with white puffy clouds sailing through the clear blue sky. The fields were laid out so neatly, their edges marked by stone walls or rows of bushes or small trees. Most of the fields looked recently planted, but there were other grassy fields that had a scattering of sheep on them, or of cows. They must have gone past a cow barn or two: somebody'd have to take all those cows for milking somewhere. Sure and there must be a bull not too far away, but she hadn't seen him. Just cows munching on grass or lying down and chewing their cud or thinking about it, she guessed.

"There 'tis!" Diarmaid was nudging her shoulder, pointing up at the top of a gentle hill. Mostly green grass leading up to it, but she could see some colors in the distance, and there were the tops of trees leading up to it, looked like, but then the road took a turn and she could only see the great stone house at the top.

"That's the house?" she whispered. Even the landlords in Inishowen had not lived in big houses that grand.

"That's it." He was looking up at it with the hint of a smile tugging at his lips. "Doesn't change much, year in and year out. It's been there for a lot of lifetimes."

"That's where your mam works?"

"Well, she's in the kitchen, and that's downstairs—not a part you can see from here. But yes, that's Kendall House, and she's the cook there."

The cart slowed down a bit as the grade of the road grew a bit steeper. The horse must've been feeling the load of three people and whatever they'd thrown in the cart. Tucked in as she was between the two men, she was hardly able to look around and see if there was more in there than the bags she and Diarmaid had brought. But just then the road leveled out, and they picked up a little speed until in a bit they slowed again.

This time it was to turn through some low gates to take a road that seemed to lead to the back of the house.

"There's some grander gates if you're goin' to the portico in front, but I thought we'd rather come in the back way." Diarmaid was shifting just a bit as if he was half tempted to jump down from the seat now.

Muirne grabbed his sleeve. The cart was slowing again, true, but she didn't want him getting off until she was ready to go with him. Her heart seemed to be pounding so hard she was surprised both men were not lookin' around tryin' to figure out where the noise was coming from.

"Here ye are," Steve said, as the horse and cart gradually came to a halt. They were in a little sort of courtyard, with the stone mass of the house on one side, and low buildings, some of stone, some of timber, on the other.

"What are all those there?" Muirne asked.

Diarmaid had been looking at the house. He cast a quick glance over in the direction she was pointing and said, "Oh, that's just for stuff that's better kept out of the house. There's the laundries there, and the shops for making and repairing what's broken or needed in the house. Some of the wagons as well, I think. The proper carriages they keep up in front in their own coach house by the stables."

Diarmaid slid down from his seat and went to lift their bags out of the cart.

She was still looking around in awe. "'Tis almost like a village here." Sure and all the land the great house and the outbuildings took up was surely more than the whole clachan had been built on. Well, except for the two circles of land surrounding it: the one for the crops and the other for the livestock. Although…

"How much land belongs to this house?" she asked.

Steve shrugged. "We've been driving over it since—well, since we got maybe half a mile from the village."

"Oh." It was vastly more than she could imagine. And one family owned it, and they not Irish at all, but English? Hard to get your mind around that.

Then she felt Diarmaid's hands around her and he was lifting her down as if she was light as a feather, which she was not. And would only be getting bigger, she thought, when she looked down at herself standing on the ground and could see the way her dress—her new and unpatched blue dress—sort of poked out a bit in front. Was that what Diarmaid's mam would see first?

She sucked in her breath, hoping it would help.

Diarmaid was over talking to Steve. Looked as if they were arguing a bit, but she quickly gathered that Steve was objecting to taking the coins that Diarmaid seemed fixed on giving him.

"'Tis your livelihood," she heard Diarmaid say.

"An' you're me friend."

"P'rhaps I'll let you take us for a ride another day. This ride was business, to get me to where me mam is." Diarmaid was poking the coins into Steve's pocket. "Get a treat for your wife, as she has one and is carrying another."

Steve shook his head but gave over arguing, and after some cheerful insults passed back and forth, he turned the horse and cart around—there was easy enough space to do that right there behind the big house—and went back down the same roadway he'd followed coming.

Muirne took a deep breath and walked behind Diarmaid toward the house. There was a door there, with a doormat on the step outside, and his mam must have trained him well, because he did a right thorough job of scraping off his feet before he opened the door.

She made it her business to do the same 'til Diarmaid got restless and groaned.

"You're going to scrape the bottoms off Thomas's shoes," he said.

She looked down at them. She'd worn those today since he'd not said how long the day would be or how much walking they'd do. Not much, as it happened, but she'd not known that. In any case, her dress was long enough so that unless someone happen to be looking, they'd never know it was a boy's shoes on her feet.

"There's plenty of sole left." She tried to keep her mutter low, so he could choose not to hear it.

He had the door open, and was looking back at her, shaking his head.

"Come meet me mam," he said.

'Twasn't only feeling it. She was sure she could hear her stomach dropping out of the middle of her. She'd not allowed herself to think it until now, but this was Diarmaid's mother she was about to meet. An' she was a cook, and a woman who knew more than anyone else about what was going on in this vast stone house—Diarmaid had told her that more than once. An' here she was, from a dot on the map in faraway Donegal County, comin' from a clachan on the Inishowen peninsula so unimportant it hadn't a real name. And already carrying a babe.

Would Diarmaid's mam be pleased to think she'd have a grandchild? Or would she be shamed to think the babe had been planted before Muirne and her son had been wed? 'Twouldn't take much figuring to get that worked out.

"Are you coming?" This time Diarmaid sounded on the edge of being cross about it, so she scrambled in behind him and walked as quick as she could to keep up.

The hall was plain, and long. The floor under their feet was timber, but it had been painted a dark grey, and obviously repainted, because there were no worn spots, although Muirne was sure many feet came this way day after day.

They could catch the fragrance of the kitchen before they reached it. An odd mixed smell it was. Baking bread, that was surely part of it, and then there was meat cooking and some potatoes—odd how you could smell potatoes before you smelled anything else. Or p'rhaps that was because she knew the scent of potatoes cooking best. But there were other delicious smells she didn't know. Then they turned the corner into the kitchen, and they were there.

She saw Diarmaid's mam first. 'Twasn't as if she was the only woman there, but she was the one telling everyone else what to do. She was covered with a great white apron, and had a wooden spoon in one hand that she was waving about as she sent one kitchen maid in one direction and another somewhere else. She had a great mass of grey hair turning white on her head—almost as untidy as Muirne's own—and her hands looked capable and well-used.

It took her a moment to notice they'd come into the kitchen, although everyone else seemed to see them at once. It was only when all the kitchen maids were looking at where Diarmaid and Muirne had come in that she whirled around to see what was going on, her face half irritated.

Then what looked like a reluctant half-smile settled.

"Diarmaid," she said. "So. You're back."

He gave her one of his finest grins. "I am. And this is me wife, Muirne." He put his hand firmly on her shoulder, claiming her.

Did the cook blink? Muirne thought she might have, for a moment. But then she was walking toward them, giving Muirne the sort of look that gave her the feeling that she'd checked her out from top to bottom and probably even knew about Thomas's shoes, hidden by her skirt.

"Glad to meet you, Muirne."

Muirne hoped her smile didn't look forced. "I've looked forward to meeting you."

She was more surprised than she expected to see, now that they were close, Diarmaid's mam was no taller than she was herself. She'd somehow thought that she would be a tall, commanding woman, from what Diarmaid had said about her.

And what was Muirne to call her? Mam? Most likely not. She didn't look like the kind of person you'd call that unless you were blood kin. Mrs.? Mrs.what? MacGuinness?

But seemed she could read minds. Now they were face to face, she took on a big smile that made her seem at once mischievous and welcoming.

"You'll call me Maeve," she said. She nodded her head in Diarmaid's direction. "He does."

HOW IT WAS MANAGED DIARMAID did not quite see, but somehow his mam's iron rule showed itself and all the kitchen maids found other places to do their work—vanished into some of the many small rooms attached to the kitchen, he thought most likely—and only the three of them were left in the kitchen. They sat on stools pulled up to his mam's huge kitchen table, drinking tea out of the thick white mugs that had been part of Maeve's kitchen forever, as he remembered it.

Muirne sipped at hers uncertainly. She'd never had tea before, of course. The clachan—and likely Inishowen itself, for all he knew—didn't run to such luxuries, and the uncles in Galway had never gotten a taste for it. Just as well, considering how many of them there were and how costly it was.

Maeve kept a watchful eye on her new daughter-in-law.

"Might like it better w' a bit of sugar." She pushed the sugar bowl over in Muirne's direction.

It was a different shy Muirne here. Diarmaid kept his smile to himself. Now that he thought of it, this was how it'd been when they first got to Patrick's house. Took a lot to dampen Muirne's quick spirit, but meetin' his relatives seemed to do the job.

Muirne carefully added a spoonful and then tasted it. He recognized her cautious smile as she looked over at Maeve. "Now it's nice."

Maeve nodded. "So when's the bairn due?"

He shared a quick glance with Muirne.

She lifted her chin in the way she had, and speaking clearly, said, "December."

"'Tis July now." Maeve looked like she was thinking things over, then turned to face him herself. "Where you going to stay?"

He had the queer feeling of being pushed over a cliff. Wasn't that he hadn't known his mam would have no place for them to stay at the big house. But in the way he'd always believed her capable of doing miracles, he must have had the hope, hidden even from himself, that Maeve would come up with some solution.

No. That was not to be.

He knew in the way he knew things he might not see that Muirne was looking to him. He needed a bit of time to pull himself together and figure something out, so he kept his eyes on the edge of the kitchen table, running his finger along it.

"Knew that would be a problem," he said. "Thought p'rhaps might be a place in the village we could find."

Maeve shook her head impatiently. "Too far. And 'tis downhill, you know that. When her day comes closer she doesn't want to be walking all the way up here. Nor would it be good if she has to spend her days all alone there. What if she starts her laboring?"

"I'd be there, too." Spoken indignantly.

"Not if you're working, and there's work to do here. Sure I am that the earl can find you a place in the stables, or mebbe the fields."

He nodded. 'Twas all true, God knew. His mind was runnin' around like a mouse with a cat after him. He was home, for sweet Mary's sake. These were his people. He should be able to think o' something.

O' course that was one thing he could do, although his spirit revolted. He could go find the earl's steward—would it still be John Bowyer? There might be an empty tenant cottage they needed filled. He could be one of the earl's tenant farmers, and live close to his mam for Muirne's sake. She'd be a help with the bairn.

But. But but but. NO. What use would he be to the cause if he was stuck into the endless circle of the farming year? He'd taken up the burden of working for the freedom of the Ireland he loved with all his heart and soul when his father had been killed by the English. He could not set it down yet. Yes, his wife and his child would need a roof over their heads, but there had to be some way of finding it without cutting out what was most alive and important in his own body and soul. He was just getting to the age where he would have a little wisdom to add to the strength of his body for the fight against England.

How could they expect him to walk away from it now?

He glanced over at Maeve, who looked back with her face showing no emotion. She knew the fight he was having. Of course she did. But would she be just as happy to have him settled as another tenant farmer, close enough so that she could be a part of his family? Yes, of course the freedom of Ireland was important to her. But she'd given Ireland her husband. Could be she was not eager to give her son as well.

Had they been ripping his skin off his bones it could not have been more painful.

Muirne sat still, waiting for some sign to tell her what to do. What was she thinking? He dared not try to guess. Maeve was standing, as always a strong pillar of a woman though a short one. He'd been surprised to see that she and Muirne were of a size.

What was he to do? What was he to do? Rat in a trap was what he was. Running round and round and round with no hope of escape.

'Twas then the faintest bit of an idea crossed his mind.

He looked at his mam and his wife, there together, and with the desperation of a drowning man, he said, "I'm off to see about something," and walked straight out of the kitchen and down the hall to the back door.

Muirne and Maeve looked at each other, equally bewildered.

Maeve pulled herself together first. "Another cuppa tea?" she asked.

"No, thank ye," Muirne said as politely as she could. Tea was all right with a bit of sugar, but she couldn't imagine drinking two cups, one after the other.

Diarmaid's mother clearly thought differently. She poured herself another cup and drank it as it was, dark and hot. Muirne's mouth almost burned, watching her.

"Where'd you meet him, then?" Maeve looked at her over the top of the cup.

"I'm from Donegal. He was there in our clachan." She thought of adding "getting a group together," but she wasn't sure what Diarmaid wanted his mother to know.

"What's a clachan when it's at home?"

She couldn't help her quick smile. "A village, in a way. Usually 'tis a family or relatives who start it. Ours started long ago—mebbe by my granda's granda?"

"You have family there now?"

Muirne shook her head. "Not now. Me mam died and—and me dad's not worth much."

Maeve gave her a quick look, but let it pass. "How'd you get from there to here?"

Well, she was Diarmaid's mam. 'Twas to be expected she'd ask questions. 'Twas to be expected, too, that she'd feel freer to ask her than Diarmaid, them both being women. Probably that was the way it'd stay.

"We walked to Galway."

Maeve's eyes widened, just a bit. "How far is that?"

Muire shrugged. "Not sure. I think I heard 'twas three hundred miles, but I'm not sure o' that."

"And you carrying a babe all that time?"

She shook her head quickly. "Not until close to the end."

"How's it been?"

Muire considered. O' course she knew so little about carrying a child. 'Twasn't anything she'd talked to anyone in the clachan about, and Kate and Rosie'd been mainly concerned with how she was doing now, not so much how she'd managed before.

"Not bad," she decided to say. "I was terrible tired at first."

Maeve smiled a smile that held memories. "I remember that."

"I feel more like eating now."

Diarmaid's mam gave her a concentrated look. "You be too thin."

"I feel more like eating now than I did then, but skinny's what I've always been."

Maeve, who had sat down on a stool when she began her questions, got up and opened one of the cupboards. Muirne almost gasped. It was just as Diarmaid had said. There was more food in there than she had ever seen in one place in all her life. Even in shops

Maeve pulled out a great loaf of bread, wheat bread from the looks of it, and took a knife out of a drawer to cut a thick slice. "D'ye like butter on it, or jam?"

"Butter'd be fine," she almost whispered. Jam? Oncet Lizzie'd been given some blackberries and she'd made a jam of them. Where she'd got the sugar from Muirne had never known. She'd had a scone with the jam thinly spread on it on two separate days, but she remembered the delicious sweetness. Dare she ask for jam here?

Maeve gave her a considering look. "Would ye like both?"

Both? Dazed, Muirne nodded slowly. When she opened another

cupboard to get the jam, Muirne was dazzled. Pot after pot after pot was in there. She couldn't begin to count how many.

"Strawberry be all right?"

Muirne was past speech. She just nodded again, watching Maeve spread first butter thickly and then jam—and the berries themselves were right there in the jam—and put the bread, cut into two pieces, on a plate and handed it to her.

She bit into the slice, and her smile escaped her. This was as close to heaven as she ever expected to get.

Diarmaid felt sick inside. The warm skin of a horse was beneath him but the worst memories of his life were suddenly alive all around him. Events he'd spent these last years trying to forget were washing around him, crystal clear and accusing. And he was on his way to stir them all up again.

He was on his way to see the Lady Anne and ask her for a favor.

Which was pretty much the way the disaster had started. He'd been off with a band of young ruffians he'd been trying to shape up into disciplined rebels. Had not been brilliantly successful at it yet; there had recently been a nasty scene, and the most undisciplined of the ruffians had announced himself their leader. Diarmaid planned to unseat him by force of arms, if necessary, and he had a store of them for himself and and his lieutenants, but he'd locked them away and given the key to his mam when Matthew McGonnagher so stupidly took the leadership for himself. Now the time was coming when he'd need them, so he sent a message to his mam.

That was where it started to go wrong. His mam decided it was an emergency and the key was needed right then. Ill luck multiplied. Maeve would've brought it to him herself, but in a badly-timed accident, she'd burned her foot with boiling water. She and Lady Anne had had a curious friendship, always had since Lady Anne had been a little child, and so it was to Lady Anne Maeve'd turned. She asked her to take the key to Diarmaid.

It was a mad idea to ask her, and Lady Anne was even more mad to agree to go. Of course she had no idea where to go or how to get there, so Patrick, the lad who was helping Diarmaid take food to the starving when he was at Kendall House, got pulled in to guide her. Fine lad,

Patrick, but only the sense appropriate to his age, which was not much. Since what he knew about fine ladies would've fit under his eyelid, he walked her through the night to near dawn, and she was close to exhaustion when they came across McGonnagher and his men— Diarmaid with them, of course.

A babe could've knocked him over when he saw Lady Anne, pale, barely walking, straight into the hands of a man as wicked and stupid as McGonnagher. Couldn't let on that he knew her or it would've been worse. 'Twere still some distance from the falling-down barn McGonnagher had made their headquarters, and on the way Lady Anne could walk no more, and he, Diarmaid the Foolish, had carried her. Patrick, thank God, had disappeared, but when they got to the barn it turned out the Great McGonnagher had decided Lady Anne was his toy, and all o' them could play with her.

Diarmaid flew at him like a man possessed, but even a man possessed cannot take on five or six fools at once, and 'twasn't a battle so much as a confused noise. There was a point when Diarmaid was near to passed out, and McGonnagher decided to begin his game. Thank God and all the saints, that was exactly when Patrick, lurking outside unseen as Diarmaid himself had done when his age, set a stick wrapped with straw afire and shot it into the barn. The barn burst into flame and the cowards did what cowards do—abandoned their prize, Lady Anne, and Diarmaid, spread out on the floor, and ran as fast as their legs would take them.

It was Patrick, showing more sense than the lot of them including Diarmaid himself, who got the two of them out of there. And it was the marquess, an English newcomer in the land who could only've been guided by Mother Mary herself, who managed to find them and take Lady Anne home with him—bruised, exhausted, but untouched by those villains—to marry her and look after her with all the love and tenderness anyone could ask for.

So was it the marquess that was about to beg a favor of her?

No, it was Diarmaid, whose fault it was the whole terrible episode had happened. And now he was going to ask them both, her and her husband (who had every reason to hate him) to take in his wife and child-to-be, into their own house.

Diarmaid knew this road that led to that house. He rode along bareback on the horse, with just the reins and bridle. In the stable they'd tried to get him to take a saddle, but he'd felt asking for the loan of a horse was more than enough. The good Lord knew he'd ridden bareback many and many a time when he was a boy. Back then he and the lads in the stable would take the horses out for a run more or less just as they were. Now, all the way he was trying out things to say in his mind, but none of them came right. Still, he had to try. It was this, or—or be turned into a farmer. His choices had narrowed to just those two.

He saw Ballymuir in the distance and kept his eyes on it as he drew closer. He'd been here a time or two before, but he'd never come to the front door, and he couldn't think of any other way to approach this house. He'd not taken the time to change his clothes at all—nor did he have a place to change them—but he'd dressed nicer than usual for the coach journey. As he was would have to do.

Had seemed longer than usual to get here, but it hadn't been long enough for him to work out in his mind what he was to say. When he reached the portico, he slid off the horse and stood for a moment, not quite sure of what to do next.

A stable boy appeared, and raised his eyebrows at the sight of the bare horse.

"Sorry," Diarmaid said. "Can you manage?"

The stable boy nodded, and took the reins, and the horse followed him down toward the stables. Diarmaid spared a single thought for what the stable boy might be thinking, and then walked up the steps to the front door. The horse had been only a means to his end. Now he had to think what he was to say.

He knocked firmly on the door.

The man who opened it, the butler, Diarmaid assumed, looked at him with no particular interest.

"Is Lady Anne at home?" He was careful to keep his tone and attitude as respectful as he could.

"Lady Anne?"

Did he not look like the kind of person who would be asking for her? Diarmaid fought down his immediate response, which would have been along the line of "who do you think I mean?" and simply nodded, and said, "Yes, please."

The butler, not in his first youth, gave him a suspicious look and opened the door enough for Diarmaid to enter.

"I will inquire," he said. "May I say who is calling?"

"Diarmaid MacGuinness." He drew himself up to his full height, and the butler, who was smaller, nodded respectfully. He took a parting look at Diarmaid—was he trying to decide how to describe the caller?—and retreated into the depths of the house.

Diarmaid waited. It was not a short wait, but in the end it was Lady Anne who came to meet him. Lady Anne—he had last seen her in ripped and torn clothing, her eyes wide with disbelief at what had happened to her. He could still feel the weight and warmth of her on his back when she had been unable to walk farther.

"Diarmaid," she said. She was as she had always been. Beautiful, he'd always thought. Her dark hair was still trying to tumble down from where it had been pinned to the top of her head. Her eyes still cast a spell on him, a startling Irish green with just a thin line of gold around her pupils. She looked very much at home in this house, as was only sensible. How long had she been married now?

He bowed. How long had it been since he'd bowed so respectfully to an Englishwoman?

"Lady Anne."

When he straightened up, she was gazing at him. Closely, but with some curiosity. It was an odd look back to all those years ago, the two of them staring at each other in the gallery.

"Why did you come here?" Well, that was like the Anne back then. She never minced around a problem.

"I needed to ask a favor."

"A favor?" She sounded genuinely surprised.

"I too am married. I have a wife who is increasing, and we expect the babe in December. I have nowhere to keep her while I am here. Would there be any way that she could come to Ballymuir to stay with you?"

"Here?" Her shock was obvious.

Well, it had been a mad errand. He'd known that from the moment he thought of it.

"I know," he said, deciding he might as well approach the problem as he felt it. "It's not very sensible. But I have nowhere for her to stay, and—and she is bearing my child in December. I can find work, but nothing that would supply a place for her to stay. Me mam, over at Kendall House, could find a space for me, but it would be harder to find a place for her to stay awaiting the birth, much less for the birth itself. You and I knew each other once. I thought perhaps if I came to you…"

He ran out of anything to say. They stood facing each other, both captives of the past they had shared. She had been desperately in love with Ireland, he had been just working out the way he could join the struggle for Ireland's freedom, and partly through his mam's misjudgment, Anne had ended in danger. That she had escaped was mostly due to her own bravery and determination to escape, but they had managed to escape together, and the marquess, her husband now, had rescued her in the end.

All water long since over the falls, but was there still a trace of the close attachment—not love, which was just as well—that had existed between them? He had gambled on it.

She sighed, and all of a sudden, like, the closeness they had dared to feel then was back, drawing them to each other.

"What can I tell Hugh?" she asked. Hugh, the marquess. Her husband.

Diarmaid shrugged. "That she is someone in need of your help? God knows that's true enough."

"What's her name?"

"She's Muirne MacGuinness. We are lawfully wedded."

Anne sighed. "I cannot have you living here officially, you know."

He nodded. "I thought as much."

"But I can find a place to put her where you could slip in, if you were careful."

His gratitude was immense. "That will make it much easier for her." He paused for a moment. "She is dear to me," he added.

Anne smiled. "As my husband and my son are to me. Did you know I have a son?"

Diarmaid shook his head.

"Well, I do. He is but five months old now, but a fine bonny lad."

He grinned. "He would be, I'm sure."

She looked at him, the memory of their adventures together clear in her eyes, and said, "I'll talk to Mrs. Brophy, our housekeeper, and find a place for her. Can you bring her here this afternoon? I can make sure she has some dinner, but I'd like to get her settled in her room before my husband is back, noticing all that's going on. He's with his steward now."

Diarmaid nodded. "I thank you."

Anne looked at him and shook her head a little. "An odd pair we are, that's for sure. But you've added richness to my life."

He looked at her, curiously moved by what she'd said. There they were, her English, he Irish, and by rights they should be in opposition. But instead there was an odd friendship between them. Always had been.

Now, because of her kindness, they would be more closely linked with one another than ever before.

29

'TWAS A NICE ROOM. MUIRNE stood in the middle of it, looking around after the Lady Anne had slipped out, leaving her alone. There was a big comfortable bed, with a pretty quilt spread out over it, and another folded and lying on the end, to use if she got cold. Lady Anne had told her that. There were two windows on one wall, and a third on the next—the room was at the corner of the big house on the ground floor, so there was a nice view of bushes and flowers in summer bloom when she looked out. Ballymuir, that was the name of the house. All these grand houses of the English seemed to have names.

Her small bag, with everything she possessed, lay on the bed. Lady Anne, when she took in that Muirne had nothing more, had said something about seeing what she could find around the place that might fit her. Muirne hoped she'd not bring some of her own fine gowns. First of all, Lady Anne was taller and for the second, her clothes were so grand that Muirne'd live in terror that something be torn or spoiled every time she put one on. Now, if one of the servants had an old dress to spare, that might be useful. Specially if the servant be on the fat side, so there'd be room for her belly to grow, as it seemed to be doing now.

That was sort of a relief to Muirne, as she'd begun to wonder if her babe was going to be only the size of her fist when it was born. Now she was less worried, because she could feel the babe move about, and sometimes she could feel it in two places at once, as if it'd stretched out. The places would be more than a fist length apart.

The Lady Anne'd shown her around a bit. There was a door to the outside one room down, and so Diarmaid could slip in there. Seemed it would be more of a problem if people knew he'd be staying there as well.

Muirne didn't quite see why, but she was too awed by the grandness of the place to ask a lot of questions. Where to eat was another hitch. As far as Muirne could tell, there was a big dining room for the family, and then another for the servants. Since she was not one nor t'other, it would be easiest to bring her meals to her room, and she had a nice table and two chairs there. Two, so if Diarmaid was around, he could eat as well.

'Twas all very odd. 'Twasn't as if people weren't to know she was there, because she had a bell to ring if she needed anything—if she was hungry, like, or wanted a bath. She'd have a maid to keep the room tidy for her. And the Lady Anne had said they'd have a horse that Diarmaid could ride back and forth. A horse *and* a saddle, she'd said.

There was even a rocking chair for her to sit in. And when the Lady Anne had found out that she could read, she'd said she'd bring some books for her.

'Twas like she was a princess or something in some old tale where the princess had to be hidden away. Certain it was she was being treated like a princess. When she thought of all the years she'd slept on the straw bed by the side of the peat fire in her da's sod house, she wondered at all the places she'd slept since she and Diarmaid had crept away together. There'd been the inn in the rain—that was a memory to treasure—and all the places they'd slept rough. She would always remember the smell of grass first thing in the morning. Then there'd been Kate and Patrick's house in Galway. She'd gotten to feel at home there, part of the family. And now this, where she wasn't part of anything, but would be living in a sunny, pleasant room with a maid at her beck and call.

What a tale to tell Lizzie in the clachan! If she ever would be there again to tell it.

There was a quiet knock at the door, and she jerked with surprise. Silly goose, she told herself, and went, stepping softly, to open it.

It was Diarmaid.

"She gave a key to me," he explained as he came into the room.

Muirne nodded. "'Twas kind of her," she said, feeling she was expected to say something.

"Will this do?" Diarmaid's voice was anxious as he looked around the room.

She looked at him in amazement. Couldn't he see for himself that she was going to be staying in luxury? "'Tis grand," she said.

"'Tis all I could think of." He still sounded somehow as if he felt he'd done something wrong.

"Just look at it. You know where I came from. I couldn't have

216

dreamed of a place like this." She sat down in the rocking chair and smiled at him.

"I know. But I wanted a place where we could stay, both of us. Like it was when we were walking—only a proper kitchen, like."

"You can be here at night. Lady Anne expects that."

Diarmaid nodded, but sighed at the same time. "Sneaking in like a thief in the night. Well, can't be helped. He has his reasons."

"Who?"

"The marquess. Her husband. She doesn't want him to know that we're here. Well, that I'm here."

Muirne almost said "why?" but then hesitated. Mayhap there were mysteries here she'd be better off not knowing. She'd never had to think about matters so complicated before. In the clachan, it had all been more straightforward. Mebbe because people there worked so hard and got so tired.

"He has no reason to like me. 'Twas because of me that she was captured by rebels and could have—could have been raped or burnt up in a fire." His voice was flat.

"What happened?" Hers was a whisper.

"'Tis a long story, but it came out well. We got out, her whole and me no worse than beat up, and I was about to send for him to come get her when he got there on his great horse." He shook his head, like he was remembering something he'd thought about a lot over the years. "He took her home where she belonged and they married. Right then and there, I heard."

She sat for a moment, fighting the question. No, she had to know.

"Did you love her?"

He shrugged at first and then shook his head. "I thought I did, I s'pose. Did have enough common sense to know 'twould never work—have to give meself credit for that. I was young and so was she. But she was a lady and would never be part of me world. Nor me of hers." He leaned over to take her hands. "I was young and stupid. Knew the word, but not the feeling. This we have is different, like. This is real."

It had to be. She had a babe now, moving around in her belly, and that babe would need to have the two of them. She looked at him, at the face she knew so well now, just the hint of freckles across his nose, the strong jaw, and the bright red hair. Would this babe be red-headed? Would be hard to escape it, she'd think.

Whether 'twas sensible or not, she loved him. Must have been at least the seed of that love from the beginning or she'd not have walked away from everything familiar to go with him into his life. So this room here, and all the complications of love and not-love that came with it, were part of that life.

She lifted her head and smiled at him. "I think this room is grand. And I love you."

He picked her up so that her feet were above the floor and kissed her. And in that kiss she thought for a moment she smelled the fresh grass and the fire boiling up their potatoes and all the past and present were there with them.

Maybe even a bit of the future.

As it had in Galway, time slipped past. As in Galway, she spent little time with Diarmaid. His days were full, but he was not arguing tactics and politics with his uncles and the other men of their shadowy organization. He was out doing the hard labor of farming. He'd come home—well, to Muirne's room in Lady Anne's house—after dark on long summer days. Usually he had eaten something in his mam's kitchen, but there were times when Muirne would ring her bell and ask the maid to bring a plate from the kitchen for him.

Muirne with a maid! She'd get hot with shame, thinking of Lizzie, who was such a good person, with her dirt floor that she swept with such care. Then she'd all of a sudden giggle at the unlikeliness of it, wishing her da could see her being waited upon.

After his supper, as dazed with exhaustion as he had been in Galway, Diarmaid would crawl into the wide bed under the quilts, curl up against Muirne, and drop off to sleep.

In Galway she had filled her days talking with Kate and, sometimes, Rosie, helping with the mending, and practicing her writing. So it was here at Ballymuir as well, only here her companion came to be Lady Anne.

Was it the third day, or maybe the day before that? Whichever day 'twas, Muirne started to say something beginning with "Lady Anne," and Lady Anne sat straight up in her chair and announced that she could not bear this, that Muirne should be stuck using a title that meant nothing to either of them.

Muirne had blinked at her, taken aback.

Lady Anne—or Anne, or whoever she was—promptly apologized.

"I shouldn't have snapped at you," she said. "I should behave more like a lady, even if I don't want the title."

"'Tisn't it right to use it? It be your name, in'nt it?"

"Please don't use it. It makes me feel as if there's some great gap between us. Makes me feel lonely."

Muirne had the sudden impulse to go over and put her arms around Lady—all right, around Anne, then.

"Then when we're alone I'll not use it. But I can't be seemin' ungrateful and disrespectful if there's anyone to hear."

Anne smiled at her and shook her head, but then she was distracted by having to pin the part of her hair that was sliding down one side back where it belonged.

Once she had it back in place, she looked over at Muirne. "How did you ever meet Diarmaid? You're from way up north, aren't you?"

That was the trouble of being in a new place. Everyone wanted to know how you happened to be there, and where you'd been before. For years she'd not needed to explain who she was, or really anything at all. Everyone already knew all about her, and probably all about her mam and da, and theirs as well.

"Donegal," she said. "Up in Ulster, that is."

"What's it like there?"

She was silent for a moment, thinking. What would it be that would first strike someone like Anne—Lady Anne that was—if she went up there?

"'Tis poor."

"Poor? What do you mean by that? The land's poor, or the people are…"

"Both." Muirne tried to look straight at Anne, to tell her as plainly as she could. "The land's not really fit for growing much, and so the people live on the scrapings." How could she go about explainin' life in the clachan to someone who lived with plenty on every side?

"Do people starve then? It was Diarmaid who told me some people starve even here." It must bother her even now. Her face was deeply troubled.

"When times are hard they do. But even when all is as good as it gets, like now, it's—" Muirne's voice stopped dead as she tried to think how to tell her. "Hard," she said. Mebbe if she told her about the food—"like what we eat. I thought that's the way everyone in the world eats. In the morning we have porridge—oat porridge, because oats grow better there than wheat. Wheat's not meant for so far north, or maybe it's being too close to the sea and the salt wind. I don't know." She looked at Anne, who was watching her face intently. "Then for dinner we have potatoes. Boiled. An' some buttermilk. Buttermilk's nice."

"That's all?" For some reason her horrified voice stung Muirne a bit. 'Twasn't as if they'd had much of a choice, and potatoes and buttermilk were better than nothing.

She nodded. "Then there's supper. That's porridge again. Unless we have something special. Kitchen, that's what we call the special things. Diarmaid brought me an egg once. Or I've found fish down at the shore. Or if someone has to slaughter a cow, there's a bit of kitchen for all of us in the clachan. But that's not often."

"But that's horrible!" Anne's voice almost trembled. "That's *all?* Day after day and week after week?"

Muirne shrugged. "It's what's there."

"Has it always been like that?"

Muirne tried to remember what she'd been told. "I'm not sure if it's just old men's tales, but I've heard tell that we used to be farther east. This was back in the days of the Catholic earls, who owned most of the land. But they got mixed up with the English politics—no one's ever explained it all to me. There was a King James? And another king— William, mayhap? Anyhow there was a battle at the Boyne River and the Protestants won, and when the Irish earls left, William and the English gave all the land to Protestants. Brought even more over from Scotland, they did. So the Catholics were pushed west, to what's now Donegal. I've been told they even gave land in Donegal to the Scots and the English Protestants, but it wasn't much good as farming land so they didn't stay. We got it in the end."

"So you're Catholic?"

"Aren't most all the Irish? They are where I come from."

Anne sat silent for a moment. Then she said, "So you scrape a bare living. Is there nothing of value there?"

Muirne sat quiet while she thought. Then she remembered. "Peat bogs. We've fine peat bogs. That was my job. I worked at cutting turf."

"How did you get here?"

Maeve had wanted to know about that, too. Pity she hadn't seen Maeve since she'd come to live at Ballymuir. Seemed she should be getting to know Diarmaid's mother.

Well, that was for another day. She smiled at Anne, and began the story. Again.

"We walked."

"All the way from Ulster? How far was it?"

"We walked to Galway. Diarmaid's uncles live there. I think it's about 300 miles."

"You walked 300 miles?" Anne looked as fascinated as if Muirne had been telling her tales of leprechauns and fairies doing mischief.

Muirne nodded. "'Twas a long way, but that's when we got the chance to really get to know each other."

"I expect you would." Anne was silent for a minute or two, thinking something over by the look on her face. "You know, it was Diarmaid who first told me about how the Irish really live here, and I thought it was terrible. Nobody had ever told me before. But it sounds like the Irish here have it better than your people in Donegal."

Muirne remembered some of the things Diarmaid had told her of what life was like for the ordinary people who didn't live on the great estates and were left to scrape a living however they could. How he had taken food to them from Kendall House.

"Well," she said, "I s'pose starving to death is just about the same whether you do it in Meath or in Donegal. Life's hard for the Irish."

"But my father's fair to his tenants. Even Diarmaid says so."

"That's what he told me, too. That the earl is fair and honest." But she couldn't leave it at that. She had to tell Anne the truth as she knew it. "But not all the landlords are. Diarmaid says many of them live in England and never see their tenants to know if they're starving to death or not. They have men—what do they call them?"

"Middlemen," Anne said, her tone flat.

"An' all they're concerned with is getting the rents. In November it is in Donegal. D'ye know when it is down here?"

"No," Anne said.

They sat in silence for a bit until there was a bit of noise outside Muirne's room. Anne sighed and came to her feet.

"I'd better see what's going on," she said. "Are you all right?"

Muirne grinned at her. "Sittin' in the lap of luxury, as you see. My belly's gettin' bigger, too."

As Anne moved toward the door, it opened and Diarmaid let himself in.

"'Tis early," Muirne said in surprise.

"'Tis," Diarmaid agreed. He bobbed his head to Anne—well, Lady Anne now that there was someone else here.

Lady Anne was suddenly brisk, and the lady of the house again. "Have you had your dinner yet?" she asked.

Diarmaid shook his head.

"I'll get them to send you something special from the kitchen," she said, then turned to Muirne and looked at her with a special light in her eyes. "Some kitchen from the kitchen," she said, and the smile that was trying to break through grew into a grin.

Diarmaid looked back and forth between them, puzzled, which delighted both Anne and Muirne enough so that they were giggling as Anne slipped out into the hall.

He was frowning, still confused, when Muirne went to him and put her arms around his neck, pulling his head down so that she could kiss him and nuzzle her face against his nose.

"It's good you're here," he said.

30

THE DAYS PILED UP, ONE after another. For Diarmaid, it was almost like being thrust backward to the days when he had gone adventuring from Kendall House. Some mornings when he slipped back into the big house—through the secret passage that led out through some of the shrubbery at the back—he almost felt he should go find what had become of the long strips of bed linen he'd used to conceal the food he took from the house, wrapped around his body, to give to those who had none. Well, to start the food on its journey. He'd meet Patrick, who'd take as much as he could carry on his much slimmer boy's body, and make his way to the settlement just off the boundaries of the estate. They'd hide the rest in one of the dry stone walls, for Patrick to pick up on a second trip.

Only now Patrick must be close to grown, and as his mother was a widow with other children, he was most likely making his own way, needing to earn enough money to feed all of them. No, it had been something for Diarmaid to do while he tried to see what was possible in the way of gathering together a band of rebels devoted to harassing the British.

'Twas then he'd learned the futility of such hopeful, pitifully small ventures. First of all was the problem of finding men—boys, really most of them had been, growing their first beards and thinking themselves the raw material of heroes. More than one of them had liked the excitement of battle more than they cared about what happened afterward. Simply liked to fight, they did. He'd taken a bashing or two himself—had handed out more—because they got impatient with his wish to wait until they were stronger. Oh yes, he'd been a fighter himself back then. Hadn't gotten smart enough to figure out that whereas you might beat someone into goin' along with you, he'd stay with you longer if you'd convinced him there was sense in it.

It'd taken the uncles in Galway to teach him that.

The hidden door outside led to a passage goin' straight to the kitchen. Well, 'twasn't all that well-hidden, it seemed. That Lady Anne had somehow sussed out that it existed, and near to gave Maeve a turn of her heart by popping through the door, all unexpected like. Had its purposes even so. During these months when Diarmaid was sleepin' down at Ballymuir and comin' back up to Kendall House to do whatever the steward, John Bowyer, set out for him, the passageway was what kept where he was at any one time vague enough so that no one was full aware of where he'd be.

'Twas better so. Better for his mam, Maeve. Diarmaid had messed up his copybook for the people in the house by Lady Anne's impetuous walk through the night to bring him a key his mam was convinced he needed. Been long enough so that he couldn't remember all the ins and outs of it, but somehow something he must have said made Maeve think he had to have the key then, and she'd entrusted it to Anne, figuring that she, being English and the earl's daughter, would be safer carrying it across country.

Which of course she'd not been. The band of those who liked to think they were dangerous rebels had been with him when Anne found him, and of course they had to take her prisoner. Daft fools. When the self-appointed leader decided to share her around with all the men there, Diarmaid had taken exception and gotten beaten to a bloody pulp. 'Twas only the self possession of Patrick, who'd guided her there, that saved them all. He managed to set a brand afire, and threw it into the straw-filled abandoned barn they called their headquarters. The brave men, o' course, ran off in all directions to save their own skins, and Patrick managed to get the two of them out of there to safety.

Had not been a brilliant success from any viewpoint. Except that the Lady Anne was alive and unmolested, and the marquess had managed to find her—that had been heavenly intervention if any of it had been—and took her home. Only by then 'twas morning, and her family at Kendall House had discovered her missing, and there was hell to pay.

'Twas not hard to understand why for the earl and his family the continued existence of Diarmaid himself was not much of a blessing. 'Twas simply a stroke of good fortune that the earl'd become addicted to the quality of Maeve's cooking, and her relationship to Diarmaid was overlooked.

Seeing the way the wind was blowing, Diarmaid had figured for his mam's sake and everyone else, the big house would be better off without him, and that was when he'd set off to Galway to find the uncles he'd heard of but never met.

The whole adventure showed how the hand of the Good Lord, or mebbe the understanding of the Blessed Mother, had taken everything that'd been part of the unfortunate mess and made of it something good for them all. He'd found his life work with his uncles. Lady Anne had been properly married off and had a fine son now. The more savage members of the "rebel band," as they had called themselves, were removed from the area. Diarmaid hoped that was partly due to the detailed information he'd left behind before he disappeared on the road to Galway. Maeve still organized most of what went on in the big house from her cockpit in the kitchen.

'Twas into that kitchen he popped now, but no one took much notice. Maeve was at the table fussing with something for breakfast—the people in the big house had a lateish breakfast, most of them being up and around for a couple of hours before they had a proper meal. A cup of tea here or there, yes, but the food wasn't set out in the breakfast room for them to help themselves 'til ten or later.

One of the more flirtatious kitchen maids twinkled at him. "Morning, Diarmaid."

He nodded shortly at her. 'Twasn't the kind that would attract him if he was in the frame of mind to be attracted, and things bein' as they were now, the only looks he fancied were those of a woman with barely tamed bright red hair, blue eyes that could cast a spell, and an enormous belly, given her overall size.

Maeve swiveled around to look at him. Had she not heard him come in? "How's Muirne then?"

He shrugged. "Finding it hard to sleep. Says she tastes everything coming up in her throat when she lies down. We've gotten her two or three more pillows, and she sits more than lies."

Maeve nodded. "Getting close, it is."

He was less than certain. If 'twere not the middle of breakfast preparations, he'd pour his mam a cup of tea and try to talk to her about what he should do when it started. It. He had no idea really, of what was to happen, except that a whole baby was going to come out of a very small body, and from a place where there didn't seem to be much space available under any circumstances. He almost wished that when it all began he'd be at the far end of one of the fields and by the time anyone could find him to summon him, the whole business would be over and th' baby born. That'd be his choice.

But Muirne had asked him to keep her company, and so he would. After all, he'd had a part in putting it there, and as she had to do all the work of getting it out, the least he could do was to be there holding her hand. Or whatever else she needed. That was the part that worried him. How was he to know what to do?

What he really wanted was to take his mam by her elbow and take her to her bedroom here, just down the hall, and sit her down and get all the information she knew. She'd had him, had she not? He'd been planning on doing just that for a good time past now, and the chance never seemed to arise, and he had a horrible tense feeling that it never would, and there he'd be, full of love but witless as a worm.

"I'll try to run down to see her today or tomorrow," Maeve said, turning back to whatever she was doing.

"That'd be good." He looked about. "Seen any sight of Mr. Bowyer yet?"

"He be at the stables." That kitchen-maid—Biddy, was she? Half of them seemed to be named Biddy—must've had eyes in the back of her head. Always knew where everyone was. An alarming skill, that.

"Thank ye." He touched his cap and set off down the proper corridor, walking to the back door. Hoped Mr. Bowyer had a lot of work to be done far, far away.

How would she know when it had started? That's what Muirne had asked Anne, over and over again. Anne kept protesting that she could only tell her how it had started for her, and all she had was one experience of it.

One time when they were discussing it, Anne's little boy, Charlie, had been crawling around Muirne's room trying to pick up a dust bunny he'd found under the bed. Anne was horrified, and promised Muirne that her room would be cleaned more thoroughly in future. Then she'd taken the dust bunny from him and thrown it into the basket for waste paper, and Charlie had waited patiently until they were talking intently again and then had crawled over to the basket and carefully retrieved it with his thumb and one finger—Muirne had to admire his expertise, although she didn't point it out to Anne—and then sat down on his fat bottom to inspect it carefully.

Would this babe in her belly be like Charlie someday? Or would he—or she—be like Diarmaid or like herself? It seemed very hard to imagine a babe being like either of them. Red hair she was prepared for, but it was hard to imagine anything else. Well, there were eyes. Hers were blue; his were brown. Which would the babe have? And although Anne often told her that Charlie was very like his father, Muirne couldn't see how a babe, lying in its cradle and unable to move except to kick now and again, could be much like a grown person. She'd think about it in the night, when she was wakeful with the horrid feeling that whatever she'd eaten most recently might suddenly come up to her mouth and out again. She could already taste it a great deal more than she liked. Sitting up helped, but it did little to let her sleep peacefully.

She sat there with the taste of food in her mouth and watched Diarmaid, a lot like a little boy himself, sprawled across his side of the bed and half across hers, deep in sleep. It always reminded her of that time when they had first slept outdoors, and she'd wakened in the morning to find him spread-eagled on the grass.

Ages ago, now. Time had moved slowly in the clachan, where not much changed from day to day, but it seemed to speed forward here. They'd come here when? In July. And somehow August and September had sped past, and October was nearly gone, and then it would be November, and then time for the babe. Anne had brought around a midwife, the one who had helped her when Charlie was born, and she had horrified Muirne by telling her the child was of a good size and might arrive at any time. But he couldn't! She remembered that night in the rain in Donegal town, and that had been the first time. Before then they had slept quite separately.

But she couldn't find the words to tell Anne that, and so Anne had been busy preparing everything she said they needed. She'd found a new nightgown for Muirne to wear afterward, and there were piles of towels and plain cloths standing ready. She'd said Muirne might like some ice, and so had made sure the ice-house was operating as it should. If all were as usual, she told Muirne confidentially, they would just let the water there freeze or not, depending on the weather, as they really only used the ice during the summer. But there would be plenty for Muirne if she fancied some.

Muirne could not imagine why she might.

Finally, even Anne had to agree all was in place, and there was naught to do but wait.

That was the hardest part, because Muirne could no longer ignore what was happening in her body. There was the misery of wakefulness at night. Even when it was not the taste of food disturbing her, the strange foreign object within her seemed unaware of night—well, how could he know it was dark?—and thrashed around with force and energy, and how could a body sleep with that going on? Nor did she have any control over it, and that was almost the strangest part. She could put her hand firmly on her belly trying to hold the babe in one place, and he paid no attention to her at all. He would wriggle away from where she had placed her hand—she could feel him doing it—and once free, go back to whatever kicking or bumping he'd been doing.

Would it be like that when he was out and born? She'd asked Anne that once, and dear patient Anne had looked at her for a moment, opened and closed her mouth a couple of times, and then just plain laughed. And laughed and laughed. Which seemed to be all the answer Muirne was to get.

In the end, it began in the middle of the night in the messiest possible way. Muirne, sitting up, had at last drifted off to sleep, and Diarmaid suddenly woke up, claiming loudly that the bed was wet. As it was. They both got up, and, puzzled, looked at the mess, until Muirne at last remembered that Anne had said something about "breaking of the waters," and maybe that was it.

"Mebbe it's started," she said uncertainly, and just then her whole midsection seemed to tighten up like a fist.

"Oooh!" she gasped.

"Has it?" Diarmaid asked looking at her in a way she'd not seen before.

She nodded.

"I'll go get someone," he said.

Her eyes had been half-closed, waiting for whatever would happen next, but they popped open then. "Not as you are," she told him. He seemed to have forgotten he was bare naked with nothing on him at all.

"Oh," he said, with a bashful grin. He'd been already on the way to the door, but he turned around sharpish and went to grab the clothes he'd worn the day before. In this new grand style of living they'd come to, Muirne thought in passing she should get him a clean shirt and drawers, but just then her whole middle seized up again and what Diarmaid wore lost all importance.

Diarmaid stopped where he was to watch her, as if she were a pot that might boil over.

"Are you all right?"

She shook her head, because she wasn't, and then nodded, because she needed him to get some help and was afraid he wouldn't go if he thought she needed him. She certainly needed someone who knew what was happening. Diarmaid did not seem to be that person.

"Just go," she whispered, and he threw open the door and went barging down the hall, banging against a wall once or twice. Muirne came to her feet and walked carefully over to the door and shut it.

Who would he find? Who was there to find, wandering through the house in the middle of the night? She'd be surprised if there was anybody around at all. Mebbe she'd have to wait until dawn, whenever that was. What was the chance that the babe'd tear her apart trying to get out? Mebbe when Diarmaid came back, she'd be torn and ripped on the floor.

She sat down abruptly on the bed when the tightening began again.

It had happened twice more by the time Diarmaid came running back with one of the kitchen maids, still in her nightclothes.

"Oh dear," she said, clearly not knowing what to do any more than the two of them. "Just a minute. I'll get Miz Brophy."

The housekeeper. Well, if she knew where Miz Brophy was, that was better than what either of them could have done.

"I'll stay with you," Diarmaid promised, and somehow with his arms wrapped around her Muirne felt that maybe she'd manage to get through this one way or another.

"Where did you find her?" Muirne murmured, leaning against him.

"Started bangin' on doors." He smiled at her and kissed her temple. "Thought that would wake someone."

Who had obviously woken others, because there was getting to be a fair old hubbub outside the room. In a minute or two the door opened and an assortment of women came in, some dressed properly and some having tossed whatever was closest at hand over whatever they slept in. Mrs. Brophy was there and so was the kitchen maid they'd begun with, and a bunch of others. To start, Mrs. Brophy sent off one o' them to get clean sheets, and they stripped the bed and made it up dry and proper. Muirne was placed in it with all the tenderness and care she could have asked for, and Diarmaid settled right next to her, but on top of the covers.

The dirty bedclothes were being removed when Anne appeared, in a dressing gown and her hair in a great braid down her back.

"I've sent for the midwife," she said.

Muirne said nothing—her belly was seizing up again—but at least now there would be somebody there who knew what was happening. It was a great relief.

It then settled into a kind of pattern. There would be the dreadful tightening—that part hurt—as if something was rippling up her midsection tighter and tighter until she thought she'd die of it, and then it would gradually, gradually let loose until it started again. But the starts were happening more and more often, and the rest bits were shorter.

Diarmaid held her tightly, his hold getting stronger and stronger as the pain increased, and then he'd relax, too, as she did. She could see the strain of it on his face. Poor man. How would she feel if it was him sufferin' there where she could see it, but do nothing to help? When there was a brief pause after three pains that had come almost in a single agonizing whole, she managed to find Anne's face among all the others.

"Please?" she asked. Please, please, let Anne know what she meant.

She did. She came over to t'other side of the bed, and whispered something to Diarmaid.

He looked surprised, and turned to Muirne.

"Do you want me to stay?"

Muirne shook her head wearily. "I can do the rest meself, with all the women here. You go and get some peace."

"I can stay here."

She shook her head again. "No. Go. This is women's work."

Anne said very clearly, "Ashbourne's in the library with a full bottle of whiskey. You'll do better there with him."

Surprise, resignation, relief—she saw all of them cross Diarmaid's face. Muirne managed a smile and kissed his hand as he let go of her. He came to his feet, still uncertain, and Anne bustled him out of the room before he got the chance to argue further.

Once the door closed behind them, Muirne looked up and met the eyes of the midwife, looking down at her with approval.

The tightening was beginning again. She wouldn't yell now, but if she wanted to, she could. She let the tightening roll up tighter and harder and settled into the work of it.

THE LADY ANNE LED HIM through a warren of corridors, past doors that were mainly closed but when open showed rooms used for storage. Food in some—bags of flour, potatoes, who knew what else. Spare furniture in others: chairs stacked together, tables, rolls of rugs. Hard to imagine how much was there, ready to lay hand on when needed. If needed. And not that far off Irish people living on the edge of starving, with loose straw for their beds on dirt floors and no more'n a stool for sitting. Diarmaid pressed his lips together.

Then up a short flight of stairs—how many levels did Ballymuir have? Down a short passage and through a door, and there they were in the grand part of the house.

Even in the midst of all that was goin' on around him—and now he was out in the rest of the house he could feel he'd been sweatin' as he held Muirne—he couldn't help looking around to see what all was there. He'd never been in a Big House except Kendall House, of course, and whereas 'twas plain Lady Anne was her mother's daughter the way her house was arranged, it was somehow a lighter place. Curtains here were much paler in color and not so heavy as whatever they were at Kendall House.

Of course he had no idea where the library would be, so he kept close to the Lady Anne's heels, doin' his best to keep from swiveling his head to see both directions at once. Now they were slowing down, and he could tell they were near wherever it was they were going, he had a moment or two to think.

'Twas clear the marquess now knew that Muirne, and presumably Diarmaid himself, was in the house, and there'd been no trouble that he'd heard of. Still, let it be said now the only time when he'd be going voluntary like to sit with the marquess—what had the Lady Anne called him? Ashbourne?—would be when the other choice was watching his wife suffer.

They were there. Lady Anne opened the door, and inside the marquess jumped to his feet. He'd been sitting in one of two leather chairs in front of a long narrow window that went from the ceiling to the floor. 'Twas a little table between them, with one o' those squarish glass bottles etched with fine patterns, well filled with whiskey, and a little glass, patterned like the bottle. There must have been two to begin with, because the marquess had the other one in his hand.

"MacGuinness," the marquess said and bowed his head.

Startled, Diarmaid managed a full bow, or as close as he could come, given that no one had ever taught him how to do it at all. "My lord."

The marquess smiled, not at all a mocking smile. "Come now, we don't need formality here. Have a seat. Would you care for a whiskey?"

"Yes, sir." Diarmaid spoke with deep honesty.

"If you're both settled, I'll leave you here," Lady Anne said. Diarmaid looked round with some surprise. He'd figured she would have left and returned to Muirne as soon as he'd gone into the room. But she disappeared now.

The marquess sat down in one chair, motioned to the other, and poured a generous amount into the glass. Handing it to Diarmaid, he lifted his own glass slightly and said, "May all go well."

Diarmaid would have known what to say had he been in a pub, but this encounter was out of his range of experience. "Yes, sir," he said. He sipped at his drink. He would have taken a comforting swallow, but this marquess fellow had more 'n likely heard little enough good about him, and there was no need to lead him to thinking he was a drunkard as well.

"How was it going?" the marquess asked.

Diarmaid shrugged. "Don't know. Never been around a birthing before. Muirne—me wife—was in pain. I could tell that. Not pretty to watch, it's not."

The marquess drank a bit of his whiskey, nodding his head. "It's not," he said. "I knew nothing about it either. Men don't, do we? It's not until our wives are giving birth that we find out anything, and that makes it too late for us to do much except get out of the way."

So there were some times when it didn't matter how much gold a man had. 'Cept it was sure easier to wait in a nice room like this one w' a glass in your hand than standing in a house w' a dirt floor and the wind whistling in through the cracks by the door.

Although you might have some poteen in your mug instead, and Donegal poteen, made of barley and distilled in a copper still, took a lot of matching.

"So my wife tells me you've been in Galway," the marquess said.

Diarmaid took an assessing look at him. Was this just pleasantry, or was there some purpose in his talk?

"I have been," he answered as pleasantly as if it didn't matter. "Me uncles are there."

"What's Galway like? I've never been that far west."

Had he not? But then Diarmaid remembered that he'd just come to Ireland about the time he'd been surprised by Lady Anne in the gallery. Or perhaps he should say they'd surprised each other.

"Windier, I'd say. Comes howling over the Atlantic, it does."

"I suppose it must do." The marquess sipped again at his whiskey. "My wife tells me you're the one who taught her almost all she knows about Ireland."

"I doubt that." He kept his tone careful. This ground could go marshy on him at any moment. "She'd been in Ireland her whole life."

"But she didn't know about it, she says, and from what I've observed, the English here don't go out of their way to learn about the Irish and the way they live here."

The truth pressed against his lips, coaxing him to speak. P'rhaps, if he stayed careful...

"S'not so much that they don't try to learn as that they choose not to even open their eyes and look," he said. "Starvin' children don't add nice color to the English garden plantings."

More than knowing he had it, he could just about feel the marquess's startled attention, and inside his head, muttered to himself, "Ye trying to make sure the hangman's noose will fit? An' what'll Muirne and the babe do then?"

"It's as bad as that?" The marquess sounded shaken.

"Better here than many places. The want in Donegal was new to me."

"You've been there?"

"That's where Muirne comes from." Step away, you fool, his brain warned him. Your tongue will get you into more trouble than knowing fine folks can get you out of.

"What is it like there?"

He scrubbed through his mind. "Bare mountains. There's many hills and small villages, only they call them clachans. More peat bogs and rocks than land for growing much, and what soil there is not as fruitful as down here. Just to look at I guess it's beautiful, but it's a hard place to make a living." He thought for a moment, and then added, "To try to make a living."

The marquess frowned. "Why do the people stay there, then?"

Diarmaid did his damndest not to sigh. Seemed a nice enough man, this marquess, but the English were all alike. Had no idea of what real life in Ireland was like.

"Where else to go? Being Catholic, they got pushed west by the plantations. They tried to give some of that western land as well to the Scots and English, but they didn't stay. Couldn't make a living on it. 'Twas only the Irish who had nowhere else to go who stuck there. They're still there."

"Why didn't I ever know of all this?" The marquess sounded like he really was looking for an answer.

"'Twas a triumph, wasn't it? Battle of the Boyne and all that. That's when the English and their Scots allies won for all time. Ye must have heard of that."

"That was more than a hundred years ago!" 'Twas bewildered the marquess was, more than angry.

"Where there's winners, there's losers. Ye were the winners. We who were born and raised in this green and beautiful land were the losers. Still are." And when will ye learn to keep your mouth shut and what you believe to yourself? Diarmaid drank the rest of the whiskey in one swift swallow. Mebbe if this chat came back to haunt him he could claim he was drunk at the time. P'rhaps they'd even believe it, given that his wife giving birth at the time.

His wife! What was happening with Muirne? He almost came up to his feet. "Me wife…"

The marquess smiled at him, and gestured for him to sit. "They'll come to let us know when there's news." Without asking, he took the etched bottle and re-filled Diarmaid's glass. "Take this and settle back."

"'Tis hard to wait." Diarmaid allowed himself a small sigh.

"It is indeed. English or Irish," the marquess said, a smile flirting around his mouth.

Well, and who would have believed this? Here he sat, being treated like he was English and rich himself in a Big House. How had such a thing ever happened? Less comfortably, what would his people in Connemara and the clachan in Inishowen think of him now? Would they have the sense to know it was not every day he had the chance to talk to one of the English—and an English estate owner, no less—about what it was like to be mastered in your own land?

So when his babe was born—pray God it be soon—what sort of world would he have? Or what would her life be like should it be a girl? Dear God, how was he to know how to raise a girl?

The time was coming close when he would have to look at what he'd chosen not to look at ever since he'd known Muirne was pregnant. What were the two of them to do with a baby? What'd he been doing the last year or so? Been going from place to place, sleeping where he found a flat spot, inside or outside. Working with the commonest of men, talking and persuading them to move from their places of safety to the edge of danger. And then to find Muirne, who could do that with him, had been the best part. He knew she would. Three hundred miles she'd walked with him, and when he thought of it, it'd been the best part of his life.

But with a baby? 'Twasn't possible. Remember that day when it had rained the whole day? What would they have done with a bairn? They were out in the middle of nowhere. How could they keep a babe safe when something like that happened?

He and Muirne would have to talk. Mebbe they'd need be like the uncles, who'd left their families to fend for themselves for months at a time, while they'd done the travel that now they'd turned over to him. Would Muirne do that? Stay at home with the wives?

It made his head ache. How'd he ever been stupid enough to let her into his heart and his life so there'd be a great gaping hole if she were not with him? But how could she be with him if there were a babe to shelter and care for?

"Every hour lasts like two."

It was a voice bursting suddenly into his mess of thoughts and took him a minute to know who 'twas. Oh, yes. The marquess, no less. Fine guest he was turnin' out to be. Here this Englishman was, trying to do him a kindness, and his thoughts were scramblin' all over the place. And not one o' them could he share.

"That it does," he muttered. His glass had gone dry somehow, and the marquess was lifting the sparkling glass bottle again. To his own surprise, Diarmaid put his hand over the glass.

"Thank ye," he said. "'Tis not the time for me mind to be fuddled."

The marquess lifted one eyebrow and smiled. "I found it helped."

Perhaps he'd had too much already, because all of a sudden like it came to him that the titled Englishman sitting there with him—the one with Irish tenant farmers, who worked on the land their ancestors had tilled but he owned now and they paid him rent for the privilege of doing his labor—*this* Englishman was a good man, one who cared about the people around him.

Did he know that Diarmaid had promised not only himself but all the men he worked with to give his life to the cause of dispossessing this good man of the property he was tending with care and fairness? Did Diarmaid himself care that this good man did not know, had never been told, the price his Irish tenants—and Irishmen all up and down this beautiful, green land—paid for the comfortable life he lived here?

He most likely would have groaned aloud except that just then there was a sound on the far side of the door and it was thrown open. Lady Anne, still in some loose dress with her thick hair in a braid down her back, stood there with a smile as big as her face could manage.

"Diarmaid! You have a son!"

He would not have been astonished if his knees had failed to hold him as he struggled upright.

"And Muirne?" He had to know.

"She's fine. Tired, but wants to see you now."

The marquess extended his hand and gave Diarmaid a hearty handshake. "Congratulations to you both."

"Thank you, sir," he said, still convinced that somehow his feet were floating some distance above the floor. Was that what good whiskey did, or was it relief, or was it just what happened to a man who'd had a son a few minutes before?

"Come along," Lady Anne told him. "She's waiting for you."

Diarmaid followed stupidly along behind her. The distance from the library to Muirne's room had seemed long enough on the way there. It had doubled now, for no reason he could explain. But after endless walking they were in the corridor leading to her room—he could see the door to the outside just beyond, so familiar to him now.

The Lady Anne moved out of the way so that he could take the door handle in his own hand. He looked over his shoulder at her, still half muddled by what all was happening.

"Go ahead. Go on in," she said, and her smile was near as wide as it had been before.

The handle was cold to his hand, but he pressed it down and the door opened. There was the bed he'd shared with Muirne. She was sitting in it now, looking all fresh in a white nightgown with lavish lace around her shoulders—he'd never seen her wearing anything like it before.

But all that he took in with a glance. What he saw next and could not look away from was the babe wrapped in a blanket in her arms. His son, a wondrous pink color and with a great mass of what looked like black hair on his head.

"Diarmaid, your son," Muirne said in a voice as soft as a whisper that nevertheless went straight to his heart. When he remained frozen there by the door, she smiled at him and said, "Come see him, me love."

Was there anyone else in the room? He would never know. He walked straight to Muirne, and sat down on the edge of the bed nearest her. Her eyes looked tired, but she was as beautiful as he'd ever seen her.

"Are ye all right?" He had to know that.

"Proud," she said and the smile turned into a grin. "I did know how to do it, you see?"

He nodded slowly. "Did it well, too."

"He's perfect," she said, and started to unwrap him. Someone—so there *was* someone else there—came forward in protest, and Muirne waved her away. "Room's warm," she said. "Diarmaid needs to see."

Then the blanket was open and there was this wee babe on it, kicking. Did he not like the cooler air? But Muirne had fished out his tiny hands and was counting the fingers. Five on each hand, just as they should be— but so small, so fragile looking. And his ears—he had two. Then she pulled off the wee socks from his feet: ten tiny toes, looking more like beads.

"Wrap him back up, love," Diarmaid said. "Like you said, he's perfect." He was relieved when the socks were back on the babe's feet and the blanket wrapped round him again. He did not like the feeling that his son might be cold.

"What shall we call him?" Muirne looked up at his face. "You'd not say before."

"Had to see what he was, didn't we? What if we'd decided to name him Deidre?"

She shook her head. "Silly," she said but the love was rich in her voice.

"He's Dubhán." Diarmaid's voice was firm.

"Dubhán?" Muire asked.

"For sure. Means dark-haired, and 'twas me da's name. His hair was black, too."

Muire bent over to kiss his head. Now the babe was wrapped again, he'd settled and looked likely to fall asleep. "My Dubhán boy," she said, cuddling him in her arms.

"I didn't look at his eyes!" Diarmaid protested, as small Dubhán's eyelids slid down. "What color be they?"

Muirne ran her fingers through the baby's hair. Dark 'twas indeed, and a lot of it, all standing straight up, soft as it was. "Blue," she whispered, as if her voice might disturb him.

Diarmaid smiled. "That's good. It's fair wonderful to look in your eyes, and when I look at him, I'll see you."

Muirne said nothing, but just looked at him, his son in her arms, and Diarmaid knew his heart, for the very first time, was all the way full to overflowing.

32

HE WAS SO SOFT. SO fragile. Not connected together the way people—even children—seemed to be. His arms, not to mention his head, seemed to be only loosely joined.

Diarmaid had gone to sleep. He'd said, almost as if he was begging her pardon, that the day had near done him in. But Dubhán seemed ready to spend some time looking about at this new world he'd slid into, whether he meant to or not, and Muirne had taken him out of his cradle by her side of the bed, and laid him on her lap.

How could she love him so much already?

There he was, not a day old yet, unless you counted the hours before he was born when she and Diarmaid'd been working on it in the middle of the night, neither of them having the barest idea what they were supposed to do. Almost comic, that, looking back at it. Like so many other parts o' life, not comic at all at the time.

So when had she fallen in love with this small new person, then? Was it when he came slipping out of her body, as she gave one last great groan of effort? Didn't remember that clear enough to know, but most likely not. But when they'd taken him away, so as to clean him up a bit and clean her, too, for both of them needed it, it felt like they'd walked off with an arm of hers, or a leg. So had she loved him then?

Seemed likely. And she would never, ever let him go.

Which faced her with an ugly thought. Had her mam loved her then, when she'd been lying in her arms just after birth? If she had, why had she stopped? Did that mean someday she, Muirne, would be capable of walking past her child's arms the way her mam had walked past hers, time and time again? How had the change come over her—little by little over the days, or all at once, and if all at once, how'd that happened?

'Course, could have been the poteen. Her da had few other virtues, but he made fine poteen. Everyone said so. Her mam had been unsteady on her feet, that Muirne remembered. Unsteady on her feet and paid only enough attention to her bairn to make sure she'd not starve to death and had something in the way of clothes on her body. And to wobble past the child when she reached out for her. That be a memory of Muirne's, too.

They'd found her dead body at the bottom of a pile of stones, someone told Muirne once. Had she been up hunting the copper still where Muirne's da was making the fine poteen and missed her step? Muirne didn't know and it didn't matter. She'd still been a child then, but old enough to make porridge and boil potatoes and that was all that her da needed.

It was only now, with her own small Dubhán on her lap, that Muirne wished she could reach through the years and try to figure out her mam's thinking. When had it changed? Or had she just stuck her new bairn in a cradle—or a box?—and left it there? Had the feel of her child sucklin' at her breast meant naught to her?

'Twas most likely impossible ever to know. But for sure she'd learned one thing from the woman. She'd never allow so much as the poteen on the tip of a finger near her lips. Good it may have been, from all she'd been told, but it had been the ruin of two people's lives and most likely a good many others as well.

Dubhán, warm wrapped in his blanket, turned his eyes from the candle—the light had drawn his gaze—and looked up at his mother. His eyes were indeed a deep blue and for a moment she thought she saw the world in them. As would he.

What would his world be?

His eyes gradually shut. He'd thought he wanted feeding, so she'd tried to feed him, but he'd not taken much. The midwife'd told her he most likely wouldn't, that it'd take a day or two for him to find his appetite, which gave her body time to make his milk. Seemed funny to think the two of them were still so linked.

Odd. Was her body empty without him now? She lifted him with gentleness she'd not known she had and put him back in his cradle. It barely moved, so she touched the end to encourage it to a gentle rocking, and lay down on her side, watching him for the minute or two before she blew out the candle.

That was the end of the first day. Or so she thought.

Didn't know until some later that Dubhán didn't yet know it stayed dark all night and other people slept. He woke up to see what was going on two times more. He did not really want to nurse, and Muirne found herself short of energy and patience to deal with this stubborn small person who stopped wailing as soon as she lighted the candle and picked him up. What he wanted she had no idea. Once she had him in her arms he was happy just to look at her. At least she hoped he was happy. She didn't know when he could smile, but for sure it wouldn't be yet. But when she put him to her breast he turned his head away and looked at the candle.

She was staring at him wondering what to do with him when Diarmaid roused.

"Is 'e hungry?" His voice was thick with sleep.

"Don't think so." She pulled closed the nightdress Anne had loaned her, and Dubhán followed the movement and settled back to staring at her. "I tried to feed him and he didn't want it."

"What does he want?"

For no good reason Muirne was close to tears. "I don't know."

"Ah, there, a ghrá." With a great heave that shook the bed—Muirne hastily tightened her hold on her son—Diarmaid managed to get sitting up. His hair was wild around his head and he looked like he'd been deeply asleep. "Give 'im to me."

"What can you do for him?" She still sounded tearful.

He smiled at her, even though the smile was crooked. "As long as he's not wanting feeding, I can do all for him you can."

"That's true enough," she admitted.

"This the first time he's been up?"

She shook her head.

"Then I'll come around t' where you are, and you just move over here. Mebbe you can get a bit of sleep and I'll have a talk w' him."

She couldn't but smile at that, and Diarmaid took Dubhán in his arms and she wriggled across the bed. The pillow smelled of Diarmaid as she nuzzled into it. For the moment before she slid into sleep she thought everything in her life was finally coming straight.

When he woke at the usual time, or close to it, Diarmaid wished for a moment he could roll over and pick up more of the sleep he could feel was missing, but the force of habit was strong, and he eased out of the bed—Muirne was still sleeping, and so was the bairn—and put on his clothes as silently as he could.

Riding his horse back over to Kendall House, he was more than usual like grateful for the loan of it. 'Twould have been a long walk to get there today, though he'd walked it, or distances like it, in the past without a thought. Went straight to the stable, where by the grace of God a stable boy was free and said he'd take care o' the horse for him, although he didn't need to do that. Another day Diarmaid would've liked the looseness in his shoulders and arms from dealing with the saddle and brushing the horse's coat 'til it shone, but not today.

'Twas enough effort just walking out to find John Bowyer, and get stuck into whatever it would be he'd be doing that day.

Found him easy enough. He was still close in to the house.

"Hear congratulations are in order," John Bowyer said.

Diarmaid nodded, feeling the proud grin spreading across his face.

"How're they doing?"

Diarmaid pursed his lips for a moment. "Fine, it seems, but the bairn don't know about sleeping at night yet."

John Bowyer laughed. Well he might. It took doing a night like the last one to understand why a new mam or da might look drowsy like.

"Come w' me," he said. "My office's just here. I wanted a word with you."

He led him to a large timber hut, built alongside the stable, and brought him in. There was a desk and chair there and a big table with papers spread over it, and another chair set opposite the desk. John Bowyer motioned for Diarmaid to sit there.

"There's a tenant cottage come vacant," he said. "One o' the new ones. Nice, with a piece of good land attached that'd feed you and your family well."

Diarmaid felt something like a great weight descend on his shoulders. So here it was. The time to make his choice. "I see," he said, because he did.

"Do you want to talk it over with your wife?"

Diarmaid nodded, dumbly. In one way his mind said no, because whatever was decided would set the pattern for what their life would be. In another way yes, because they had to choose, and it seemed the moment for choice was thrust upon them.

"Now?" John Bowyer asked. "If you want to go talk with her, you may."

Diarmaid shook his head. "Can't, now. She was kept up most o' the night." Which may have been true, but was not the reason. He had to get straight in his own mind what he could live with, what he could bear to give up.

John Bowyer grinned, and nodded. "Where were you working yesterday—no, I guess the day before?"

Diarmaid dragged it out of his memory. "There's more to do there," he said, because there was, and the doing of it required the strength of his back and shoulders, not his attention.

"Then do it."

'Twas far enough distant that he could have taken the horse, but he chose to walk. Walk and think.

So the choice was there. 'Twas possible to stay here, on the earl's estate. The earl and his steward, John Bowyer, were fair, both o' them. The house'd be a good one, and he'd know the land, what he farmed himself, would be good soil. Better than anything Inishowen way, and that for certain. His mam would be close if Muirne needed anything with the bairn—no, Dubhán. He had a name, now.

But could he continue to work for Ireland's freedom? No. All he could do would be to send money—what extra he might have—to his uncles, to help with their work. And cold fact was tenant farmers were less'n likely to get rich, so not enough money to be much help.

True, lookin' at it w' a cold eye, was it likely that whatever he did for the freedom of Ireland, would he see that freedom happen in his lifetime? Was he willin' to throw all else away—a home, a family, his own first son—to keep scrabbling in small ways for the independence of this land he loved with every fiber of his being to come someday? Even if 'twould only be Dubhán's son's son who might ever seen it happen?

He'd made up his mind it didn't matter before. Did it now?

But say it did not. Say that he turned his back on the tenant cottage and went back on the road. Where'd Muirne be? Dubhán? 'Twere it just Muirne, the two of them could manage, in a way. Oh, p'rhaps choosing an inn oftener than they'd done coming from Donegal to Galway, but sleepin' rough most o' the time. When they got to where they were going, find somewhere no one else was usin' to serve as a place to sleep, as he'd done in the clachan. There'd always be somethin' wrong w' it, like the roof coming down on his place there, but 'twas surprising what ye could live with. Could Muirne live w' that?

'Course she could. But that wasn't the question. Could Dubhán? 'Course not. A babe needed warmth, and shelter, and a place to learn to walk about that was safe. Could he promise any of that if they were travellin'? No. 'Course not.

Mayhap they could leave him somewhere safe. Promise to come back soon as they could. How long had he been in Connemara? A year, or a bit more. Could they leave Dubhán for a year, and come back to get him? Could he? Didn't know. Caught him in the gut somehow to think it.

Muirne?

Never. He didn't need to ask her to know. So it came down to that. Him staying with them, leaving Ireland to get on as she might, or him choosing to do whatever he could for his country, and letting Muirne and Dubhán get along as they could.

He'd not expected this boiling anger, this feelin' he was being torn bone from bone. The work he'd been given was hard work, clearing out a field that had been left fallow, and the soil was good enough so that all manner of unwanted weeds and plants had taken over. To clear them out was almost more than he would've thought he had strength or the will to do, but he attacked it with all the power of his anger and misery, and when he stopped, the field was clear.

He made his way back, still seething. Would have walked to Ballymuir to burn off more of his temper, but remembered he'd need to get back in the morning, and wasn't sure when this wild strength would leave him. Rode th'unfortunate animal home at a gallop, and then spent more'n an hour wiping him down, feeding 'im, and settlin' him for the night.

Then, spent, he walked to the house, hopin' he'd not terrify his wife and child.

It'd been a quiet day for Dubhán MacGuinness on his second day on earth. He and his mam spent the whole day together, although Anne had come in to keep Muirne company for most of it. She sat in the rocking chair, doing needlework or some such, while Charlie played at her feet with the bag of toys she'd brought along. He was almost as interested in the bag as what was in it, and the game of taking toys out and putting them back seemed to occupy him for hours.

Muirne sat on the bed next to Duhán in his cradle, glad of the chance to rest.

"I think you have another visitor," Anne said, looking out the window.

Muirne looked up, surprised, just as there was a knock on the door. "You can come in," she called out.

The door opened, and it was Maeve, still with her apron on from the kitchen, but she'd thrown a cloak over her shoulders.

"So this is him," she said, coming straight to the cradle.

He was asleep, but Muirne picked him up anyway and handed him to his grandmother. Maeve shrugged off her cloak—Anne caught it, and folded it over the back of her chair—and stood there, looking down at him in her arms.

"What's 'is name?" she asked.

"Dubhán," Muirne said.

Maeve glanced up at Muirne, and murmured, "His grand-da's name." She sat back on the end of the bed, still watching the baby, rousing now that he was out of the cradle. He must have opened his eyes, because Maeve made a cooing noise at him, and looked over at Muirne.

"He's got your blue eyes," she said.

"For now. The midwife told me they might change. Were Diarmaid's eyes brown at first?"

Maeve smiled, a little sadly. "Would ye believe I don't remember? You think it's all burned into your mind and you'll never forget. But you do. Do you know how to write?"

Muirne nodded.

"I learned a bit, later, but didn't think to put anything like that down. Write it down now, me daughter. You'll be glad you did when you're scrubbing your memory and can't find what you want." She picked up one of his curled hands, and let it lie in her palm for a moment. "I do remember his hands, right from the beginning. This little Dubhán has Diarmaid's hands."

Muirne, who'd been sitting propped up against the head of the bed, leaned forward to see. "Yes! They are." She could hear the joy in her own voice. "I hadn't thought of that."

"Bit smaller," Maeve said, smiling as well. "But as I remember them. Only now he's got a scar on the back of the right 'un where he fell off the roof."

Muirne gasped, just a little. "When was that?"

"He was seven years old, eight—something like that."

"How'd he get to the roof?"

"Might as well ask the wind," Maeve said. "He'd ne'er admit he'd climbed up there. Just stood there bitin' his lip so he'd not cry with a big slash acrost his hand."

Muirne nodded. Sounded like him. She'd asked him about the scar once, and he'd dismissed it as nothing much, happened years ago. Would her Dubhán climb up to roofs and then not admit it nor say when he was hurt? Seemed likely. She looked at Maeve and wondered how a mother could bear it. Bear it and go on caring and knowing e'en worse things might happen.

"How'd he fall off the roof and get nothin' worse than a cut on his hand?"

Maeve shrugged. "The angels must've protected him. God knows I prayed to them often enough."

Anne giggled and put her hand over her mouth. "Do you mean my Charlie might try things like that, too?"

Maeve looked over at her with a long affection written all over her face. Muirne watched them, remembering Anne telling her how as a child she'd run truant down to the kitchen to listen to Maeve's tales. "Course he'll be a gentleman," Maeve said. "Haven't been around a lot of those when they're small."

"Much the same, I'd think," Anne put in. Muirne looked back and forth between her and Maeve. Maeve was right, of course. Anne's Charlie and her Dubhán'd be walking separate paths right from the beginning. As would she and Anne as soon as Diarmaid decided when they were to go. This was just a golden peaceful time they had together— nothing that would last.

But there was still the warmth between Anne and Maeve. So p'rhaps something might remain.

Maeve couldn't stay much longer. There was dinner to prepare, and she needed to be in her kitchen. Seemed Anne had sent the carriage for her, and it was waiting to take her back now.

Maeve handed Dubhán back reluctantly, and kissed Muirne's cheek.

"Get word to me if there's aught you need from me," she said, running her hand over the babe in her arms.

Muirne nodded. How did there come to be tears in her eyes?

Maeve nodded to Anne as well, and then quickly walked out of the room, through the back door Diarmaid used, most likely, to get the carriage and go back to her life, so separate from Muirne and Diarmaid's. And Dubhán's too, of course. Muirne tried to cast out the resentment in her heart. How was it that Anne's mother, the countess, was able to see as much as she wanted of her grandson, and Maeve had to work in her kitchen and so could not?

But she still had Dubhán in her arms, and he looked willing enough to sleep more, so she laid him back in the cradle.

Charlie was less accommodating. He'd lost interest in the bag or his toys, or even the bits of who-knew-what from the rug he was trying to pick up. Fast as he got them, of course, Anne leaned over and took 'em away. 'Twas hard to know how much of this he'd go along with, but he knew and when he'd had enough started a high-pitched screech.

"Goodness!" Anne said and snatched him up. "I think it's time to feed him or something. Will Diarmaid be here for dinner?"

"Don't know," Muirne said. "S'pose it depends on what he's doing."

Anne hesitated at the door, her bag and the toy bag in one hand and Charlie hanging over her other arm. "Well, it's not as if we lack the food. I will ask them to send enough for two. If he has eaten already, send it back."

"I'll do that," Muirne said, but as she watched Anne out of the door and saw it close behind her, there were few she could think of who could deal with food so careless, like. No wonder Diarmaid could take so much of it to share out w' those who had none. What were they doin', now that he wasn't bringing the extra from the Big House?

'Twas hard, sometimes, to stand with one foot in each o' two worlds.

33

WHEN DIARMAID CAME IN, MUIRNE had just picked up her dinner tray and had it in her hands to put it outside the door. That way Dubhán would not be disturbed by someone coming in to take it back to the kitchen.

She stopped where she was. "There's dinner for you here," she said.

Diarmaid looked at her. The fury of emotion he'd felt all day had most all left him, and in its place was a deep, deep tiredness. But they had to talk, and they had to talk now.

He sank down heavily at the foot of the bed, and took the tray she handed him. The last thing he wanted just then was food, and yet if he had to choose between talking and eating—and right now he did—he'd eat.

"Your mam was here today."

He looked up at her for a moment and nodded.

"Did you see her?"

He shook his head.

"She couldn't remember if your eyes were brown at the beginning, but she said his hands are like yours."

Diarmaid lifted one hand, the one without the fork, and looked at it for a moment, managing a smile. "Did she?"

"She did. And she told me you got that scar falling off the roof."

He glanced at the back of his hand and nodded again.

"It was good to see her." Oddly, to his ears Muirne sounded a bit anxious.

He set down his fork on the plate and ran his hand over his face. "We could live here, close to her, if you want."

What alarmed her? She moved back, away from him suddenly. She might've been a terrified bird. She sank down on the edge of the rocking chair, those frightened eyes staring at him.

"What do you mean?"

"John Bowyer told me today there's a tenant cottage we could have."

"But if we did that, how would you work for the cause?"

"I couldn't. Well, not the same. But we'd be here and together."

Her hands were over her chest, clasped. She shook her head, dropping her hands. "You'd hate that. You'd not forgive yourself for giving up."

"But we have a bairn now. How can we wander about the countryside with a babe?"

"Dubhán. He's got a name."

He nodded. "Dubhán. But he needs somewhere safe, and warm, and dry. He needs to be with you." He made an attempt at a smile. "I need to be with you."

"But to give it up—it would kill you."

He tried to shrug. "Mebbe I could do bits and pieces for me uncles."

She jumped to her feet, leaning into his face. "Bits and pieces? 'Twould destroy you, Diarmaid MacGuinness, from the inside out. And I'd have to watch it. Never. Never."

He felt his own temper beginning to rise again.

"What would you want me to do? At least I'd be with him 'n you." He ran his hand through his hair. "How could I do more than bits and pieces livin' here? You want me to try to gather people together, *here*, to overthrow the earl and Lady Anne's husband? You know as well as I do those two are about the fairest and most careful of the English. They give a thought to the Irish working for them—even the Irish living near them. May sweet Mary bless them, they reach a hand out to me, who between me and my mam came damn close to getting the Lady Anne raped and God knows what else. You think John Bowyer didn't talk it over with the earl, about givin' me the tenant cottage? An' Anne's given you food and a fine room for you to stay in and taken care o' you when the babe— when Dubhán came. And the marquess, who had to rescue her from the folly of me and my mam, wasn't it he stayin' wit' me while Dubhán was being birthed and I was half mad with worry? You want I should live on their land and betray them?"

His voice had risen louder, and she glanced, nervous-like, at the door.

"No," she whispered. "No. No."

"Well then." He picked up the tray and went to the door with it, glancing around the space outside as he set it down on the floor. The saints, with their mercy, had blessed him again: there was no one within sight. Or within hearing, please God.

He came back inside, shutting the door firmly.

She was standing there, pale as the sheets of the bed. "It's Dubhán who's the trouble, in'it?"

He shook his head wearily, making a meaningless sweep of his hand.

"I'll ask Anne, if she'll take 'im."

"What?" The word escaped as a great roar.

"If'n it's just me, I can go anywhere with you. I don't mind if it's wet or cold or we sleep outside or within. May need a new pair of shoes from time to time"—she made a weak attempt at a grin—"but otherwise I'm fine. An' mebbe from time to time we can come to Meath and visit 'im."

"Are you crazy?" Was he goin' mad himself?

"Don't yell so. You'll wake 'im up and half the house with 'im." She gave a casual glance into the cradle, as if it didn't matter, and looked away.

She'd been standing. Now she sat down on the rocking chair, on the edge of it, so that it didn't rock and her back was as straight as the wall behind her. "Wit' the two of us working as hard as we can, mebbe we can get Ireland to freedom that bit sooner."

He shook his head, but instead of stopping after the first back and forth, he kept moving it from side to side, side to side. "It'd kill you."

She shrugged, but when she looked at him there was something dead in her eyes. "I don't know. Mebbe I'm as bad as me mam. She was a terrible mother. I know she never loved me, but I don't think she liked me much, either. Might be something in the blood. P'rhaps Anne would be a lot better at it. She does a good job with Charlie."

"Muirne—don't. You're killing me."

"O' course, with me mam it was the poteen." She was going on as if they were talking about how many potatoes to cook, or whether she should carry the shawl in her bag rather than his. "But there must've been something inside what went wrong, don't you think? Mebbe the same thing'll happen to me. But the earl's lady is fine, and so will Anne be. It'd be better for the bairn."

"*Dubhán.*"

"Dubhán, then."

"And so we go off and what if there's another?'

Her mouth tightened. "There won't be. I'll make sure."

His world—his world that had been so whole such a short time ago had become nothing but random sticks and brambles. And how had Muirne, his love and his treasure, disappeared into this blank-eyed stranger, and how was he to coax her to come back?

"My love, my own—leave it with me. I'll find a way." He was begging her. How was there no blood on the floor? Seemed to him there ought to be about a pint of his own already.

But what was Muirne doing?

She was standing up again, up from the rocking chair, and pulling some sort of silky thing over her shoulders, still with that dead, dazed look in her eyes.

"I'll go talk to Anne now."

He grabbed at her, managed to catch her hand. "Muirne, what are you thinking? It's evening. They may have gone to bed."

She shook her head. "Not this early. Better to get it settled now, so I can get used to it."

"Where did you get the crazy idea you could just give away my son?"

She turned her head, slowly, awkwardly, to look at him. Her lips were trembling. "But don't you see? 'Twill break my heart to lose you, and if I have to watch you bein' all hollowed out on account o' tryin' to hide what's most important to you, I'll have killed you, and that'll kill me. Dubhán is new. He doesn't know me yet, nor you. Anne will love him, I promise you she will. I'll ask her now."

He was still in his working clothes, and the shirt that had been wet with his sweat was damp and cold against his skin. There was times when that might matter, but not now. "If you're goin' to talk to her now, I'm comin' with you"

She shook her head. "You're being daft, you are. If you're there, how do I explain how we can't stay here? Well, you see, Diarmaid is gettin' together bands of rebels to start the war for Ireland's freedom, and so we can't stay here. He has to go from place to place to gather his rebel fighters. But we can't take Dubhán, so we need to leave him with you. Can't tell 'em *that*. You'd wind up in gaol or hung, more likely."

He started to ask what the hell she was going to tell the Lady Anne that would be different, and then he wiped it all away with his hands in front of him.

"And does whatever crazy story you're going to tell make better sense?"

Her shoulders drooped, and she started to weep. More'n just a tear here and there. Great gulping sobs and she shook all over and her nose set to running.

Her sobs were so loud that Dubhán in his sleep roused and started to cry as well. Diarmaid moved toward the cradle, but Muirne had spun round already and held him tight against her, both o' them wailin'.

"I can't do it, Diarmaid," she wept, between hiccupping from the sobs. "I can't give him away. What are we to do?"

Dubhán clearly had no sense of what was going on, but Diarmaid could see what mattered to him was that his mam was there and he could smell the milk and wasn't gettin' any. He raised the volume of his bawling.

"Got good lungs, he has," Diarmaid said. "Now sit back down i' the chair there and feed the poor babe, and we can talk without goin' deaf."

Muirne's hands were shaking so that Diarmaid went down on his haunches next to her and helped her unbutton and make herself ready. Dubhán latched on with a great smack, and there was suddenly silence, if a body could ignore the gulping sounds.

"There," Diarmaid said, with obvious satisfaction. "One o' us is happy, at least."

Muirne took a long shuddering sigh. "We can't stay here. You're not a farmer, Diarmaid MacGuinness. Nor do you want to be."

"That's true enough." He sighed, and sat down on the bed. "So we've got as far as decidin' that." He ran his hand through his hair again. "So if not here, what?"

"We go to Galway."

He nodded. "Galway. There's sense to that."

"D'ye think I could stay—Dubhán 'n me—with Patrick and Kate?"

"Fair certain o' that." He leaned a bit against the end of the bed, lovin' the softness that came over her face when she was feedin' Dubhán. No wonder there was so many paintings of mother and child. He'd do one himself if he had the gift. "An' what do I do?"

"You go where you're sent, and do what's needed to be done. An' when you're done, you come back to us."

"But not as before." He could hear the firmness in his own voice.

"What d'ye mean?"

"No longer bein' gone a year and more at a time. I need to be around you and 'im"—he pointed at the babe at her breast—"more'n that. If it's too far away to be able to travel easy, then we take enough money to rent a place for you and Dubhán to stay w' me. I'm not wanting you to have to explain to him who I am over 'n over."

The faint smile on her lips was growing to be more like the smile he knew. Dear God, was this what real marriage was like? To have someone who could twist your heart about until you thought 'twas about to crack and at the exact same time have you longin' to do whatever you could to ease the heartbreak she was suffering?

"To Inishowen again?" she asked.

He shook his head. "Don't think so. Patrick and Con and me'll talk it over, of course. But life there is harder than I want it to be for you and 'im while he's so little. Maybe back to Connemara. Maybe someplace else." He grinned at her. "Maybe Galway. You never know, do you?"

"If it's not, I'll miss you every day you're gone."

"And me." He took a deep sigh. "Feel as if I climbed seven mountains today."

"Eight." Muirne took Dubhán, already half asleep, and lifted him to her shoulder. Drowsily he looked around, milk still around his mouth.

Diarmaid leaned around so he could see him. "Who'd think you'd get so attached in two days?"

"Y'know, if we had given 'im to Anne, he'd have to be Protestant." Muirne patted his back, and he produced a big bubble of milk, closed his eyes, and from all they could see, went back to sleep.

"That wouldn't have done," Diarmaid muttered. "Me da would have turned in his grave. If he had one."

"Didn't he?"

"Don't know. It's not the sort of thing th' English were big on letting the families know. I think me mam was told maybe two, three months later that he was dead. Lucky that she'd already heard from friends who knew about it. Didn' say anything 'bout where he was buried. Someday I'd like to look round and see what I could find out."

"Dubhán MacGuinness. Wouldn't think there'd be too many of those."

Diarmaid gave her his best crooked grin. "Know of two, at least."

"They should have told her." Muirne stood up, their son in her arms, and went to put him back in his cradle.

"'Tis a lot harder when you know people on both sides. The marquess, had he been around then, would have told her."

"Or the earl. What d'ye think'll happen to them?" Muirne stood up and stretched.

"Dunno. Most likely they'll die in their own beds. But the day'll come. I promise you that."

Muirne pulled back the coverlet on her side and kicked off her slippers before climbing into their bed. "As long as you die in yours, that'll suit me."

MAKIN' GREAT DECISIONS WAS ALL very well and good. But life went on between times.

When Diarmaid wakened the next morning and slid out of bed to ready himself for work, Muirne roused just enough to remember he had gone. Dubhán slept on, and Muirne let herself sink back into her pillow.

So when her baby decided he was ready to begin the day, she already knew Diarmaid was gone. She pulled herself up to sitting on the side of the bed and looked down at the bairn. He was twisting himself about, wailing. Her Dubhán wasn't the patient sort, it seemed. She picked him up, and the movement quieted him, but not for long. The movement was a change, but not enough of one. His small face crumpled and his mouth opened and he went back to yelling.

Should she change him, angry as he was, or should she feed him first? If there'd been anyone to ask, Muirne would have, but she and Dubhán were going to have to work out those things for themselves. She decided the noise was more than she wanted to listen to while she changed him. Anne had brought her a pile of toweling squares, and although they looked a great deal bigger than Dubhán himself, there had to be some way of wrapping them around him, and when he was not howling she would figure it out.

Once she put him to her breast he was smart enough to latch on at once, and the howls changed to hungry gulps. Seemed to her he was getting as much air as milk, and didn't you put the baby over your shoulder or on your lap and pat his back to bring the air up? Had Anne said something about the air hurting him inside? Muirne thought she remembered that. But was there some way to stop him from gulping so?

She looked down at the small determined face and tried to imagine how you'd do that. His eyes were shut tight and he had the air of someone who knew what he was about, not someone lookin' for instruction.

And indeed he managed quite well. When he was done, he opened his eyes and his mouth and gave out one great belch that brought up some milk with it. He watched her, eyes as blue as her own were, while she wiped him off and began to undress him so she could change him.

Anne knocked once and then peeked through the door and laughed as she saw what was going on. Muirne had one of the toweling squares and was trying to figure out how to fold it so the thickness would be where needed and not on his back, where she now had it.

"Here," she said, coming rushing across the room. She whipped the square away from Muirne and folded it with swift ease. "See?" she said. Muirne looked at it dubiously. It still looked like a great deal of cloth for a rather small babe.

"You fold it this way, so the thickness is at the front," Anne went on to explain.

Muirne nodded, wishing she'd thought to reach for another square herself, so she could practice. Then she decided Anne knew how to read minds, because Anne unfolded it and handed it to her.

"Now you try."

Muirne frowned with concentration as she tried to copy what she'd seen. She glanced over at Dubhán, lying there contentedly on the bed kicking his legs, and then suddenly there was a small fountain.

"Oh, look at you!" She grabbed the square, which immediately unfolded and used it to mop up the fountain. Dubhán looked at her solemnly and went on kicking.

Anne was laughing. "That's the trouble with baby boys," she said. "It just happens. There's nothing you can do to stop it. Except, I guess, being so fast that there's not long when there isn't a cloth in place. Charlie's nurse moved like lightning." She handed Muirne another square.

Muirne frowned. Clearly from now on she'd need two squares at hand. One to cover him while she folded the other. Hopefully, that wouldn't mean she'd need twice as many. This couldn't happen every time. It was all very well for Anne, who had a nurse as well as an unlimited supply of squares, it seemed, but she was going to have to be careful, herself. The lifetime she and Diarmaid would share would not be a luxurious one.

"Charlie and I don't really need the nurse all the time," Anne said. "Would you like me to send her down to you?"

Muirne shook her head firmly. "It's different for me," she said. "I'll have to do it meself, so it's better for me to figure it out from the start." She held up the square she'd been folding. "Is this right?"

Anne looked at her for a minute, and then reached over and gave it a twitch. "There. Yes, that'll do. Here's a pin." She held out one from the sleeve of her dress.

Muirne was busy trying to arrange Dubhán on the folded square without it unfolding. A bit did, so she tucked it under as best she could and then looked at the pin in her hand.

"How do you keep it from prickin' him?"

Anne pulled a bit of wadded cotton from inside her sleeve. She tore off a very small bit. "I put this on the tip of the pin. Doesn't work all the time, and if he seems to be fussing for no reason, it's a good idea to check, but there's lots of layers and it doesn't prick him often." She replaced the cotton wad in her sleeve

Muirne nodded, and carefully pinned the square. Made her a bit nervous to be plunging the pin towards him, even if she had her finger there to stop it first, but in the end she had it more or less fastened. She'd get faster at it, she promised herself. 'Twould just take her some time.

She held up the dampened square she'd covered him with. "Where d'you want me to put this?"

Anne reached out for it. "Funny," she said, "it's barely damp. When Charlie wets his now, it's wet. You'll see."

Muirne picked up Dubhán and held him close. "When he's as big as Charlie, we'll be far from here."

Anne looked up at her sharply. "When?"

"Soon," Muirne said. "Mebbe a week or so. Diarmaid's not said for certain."

"But I thought he was going to take the cottage here!"

So it had been a family decision that everyone knew about. They were good people. But as Diarmaid had said, 'twas impossible.

"His uncles need him," she said, which was true enough, but she could never explain. "We'll be heading back to Galway soon."

"I'm used to having you here." Anne's voice was forlorn. "And you shouldn't be traveling around yet, should you? My mother insisted my confinement should last at least a month."

Muirne laid her cheek against Dubhán's head and smiled at Anne. "That's for those as can manage it. If my people stayed away from work an' all for a month, the rest of their family would starve, at least. No, I think I'm favorin' myself to ease back for a week. Then it'll be time for us to go."

"Will you be staying in Galway?"

Careful, Muirne, she warned herself. This is where t' speak too fast could be dangerous. "Most likely. We'll see," she said, keeping her voice light.

"What do his uncles do?"

The question was innocent, just honest curiosity because she cared where they were going, Muirne reminded herself. No need to be too mysterious. "They build things," she answered, thinking to herself, networks, conspiracies, revolution, and rebellion. That was the world she was going back into, the world where she and Diarmaid, and eventually, she hoped, Dubhán lived. But pray God spare these good English people, their friends.

"That's good," Anne said happily. "People who can build things are always needed."

They are indeed, Muirne thought, holding back her smile. What they were saying went back and forth between them, when what they were talking about couldn't be more different. 'Twas safer for her, certainly, and for her dear friend Anne as well that that's the way it should be. Yes, it would be much better for her and Diarmaid to be off on their own again.

"Twas too confusing to be in the midst of what had to be the enemy, specially since these enemies were so dear to their hearts.

John Bowyer did not take Diarmaid's choice not to remain lightly.

"Are you sure?" he asked more than once. "The earl's a generous man."

"I know that," Diarmaid said. "Thank him for the offer. It's very kind of him—and of you. Had you not put in a word for me it wouldn't happen, I do know that."

"Oh, aye," Bowyer said. "Nothing but self interest was what it was. You work harder than any of the other tenants round here. 'Twould make my life easier if you'd stay."

"That's what me uncles say about me comin' back to Galway." He pulled off his cap and ran his fingers through his hair. For all it was late November, this was an unseasonably warm day. Had more of the feel of September, though the trees were stripped of their leaves. The leaves were still blowin' around where they'd not been raked away.

"When d'you think you'll be leaving?"

"Next week, most likely."

"So soon?" John Bowyer looked surprised and disappointed. "Will ye be working until you leave? I'd be able to give you a comfortable bit to set off with, since you'd not have the cottage as a benefit."

"Yes, I'd like to work." Diarmaid's fingers went automatically to his cap. "And I thank you."

"How'll you go?"

"I'm a family man now." Diarmaid grinned. "So I s'pose it'll be the coach. Can't quite see Muirne walkin' along with the babe on her back."

"I'd hope not," John Bowyer said with barely concealed disapproval. "I'll get you a schedule if you'd like."

"I'd be grateful." Diarmaid took a deep breath, trying to fit the goodness of the people here with what he'd seen and heard of the English elsewhere. Of course, John Bowyer wasn't English either, but at this point after years of working with the earl, he might as well be. Come the revolution, would there be time to sort out the ones who should be swept away from the ones who had earned some place on the land—not as landlords, perhaps—from years of honesty and fair treatment of those who'd worked for them? The truth was probably not.

And yet was he going to work for the revolution? Of course. And hope there'd be time for him to get back here and warn and protect these people. Asking for perfect justice from the English or the Irish was a fool's game.

In the end, it wasn't the coach that took them west to Galway. They went by carriage and four, and very nearly had two carriages to choose from. Fortunately, John Bowyer managed to straighten out a muddled message and stopped the stable at Kendall House from preparing the carriage to take the MacGuinnesses, since the marquess had already ordered his carriage to be made ready at Ballymuir.

In fact, Diarmaid was some taken aback when he came out to see how much had been loaded onto the coach ready for the journey. Dubhán's cradle was tied to the top; there were easy twice as many bags as they'd arrived with, and an enormous picnic basket that had enough in it to feed a family of ten sitting by the carriage door, ready to be lifted in.

He took a look around and went inside to see if he could have a private word with Muirne.

Mercifully, Anne had run off to pick up something else she'd forgotten to pack, so Muirne was sitting on the bed feeding Dubhán just before they left.

"Have you seen what's out there?" Diarmaid demanded.

Muirne nodded. "Not all in one place, but Anne's been runnin' back and forth with half the maids in the place taking things out."

"What're we going to do with it all?"

Muirne shrugged and smiled at him. "Patrick and Kate have a pile of young 'uns, and then Con and Rosie are there, too. We'll find a place for it all. After all, it's just good people who have a lot being generous. We can't tell them to take any of it away."

Diarmaid blew out a long breath. "That's the truth of it. But, dear God, when I look at that carriage and think of the good folk in the clachan in Inishowen—"

Muirne's smile faded. "You're right. But 'twould do them in Inishowen no good if we handed it back and there's no reason to hurt the family's feelings. There'll be plenty o' people in Galway who can use the extra."

So all of it went with them.

Loading themselves into the coach at Galway had been a simple business, mainly because the coachman was determined to leave according to his schedule, and it was up to them to get themselves and their bags into the coach in the time allowed.

The carriage at Ballymuir was another business entirely. First of all, everything had to be stowed in the best possible way for them to have space during the journey, although there were only the three of them this time, and one of them took up hardly any space at all—although all the equipment Anne had collected for him did have to be fit in.

This meant that Anne and Muirne were popping in and out of the carriage checking on what was there and rearranging it. John Bowyer had come down for the departure as well, and to Diarmaid's amazement, the earl as well. The marquess was fussing around with the horses, making sure everything was as it should be.

At what seemed like long last, John Bowyer pointed out that they'd better be on their way or they wouldn't be arriving in Galway at a civilized hour.

Anne threw her arms around Muirne, and gave her a long and heartfelt embrace.

"Will you come back to see us if you're ever over on this side?" she asked, and Muirne was surprised and touched to see Anne's eyes were bright with unshed tears.

Muirne blinked rapidly, and looked at Anne, realizing what she was feeling was a lot like love. "I promise," she said, and, handing Dubhán to his father, put her arms around Anne as well. "You'll never know how much you did to make this such a happy time," she whispered into her ear. "I'll remember it my whole life long."

"Come along," Diarmaid said. He shook hands with John Bowyer, and the earl and the marquess both nodded to him with respect. He had his son in his arms and Muirne, glancing in his direction could see how taken aback he was as he held Dubhán's head against his shoulder and bowed to them in return. Not a formal bow, perhaps, but the best he could do under the circumstances.

"You come along," she said, and shepherded him and the baby into the carriage. She took one last look at Anne—who had a couple of tears streaking down her face now—and climbed through the door herself.

John Bowyer shut it, giving them both a nod of farewell. Muirne scrambled across the seat and managed to be sitting properly before she reached out for Dubhán. She turned the baby so that Anne would be able to see him through the window.

"Say goodbye," she whispered to him, and the carriage jerked into motion.

The little bunch of people standing in the drive gradually got smaller and smaller as the carriage rattled down the drive. Finally, the carriage took the curve, and they disappeared altogether.

"So it begins," Diarmaid said.

Muirne turned to him. "What begins?"

"The rest of our life," he said, and put his arm around her and their son. She leaned her head against him, and the carriage drove on.

Note To Readers

As you turn the last page over, let me thank you for reading this story of Diarmaid and Muirne and the Anglo/Irish aristocracy with which they were so incongruously meshed. If you've enjoyed the glimpse you've had into their lives, I would greatly appreciate it if you would do two things: first, recommend it to your friends, because nothing is as convincing as hearing someone talk about a book they were glad they read, and second, leave a review at the site where you purchased it or at Goodreads. I'm always grateful for new readers, and as a devoted reader myself, it's always wonderful to come across a review that introduces me to a book I might not otherwise have noticed.

This book is the first of a new trilogy, one that is related to *The Heart Trilogy* already available at Amazon. The other two books will be released later in 2015.

The Reluctant Heart is the story of Emmeline Hawthorne, the young sister of Ethan, who has remained in Ireland with his uncle, the Earl of Kendall, as he will inherit his uncle's estate. Emmeline has had enough of the attractions of London after two seasons, and decides to follow her brother to Ireland even though her horrified mother points out if she doesn't marry she might live her life as a mere attachment to Ethan's household rather than having a family and house of her own. Emmeline says she doesn't care and flings off to Ireland. There she almost immediately acquires, of all things, a suitor who had idled his way through the pleasures of the Seasons in years past when his great friend Ethan was also footloose and frivolous. Emmeline has seen far too many men like Viscount Oliver Sheffield in London herself, and is uninterested. The viscount, on the contrary, is instantly attracted, and *The Reluctant Heart* is the story of the viscount's dogged pursuit and Emmeline's determined attempts to escape.

The constant heart belongs to Lady Dorothea Robinson, the daughter of the Duke of Apthorp. At one time she and Lady Caroline Hawthorne had been sisters-in-law, during Caroline's brief and tragic marriage to Dorothea's brother. So when Caroline, now living in Dublin with her Irish husband, comes across a brilliantly talented young Irish artist who hopes to make his way in London, she sends him to Dorothea, to see if her connections might open doors for him.

The first door that opens is Dorothea's own heart. Their story tells of the struggle between a wealthy and titled young woman who wishes she could give the world on a string to Patrick Monaghan and Patrick's proud determination to find his success himself, complicated by his attraction to Dorothea.

ELSBETH

Book Four – The Daughters of Alastair MacDougall

by Lane McFarland

Set in late thirteenth century Scotland, this series tells the stories of Laird Alastair MacDougall's four independent and oftentimes, headstrong daughters coming of age in a country fraught with war and feuds amongst rival clans. Follow his daughters as their lives become intertwined with four fierce, rebel highland warriors bent on eradicating the English soldiers from their homeland.

Elsbeth – to be Released Fall 2015

Elsbeth MacDougall recoils at the violent Scottish rebellion and the bleak plight of orphans. Vowing to protect the homeless, she embarks on a journey to Scone and sets her course to become a nun, sheltering children from the cruelties of war. But when Brandon McLeod arrives at the Abby, he shakes her convictions and stirs provoking emotions she buried long ago.

After English soldiers murder his family, Brandon McLeod determines a course of revenge and leads numerous clans in Scotland's fight for freedom. Bent on the annihilation of English oppression, he is resolved to a life of solitude, vowing never to marry and chance the pain of losing loved ones again. However, that was before he met the enchanting Elsbeth.

Methven Abbey, Scotland
March 1300

"YE'VE FAILED."

Dread churned Elsbeth MacDougall's stomach as she braced herself for the abbess's harsh reprimand.

The reverend mother clamped her thin lips into a tight line, effectively letting the two simple words sink in. She sat in a heavy wooden chair perched on the raised platform, and peered down her nose at Elsbeth with an undeniable air of superiority. A crucifix hung behind her on the drab stone wall, the only adornment to the chamber.

Dampness and the incessant cold permeated the abbey solar, and chill bumps peppered Elsbeth's arms. Hands clutched in her lap, she dug her fingernails into her palms in an effort to stop her nervous tremors.

A starched white wimple outlined Abbess Mary's face, squeezing her loose porcelain skin into an array of sagging wrinkles. Her upper lip curled in disdain, and disappointment emanated from her pale grey eyes. "Regardless of the close bond I shared with yer mum, yer outlandish actions will no longer be tolerated. Ye have set a bad example for the orphans."

Elsbeth raised her chin. Occasional late nights spent before the solar hearth, furtive moments in forbidden baths, and a cheerful countenance could hardly be considered outlandish. The woman made it sound as if Elsbeth was an unscrupulous trouble-maker.

Silence filled the stark room. The solar's cold hearth and dreary shades of grey and brown added to the disheartening atmosphere, attesting to the self-imposed denial of luxuries. How senseless. Prohibiting bright colors and suffering bitter temperatures embodied the abbey's strict code of conduct and commitment to the vow of poverty. Elsbeth struggled to believe God demanded martyrdom as proof of devotion to the church.

The candle's yellow beeswax trickled down the squat wrought-iron candelabra and dripped onto the oak table between the women. Partially translated manuscripts covered the abbess's desk, and the smell of ink resin mixed with the taper's honeyed scent filled the dim chamber.

"The sisters' concerns have reached a level I can no longer ignore. Yer willful, carefree ways must end." The abbess leaned against her straight-backed chair, the wooden slats creaking under her ample frame. "I expect ye to take yer vows."

Defiance flared inside Elsbeth. The abbey biddies remained trapped within rigid self-righteousness, their unyielding intolerance abhorrent. She swallowed the retort perched at the end of her tongue. "With all due respect, Reverend Mother, I care for my charges, and do not feel I adversely affect them with willful actions."

The abbess's gaze sharpened. "How can ye sit there and tell me what ye do does not affect the children? Yer role is to teach God's law by example. I've never allowed a novice longer than a year before taking her vows, yet ye've had well over two. I more than met yer mum's request to give ye time. Last night, Prioress Ethelinda informed me ye missed Compline *again*. Ye are well aware of the rules, Elsbeth. To the detriment of the sisters and yer charges, I've been much too lenient with ye."

Elsbeth squirmed under the woman's scrutiny. The abbess had admonished her many times before, but Elsbeth sensed a difference in this scolding—a foreboding of dire consequences. "I attend most services, and always ensure the children are present for their lessons."

"Are ye suggesting yer actions represent an adequate commitment to Christ?"

With the rigid convent rules and severe religious practices, Elsbeth was no longer sure she wished to devote her life to the church. But if she didn't, how would she help the orphans? "I'm merely stating the children attend services daily. They're cared for, fed, and clothed." *And loved.*

As if on cue, the sisters' monotone chanting in the adjoining chapel drifted into the solar. "Defiled by misguided deeds, wretched as I am, I am unworthy, O Christ. Wash me thoroughly from my iniquity, and cleanse me from my sin."

The abbess thrust out her pudgy chin, and her mouth twisted into a disdainful smirk. "God will punish the wicked for their iniquity."

Wicked? A gush of indignation threatened to spew forth. Elsbeth forced restraint. Her leashed anger teetered on the verge of an irreparable blunder.

"When ye arrived, did I not explain every candidate seeking admission to the order must take the vow of obedience?"

"Aye," Elsbeth acknowledged, the outrage in her voice barely contained. She'd not given a whit to pledging chastity. She would never lose her heart to another man. No one could take Fabien's place. She also embraced the second pledge, one of service. After all, devotion to helping orphans had become her life's mission. But the oath of absolute poverty—deprivation of basic needs, self-infliction of unforgiving hair shirts, and abstinence of sinful indulgences such as cleanliness—went too far.

"Yet ye renounce shearing yer hair, ye ignore the pledge to carry out yer duties in silence, and ye refuse to retire until well past Compline."

Those were not God's rules. These restrictions were drummed up by men who sought to exert control over the masses and repress mortal desires. "Surely, God does not expect us to live under such harsh conditions. Our work would be no less effectual for speaking, laughing, and cheering the blighted."

"That's quite enough. Commitment to the Holy Father requires taking up yer cross, forfeiting yer dreams and belongings, even yer verrae life for the cause of Christ." Anger sparked from the abbess's eyes. Tension between the women stretched as tight as the rack's victims. "Yer mum spoke on many occasions about yer future. Before she passed, she asked me to watch over ye, educate ye on God's law, and ensure ye become a righteous apostle to spread The Holy Spirit's word."

Bringing Mum into the chastisement to jerk the guilt strings taut was Abbess Mary's standard practice. She ought to be used to the assertions, nevertheless she bristled under the woman's loathsome tactics. The abbess twisted Mum's words. Entering the convent was merely a means to care for the orphans. It would do no good to point out the abbess's divergence from the truth.

"And, although yer da isn't a man of unlimited means, he fills our coffers because of his high expectations for yer commitment to the church. Ye don't want to disappoint him, do ye? What would yer mum say, God rest her soul, if she were alive to witness yer unruly behavior?"

Elsbeth's ire rose over the abbess's attempt to shame her into submission. Mum had encouraged her to follow her dream to aid displaced victims of war. However, she would not expect her daughter to live a life of misery closeted behind these cold, dreary walls.

Abbess Mary folded her arms into the flowing sleeves of her dark robe. "I suggest ye retire to contemplate a life without the orphans."

Elsbeth's breath caught as she stood on shaky legs. "Without the orphans?" Her voice struggled past the lump in her throat.

"If ye cannot abide God's rules, ye must leave."

Tears stung Elsbeth's eyes as she escaped the solar and hurried toward her dismal cell. Her sandals slapped the cloister's stone slabs. Golden flames from the wall sconces flickered in her wake, and her black habit billowed behind her. She'd known the day would come when she'd be confronted with making her pledge, but she hadn't been prepared for the ultimatum to take her vows or leave the children.

Several sisters huddled in muted conversation, turned toward Elsbeth. She averted her tear-filled eyes to the floor, and rushed from the covered walkway into the narrow hall alongside the dormitory. She wouldn't give them the satisfaction of knowing they'd hurt her. The worn oak door to the cell she shared with Beatrice, her childhood nursemaid, stood ajar. Elsbeth slipped inside the room, shut the door, and leaned against it as she inhaled deeply to quell her frazzled nerves. Musty stale air filled her lungs, and her nose wrinkled in protest of the repugnant smell.

"Are ye all right, child?" Bea asked. "Ye look pale."

Elsbeth huffed, her breath forced loudly from her nostrils. "No. No, I am not all right."

She studied the austere chamber. Two straw mattresses were flanked by inhospitable rocky walls. The main source of light—four candles secured in a taper holder—hung from a black iron chain suspended from the ceiling. A wobbly wooden table, the uneven surface rippled with frayed timber, and two coarse benches scarred with unforgiving splinters completed the room.

Elsbeth pushed away from the door, dropped on the seat adjacent to Bea, and propped her back against the rough mortared wall. The older woman wore her usual worsted tan robe with a woolen rope tied at the waist. She had wound and pinned her white braids atop her head, and her brown eyes held concern.

She placed her sewing on the table. "Tell me what's troubling ye."

"The abbess's patience has run out. She demands I speak my vows or return home."

"I see. And ye are still uncertain of making the commitment?"

Elsbeth's eyes cut to Bea. "Ye know I only remain here because of the children."

"Have ye told the abbess?"

"No." Elsbeth blurted the word more forcefully than intended. She rubbed the undeniable throbbing in her forehead. "Oh, Bea, what am I to do? I thought I'd grow accustomed to this...this *sheltered* existence.

When we arrived, I looked forward to devoting my life to the church, making a difference." She swallowed emotions threatening to erupt. "After losing Fabien, it seemed the perfect solution. Now, I'm not sure…"

"Ye must tell Abbess Mary the truth," Bea insisted. "It's unfair to her and the sisters."

"I can't."

"Beth…" Bea's disapproving tone rankled.

Pain sliced Elsbeth's heart, and her voice trembled. "What would ye have me do? Tell the abbess I no longer desire to devote my life to the church only to be ushered from the convent walls, never to see the children again?"

Sleep eluded Elsbeth. She flipped over and punched her lumpy pillow. She should've expected the abbess's ultimatum. It'd been coming for quite some time. In the past the abbess had granted Elsbeth special favors. She even gave Elsbeth the responsibility of her own charges. Never before had a novice held such trust. If only the shrews hadn't fussed. Perhaps the sisters felt Elsbeth selfish and privileged, but her time here was about the children, not about devoting her life to a religious order or garnering acceptance from the somber sisters.

Contemplate a life without the orphans.

How could she? After caring for them nigh on two years, she loved the little family as her own and would be heartbroken without them. She had helped them. Because of her, they were learning to trust again.

And…they helped me. While she fostered them, they healed her heart. God knew she needed them as much as they needed her.

Despite the fact she'd been forbidden from staying up past the last evening service, desire to be with the children washed over her. How could checking on her charges in the still of the night be considered sinful? After all, they were her responsibility, and if she was quiet, no one would be the wiser.

Easing the thick blanket aside, she placed her feet on the icy stone floor. Shivers racked her body, and the hair on her arms stood on end, dotting her skin like one of Cook's plucked chickens. The frayed nightdress offered little protection against the frigid air, and Elsbeth rubbed the chill from her arms. As she stood, she glanced at Beatrice stretched upon her straw pallet. Her dear nursemaid would not be pleased if she learned of Elsbeth's late night transgression.

Her drab habit draped the chair at the foot of her mattress. She snatched the wretched garment and shoved her arms into the voluminous sleeves, then slid her feet into her sandals. The thought of donning the suffocating coif caused her nose to scrunch. However, remembering the abbess's reproach, Elsbeth tugged the cloth over her head and tucked away any sign of her forbidden hair.

Once properly clothed, she crossed the room and eased open the door. Rusty hinges creaked like a screeching owl. She froze. Beatrice coughed and turned over. Elsbeth's heart pounded. What she'd give for King Arthur's mantle of invisibility.

Finally, the older woman settled. Elsbeth released her held breath, and with a last glimpse over her shoulder, she hurried down the damp corridor toward the children's chamber.

Unrelenting wind battered the abbey. The howling gale scraped tree branches against the ancient walls, the scratching sound eerie. She prayed there'd be no damage caused by the intense storm; however, the barrage would drown out noises she made. Elsbeth grinned and sent up a silent prayer of thanks for her good fortune.

Tiptoeing inside the children's sparsely-furnished chamber, she made her way to the area sectioned off for the lasses. Light shining through a single window cut high in the thick wall bathed the three sleeping sisters, lying side by side. The cramped space was filled with straw mattresses, a table surrounded by five chairs, and a plain wooden chest containing the children's meager belongings butted against the far wall. A brown woolen privacy curtain suspended from the ceiling, divided the chamber in half, making the space even smaller.

Peaceful soft snores met her as she eased to Lena's side. The young one had kicked off her blankets, leaving her legs exposed to the chilly night air. Elsbeth stooped beside her, gently tugged the worn cover over her body, and tucked it around the young lass's shoulders. Lena's mouth puckered in her sleep. At barely five years, the troubled child held a special place in Elsbeth's heart. How she wished Lena would speak. What evils had the child witnessed? Elsbeth ran the back of her finger across the little one's baby soft cheek, then placed a kiss on her forehead.

She straightened and turned to Alainne. The lass lay on her side. Her small hands cushioned her face, and her soft blonde hair fanned out behind her. Elsbeth prayed for guidance in helping Alainne get past the horrors of the rebellion. The girl never spoke of the attack on her village and the murder of her parents, but the fragile façade she'd raised couldn't hide the anguish that smoldered just below the surface.

Morgana, the oldest of the three sisters, slept beside Alainne, the blankets covering her dark head. At eleven years, she had grown up much too quickly. As with the other siblings, that Morgana had experienced horrible atrocities at such a young age broke Elsbeth's heart.

Elsbeth ducked around the other side of the brown woolen privacy curtain suspended from the ceiling, hanging at Morgana's left. The two brothers burrowed beneath thick furs. At three and ten years, Tristian was the man of the family. He kept an eye on his brother and sisters, and protected them with his life. She glanced at Bodwyn, who worshiped his older brother and strived to do everything Tristian did.

How blessed she was to have these children. Surely the superioress would not make her leave them. But Abbess Mary had never acted so resolute in her scolding or handed down such a harsh edict as she had this evening. Despair punched Elsbeth's stomach. A sob escaped her lips, and she covered her mouth. She would not have the children awaken to her pitiful cries.

Elsbeth hurried from the chamber and stumbled down the drafty hall. Candelabra cast eerie shadows, stretching along the darkened cloister. The old abbey's wooden beams creaked in protest of the violent blizzard, however even the fierce tempest could not match the turmoil churning her stomach.

She slipped into the front solar, closed the door, and leaned against it. Used for the reception of visitors, the room held a fireplace, and comforting warmth often filled the intimate space. An aroma of peat invoked wistful memories of MacDougall Castle. How she missed Da and her sisters. She shoved away from the door. Red embers from the early evening fire still glowed, beckoning her closer. Elsbeth grabbed a small log from the wood holder and tossed it onto the grate. An array of gold flecks swirled up the chimney. Orange and yellow flames flickered over the timber.

The chamber was quiet save for the occasional fire pop. She sank onto a rough-hewn bench before the hearth and crossed her arms. How could she take a pledge she didn't believe in, give up her freedom, and live a life secluded from the rest of the world?

Leaving the children was not an acceptable option. She was caught— a rabbit in a snare with no easy way out. Bitterness festered like a thorn jammed in her foot. The English and her brethren Scots were to blame. If they resolved their differences, there would be no need to care for a vast number of parentless children, and she'd not be forced to take her vows. Why couldn't they get past stubborn pride and come to an amicable agreement? The rebellion exacted a high price of rape, pillage, and murderous retaliation from the English soldiers. Nay, she didn't like the never-ending aggression, but how could anyone argue this fight was worth the havoc and suffering inflicted? The Scots' rebellious attacks on King Edward's minions caused resentment and hatred which fueled a vicious cycle of continued violence and mayhem.

Images of the frightened children plagued with nightmares, clinging to Elsbeth, and trying to show bravery in the face of terror, flashed before her eyes. Her heart was heavy, but her decision was clear. She could not leave them. She'd *take up her cross*. The sacrifice would be hers to bear. She would come to terms with the strict rules and abide them.

Bowing her head, she closed her eyes and whispered, "Lord, I pray ye give me guidance."

A loud bang sounded outside.

Elsbeth jumped from the bench and spun toward the solar door. That was the courtyard gate. Who would arrive at this time of night in a blizzard?

An insistent knock rattled the heavy front door. The urgent noise reverberated down the corridor. She eased from the solar. Legs shaking, she hurried across the hall and peeked out the small window overlooking the courtyard. Her gaze swept the interior walls. Dense snowfall hid any sign of intruders. Nothing appeared out of the ordinary.

Someone beat the dark wood again. If a traveler trapped in the storm sought shelter, she couldn't deny sanctuary and leave them in the fierce squall. With a deep breath, she shoved the iron bolt to the right and eased open the door.

A gust of wind buffeted the heavy door and shoved it against her body. The turbulent storm swirled a blanket of snow, and stinging ice crystals pelted her eyes. She held up a hand to shield her face and squinted into the courtyard.

Large men shrouded in darkness appeared just beyond the landing. One man stepped forward. His fur-cloaked shoulders spanned the width of the door, and his piercing dark eyes peered over a thick woolen cloth wrapped around his face. He pushed the hood from his head. Snow and ice covered him from his shaggy hair to his rugged boots, and the hilt of a sword protruded over his back, another dangling from his hip.

He's a warrior. Familiar resentment bubbled into her throat, and she choked on the bitter taste.

As he advanced, his gloved hand tugged the cloth from his face. Her breath caught at his intense scrutiny, his commanding presence. An overwhelming urge to slam and bolt the door nearly overcame her, but her feet remained rooted to the spot.

"Sister, there's not much time," his deep voice resounded. "Yer life is in danger. Ye must flee!"

Lane McFarland is a best-selling author of historical romance stories full of feisty heroines matched with courageous heroes and the passion that flares between them. She's the author of Scottish medieval series, *The Daughters of Alastair MacDougall*, where her readers escape into a world of brawny Highland warriors and smart independent lasses fighting for their independence. Join the sisters' adventures and transport to an era filled with strife and hardship, only to be overcome by everlasting love.

For more information on Lane, please visit her at lanemcfarland.com.

ABOUT THE AUTHOR

Beppie Harrison lives in southeastern Michigan with her husband and two slightly addled cats, their four children having grown up and flown the coop. They live a somewhat cross-Atlantic lifestyle. Her husband is an English architect and they began their marriage living in London, only moving to the States when they had young children. In many ways, England still feels like home.

For Beppie, the pull from across the Atlantic comes not only from old friends and familiar places in England, but from Ireland. Did it start with its literature, its history, or its wonderful garrulous people? However it happened, she is addicted now.

Her first fiction trilogy, the *Heart Trilogy*, is placed primarily in Ireland during the Regency period. *The Grandest Christmas*, a novella for the holiday season, is a warm and cozy read for Christmastime. *The Abiding Heart*, the first of the second *Hearts Everlasting Trilogy*, takes place mostly in Ireland as well.

Visit her online at www.beppieharrison.com.

www.ingramcontent.com/pod-product-compliance
Lightning Source LLC
Chambersburg PA
CBHW050014180626
46810CB00002B/409